By the same author

The Summer Before the War

Major Pettigrew's Last Stand

The Hazelbourne Ladies Motorcycle and Flying Club

The Hazelbourne Ladies Motorcycle and Flying Club

Helen Simonson

BLOOMSBURY PUBLISHING

LONDON · OXFORD · NEW YORK · NEW DELHI · SYDNEY

BLOOMSBURY PUBLISHING
Bloomsbury Publishing Plc
50 Bedford Square, London, WC1B 3DP, UK
29 Earlsfort Terrace, Dublin 2, Ireland

BLOOMSBURY, BLOOMSBURY PUBLISHING and the Diana logo
are trademarks of Bloomsbury Publishing Plc

First published in the United States by The Dial Press, an imprint of Random House,
a division of Penguin Random House LLC, New York.
First published in Great Britain 2024

A catalogue record for this book is available from the British Library

ISBN: HB: 978-1-5266-7023-6; TPB: 978-1-5266-7022-9;
eBook: 978-1-5266-7021-2; ePDF: 978-1-5266-7020-5

2 4 6 8 10 9 7 5 3 1

Typeset by Integra Software Services Pvt. Ltd.
Printed and bound in Great Britain by CPI Group (UK) Ltd, Croydon CR0 4YY

To find out more about our authors and books visit www.bloomsbury.com
and sign up for our newsletters

In memory of
Susan Kamil
Alan Phillips

Chapter 1

IN THE FIRST PLACE, IT DID NOT SEEM QUITE RIGHT THAT a girl that young should be free to wander the hotel and seaside town without a chaperone. She looked respectable enough, though she was pale as alabaster and thin as a wet string. She was clothed in a brown wool dress, perhaps a bit too big, that fell decently to the ankles, and her leather boots still had a shine of newness on them. She was some sort of connection and companion to Mrs Fog, an old lady from a grand family in the shires, but it seemed to Klaus Zieger that the old lady encouraged far too much independence. Since her arrival at the Meredith Hotel, the girl was always to be found tripping through the grand public rooms alone, or curled up in an armchair deep in a book, oblivious to all. And now, with the old lady having ordered dinner in her room again, the girl wished to be seated in the Grand Dining Room alone.

'I hoped, because it was early . . .' she said, peering past Klaus into the high-ceilinged room, which functioned as both restaurant and ballroom. She spoke respectfully but there was a firmness to her tone and a faint lift of the chin. 'A quiet corner somewhere?' Only two tables were occupied; each with a pair of elderly ladies nodding their hats at each other. The room echoed a little. Silverware pinging against glass, shoes loud against the parquet floor. The tall potted palms stirred in an unknown draught and from beyond the tall French windows came the murmur of voices from the seafront and the low booming of the sea against the pebbled shore. Later would come the dancing crowds, the loud hotel orchestra and the crude drunken Saturday night carousing – all things that would never have been countenanced before the war.

'I'm very sorry, miss,' Klaus repeated, drawing himself up. He was the lone waiter at this hour, and in the absence of the headwaiter, who was having his own dinner in the kitchen, he felt keenly the need to defend the ragged standards that were left. 'Can I arrange to have something sent to your room?'

'Please don't be sorry,' the girl said. 'We are all bound by our duties, are we not?' She gave him a brief smile and walked away down the long marble floor of the glass-enclosed Palm Terrace. Her smile made him ashamed. Not answering him about the dinner tray made him irritated. Turning away a hotel customer added a new string to the vibration of anxiety that hummed in his veins.

He tugged down surreptitiously at the sleeves of his black jacket, now a little stiff from age and mothballs, and rubbed the arthritis in his knuckles, wondering if he should have relented. Would this quiet young woman eating tonight's chicken quenelles behind a potted palm have been more scandalous than the women who would come later in the evening to dine intimately or in great parties, with men, laughing open-mouthed over champagne and bending the fringed edges of their décolletages into the mock turtle soup?

He cast a discreet eye over his tables, looking for the dropping of hands, the setting down of cutlery that would signal he was needed, and sighed. Everything was confusing now. He had recognised one of the pair of diners from before the war, the widow of a wealthy brick manufacturer and her spinster sister, who lived in a large villa on a hill above the town. Kind women who appreciated fine service, who blushed at a carefully dispensed compliment, who always left a little gratuity hidden under the napkin. He had made a mistake today, exclaiming at seeing them after so long, trying to kiss their gloved hands. They had responded with squeezed lips, their eyes darting and anxious. Like a blow to the ribs, he understood why the hotel manager had been hesitant and cruel in hiring him back. Two months' trial only and an instruction to keep his mouth shut as much as possible. Klaus had been hurt, almost to the point of refusing.

Before the war, a German waiter commanded the greatest respect. But what was the point of standing on his pride? After six humiliating months in the internment camp, and banned from returning to the coast, he had nearly starved in London, scratching for whatever job they would give to a German. He remembered the long steaming hours at the sink, washing dishes in a men's hostel; waiting tables at an asylum where an inmate might thank you for the supper or throw it in your face; a pallet on the cellar floor in exchange for working in a boarding house dining room. To return home to Hazelbourne-on-Sea he needed this job and the room that came with it. He wondered, as a tremor ran down his spine, where he would go now if the two women, or the young girl, made a complaint.

IN THE LOBBY of the Meredith Hotel, Constance Haverhill paused, pretending to admire the flowers in the towering urn on a marble table at the foot of the grand staircase. The reception desk seemed busy with a large party arriving and two or three gentlemen chatting to the concierge. Her rejection from the dining room fresh, she felt too humiliated to push herself forward to the centre where the clerk would offer her the menu of the day and she would be forced to publicly decide between broth or fish paste on toast and then accept the plain dinner and one of the three rotating puddings, most of them custard. On their first night, she and Mrs Fog had dined together, but dinner had been taken in her room these last three days, and Constance was tired of the lingering smell of gravy and the awkward waiting for the used tray to be removed.

There would be plenty of time in the years to come to feel the limits of a life as a spinster. Lady Mercer, who fancied herself Constance's patron and had sent her to the seaside to look after Mrs Fog, her mother, had been loud in her opinion that now, with the war over and women no longer needed in men's professions, Constance would be well advised to take up as a governess. Joining the family once a week for dinner with the children, trays in one's room when important guests came to dine, sharing one's room on occasion if there were too many ladies' maids at a weekend party. Constance shivered at the thought. As a young girl, she had seen the governesses come and go, for Lady Mercer couldn't seem to keep one. And when one left, Constance's mother would be called in to help during the transition. On those occasions, Constance would go with her mother to the big house and join in the lessons with Rachel, their daughter.

Her mother and Lady Mercer had been schoolgirls together, and though the former married a farmer and the latter a lord, they maintained the fiction of a lifelong affection of friends and equals by never allowing the crudeness of money to come between them. Constance's mother had never received a wage for the many services she had provided under the guise of friendship and the patronage of the Clivehill estate. Instead there was always a small velvet bag of sovereigns at Christmas, the discarded dresses of prior seasons, a supply of preserved fruit that she and Constance helped the kitchen put up every summer. There were invitations to hunt balls and to fill out the numbers at some of the less distinguished dinners held in Clivehill's magnificent dining room. Constance herself had plenty of training in working for, and being grateful to, the Mercer family, including having run their estate office for most of the war. But with the Armistice, it had been made clear she was surplus to requirements and her need for paid employment was now pressing. As a thank-you, she had been promised these few short weeks at the seaside, during which she might float in the luxurious anonymity of hotel life. But her rejection from the dining room made her uncertain future seem all the more immediate.

Her reverie was interrupted by the slightest ripple of tension in the lobby. There were no raised voices but only the urgent cadence of a disagreement being conducted discreetly by the open French windows. The hotel's undermanager, a shy youth of some relation to the hotel manager, was bent to converse with a woman about Constance's age, who was sitting half-concealed on a settee, reading a newspaper. There seemed to be some issue regarding the woman's ordering tea and Constance drifted closer with all the natural curiosity of someone fresh from her own humiliation.

'Oh, don't turn me out, Dudley. I'm having dinner here with my mother later,' said the young woman. 'Just bring me a tea table and I'll promise to hide behind the tablecloth.'

'But we cannot serve you, Miss Wirrall . . .' said the undermanager, his face reddening at her familiarity. He seemed like a man on the third or fourth round of saying exactly the same thing. Constance could see that the young woman, though discreetly tucking her ankles under the seat and partly covered by the day's headlines, was wearing slim brown wool trousers tucked into the tops of thick black knee boots. A green tweed jacket and white silk scarf completed the ensemble. A leather helmet and goggles lay abandoned on a low table. The woman's chestnut hair was fuzzy and loose in its pins, no doubt from wearing the helmet, and gave her a slightly disreputable look.

'Take pity on me,' said the girl, but the undermanager shook his head. She seemed to catch sight of Constance in that instant and grinned before tossing the newest of her long list of arguments. 'I'm liable to die of thirst, Dudley.'

'May I be of assistance?' asked Constance. 'I didn't mean to eavesdrop, but if the lady needs a companion for you to bring her tea?'

'We only serve ladies on the Palm Terrace,' said Dudley, his face stiffening. 'And afternoon attire is required.' Constance was distracted by his Adam's apple bobbing awkwardly above the too-large ring of his stiff shirt collar. Everywhere she looked these days it seemed that the people, at least those not swathed in the comforting blanket of rank and money, had become smaller than their clothes. Hollowed out perhaps by the rationing, the ravages of influenza, the usual ailments of the British damp. But maybe it was just the long years of the war itself, which could not be sloughed off in a few days of Armistice celebrations. Everywhere, she saw the cinched-in belts and frayed cuffs, the stiff shoulders and old-fashioned clothes. Everywhere in the gaunt but cheerful faces, the flickering ghosts of loss. The young undermanager's face might have shown a hint of disdain at Constance's interference, but she saw the war in his eyes too and could not resent him.

'Bless you, but I'm unchaperonable,' said the girl, laughing. Her cheeks were pink, but from fresh air not from blushing; her posture was relaxed and her blue eyes were clear and full of mischief. She really did not look as humiliated as the situation seemed to require, and Constance realised she was only playing with the poor youth. The girl was amused and Constance felt a slight indignation creeping inside her.

'I shouldn't have presumed,' she said stiffly. 'I didn't mean to interfere.' She turned on her heel, anxious to escape.

'I say, is there any chance you would help me?' said the girl, jumping up and extending a slightly oil-stained hand. 'I'm Poppy Wirrall. I've been out all day on the motorcycle and damn it all if I didn't leave my bag behind at home. My mother is still out visiting and the powers that be here have decided that after four years of war and pestilence they should still have the vapours over a woman having tea in trousers.'

'I foresee no chance of either of us persuading them as to any softening of the rules,' said Constance, shaking hands.

'Yes, but could you be an absolute saint and lend me a skirt for an hour?' asked Poppy. 'Probably be a bit of a squeeze for me but I take it you have pins?'

'Well, I . . .' Constance paused, her mind racing. How was one supposed to respond to a complete stranger asking to borrow from one's small stock of clothing? And when most of the clothing is not yours to begin with and the only good skirt left would be one's best . . .

'It's too much, I know,' said the girl. She began to cheerfully tidy up the newspaper and handed it to the young man. 'Not to worry. My mother will be back for dinner and she'll be only too delighted to stuff me into something frivolous of hers, perish the thought.' She sighed. 'I'll just have to slowly dehydrate in the gardens until then.'

'I'm very sorry . . . but we just cannot make exceptions . . .' babbled young Mr Dudley, flushed and confused. He waved his hands as some sort of deflective protection. 'I'm sure you understand.'

'Yes, the floodgates will open and tea will become a bacchanal of oddly dressed bohemians and suffragettes.'

'Exactly,' said Dudley.

'I'll lend you something,' said Constance, leaping in as much for the poor undermanager as for the strange girl. 'I know something about how awkward hotels can be.'

'Would you really? You are a lifesaver,' said Poppy, as if the whole thing was Constance's idea. She began gathering her helmet and goggles. 'Shall we go to your room?'

'Of course,' said Constance, quailing at the thought, as she couldn't quite remember if she had left the bedroom absolutely tidy. It was quite a large room in the back of the hotel but there might be books and papers on the bed and floor. There might also be stockings drying over a chair, slippers abandoned under the dressing table and a pear ripening on the windowsill.

'While I'm dressing, could you arrange a late tea for two on the terrace, Dudley, and charge it to my mother?' said Poppy. She stopped and raised an enquiring eyebrow at Constance. 'Would that be all right? You will have some tea with me, won't you?'

'Oh, that's not necessary,' said Constance, though she felt suddenly desperate for the chance to talk to someone so interesting and of her own age.

'Nonsense!' said Poppy. 'I insist you let me treat you. It's the least I can do.'

'Well, that would be lovely,' said Constance. She did not look to see if the undermanager was raising his eyebrows at her.

'As well as tea, we'll have sardines on toast, some deviled eggs and two glasses of sherry,' added Poppy to the undermanager. She tucked her arm beneath Constance's as if they were old friends and added, 'We wouldn't want to faint from hunger before dinner.'

⇥⇤

CONSTANCE'S ROOM WAS bigger than she had expected it to be, and she was grateful it was not some narrow attic reserved for ladies' maids and children. It faced a small, fern-filled courtyard and was furnished with only a bed, a dressing table with a triple mirror and two small gilt chairs, all in the French style. It seemed to shrink with Poppy in it, and Constance, hauling her best lilac silk skirt from the wardrobe and laying it on the bed, wished she had the elegance of a screened dressing area or a full-length mirror to offer.

'What's that blue skirt in there?' asked Poppy, peering brazenly into the wardrobe. Constance, busy whisking the dried stockings out of sight, stiffened at the casual sense of entitlement, a hallmark of the wealthy so familiar to her from many years' acquaintance with Lady Mercer. But in Poppy's case she was charmed to see that it seemed to come without criticism.

'The blue is really a walking skirt; the lilac is more formal,' said Constance. She took out the plain blue wool skirt, trimmed with a narrow black ribbon around the hem, and laid it alongside the lilac skirt she had not yet worn. It was worked around the hem with embroidered sweet peas and caught up at one side to reveal an underskirt of darker purple. It was really too fine for her and she had hesitated to wear it. Perhaps she would wear it tomorrow, Sunday, when a string quartet would play on the hotel's terrace at teatime. The wardrobe also contained two white summer dresses she hesitated to dirty, several blouses and a stiffly boned, dark-blue lace evening dress. Some of the clothes were cast-offs of a decidedly old-fashioned cut, retrieved from dusty trunks and hastily altered to fit Constance. But some were more fashionable. They had been ordered for Lady Mercer's daughter, Rachel, early in the war, but when the first Zeppelin raids on London appeared in the newspapers, Rachel had been rushed away to wealthy friends in Virginia. There, she had apparently made quite an impression on American society and presumably acquired a new wardrobe along with a fiancé from a prominent political family.

Rachel and Constance called each other 'cousin', but they were not close friends as their mothers had been. There had been help, and not a little self-congratulation from the Mercers, in securing a scholarship for Constance as a day girl at the local boarding school. But Rachel had been sent away to a much more prestigious boarding school, and they had naturally, or by design, grown apart. Now Constance fingered the blue silk knots that decorated the evening gown's bodice. 'If you're having dinner later would you prefer to borrow an evening dress?' she asked. 'It is Saturday night.'

'I despise all fuss and furbelows so I'll take the blue,' said Poppy, nodding at the plain skirt. 'Do you have a scarf I can use?' She was unlacing her boots as she spoke, and then she was shimmying out of her trousers while Constance turned her back and dug in her dressing table drawer for a scarf of blue silk flowers. In another moment Poppy had slipped on the skirt, buttoning it in the front and swivelling it around to its proper position. Removing her tweed jacket, she revealed a plain white blouse with two jet pins carved into swallows at the collar. She took one and used it to fasten the scarf around her waist like a broad sash.

'You look transformed,' said Constance. 'I'm astonished.'

'I'm used to making do with very little luggage,' said Poppy, unpinning two strategic hairpins and combing her locks with her fingers.

'You can use my comb if you like,' said Constance shyly.

'Well, now I am really in your debt,' said Poppy, barely scraping her hair with the comb before loosely twisting and pinning it up again. 'Lending another girl your comb – it's sort of like my brother and his friends declaring blood brothers.'

'I would offer to lend you shoes but I'm not sure . . .'

'Oh, not to worry, I have the feet of an elephant,' said Poppy, sitting and hitching up her skirt over her knees to put on her boots. 'To my mother's eternal despair. My father would always tell her not to worry. 'In the event of a flood, Poppy will always have her own canoe,' he'd say. It really didn't help.' She shook her head, and though she gave a short laugh, her face grew soft and her eyes wet.

'Are you all right?'

'I'm sorry. My father died in the autumn. Spanish flu. I forget sometimes and then . . . well, it catches me unaware.'

Not used to such naked openness of feeling, Constance sank onto the other chair and turned her head away. In the sudden silence an unknown bird in the courtyard spilled its song into the last rays of the afternoon sun and something cracked in her usual reserve.

'My mother too,' she said at last. 'We buried her on Armistice Day.'

Constance could still hear the sounds of church bells ringing and the village band playing; see the cheering crowd gathered in front of the Rose and Crown, children waving flags and racing across the village green. The band had fallen raggedly silent as the hearse and the small band of family following it on foot had rounded the bend, heading for the church. The cheering people hushed and men removed their caps. Women nodded to her and tried to disguise a slight backing away. A pair of small girls froze where they were on the green, clutching dolls, unsure. She smiled at the girls, releasing them to run to their mother. The funeral procession was a small group; just Constance, her brother and his wife, who did not know there was worse grief to come; the Vicar, clutching a handkerchief to his nose; and two or three farmers who had been friends of the family for years, each walking carefully apart. Lady Mercer had wanted to come, of course. She made that very clear. But for the fear of the influenza and her weak heart. The Vicar had been relieved that theirs was the only funeral of the day. After they passed into the churchyard, Constance heard the cheering resume. The band struck up a march. And why not? Today marked the end of the war, and perhaps the end of the war would bring an end to the influenza, which had created so many new-turned mounds of dirt in the churchyard.

'One gets exhausted exchanging condolences,' said Poppy, and her face seemed to have lost some of its colour. 'It feels as if no one is untouched.'

'And my brother's child,' Constance added, almost a whisper. 'We lost him just before Christmas.' She could see the baby, small hands turning blue, breath bubbling as his lungs drowned. Her sister-in-law, Mary, shrieking at her, convinced that even a full month after her mother's death, it was somehow Constance's fault that the pestilence had come to the farm. That she was blameless did not stop her feeling guilty, and the crushing weight of it had helped drive her from home. She would be a governess before she would live at her brother's farm again.

'As if the war wasn't enough,' said Poppy. 'Do you think God laughs at us for our hubris?'

They sat in silence for a moment, companions of circumstance.

'Shall we go down?' said Constance.

'Don't you want to put on the pretty skirt for Saturday night?' asked Poppy. 'I'm a frump of the first order, but don't let me stop you from kitting out.'

'I'm not dressing for dinner tonight,' said Constance, smoothing at her plain wool dress, which until then she had considered appropriately demure but suitable. Perhaps if she had worn the lilac the waiter might have seated her in the dining room, she thought. 'I'll just have them bring something up later.' She turned away, touching at her hair in the mirror to disguise any blush that might betray her nonchalance.

'I have an idea,' said Poppy. 'After we have tea, why don't you do me another enormous favour and join us for dinner? Mother always has extra room at her table.'

'I couldn't possibly,' said Constance. 'It's a family dinner.'

'Well, you would have to put up with Mother,' agreed Poppy. 'But she would love the extra company. That's why she lives in a hotel.' Constance would have liked to ask where Poppy lived, but she feared it rude to ask why an unmarried daughter would not live with her perfectly available mother.

'I wouldn't like to impose' was all she managed.

'And look, my brother is a decent chap; bit morose, but he lost his leg so that's understandable,' added Poppy. 'You're not afraid of a man with one leg, are you?'

'Losing a leg? How awful,' said Constance. She had seen the broken men at the railway stations in London; leaning on crutches in their tattered coats, sleeves or trouser legs pinned up; rattling tin cans for alms. There had been a man in her carriage, all his limbs intact but rocking silently all the way to Sussex, humming low and tuneless. The war seemed to have shattered those it had not killed. Even in the seaside atmosphere of the hotel, there seemed a slight strain to the jollity, as if the same low humming vibrated behind the potted palms and between the notes of the hotel's dance orchestra. 'I'm only afraid of not knowing how to behave,' she added.

'Honestly spoken,' said Poppy. 'I know we've only just met, but I have a feeling we're going to be great friends. Do say you'll come to dinner with us. When you know me better you'll understand I find it hard to take no for an answer.'

'I believe I have already learned that,' said Constance, laughing. 'So I would be delighted.' The invitation might have been unconventional, but Constance was suddenly tired of being a dull moth. So she would let herself be drawn to this rather alarming young woman and trust that, for the length of one dinner, she was sensible enough to protect her brown powdered wings from being singed.

Chapter 2

THE SMALL ORCHESTRA WAS IN FULL SWING, MAKING ELE-
gant fox-trots out of wartime music hall songs, and the electric chandeliers glittered over a full dining room, hot with the smell of flowers and
ladies' perfume. Klaus manoeuvred carefully through the crush, holding
aloft an enormous silver tray of empty dinner plates. It was some satisfaction that he could still deftly serve scalloped potatoes between two
silver spoons, describe all the ingredients in the mornay sauce and carry
away a full table's worth of plates, glasses and cutlery with a flourish.
Despite the long-forced absence from fine dining, he could still outper-
form the large-eared young men labouring with him, who stumbled
over the names of French ingredients, slopped food onto plates and forgot how to fold a lady's napkin. In the heat of service, Klaus spun and
floated like a dancer, and tried to forget that the mornay sauce contained
only powdered cheese and that he would pay for his elegant flourishes
tonight, soaking his arthritic knuckles in a bowl of hot water and vinegar
and trying to find any comfortable position to sleep on the thin cot in his
attic room. Returning from the service area, he caught the headwaiter's
discreet sign and positioned himself at a large window table, sheltered
under a potted palm, to welcome the guests now being led, with simper-
ing ceremony, across the room.

He recognised Mrs Wirrall, who lived in a suite of rooms with its own dining room on the second floor of the hotel. She partook of dinner in the main dining room on Wednesdays and Saturdays. The wife of a local baronet, Sir John Wirrall, she had come down from London last spring and registered at the hotel without her title. The gossips said it was because she feared it might be stripped from her any day in the impending divorce mentioned in the newspapers. The baronet's sudden death last autumn – another one lost to the influenza – had saved her from scandal. Penneston, the family's country estate, had recently been returned from wartime use, but it was said Mrs Wirrall was in no rush to move in and preferred hotel living. She was also, they whispered in the kitchen, a former actress, which might explain the decided glitter about her as she glided across the carpet in her many jewels, a fur stole and the sculpted layers of a black silk evening dress.

Behind her came her two children, both with her blue eyes, straight nose and thick hair. The young man, returned from the war an amputee, was drawn and stiff around the jaw, wincing now and again as he leaned on his cane. He lived with his mother upstairs too. The young woman did not live at the hotel and Klaus had only seen her a few times. Hair barely restrained in its combs, she was bright-faced and pretty in a jolly, athletic sort of way. She seemed unconcerned that she was dressed in day clothes. To Klaus's surprise, the fourth guest, for whom he was even now pulling out a chair, was the young girl from earlier. She had changed into a tight jacket of dark blue worsted and an embroidered lilac silk evening skirt. Two bright spots augmented her anxious cheeks, but she thanked him in a calm voice, and where some might have met him with a note of triumph or spite, she threw him a smile of gratitude and friendly recognition. In that moment Klaus became as smitten and devoted as the ageing Don Quixote. Though by all reports, he thought, as he handed her a menu, the former actress was more a Dulcinea and only slightly more respectable as a chaperone than having none at all.

IT WAS A little discomfiting to Constance that she was welcomed by Mrs Wirrall, as a friend of Poppy, with a knowing air of pleasant distraction. It was as if Poppy were an eccentric child always bringing home stray puppies, injured sparrows and jars of frog spawn.

'Lovely Poppy. I'm so glad your friend has joined us for dinner. How lucky they could find an extra chair. I always have the Dover sole.' This last was confided to Constance as Mrs Wirrall slid her sable wrap from around her shoulders, as if it were necessary and perfectly normal to wear sable in late June, in a provincial English seaside town. Mrs Wirrall was thin in the deliberate way of some women who are used to being beauties and who seek to extend the fading glow through active discipline. In a perfectly oval face, now hollowing into handsome under high cheekbones, her eyes glittered below the blink and flicker of painted lashes. Her hair was curled and pomaded into shiny submission and worn in a thickly coiled and braided chignon adorned with a small crest of black feathers. She had drawn every eye as they promenaded across the dining room.

Poppy's brother, Harris, had greeted Constance with a blank politeness. He was a taller, thinner version of Poppy, with weary angles to his face and a pronounced limp. Now he caught his mother's fur awkwardly, with one arm, and passed it hastily to the headwaiter, along with his cane.

The waiter who had pulled out Constance's chair was the same thin and faded man who had refused her entry earlier. She blushed at what he must think of her, breaching the castle with company and a lilac silk evening skirt. Despite the headwaiter's imperious clicking of fingers, the waiter had taken the time to make her a short bow and to drop her napkin carefully into her lap while murmuring a welcome.

'I'm very hungry,' said Poppy, as if she had not so recently eaten a whole plate of sardines on the Palm Terrace. 'I hope you have roast beef, Klaus.'

'The chef recommends the chicken quenelles tonight,' said the waiter, in his faint German accent, filling their water glasses. 'But we do offer beef pie with barley, mushroom and parsnip.'

'That's a mushroom barley pie with a beef promise,' said Constance. 'I've eaten it twice in hopes of something more.'

'In my dreams I sometimes actually smell roast beef and horseradish,' said Poppy.

'Perhaps you should bathe more often, darling,' said Mrs Wirrall as Poppy's brother gave a reluctant chuckle. She turned to the waiter to ask, 'Is the celery fresh, Klaus? Last week it was quite limp and exhausted.'

'Perhaps it's taking lessons from Harris?' said Poppy, her eyes sparkling with the friendly malice of siblings.

'I'm glad my crippled state amuses you,' said Harris. No smile softened his response.

'You're right, I should not tease,' said Poppy. She turned as Constance raised her glass to her lips, and added, 'My poor brother was badly wounded in the war and apparently they had to amputate his sense of humour.' Constance choked on her water.

'Don't squabble, darlings. Miss Haverhill is not used to your savagery,' said Mrs Wirrall mildly. She turned to give their order to the waiter, who looked somewhat bemused as she detailed several dishes not on the menu and seemingly far in excess of the three courses allowed under the rationing rules. 'And bring us the salad after the Dover sole, and a small cheese before the pudding,' she finished. 'That way we will at least have the illusion of an adequate repast.'

Harris raised his eyes to Constance. 'You will have to forgive my awful sister, Miss Haverhill. She loves to shock. But she is right that I am abominably out of temper these days. I make a dismal dinner companion and am not to be trusted in company.' A brief smile showed he might be handsome if he cared to be.

'I am very glad for any company besides my own,' said Constance. 'My companion, Mrs Fog, often prefers to take dinner in her room.'

'That sounds wonderful to me,' said Harris. 'It would be bliss to be left alone and not dragged from pillar to post. Perhaps I shall take all meals in my room from now on.'

'You must stop moping, my dear. It's not healthy,' said his mother. She was looking around the room and nodding at acquaintances. She blew a kiss to a frail old colonel with a highly waxed and curled moustache. 'You have no idea how difficult it was to drag him down to dinner this evening—'

'No amount of dragging me to restaurants and dinner parties will make me anything other than crippled,' said Harris, interrupting. 'I think a certain amount of moping ought to be allowed, don't you, Miss Haverhill?'

'I think there is a lot of grief and pain to go around in these times,' said Constance reluctantly. 'I'm sure you're doing your best.'

'Ah, you're one of those women who is always relentlessly cheerful and useful,' said Harris, narrowing his eyes at her. 'Soldiering on to keep the home front going and all that.'

'Harris, don't be a beast,' said Poppy. Constance felt her eyes prick with angry tears to be dismissed with such condescension. It was no less humiliating because of its grain of truth.

She had hoped to attend university, but upon the death of her father, at the beginning of the war, Constance had been persuaded to stay home to look after her widowed mother. Lady Mercer had offered them a small, whitewashed gamekeeper's cottage by the stream, so that Constance's older brother and his new wife could be the master and mistress of the farm. With Lord Mercer at the War Office and the estate manager gone off to the Front, Constance had soon started to help Lady Mercer by keeping the estate's ledgers and working with the tenant farmers to run the estate. She had buried her grief in hard work and been glad to be of use and to be too tired to think at the end of every day. It was the idle times that brought her misery. But the war ended, and Lord Mercer had made it clear she was no longer required in the estate office.

'I hope I did my part,' said Constance, struggling against a tremble in her voice. She wished, just for once, that a man might praise the 'home front' efforts of women and actually mean it. 'I may not have a home to keep going any more, but I'm certainly not going to lie around all day in despair. I think that's reserved for people wealthier than I.'

'Touché,' said Harris, his face darkening as he turned away to ask his mother, 'When is that man bringing the wine?'

'No home, you say? Isn't that quite unfortunate?' said Mrs Wirrall, raising a discreet eyebrow at Poppy. Poppy smiled widely. Constance felt herself again the waif – an injured pigeon in a hatbox.

'I lost my mother in the autumn,' she said. She was too proud to tell these strangers all that she had lost. Even now she could feel the cold April afternoon in Surrey, with the rain lashing the library windows and melting the cherry blossoms from the trees outside, while Lady Mercer, keeping her face to the crackling fire, had tried to bury the bad news about Constance's future in delicate layers of elliptical language.

'Nothing could be further from my desire . . .' said Lady Mercer.

'Your beloved mother was my dearest friend . . .' she said.

'Nothing need be decided in haste . . .' she added.

Constance had already understood the rambling direction of the monologue to mean she was to be evicted from her home.

'It being almost six months since your poor mother left us, and believing your happiness will be best served, as it were, in the comfort of family . . .' Lady Mercer had blustered on, valiantly attempting to bring her point home without having to say it aloud.

'If it is a question of paying rent?' Constance had interrupted, knowing that it was not. No rent had ever been asked but, on the other hand, no help had ever been offered for the many repairs required to make the cottage livable. Instead, Constance and her mother had scrubbed and whitewashed and spent the war battling the ongoing damp in the north wall.

'Rent? No, no!' To watch Lady Mercer wriggle like a worm on a fishhook had been fascinating. Fascination and bitter amusement were perhaps not the expected emotions in such a scene but there were only so many blows to the heart one could take before becoming numb. In the country as a whole there had seemed a strange, numb resilience.

'As you know, it was such a pleasure for me to be able to offer your mother a refuge after your father died,' said Lady Mercer. 'By rights she would have stayed on with your brother and his wife, but I insisted she be the mistress of her own cosy establishment.'

'My mother and I were very grateful,' said Constance.

'No one misses her like I do.' A lace handkerchief had appeared and was pressed to the corner of a dry eye. 'When you are girls together . . .' Constance had turned her head away towards the streaming windows, biting her lip against the brief flare of pain. 'A home with your brother is, we think, a better option than to live as a young woman alone and un-protected,' Lady Mercer had said.

Now, seeing the note of pity in Mrs Wirrall's gaze, Constance under-stood the pressure to maintain a fiction of comfortable respectability.

'I have my brother. When Mrs Fog no longer needs me, I may make my home with him and his family.' She stumbled over the lie and blushed. There had been no way to explain then, as there was no way now, that while a spinster home with her brother and his wife might once have been merely uncomfortable, to live under the haunted hatred of her sister-in-law's grief was impossible. 'Until I find further employment, of course. I am considering all the possibilities.'

'Hotel living is not too bad for a season or two,' said Mrs Wirrall, distracted again. 'My husband and I spent a year on the Italian Riviera when we were young.' She sighed. 'We were different people then. Pass-ionate, carefree, childless.'

'Thank you so much for that, Mother,' said Harris.

'Of course it is so much nicer to have your own cook. Hotel cooking is all theatre and suspicious butter,' she said, as the waiter presented her a bread roll with his silver tongs and a small china pot of butter. She peered at Constance as if seeing her for the first time. 'I don't suppose it would be entirely respectable for a young woman to live in such tran-sient circumstances.'

'Mummy, Miss Haverhill is as respectable as you are,' said Poppy.

'You're not on the stage, are you, Miss Haverhill?' asked Harris. 'Though of course our mother insists the stage was much more dignified a profession in her youth.'

'I am not ashamed of my time on the stage,' said Mrs Wirrall. 'Though I was never, ever without a chaperone; even when the Prince of Wales came backstage after my Covent Garden debut, I refused to dismiss Madame Emily from the room.' She sighed. 'I might have been a princess, you know.' Poppy's laughter, hidden in her napkin, suggested this was an old family tale.

'We are just here for a few weeks' holiday while Mrs Fog convalesces,' said Constance, flustered by the interrogation. 'I nursed her through the influenza. Her family, Lord and Lady Mercer, wished to thank me.'

After her mother's death, Constance had not wanted to nurse anyone else. But the nurses wouldn't stay. Or perhaps they were too expensive or did not appreciate being banned from the servants' hall at Clivehill and their tea left in a Thermos on the back stair. And Lady Mercer was declared too fragile by the doctors, she said, to risk entering even the same wing of the house. Remembering her own mother labouring to breathe and moaning in fear, Constance could not quiet her conscience. She came to the house every day with a stout apron, a cloth mask and a basket of remedies, and took complete charge of the sickroom. Weeks after her fever broke, the old lady was still weak, with bones as fragile as a bird's, and skin so pale it shone blue in certain lights. Constance wondered privately if Mrs Fog would ever recover fully.

'Perhaps we can thank you by sending you and Mother to the seaside as soon as the weather improves,' Lady Mercer had said, just a few days after suggesting eviction. 'My father had a bath chair and a man to push it one summer. I dare say we could manage without the expense of the man as Mummy would be so much lighter to push.' Constance had been too stunned to speak and this had been taken as acquiescence.

Once again, the thanking had not extended to any definite financial arrangement. Instead, Lady Mercer had made all the hotel arrangements and passed down to Constance a small wardrobe of suitable attire for life in a seaside hotel. Constance had examined her own meagre savings and brought the largest portion with her. And the old lady had surprised her on their journey down by pressing a small purse of money into her hand and telling her a young woman should be able to buy the occasional book and hair ribbon on her holiday.

'Mercer? Surrey, isn't it?' said Mrs Wirrall. 'Near Box Hill. Ancient family fortune married into some interests from the old Barbados sugar trade?'

'Don't mind Mother,' said Poppy. 'She has Burke's Peerage entirely memorised. It's her principal hobby to know who everyone is.'

'Not at all,' said Mrs Wirrall. 'I just have an excellent memory.'

'And she does not remember that it is unseemly to talk about the finances of one's peers,' added Harris.

'Of course I do,' said Mrs Wirrall. 'I never talk money. Though I met an earl once who fancied himself above all men, and it was quite satisfying to tell him how much I admired his saving the family fortune through his early investments in patented shoe polish.'

'And she calls me incorrigible,' said Poppy.

'So how did you come to be employed by Lady Mercer?' asked Mrs Wirrall.

'It was not a paid position, more a family favour,' said Constance, her voice perhaps a little too urgent. 'Lady Mercer is my mother's oldest childhood friend. When the war broke out I was asked to help run the estate.' She paused, unsure how much to reveal. 'I understand now that Lady Mercer and my mother probably plotted together to keep me safe at home.'

'Running an estate is an extraordinary task for a young woman,' said Mrs Wirrall.

'Women worked or volunteered at all kinds of professions in the war, Mother,' said Poppy.

'If this is an attempt to get me to invest more in your little motorcycle company, I decline to engage,' said her mother. 'I'm sure Miss Haverhill would not dream of coming to dinner with oil under her fingernails.'

'My father's family have always been farmers,' said Constance, as Poppy rolled her eyes while surreptitiously examining her hands below the table. 'I grew up learning how things run.'

'So you are a farmer's daughter,' said Mrs Wirrall. 'Well, farming is perfectly respectable these days. Kept us going through the war and all that. I can't think why Harris thought you were an actress.'

'I said no such thing,' said Harris. 'Miss Haverhill is quite obviously more dairymaid than demi-monde.'

'My mother is from a clerical family,' added Constance. Then she shut her lips, for to mention her late grandfather, the Bishop, might suggest some shame of her own father. She blushed at her shabbiness.

'My fingernails are perfectly clean, Mother,' added Poppy.

Constance decided she would not let Harris Wirrall's arrogance ruin her enjoyment of dinner. All around her the restaurant hummed and glittered under the chandeliers. The orchestra played, the small dance floor was already full of spinning couples; the waiters swept in long curves between the tables, their enormous trays held high, white gloves flashing. The tinkling of many spoons against china, the splash of champagne and ruby wine into glasses, the shimmer of evening dresses against the dark of men's dinner jackets. Here and there the brass and braid of uniforms still visible. She knew it was not the most fashionable of seaside towns, nor as grand a hotel as might be found on the French Riviera or even in nearby Brighton, but she was glad to be amid such warmth and gaiety.

There were celery stalks on a long glass dish served with small silver tongs. There were dishes of small green olives, and a plate of the ubiquitous tinned sardines rolled around tiny white onions and stuck through with a cocktail pick. A broth followed, slightly cloudy. Then an indeterminate course of oeufs mayonnaise. Finally, the main course: Mrs Wirrall had ordered Dover sole for the ladies and the pie for Harris. She had commanded, and was delivered, buttered new potatoes, a dish of tiny spring peas and a carrot mash. There was even a small wedge of lemon in a muslin cloth, which the waiter squeezed over their fish with a silver tool.

'I haven't seen a lemon since before the war,' said Constance. There were one or two frowns from ladies at neighbouring tables, which indicated that not all patrons had been honoured with such an intoxicating spritz.

'My father knew the hotel's owners,' said Poppy. 'I think he invested.'

'It's not ladylike to pay any attention to business,' said Mrs Wirrall, frowning at her daughter. 'But I was offered the utmost consideration when I came here to live and I offer, in return, my loyalty.'

'Mummy won't buy so much as a cup of tea at any other establishment,' said Poppy. 'Sometimes we find ourselves at quite the other end of the promenade and as thirsty as a desert expedition, but she will insist we stagger back here.'

'A commitment must not fall to mere convenience,' said Mrs Wirrall. 'Faint hearts did not win us the war.'

'No, but bloody-mindedness cost us a few lives,' said Harris.

'Harris, you are abominable this evening,' said Mrs Wirrall. She waved a finger as if he were a naughty lapdog. 'I don't know why I allow it.'

'Because he's your favourite child, Mummy,' said Poppy. She turned to Constance. 'I on the other hand am the black sheep of the family.'

'Don't be silly, Poppy,' said her mother. 'I've always said you are beautiful when you make an effort.'

'How is the renovation of the house coming along, Mummy?' said Poppy, winking at Constance as she changed the subject. 'Less of a lost cause than I am, I hope.'

Mrs Wirrall was happy to talk at length about the improvements she was making to their country home now that it had been returned by the army. There was to be a Moorish-style garden room centred on a fountain with mosaic panels and imported orchids. A large divan draped with shawls and a round carpeted ottoman for a table. Two large palm trees flanking the doors. The architect had been so complimentary about her ideas, wondering if she had trained professionally. Constance was delighted to hear her talk, to watch her daughter spar and tease her for her extravagance and her affection for florid decoration. Even the surly Harris, with his unfocused stare and slumped shoulders, joined in with a few blistering comments, delivered in the voice of affectionate condescension that men sometimes use to convey love. Most of all Constance was relieved not to be interrogated further about her circumstances but to be merely allowed to listen to the conversation wash over her as she relaxed and enjoyed the room.

After the fish, accompanied by a thick yellow wine from Alsace, there came a salad of young lettuce and shaved asparagus brightened with vinegar and flecked with salt. Then thin slices of mild Cheshire cheese, with plain crackers and a spoonful of fig preserve. A dish of gooseberries sweetened with redcurrant jam and swirled with custard was brought to round out the dinner.

The room grew warm and loud with laughter and conversation. The orchestra broke into a waltz and the dance floor itself seemed to whirl under the crowd of dancers. Or perhaps it was just her head, thought Constance, whirling from the mingling of so many perfumes. Even the palm tree above their heads seemed to keep time to the music, nodding in a stray fresh breeze from a transom window as a stream of laughing people flowed in and out from the lobby and the terrace to join the dancing.

'Oh, Poppy, look up, there's Tom Morris and his sisters,' said Mrs Wirrall, waving at a group of young people entering the dining room. 'Lovely girls,' she added to Constance. 'Guinevere lost her fiancé at the Somme.'

'Mother, must you wave like that?' asked Harris. 'It's a little showy.'

'Nonsense! Poppy will wish to introduce her new friend,' said Mrs Wirrall.

The twins and their brother, who was dressed in the blue uniform of the new Royal Air Force, headed over to the table. A second young man, awkward in a stiff black dinner suit, hovered a moment by a potted aspidistra trying to look nonchalant before following them. Harris stood up and bowed over the hands of the two lithe, ash-blonde girls in almost matching dinner dresses of pleated pink and grey silk. The dresses came to just below the knee, with only a fringe about the young women's shapely calves. Constance was shocked but also wished that her own lilac skirt was not so long and full about the ankles. Tom Morris, very blond as well but taller than his sisters, insisted on kissing Mrs Wirrall on both cheeks, continental style, and would have done the same to Poppy had she not sent him a glowering look.

'Ah, Poppy. As lovely but impervious as ever,' said the young man. 'When are you going to sell me your barn and motorcycles and marry me?'

'When are you going to let me fly one of your aeroplanes?' replied Poppy. Tom laughed and shook his head. He shook hands with Harris and slapped him on the back. The spare young man shook hands with Poppy as Tom gave Constance a broad wink. 'May we be presented to your lovely friend, Harris, in hopes she is kinder than your sister to a poor aviator just home from the war.'

'Ignore my brother. He's just back from Russia,' explained the twin introduced as Guinevere. She shook hands with Constance, smiling. 'He doesn't understand times have changed. Evangeline and I love our motorcycle and even Father agrees it can be perfectly feminine.' She touched a hand to her smooth hair, bobbed to the chin and carefully waved.

'He's been bombing the Bolsheviks,' added Evangeline. Her hair was even shorter and tucked, with a fresh camellia, behind one ear. Her handshake was less enthusiastic, and her eyes, looking Constance up and down, seemed to confirm Constance's fear that her skirt was dowdy.

'To no great effect, I'm afraid,' said Tom. 'I'm sure if we still had Harris we'd have beaten them back to Moscow, but as it is they are proving as stubborn as mice in a barn.' An awkward pause ensued as if each were thinking of Harris's misfortune. Evangeline seemed to blush, another small difference between the twins.

'As Captain Morris is too busy talking about himself to introduce Mr Sam Newcombe, may I do the honours?' said Poppy. The spare young man bowed over Constance's hand and murmured some pleasantry – 'Very pleased. A friend of Poppy's . . .' – that was largely lost in general conversation.

'Is Constance a motorcycle fiend as well, I wonder?' asked Tom, raising his eyebrows.

'I am not, Captain Morris,' she replied, raising her eyebrows back to reprove his overfamiliarity.

'She will be as soon as I take her out,' said Poppy. 'We'll go tomorrow and I guarantee, Constance, you'll be a convert in a matter of miles!'

'If I have to hear any more about motorcycles,' said Mrs Wirrall, waving her hands. 'Your sisters must be glad to have you home, Tom?'

'If I were allowed to be home,' he said. 'They have me out dancing every night.'

'Ah, to be young and full of stamina,' said Mrs Wirrall, looking artfully wistful.

'Would you care to dance, Mrs Wirrall?' Tom bowed theatrically. 'I know you dance rings around any girl in the place, and frankly I am tired of dancing with my sisters.'

'Oh no, we don't dance,' said Mrs Wirrall. If her glance at Harris was meant to be discreet, it failed. It was Harris who spoke into the uncomfortable pause.

'My mother doesn't care to dance at the hotel,' he said. 'But if you are at the next charity dance at the Winter Garden, I'm sure she will save you a cakewalk, won't you, Mother?'

'I will save you a tango, young man,' she said. 'I will show you how we did it when it first came from Argentina.'

'We're going dancing after dinner. New club on the pier,' said Sam

Newcombe, his ears turning red at his own abruptness. 'Your party welcome, Wirrall?'

'Oh yes, do come,' added Guinevere with great enthusiasm. 'It's shockingly democratic and one dances ragtime with soldiers and airmen, shopgirls and typists.'

'Are there any farmers?' said Harris, his face neutral. Poppy punched him in the arm.

'One doesn't have to dance with any of them,' Evangeline assured Constance. 'A polite refusal and they leave you alone.' Her pretty bowed mouth made a small moue of distaste.

'Evangeline is such a snob,' said her sister. 'No one cares – we even dance with each other. Since the war, no one thinks twice about two girls dancing together. It's quite liberating not to have to worry about a man.' Mr Newcombe gave a small cough and she giggled. 'Oh, we don't mean you, Sam.'

'You should come with us,' said Newcombe. 'Absolute fun.'

'Or perhaps another time,' said Evangeline, her tone cool, as if slightly bored. 'Don't push so, Gwinny.' She turned to wave at a friend on the dance floor as Gwinny blushed, and Constance thought that, while it might be hard to tell the twins' pretty faces apart, one might know them easily by their manners.

'I trust Mrs Wirrall knows my sisters are only pretending to be entirely disreputable,' said Tom. 'Come, girls, we will remove ourselves to the dance floor and leave these good people before your reputations are quite ruined.'

'Sometimes it seems the world has gone mad for dancing,' said Mrs Wirrall, as the foursome joined the dance floor. 'Last week I found my maid and the hotel housekeeper waving pillowcases around and doing the Lambeth Walk in my rooms. I had to have a strong word.'

'If you don't mind, Mother, I think I would like to withdraw,' said Harris, still looking after the Morris twins as they were swept away in the circling crowd. His brow furrowed and he closed his eyes briefly against the glare of the chandeliers, as if threatened by a headache.

'Is it too loud for you, dear?' said Mrs Wirrall. She gave him a smile but her eyes flickered with worry as she patted his hand. 'Shall we go upstairs directly?' She spoke in a voice familiar to Constance, that of nurse to invalid.

'I think I'll drop by the snug,' said Harris, withdrawing his hand abruptly as if to dispel any such suggestion. 'It's much quieter in there and one or two chaps might be in this evening.'

'Of course,' said Mrs Wirrall. 'I'm sure Miss Haverhill won't mind us being informal and letting you part with us.' With that she rose from the table, the headwaiter making a heroic effort to reach her in time to pull back her chair.

Constance rose hesitantly, while Poppy threw down her napkin in mock disgust and said, 'Suppose I wanted to dance, Mother? Does anyone think to ask me?'

'You never want to dance, dear,' said her mother. 'In fact I would be so delighted if you wished to, I might even wave my napkin and call Tom back over, despite the public nature of the room.'

'I'm sure I can find you a couple of chaps in the bar,' added Harris. 'If you want to really confound Mother.'

'Whatever will Miss Haverhill think of us?' said Mrs Wirrall. 'I'm sure in Surrey young women don't dance with complete strangers in hotels?'

'There was a war, Mummy,' said Poppy. 'We women won't stand to be treated like children any more, you know.'

'Well, I was going to have them bring some candied almonds with our coffee, but since you're no longer a child . . .'

'Don't threaten me, Mother, you know it has no effect,' said Poppy. 'I'm perfectly capable of ordering my own almonds.'

'Yes, but not paying for them, my dear,' said her mother. 'Now that would be very modern.'

AFTER THANKING MRS WIRRALL effusively for dinner, and accepting an invitation to go for a ride on Poppy's motorcycle should Mrs Fog be able to spare her, Constance went to Mrs Fog's room to see if she was still awake. She was sitting on a chaise with her feet up, reading, but she put the book aside to listen with interest to Constance's confession of her evening adventure. Of course, Constance spoke a little more of the glamorous Mrs Wirrall and a little less about Miss Wirrall's enthusiasm for the motor trade and in her shading tried to make the entire episode seem eminently respectable.

'An unorthodox introduction to be sure,' said Mrs Fog. 'But a prominent family and a young man as well. You are a clever girl, Constance Haverhill, and I look forward to seeing this Mrs Wirrall for myself.'

'The young man is not at all pleasant,' said Constance. 'I cannot recommend him as I do the mother and daughter.'

'Pleasantness must certainly be weighed,' said Mrs Fog, and Constance understood she, an unmarried girl, was not expected to weigh it very heavily against such qualities as a good family and solid prospects. It mortified her that still – after a world war, after her own service to the family, after her precious certificates earned via correspondence school – even the most well-meaning of friends and family continued to see marriage, any marriage, as her preferred future. 'Is that the time?' added Mrs Fog, looking weary. 'I shall undress directly.'

Constance was pleased to change the topic. She offered to help Mrs Fog but, as usual, was refused.

'You are not a maid, dear,' said Mrs Fog. 'And I fear to lose the use of my arms through indolence.' Constance could only smile, for there was little she had not done for Mrs Fog, or seen of her emaciated body, during her sickness. Sometimes she wished they could talk of it, for she often felt the weight of those dark days piling up on her as if she were being smothered under a pile of dank, itchy wool blankets. But it was clear that, while her efforts had been appreciated, the distasteful past was to be put away unexamined.

There were two stiff buttons with which some assistance was required, but then Constance waited in the tall room with its silk bed hangings, its suite of French furniture and its balcony hanging above the sea while Mrs Fog disappeared into the small dressing room. She emerged again in a long flannel nightgown and bedsocks and Constance rang for the hotel maid to come in to pick up her clothes. The maid had been called on their first night in the hotel to draw a bath and assist Mrs Fog in and out of the enormous tub. But the maid was rough with her hair, the old lady said, and so she allowed Constance to brush it at night; one hundred slow gentle strokes through the waist-length grey locks lying spread across the back of a padded chair.

'A woman's hair is part of her dowry, my mother used to say.' Mrs Fog peered closer at the dressing table mirror. 'She used to make me wear it in such a profusion of coils and braids it took my maid an hour a day and that was just for an ordinary weekday, never mind a ball.' For a moment the expression of a younger girl flickered across the soft white face now cross-hatched with fine wrinkles. The grey eyes, perhaps catching the electric lamplight, sparkled with a remembered energy. The old woman raised a long thin hand briefly to her cheekbone.

'There's a tea dance twice a week in the dining room,' said Constance gently. 'I'm not very good with hair but, between us, the maid and I could manage a few elegant coils?'

'Nothing looks worse than an old woman clinging to vanity,' said Mrs Fog. 'My daughter will tell you it is better to project a plain dignity.'

'Oh, but you brought your diamond combs with you,' said Constance. 'Surely we must find an occasion for you to wear them?'

'My husband gave me the combs on our honeymoon at Lake Como. Such a courtly gesture to give them to me privately, on a terrace under the moonlight, without any fanfare as to their cost, or his own hand in the design. I never bragged about them and if anyone asked me I would say they were just an old favourite and so comfortable. Then I would catch his eye and he would nod his approval.'

'That is so romantic,' said Constance.

'One didn't marry for love and romance back then,' she sighed. 'But he was a generous man and I did come to love him very much. Perhaps I will wear them once more before I cut my hair for good. One should be shorn and shriven to be ready to meet one's maker.'

'You are convalescing far too well to worry about that anytime soon,' said Constance. 'My mother was sure you would outlive us all.'

'Your mother probably said I was a tough old boot,' said the old lady. 'She was never one to mince her words. She often shocked me in her youth, but as I've aged I've sometimes wished I had her stalwart tongue.'

'So you recommend impertinence in the young now?' said Constance. She smiled, and Mrs Fog's reflection blinked twice and twitched her lips. Mrs Fog had changed. Being so ill seemed to have softened the old lady. Both physically, for she sagged at the shoulder and hip and her hands lay in her lap like two small birds, and in her character. She had become more reflective. She stopped and turned in a room as if she saw things from the corner of an eye. She smiled at waiters and spoke to other hotel guests. She had walked the length of the Palm Terrace on Constance's arm and asked other ladies if they played cards until a daily foursome was arranged. It would surely have upset Lady Mercer to know her mother had made no enquiries into who the other ladies might be. She had simply been delighted to find like minds among the potted palms. Constance hoped it was not wrong to take pleasure in what might be the effects of sickness on the brain, but she hoped the effects would be lasting, if only for Mrs Fog's own happiness.

'So you think we should attend a tea dance?' said Mrs Fog, raising an eyebrow. 'Are there any particular young gentlemen you hope will be there, or are you merely eager to help entertain the uniformed officers I see milling about the hotel?'

'I thought you might enjoy the music and the pretty dresses,' said Constance. 'The Saturday night dancing is a little loud and crowded, but the afternoons should be quieter.' She did not blush at the mention of young men, for though she thought Harris Wirrall and Tom Morris were certainly handsome, each in his own arrogant way, and though they and the quieter, plainer Sam Newcombe had brought a certain bouncing energy to the room, she was not guilty of any particular interest. She wondered if she was also affected by the sickness; if the long hours of caregiving had aged her. 'I am not opposed to dancing if you approve,' she added. 'I suppose I am a little afraid that such pleasures might be hubris. I've forgotten how to enjoy frivolity.'

'It is hard not to look at those young men and see at their shoulders all the boyhood companions who are laid in the ground,' said Mrs Fog. 'But at the same time, should these times not teach us to seize life and live it now, while we can? There is no time left to waste your youth and beauty. You must live life to the full.'

'Why, Mrs Fog, you are talking like a new woman,' said Constance. 'I only suggested a tea dance, not a revolution.'

'And you must get away from us at Clivehill. We will use you up, you know. You should make your own way. If not a husband, then a paid position. Save for a small home of your own. Just a room or two.' Mrs Fog grew animated, as if remembering such rooms. She turned to clasp Constance's hands in her own. 'It's not that we don't mean well, but we are too busy with ourselves to see the lives of others properly. You deserve more than a life of disappointment.'

'Mrs Fog, calm yourself,' said Constance, for tears hung in the old lady's eyes and she shivered. 'I am very happy to be right here with you now. I am very lucky.'

'Oh, don't listen to me,' said the old lady. 'I'm tired and don't know what I'm saying.' Constance finished the last stroke of the hairbrush and began to plait the long hair into a loose braid, which she tied with a silk ribbon and rolled up into a cotton nightcap.

'There, you are all put away for the night,' she said. 'Should I order you some hot milk?'

'We shall attend a tea dance soon,' said Mrs Fog, climbing into the tall four-poster bed and pulling the blankets to her chin as if it were January outside the windows. 'If you could just close all the shutters and curtains,' she added. 'It seems to stay light until midnight and the moon has been as bright as a lighthouse after that.'

Constance closed the balcony's shutters, the windows and the curtains. There were two additional tall windows to shutter. And then there were many electric lamps to turn off, leaving only a small lamp on the dressing table. She folded a dropped shawl and set it on the back of a settee. She straightened some picture magazines and a book of local maps on a side table. Hearing the maid leave the dressing room, she went in to bolt the external door and then returned to pour a glass of water from a carafe and set it at the bedside. As Mrs Fog asked so little help, Constance did this to feel as if she were earning her keep. Mrs Fog was already asleep and softly snoring among the down pillows. As she passed the small writing desk Constance saw, under a sheet of white paper, that Mrs Fog had left a finished letter, sealed, addressed and waiting to be posted. An unfamiliar local address and an unfamiliar name, a Miss de Champney. It was not her place to look at Mrs Fog's letters, but she could make sure that it went to the front desk to catch the earliest post tomorrow morning. Another small way to be a good companion. She gave one last glance around the room and let herself out the heavy door.

Chapter 3

⟶

THE SEASIDE PROMENADE BLAZED WITH COLOUR UNDER a bright blue sky on a day so windy everything seemed to be streaming sideways: flags, hat ribbons, coat-tails, the canvas seats of unoccupied deckchairs. A woman in a billowing white coat, a white hat clutched in one hand and a leashed pair of long-haired white hounds in the other, blew by like a clipper ship under full sail. On the pier, pennants flapped from spikes atop every domed kiosk roof, and at the bandstand across the street from the hotel, the halyard beneath the raised Union Jack slapped and bounced against the flagpole as if drumming out a tune. It was as if the world had been washed with rain and was now being dried on a laundry line, thought Constance as she buttoned her linen jacket at the throat and checked the security of her two long hatpins. It would not do to lose one's navy straw cloche and be forced to run down the prom-enade like a child chasing a hoop.

It was a day to lift the spirits and admit the future. As she left the shelter of the hotel's portico to join the other people beating upwind on the promenade, she did not flinch when Hazelbourne-on-Sea's newest sightseeing attraction came into view. Leaning on its side against the steep pebbled shore, the stranded German U-boat had attracted a larger than usual crowd. When she first arrived in Hazelbourne, the sight of it, higher than the pier, had been a shock to Constance, as if the war had appeared to menace them again. It seemed incongruous and slightly offensive the way families posed for photographs in its hulking shadow and hardy men paid tuppence to climb its rusting steel flanks and walk about the sloping decks.

The captured submarine had broken its lines months ago while being towed to scrap and this morning it was finally to be towed off the beach again by the Royal Navy. The sightseers were being herded back like recalcitrant sheep by some constables. Out at sea, two tugboats and a small navy cutter rolled and belched smoke into the breeze as they struggled to maintain their positions. At last a whistle sounded, flags were waved and a loud klaxon caused the crowd to scramble backwards towards the promenade. Tow ropes tightened, emerging from the sea in a spray of water, and the belching of smoke and the grinding of engines grew louder. The U-boat let out a slow groan and shifted infinitesimally more upright on the beach. A railing bent, a rope snapped loose and flew out to the sea. More whistles, another howl from the klaxon, and the lines went slack amid a general waving of signal flags and shouting. Constance turned away. As fascinating as it was to watch, it seemed liable to be a long process. Plenty of time to take her daily walk.

At the end of the promenade, where the town tried, but failed, to climb the green flanks of the high chalk Downs, Constance broke her brisk stride to duck into one of the ornate ironwork shelters that dotted the seafront. Her eyes were blurry, her cheeks roughened, and her hair had escaped in tendrils to whip about her face. Through the slightly fogged windows she could see the English Channel throwing lace handkerchiefs of foam up onto the beach. A fishing boat, draped with black nets, sailed towards the other end of town, a huddled low village, where workers and their hard-pressed wives lived in narrow, twisted alleys, and the beach was studded with black-tarred net-drying huts, beached fishing boats and a few market stalls selling the fresh catch.

The town seemed to grow in prosperity from east to west. The Meredith Hotel, the pier and the black interruption of the U-boat marked the centre point, and the houses beyond became larger and more fanciful – several Palladian villas and a redbrick castle with twisted turret and gargoyles studded like jewels among the lush ornamental shrubberies. On the beach here, men were adding extra ropes to the red-and-white-striped bathing tents as they flapped in the wind. Further along, a set of railway ties formed a short ramp into the water and a tall ladder contraption lay on its side, bolted to a stanchion. On less windy days, two red seaplanes alternated buzzing in and out from here, taking more affluent visitors on aerial tours of the beachfront. Above the western end of town, the smooth swell of the Downs rose, carpeted in grass and shaggy groupings of gorse, now blazing with yellow flowers. The white chalk edge of the cliff was thick and sharp against the blue sky, like a child's drawing.

'Harrumph.' A loud cough startled Constance. A man had slipped into the shelter and was standing at the far end. Her heart beat from the surprise but, she reminded herself, the promenade was crowded and the day was bright. She was quite safe. She stared hard and the stranger silently raised his hat, a gentleman's signal that he would welcome but not insist upon a conversation. He was young, slightly plump about the waistcoat, and had a thin moustache. He looked nervous and Constance realised she was glaring at the same moment she felt the wheels of her memory slowly click round and fall into place.

'I'm sorry, Mr Newcombe, isn't it?' she said. 'I believe we were introduced last night?'

'Didn't think you remembered,' said the young man in his slight stammer. 'Bit leery of greeting ladies in the street, but not polite to cut them either. Saw you coming up the way. Friend of Poppy's, I thought.'

'Sorry, I was lost in my thoughts,' said Constance. 'I didn't mean to be rude.'

'Not at all,' said Sam. 'Presumptuous on my part.'

'Won't you sit down?' she asked.

'I had hoped to see you at breakfast.' He spread a handkerchief on the painted bench and sat down on it. 'That is, I thought I would see you. Not to accost you, understand . . . I mean just across the room . . . as one does.'

'I breakfast early,' said Constance. Mrs Fog had preferred her breakfast in bed today and Constance had eaten alone. 'You'll think me silly, but I find it hard to concentrate on my boiled egg with too many eyes looking at me over the rims of teacups.'

'Quite right,' he said. 'Better eating alone. Indigestion is the worry.' And it seemed to Constance that he peered at her with a new degree of interest.

'Are you from Sussex, Mr Newcombe?' This bland question, which disguised an idle but pressing interest to know why he was staying at the Meredith when he had friends in the neighbourhood, made her the very definition of a gossip, thought Constance, but she smiled encouragingly in the hope of a detailed answer.

'From north of London,' he said. She noticed he did not say where exactly, but underneath his educated accent she caught the faintest inflection of somewhere well beyond the home counties. 'Tom Morris and I were at school together.' He stopped, standing up to raise his hat as a woman pushing a perambulator stopped to peer into the shelter. She looked annoyed at the idea of sharing the space with others and went away, frowning.

'You were telling me about Tom?' prompted Constance.

'I used to come down in the holidays. Very kind family,' said Sam. 'But I like to stay in the hotel now. Telephone in my room, you know. No one looking askance if it rings in the middle of tea.'

'You're in business, then?' asked Constance.

'Newcombe Foundries. Started by my grandfather. Motorcycle and aeroplane parts mostly,' he said. 'Spent the war making munitions.'

'I see.' She tried not to see again the newsreel images: yards and yards of pointy shells, the grinning faces of girls poisoned by yellow sulphur, the bombs falling soundlessly from beneath an aeroplane towards tiny rooftops.

'What did you do in the Great War, Daddy?' he said, quoting the recruiting posters that still hung, tattered and faded, on streets across England. There was a note of unexpected bitterness in his voice.

'We all had our part to play,' said Constance.

'Wanted to go, you know,' he added. 'Essential service, they said.'

'They didn't take my brother either,' said Constance. 'He had a large farm to run. I know something of what he suffered, feeling left behind.' Dark days in which she felt the weight of responsibility thrust too early on his shoulders and saw his desire to go to the war thwarted. Yet they did not speak of his conflict or of hers, for she too had dearly wanted to go, if not to university then to a typing pool in London or to train as a nurse. She had retreated from him, the unmarried sister leaving his welfare to his wife and being careful not to meddle. But underneath, she was ashamed to acknowledge, there ran the faint rubbing of a resentment that the farm had been left to her brother alone. Her mother's small life savings were also bequeathed for the farm. Constance, being left no monies, went unmentioned in both her parents' wills and was more hurt by the absence of her name than the absence of funds.

They were quiet for a moment. Outside, the happy shrieks of children running barefoot on the narrow strip of low-tide sand, and the braying of a donkey pulling plump tourists in a small wicker cart, mingled with the sudden roar of an automobile and the faint murmur of strolling pedestrians. A breeze carried the distant carnival sound of an organ-grinder and the smell of cherry ice cream.

'Morris's company, Hazelbourne Aviation, is a big customer,' said Sam. He reddened. 'Not supposed to mention it, I suppose. Being gentlemen, you see.'

'I plan to take up paid employment soon,' said Constance. 'I suppose I shouldn't bring that up either?'

'No, exactly,' said Sam. He seemed relieved and nodded several times. 'Poppy Wirrall doesn't mind,' he added. 'Good head on her shoulders.'

'She's very kind,' said Constance. 'We're going for a ride this afternoon.'

'Stern constitution, I hope? Bags of fun but bit of a jaw rattler.' He chuckled. 'Not one of ours, you see. I told her it needs dampening in the suspension.' He peered closely at her again. 'Wouldn't let her corner that contraption above ten miles an hour, Miss Haverhill.'

'Are you saying it's unsafe?' she said.

'No, no,' he said. 'Just keep your teeth apart and wave your arms like this. Only if she gets out of control.' He made downward waving motions with his hands.

'I'm sure Poppy means to transport me at a decorous pace,' said Constance doubtfully. She had imagined the sidecar like a small carriage and the motorcycle its stalwart pony. She had planned to wear her best hat and perhaps a light shawl. 'You don't think I'll have to wear a cap and goggles, do you?'

'Not one to impose,' said Sam. 'Not my place. But perhaps I should be there. Have a word with Poppy and see you off.'

Sam raised his hat and went away. Constance smiled, for though he was shy and abrupt she liked his earnest manner. As she walked back towards the hotel, she could see that at the pier the towing party seemed to have given up. The navy cutter was gone and the last tugboat was steaming out of view. As she leaned on the seafront railing, Constance wondered why they were in such a rush to have the war towed away and tidied up anyway. Memories faded, scabbed over by the layers of time. Perhaps a lasting peace required some rusting reminders of carnage?

The U-boat remained, as sad as an old beached whale; visitors once more picking their way like ants along its tilted decks and small boys throwing rocks at its black steel underbelly.

THE MOTORCYCLE AND sidecar parked at the front steps of the hotel were shiny with brass and navy paint with details and curlicues pricked out in scarlet. The sidecar, with its double-folding black fabric hood, did resemble a miniature landau carriage. Lettering on its lower body said, WIRRALL'S, and a wooden plaque screwed in with brass-headed screws said:

LADIES
CABRIOLET CONVEYANCE

Such long words necessitated small letters so that the sidecar appeared to say only WIRRALL'S LADIES, and quite a crowd had gathered as if waiting for a procession of miniature ladies to emerge from its small door. The hotel doorman looked away to the promenade as if there was nothing to see in front of his hotel. Poppy Wirrall, in leather flying coat and trousers tucked into her boots, her leather hood and goggles slung around her neck atop a yellow silk scarf, was happily passing out small handbills. She ignored Sam Newcombe, who seemed to be speaking to the back of her head in a low, earnest fashion.

'My lady chauffeurs are all highly experienced and will take you anywhere within twenty miles, ladies. Perfectly safe and discreet. Telephone us from home or ask right here at the hotel,' said Poppy, by which Constance understood that the doorman was a party to the arrangement. 'We guarantee to pick you up within an hour or the ride is free.'

'Do you take small children?' asked a lady, slipping the handbill into her pocket.

'Do you have a husband?' called a man in a broad-striped jacket and straw boater. 'Is he in there?' A laugh gusted through the crowd.

'You should leave it to the men, dear,' said another woman, handing back the paper. 'They need the jobs, poor dears.'

'All our ladies maintain their own machines,' added Poppy, more loudly now. 'Some are war widows with children to support.'

'Fine example for children,' snorted a matron trailing a gaping adolescent son.

'Perhaps you'd be more comfortable in the side alley?' said the doorman in a low voice. 'More private like.'

'No, thank you, we must demonstrate the future if we are to win it.'

Constance did not realise she was actively shrinking away until Poppy caught sight of her and waved. 'Yoo-hoo, Miss Haverhill? Your chariot!' She opened the door with a flourish and Constance had no choice but to step forward and try not to redden under the critical gaze of the crowd.

'Don't be afraid, Miss Haverhill,' said Sam, coming to offer her an arm to the door. 'Poppy has agreed to be circumspect.' He gave her hand an encouraging squeeze.

'Just hop in and sit down facing front,' said Poppy. Raising her voice, she added: 'Now to really take in the views we just lower the hood.'

'I'm perfectly fine with just the side window,' said Constance, eager to disappear from view.

'Nonsense!' whispered Poppy. 'Just sit down and I'll show you how it works.'

Bending in half to enter, Constance tucked in her skirts and managed to squeeze onto the padded red leather bench in the rear. It was a tight fit and she had to tuck her head to keep her hat from pressing against the cream fabric lining the roof. Her knees reached to a similar bench at the front and she wondered what it was for as there seemed no possibility that two people's knees would fit in the centre. Poppy shut the door, and for a moment Constance was a small child again, tucked into the perambulator with her brother, pulling a blue crocheted blanket over her knees and peering out over the buttoned-up cover at her mother as English rain streamed from the hood. A brief image, but so powerful she had quite forgotten to feel claustrophobic in the tiny dark space when suddenly the sky opened. Poppy Wirrall, still showing off for the crowd, lowered the front hood, snapped down and secured the top half of the door, and then lowered the rear, in one smooth display. Constance, revealed like a jack-in-the-box, blinked under a smattering of applause.

'Hold on to your hat,' said Poppy, climbing astride the motorcycle and pulling on her helmet and goggles. With a flourish of her scarf and an abrupt down kick, she brought the machine to ear-splitting life.

'Good luck!' called Sam. There was a smell of petrol and a rush of smoke from the exhaust, a stepping back of the crowd. Constance clutched her hat in terror . . . and Poppy pulled away in stately fashion, waving goodbye as she piloted the machine as slowly as if there were a glass of water balanced on the handlebars. Constance, undoing the death grip on her poor hat, sat straighter and looked back. Sam waved. He looked rather sad to be left behind. The doorman lifted his hand to his cap. The onlookers cheered, and Constance risked a small wave and a smile as her chariot moved smoothly away along the promenade.

It was too loud to talk and, even at a slow pace, the wind streamed under her hat brim and threatened to dislodge her hair from its pins, but it was such fun to be whisked along the seafront. Children whooped and cheered as they passed, and all manner of heads turned to look. They surprised a donkey cart, overtaking it in a spurt of smoke and causing the donkey to bray and stop short. They overtook the seafront tram and waved at the holidaymakers on the top deck. At the public gardens, Poppy rode even more slowly, perhaps so the groups of ladies, promenading among the lush flower beds under parasols, might read the sign on the sidecar. Finally, just where the road turned inland and uphill, Poppy pulled to the side and throttled the machine lower until it idled, growling like a dozing bear.

'Are you enjoying it?' she asked. 'If so, I thought there's plenty of time before tea and maybe I'd take us on a run up on the Downs and then circle back to Penneston. Show you my ladies' barn?'

'I'd love it,' said Constance. 'It's a beautiful day to be chauffeured about the countryside.'

'Time to secure your hat and put on your goggles then,' said Poppy. Reaching down, she raised the little front bench and pulled from a hidden compartment a thick muslin shawl and a pair of goggles. 'Put these on, and tie this in a double knot under your chin or you'll lose that hat.'

'But it's been so comfortable this far,' said Constance, draping the shawl over her hat. 'I hardly see the need.' Though loud, the machine felt scarcely more dashing than a pony trap driven at a fast trot and Constance felt quite proud now of her own bravery.

'I'm going to open her up a bit when we get up on the Downs,' said Poppy. 'Best to be prepared.'

The motorcycle slowed as the hill grew steep. Poppy changed gear and the roar of the engine turned lower, the power seeming to coil beneath the springs of the sidecar and vibrate through Constance's heart as the machine clawed its way to the top. When they emerged from the low trees and gorse, the high banks of the road fell away. The hammered blue sea lay to their left and the full patchwork quilt of the Weald's farmland fell away to their right. In front, nothing but the rolling spine of the Downs, a horizon of grass and intense blue sky. For a moment all seemed to hang still, then the machine burst forward over the crest. Poppy let the motorcycle have its head, like an impatient horse, and they began the blurred, screaming race downhill.

At some point Constance realised her scream was real, torn away by the wind so she could barely hear herself as she clutched the edges of the sidecar. She dared not reach for her hat, which strained away from her head, the muslin shawl pulling at her chin. She could smell the tar and the hot, dry stones of the road that ran inches beneath her toes, waiting to tear her skin from the bones should she bounce out of her seat. The grass ran by like a green river and she could smell that too, the fresh broken ends cropped by rabbits. The wind buzzed hard in her nose, something catching in her throat, her ears singing, and her breath caught at scream's end. That she had thought motorcycling as staid as a carriage ride now seemed hubris. Fainting seemed her inevitable punishment. But then, over the crest of another hill and down, she drew in a breath, a deep breath, and screamed again, this time more easily, and felt the joy of being able to scream unheard.

Two hills, three hills, and Constance felt her body accommodating itself to the up-and-down motion, as if riding a horse or bending into a dance. She screamed some more, and whooped, and thought it strange to be crying for joy. It felt so good to let go of the tired world for a moment, grief and pain flushed from her body by the pummelling air. She unclamped her fingers from the wooden edges and threw her arms in the air like a child to press her palms to the wind. She felt as if she were growing lighter in her body itself, and the motorcycle went on, faster and smoother, until it seemed they must surely have left the ground and be flying several inches above the Downs.

When Poppy finally pulled the machine over and stopped the engine, on a chalky patch of dirt on the clifftop, the silence was deafening. Constance removed the shawl from her head and pulled down her goggles.

'You're crying,' said Poppy. 'I've done it again. Gone too fast.'

'No, no,' said Constance, blinking hard as she struggled to pull her handkerchief from a crushed pocket. 'I'm not crying. I mean I am, but it feels so good.' She could not explain the release in her body, the sensation like the breaking of a fever.

'Really? Because I've frightened three friends and a housemaid just this month,' said Poppy. 'My record of persuading women to adopt motorcycle transportation is pretty dismal at this point.'

'It was wonderful,' said Constance. 'Truly petrifying at first, of course, but once you let go, something shifts inside.' She flexed her fingers, which were stiff from her initial wild clutching. 'It feels like freedom.'

'Yes, and it's completely worth the awful red rings round the eyes and swallowing so many insects,' said Poppy. 'If you're quite sure you're all right, I promise to motor us down more sedately to Penneston.'

'What?' Constance clamped her lips shut as she put on her goggles. This time she wrapped the shawl across her nose and mouth before knotting it. The taste in the back of her mouth could not possibly be grasshopper, she thought, but she gagged a little anyway.

WHERE THE DOWNLAND tumbled lower, into the comfortable rolling farmland that surrounded Hazelbourne, the manor house of Penneston stood on a low bluff, looking over the town towards the sea. It was a compact Regency villa, though its rectilinear severity and symmetrical façade were compromised by a heavily decorated Victorian addition. The curving bay window, porch outlined in scalloped wrought-iron, and its collection of oddly shaped windows set back in bulging brick surrounds gave the impression that the original house was being devoured by a fat, copper-roofed snail. A long curving driveway gave a partial view of the house's plain side and a walled garden. A glimpse of an open sheep field to the rear suggested there would be the usual terrace and lawns protected by the sunken wall of a ha-ha. As the motorcycle grew nearer the gravel sweep at the front door, Constance could see scaffolding poking above the edge of the snail. No doubt the Moorish garden room was somewhere there behind the fat yews and neatly trimmed flower borders. The house was closed up, all the windows shuttered, and the front door sanded to bare wood, with shadows for hardware.

'I'd take you inside but Mother's determined no one shall peek until her work is finished.' Poppy kept the machine ticking over; the sound of the engine vibrated gently against the warm yellow stone of the house.

'Did it need a lot of work?' asked Constance.

'I didn't think so,' said Poppy. 'But my mother always needs a project and this way she gets to show off her unrestrained taste and at the same time eliminate my father from every major room.'

'I'm sorry.'

'Oh, my father did the same thing to the London house when my mother had enough and left him. Not a photo or a trinket left in the attic. Dramatic of course. They prided themselves on their passionate natures.' Poppy sighed. 'They couldn't stand each other at the end, but they had loved each other so much. I think competing with him now is her way of keeping him with her.'

'I'm so sorry for you and your brother,' said Constance, who was not used to such frankness and so retreated, somewhat ashamed, into platitude.

'Only a year ago the divorce seemed such a scandal even I worried about us,' said Poppy. 'I was so angry at my father, and then he died and everything became so very unimportant. If necessary, I shan't mind getting divorced a half dozen times now.' She stood astride her machine with a belligerent frown, a smudge of oil and the red marks of goggles on her cheeks, and hair wildly frizzing from her helmet. Constance could not but laugh.

'You have to get married first,' she said. 'And if we want husbands I think we both might have to wash our faces.'

'We'll go to my barn now,' said Poppy. 'It's got quite rudimentary facilities, but I think you'll find it very cosy. If there's time after, we'll come back and peek at the gardens.'

THE SMELL OF motor oil and fried onions was unexpected. After the brightness of the day, Constance blinked her eyes against the cavernous darkness. The barn, a quarter mile downhill from the main house and set a short distance from a tidy farm, seemed more motor garage than agricultural building. There were several motorcycles under a canvas tarpaulin and two navy-painted sidecars, their frames propped on bricks. One was already trimmed in scarlet, the other was blank, a pot of paint and a brush abandoned by one of its wheels. Along one wall a lengthy plank table was strewn with parts and tools.

In the rear a staircase led to loft rooms under the soaring tile roof. Under the loft, a lumpy old sofa and some equally disreputable easy chairs made a strange parlour, set around an iron stove. A kettle steamed on the stove top. By the table, two women were working on a partly dismantled engine, their faces and gloved hands oil-smeared. One, tall and angular with the hollow-cheeked face of a medieval saint and long red hair escaping from under a mechanic's cap, stood smoking a cigarette in a short holder while attacking some small part in her hand with sandpaper. The other, short and plump, with a round freckled face and fluffy light brown hair, sat on a low stool, peering intently into the engine from behind small wire-rimmed glasses. The tall woman looked up at their arrival and narrowed her green eyes against a trickle of smoke.

'Look out, Tilly, Poppy brought a visitor.' Her tone was cool, amused. The other woman jumped up, flustered, and wiped her hands on the legs of her coveralls.

'You could have warned us, Poppy,' she said, transferring a smudge of oil to her hair as she pushed it back under her cap. She indicated their attire. 'We're hardly dressed to make a good impression.'

'Constance Haverhill, this is Tilly Mulford and Iris Brenner,' said

Poppy. 'We were despatch riders together in the war and now we are trying to keep all our girls riding.'

'How do you do,' said Iris, tipping her head back to blow smoke at the roof.

'I suppose I'd better go and wash my hands and make some tea,' said Tilly.

'Pity you missed Tilly's famous bacon and fried onion sandwiches for lunch,' said Iris.

'Tilly is our quartermaster,' explained Poppy. 'She's a whiz at logistics and supplies. Probably because she's a librarian. Don't ask me how, but she kept us in bacon many a long night in the war.'

'"Don't ask me how" might be the unofficial motto of Poppy's barn,' said Iris. 'We are always scrambling for something.'

'Don't call it that,' said Poppy. 'We are now the Hazelbourne Ladies Motorcycle Club, remember.'

'A fancy name, which Tilly uses as a cudgel to browbeat some poor tradesman into selling us extra tea rations.'

'We offer our repair services, social rides and racing support,' said Poppy. 'It's a way to encourage women riders and to shield them with numbers. Many girls riding together makes each of us seem less odd.'

'We shouldn't need it,' said Iris. 'After all we did in the war.'

'Iris is a racer so she's a bit of a snob about our purely social riders,' said Poppy. 'But it's girls like the Morris sisters who add the social lustre that blunts our critics.'

Iris made a less-than-discreet snorting sound. 'I hardly think the Morrises' wicker basket contraption counts as motorcycling. It's like an overgrown perambulator.'

'Now, now, Iris. Their particular feminine conveyance has already brought us a new respectability and several new converts.'

'I thought you were Wirrall's Conveyance?' said Constance.

'Wirrall's is a separate new concern,' said Poppy.

'Not all the girls are quite so comfortably off,' said Iris and her eyes flickered to where Tilly had disappeared into a small kitchen under the stairs. 'Since the war ended and the despatch riders were disbanded, Poppy's trying to find a way to keep us all on the road.' She went to the table and picked up two small wooden plaques that said:

DELIVERIES

WITH A WOMAN'S TOUCH

MOTORCYCLE

LESSONS FOR LADIES

THE FREEDOM OF THE ROAD

'Oh, they're interchangeable,' said Constance. 'How clever.'

'Pop out two brass screws and we're ready to do anything,' said Poppy. 'Girls can work when they want. We have a schedule.'

'I'm just volunteering to help with the lessons,' said Iris. 'But Poppy has plans to be a captain of industry. Perhaps one day Wirrall's will sponsor my racing.'

'Iris is the amateur ladies hill-climb champion of the South-east,' said Poppy. 'She'd also be a speed champion but they don't let women in any of those races.'

'If I had a large sponsor they could help me get in,' said Iris. 'But since I can't race I can't attract a sponsor.' She sighed. 'It's a conundrum but I have a few ideas up the sleeve of my motorcycle leathers.'

'Tilly has really spiffed up Iris's engine,' said Poppy. She nodded as Tilly came back bearing a large tea tray. 'She rides but her passion is the mechanics.'

'With a few more pieces of equipment we can really turn this place into a proper full-time repair shop,' said Tilly.

They sat down, Constance settling gingerly into a flower-covered chair that sprouted stuffing from several holes.

'It must be wonderful to have families that support you in such novel endeavours,' she said. It was more a question than a statement and the hearty laughter of all three women gave her the answer.

'You see, it was all very well and patriotic when we were freeing up men for the services,' said Iris. 'But now we are just behaving oddly and diminishing our chances of snatching up one of the few available husbands.' Constance admired how the young woman sprawled in her chair with the ease of a man, blowing smoke rings and stretching her legs, boot soles tipped up. But she wondered if such a free demeanour might hold Iris back more than her occupation.

'Iris keeps her aunt in a permanent state of livid disapproval,' said Poppy.

'She thinks it shocking now that I live here with Poppy, despite the fact we and the other girls bunked here in the war with no complaints.' Iris chuckled. 'Fortunately she has no control over my trust, and she'd still like to coax me home, so she limits herself to apoplexy only once or twice a week.'

'I'm just here part-time and my mother still doesn't think it becoming to me as a librarian,' said Tilly. 'She worries what the trustees will think, but I tell her I'll do anything to keep riding.'

'I didn't realise one could live in here,' said Constance, looking with some doubt at the dusty brick floor and the rickety stairs to the loft.

'It's as cold as a crypt in the winter,' said Poppy. 'But it's the price of freedom.'

'But as girls alone?' Much as Constance chafed against limits on her own freedom, she found herself slightly shocked at such a lax arrangement. Or perhaps she was just jealous, she acknowledged, and she saw again her mother's whitewashed cottage. How naïve she had been to think she would be allowed to live there on her own.

'My mother has her own eccentricities, so she really can't complain too much about mine.' Poppy sighed. 'We have a nominal chaperone in the farmer's wife next door, but with all the worrying about Harris, Mother is far too busy to really interfere.'

'What your brother needs is an occupation,' said Iris, changing the subject. 'It's all well and good to have money, but there's nothing like hard work to get one's mind off of one's troubles. Even an injury like his.'

Poppy shook her head. 'The leg was an awful blow but my brother is not a coward. He would face up to it,' she said. 'But he can't seem to shake this dreadful melancholy. I think it's the whole thing: the war, the people we've lost.'

'I've asked myself at times, how do we go on,' said Constance. 'For the men who had to see the war itself, it's ten times worse, of course.'

'Or perhaps women are just more resilient,' said Iris. She sat up straight, her jaw a sharp line in which a muscle flickered. 'I was a nurse in France for two years and what I saw would shock the most hardened of men. But I've not taken to my bed.' For a moment a grey shadow turned her face to marble and the cigarette holder trembled in her fingers.

'I'm sorry,' said Constance. Iris shook her head and a grin brought her face to life again.

'They sent me home with pneumonia and despatch riding was the saving grace of my convalescence,' she said. 'But that's all water under the bridge proverbial. Best forgotten.'

'On a beautiful day like this I try to forget the past and the future for a few hours,' added Constance. She looked to the large open doors of the barn and blinked at the dazzling glare of the green countryside beyond the dark frame.

'We tried to get Harris interested in the motorcycles,' said Tilly. 'I rigged the clutch on Poppy's machine. With a sidecar he could ride by himself.'

'But I can't get him to even try it,' said Poppy. 'Men! They are as fixed on their brooding as on their ambitions.'

'It's not easy to find an occupation, of course,' said Tilly. 'I have a cousin who lost his left hand. They won't give him back his old job as a draughtsman even though he's right-handed and perfectly well able to draw. It's not fair.' She frowned and Constance saw in her face a caring and a warmth of spirit. Tilly might appear the quieter and more biddable of the three women, but Constance suspected her compassion gave her a dogged strength when needed.

'At least Harris is a man,' said Iris. 'They've let go all the women at the bus company, except for the lady in the office, and Hazelbourne Aviation just laid off all the women in the paint and dope shop.'

'You can't mean it?' asked Tilly. 'I can't believe Tom Morris and his father would do that. They can't be that unfair.'

'Yes, I thought business was booming?' said Poppy. 'Hazelbourne Aviation is owned by the Morris family,' she added to Constance. 'You've seen their seaplanes on the beach giving rides.'

'He's hiring the men coming back,' said Iris. 'The government says we should. They're going to pass a law soon; no room for the girls any more.'

'We should do something,' said Tilly. 'I know several of those girls.'

'We can see if any of them want to ride for Wirrall's,' said Poppy, patting her arm. 'I'd have to get some new machines.'

'Couldn't Tom's father give Harris a spot as a pilot?' asked Tilly. 'He and Harris were always friends, weren't they?'

'I think there was some concern about it being hard to get in and out of the seaplanes,' Poppy spoke carefully now, retreating. 'I know they spoke a couple of weeks ago but Harris wouldn't talk about it.'

'They are pretty high off the ground,' said Iris. 'I'd love to go up in one but I'll be damned if I'm going to show off my legs to every Tom, Dick and Harry crowded around that ladder they use.'

'Mostly Tom you mean,' said Poppy. 'We saw him last night. He was on Constance like a wild boar on a truffle.' The women laughed, open-mouthed and rolling in their seats.

'He only kissed my hand,' said Constance, feeling herself blush. 'I didn't encourage him.'

'I would brave Tom's ladder,' said Tilly. 'Wearing my thickest lisle stockings and a pair of plus fours. But I can fill up the motorcycle three times for what they charge for five minutes' flying.'

Over tea, cheese sandwiches and a plate of misshapen scones studded with leathery currants, the three women talked with animation and at a great pace, crumbs spilling unheeded down their blouses. The topics of motorcycles and club business were declared off-limits for Constance's sake, though she protested. So they compared books they were reading – the racier of which, Constance learned, Tilly sneaked out of the library so their names would not be recorded. They talked of life in town and what Constance might think of their limited social opportunities. She held her tongue and did not disclose the vanishingly small nature of her social life. They were not as fond of clothes and dancing as some – here the Morris twins came in for some gentle filleting – but they were looking forward to the prospects for peace and a summer peace celebration, which, in addition to a ball, would include a parade in which a contingent of lady motorcyclists might be allowed. The difficulty of it was persuading the town's Victory Committee of the utter gentility of such a group and persuading Iris and some others of the flowers and white dresses that such gentility might demand. The discussion was loud, frank and punctuated with laughter and spilled tea. It was like being back in school, enjoying a raucous half hour of free time in the common room, and Constance felt herself relax and disappear into the noise. She had forgotten the pleasures of such uninhibited female conversation.

'Since you're here for a while, you really should come out with us on one of our outings,' said Tilly, as the talk edged back around to the club. 'They are a wonderful bunch of girls.'

'You should learn to ride,' said Poppy. 'Iris is the expert on training, but if you like I'll give you a go in the saddle when we leave. See what you think of it.'

'Perhaps you should make a run for it now,' said Iris. 'Poppy and Tilly are absolute zealots in looking for new recruits.'

'I'm not sure I'm looking to learn,' said Constance. She had an inkling that riding motorcycles might be a more expensive hobby than someone in her position could afford. But she also wished to continue the acquaintance with Poppy, so she temporised. 'But I'd love to come out with you sometime if you'll have me.'

'Twice a month we go and visit the soldiers who are still at the convalescent hospital and take them out for spins,' said Tilly. 'We could use more hands to pass tea.'

'I'd be honoured to join you,' said Constance.

'Better still, the Saturday after next, we've a club outing to the motor racing at Polegate to watch Iris defend her hill climb record. You can ride with me,' said Poppy.

'We're going to declare ourselves a club for the first time and both Poppy and I are going to race as members,' said Iris. 'Which all makes Tilly very unhappy.'

'It will make my mother unhappy too,' said Poppy. 'She doesn't approve of ladies racing.'

'I just think declaring ourselves a club means we have to worry about how we look and what people think of us,' said Tilly. 'As if there weren't enough scrutiny usually.'

'We will drape ourselves in floral garlands to compete in the Rig and Rider Parade of Elegance,' said Poppy. Iris signalled her disgust and Poppy added, 'For Iris, we'll make a swag of hemlock and dead grass.'

'It's all very well to joke about it,' said Tilly. 'But when we appear in the newspaper we may lose as many members as we gain. I know my mother still believes no lady should appear in the newspaper outside of her wedding announcement.'

'I'm not at all sure I would be able to get away for a whole day,' said Constance, searching for a polite way to refuse such an outing. Respectability was the currency in which Constance knew she must trade for the foreseeable future. She understood Tilly's concern and did not have Poppy's wealth and position from which to defend herself against notoriety.

'I'm sure Mrs Fog can spare you a single day,' said Poppy. 'I could ask my mother to look after her.'

Chapter 4

Harris sat in the dark, an open book on his lap, and
listened to the library creak. There were tiny cracking sounds at random
intervals, as if the books were standing very still but occasionally had to
shift their weight to ease some geriatric pain. He shifted his own left knee
in sympathy and held his breath in anticipation of the next noise. Dust
motes waited too, hanging in a narrow band of light where he had
cracked open the shutters and raised the window two inches for air.

A dull thump vibrated through the room. Both he and the dust startled then resettled as the books dampened the tail end of the sound.
It was the workmen, back from their tea break, laying stone floors on
the other side of the house. He breathed slowly, calming the pulse in
his leg, which threatened to bloom into pain at a moment's notice. He
had lost track of time again, sunk in a doze, the wing chair cradling his
head.

Somewhere back before the war he had craved more hours in every
day for flying lessons, for air and automobile racing and for the usual
young man's round of parties and friends. With plenty of allowance in
hand, and his father not yet pushing him too hard to go into the bank,
life had seemed to brim over. He had thrown himself gladly into every
new day's adventure. But that boy was gone, sloughed off like an old
snakeskin.

He was a broken man now, subject by turns to pitying stares and careful lookings away. His body still echoed with the shock and rage of the first time a kindly hotel guest had asked his mother how he fared – while he sat at her shoulder with crutches. His short temper and acid tongue had since been kept busy struggling to prevent people from treating him as an idiot child. But what was the point now? Only a couple of weeks ago Tom Morris's father had made it clear that he would never be treated as anything but a permanent invalid.

Harris had gone to the airfield, asking to take a machine up for a flip. He was eager to prove his competence, to himself as much as to them. He knew he would never fly in combat again, or join a crew working to be first across the Atlantic. But it would be enough, he thought, that he might trade flying time for some teaching and test-flying at Hazelbourne Aviation.

'Of course you can go up.' Tom's father, Mayor Morris, had been jovial in the hangar, clapping him on the back. 'Tom is coming soon. He's promised to take over some of the lessons this afternoon. How about we have a spot of lunch together and then he can take you up before the students arrive?'

'I'm perfectly fine to take myself up. It's only on the ground I stumble about.'

'You're doing wonderfully of course,' said Mayor Morris, frowning. 'No one doubts your heart, my boy.' He paused, working his jaw about as he looked for the right words. 'We'll just have Tom take her up and then you can have a go on the controls.'

'Climbing into the aeroplane is likely to be my only struggle,' said Harris. 'After flying Camels for so long, I think I can manage the rudder on an Avro.' He tried to keep smiling though humiliation began to curl like a poisonous smog through his body. 'And once I prove it, I hope you'll consider taking me on to give lessons too?'

'No need for that,' said Morris. 'Even if we were not like family, after all you've sacrificed for your country . . .' He took out a handkerchief and blew his nose to hide a sudden emotion, as if Harris had died, rather than been wounded.

'I need to fly again,' said Harris, trying to resist the urge to beg. 'I'd like to earn my flying time.'

'I fear giving lessons would be far too taxing for a man in your condition,' said Morris. 'Much better to go up with Tom anytime you want, my dear boy.'

'You know I'm more than qualified and I work hard,' said Harris. 'My doctors say it will do me the world of good to be occupied.'

'And I wish I could help,' said Morris. 'But, look here, I'll be frank with you. I can't afford to take on more pilots right now. And what kind of advertisement would it be to have a pilot who reminds our customers so clearly of the dangers of aviation?' His eyes seemed to cross as he studiously avoided looking at Harris's leg.

'You have some pretty ragtag pilots running your seaplane rides,' said Harris. 'My experience and my reliability must surely outweigh my deficits there?' He knew his desperation was showing at the edges now, but he was sure Morris would jump at the chance to have a pilot of his skill and reliability sit in one of the silly red seaplanes and take squealing visitors for endless rides up and down the coast.

'Even if you could fly again, there's the getting in and out.' Morris shook his head. 'And we mustn't frighten the children. You must see the impossibility of my position, dear boy.'

'Even if I could fly?' repeated Harris. And he had seen, in that moment, that no matter how hard he tried, he would always be the crippled invalid and they would never let him fly again.

As there was no shape to his future, he liked to lose the days, drop them behind him, fail to mark their passing, shorten the time between getting up and dressing for dinner. The dinner bell he didn't mind. It called him to the chilled cocktail, the shared bottle of wine, the after-dinner brandy. A drink muffled the dinner table chatter, which irritated his ear. It softened the electric lights that struck against his eyes. In some moments, it dulled the ache in his leg until he forgot his loss. Then he did not flinch at the stares. It made it almost bearable to watch lovers strolling by the sea, dancers swinging past in their partners' arms; Evangeline, who looked through him now, dancing in Sam Newcombe's arms last night. He had strongly considered drinking during the day so that he might also become pleasantly numb to the men playing cricket on the green, young boys racing carelessly through a crowd in the street, the workmen nimble on their scaffolds, poised with heavy hods of tile on their shoulders. But he would not. He would hold the line because while there was comfort in the dark fog that rose about him, it was better to remain suspended in it than to fall entirely into the pit below.

The guttural sound of an engine came in at the window. He got up and stood in the shadow of the heavy curtain to peer out into the painful, bright afternoon. His sister again, but this time she was standing in the sidecar, like Boadicea in her war chariot, while her new friend hunched over the handlebars, her face frowning in concentration, as she guided the machine at a snail's pace around the gravel forecourt.

'You are a natural!' He heard his sister exclaim. 'Now let the clutch out gently this time.' The motorcycle coughed and lurched forward. To give her credit the girl did not shriek or otherwise break her stare. As they made another circle, he could not but admire her shapely, white-stockinged calf, displayed beneath a hitched-up skirt. 'A club member if ever I met one,' his sister proclaimed as they came to a halt close to the house.

It was sad or charming, he couldn't decide which, the way his sister made friends so quickly and indiscriminately. There was no guile to the girl, and she was stubborn too. She lost friends just as easily. Or rather they dropped her when she refused to close ranks with them or conform to some rule. As the man of the house now, he was aware he should help her, advise her. But she lived out there in a world of sun, noise and constant motion, while he lived in a strange, shadowed half-life where he couldn't summon the energy to save himself.

The motorcycle remained idling. He hoped they had not noticed the shutter ajar. Perhaps they had only paused for one last look at the house.

He stepped back from the window and held his breath, listening for the spurt of gravel that would signal their departure. Instead his sister's clear voice echoed.

'The workmen really shouldn't be in this part of the house. I should check.'

She switched the machine off and he heard their feet on the gravel. There was no refuge for him now. He raised the sash and pushed the heavy shutters as far as he could, one at a time, with his free arm.

'Hello,' he said. A cheerful wave seemed beyond him so he settled for supporting himself with a palm against the window frame and his good knee braced against the broad stone sill.

'Sitting in the dark and dust covers on such a beautiful day,' said his sister. 'You really are becoming a mole, dear brother.'

'It's called a library,' he said. 'It's where one reads books without covering them in egg salad and dropping them in the sea.'

'I did a bit of damage to poor old Milton,' Poppy explained to her companion. 'But I was fifteen and if you ask me, it was jolly impressive to be reading Milton on the beach for fun.' The girl laughed and he allowed himself a long look at her. She was pink from the wind, with two absurd half-moons printed across her cheeks from the goggles. Her face was a little thin, but her smile was genuine and her brown eyes looked intelligent if perhaps a little too penetrating. 'You remember Miss Haverhill?' added Poppy.

'Many women introduced under the glitter and candles of a Saturday night look quite different in daylight,' he said. 'But I did manage to recognise Miss Haverhill. She looks the same.'

'That's what Harris thinks is a compliment,' said Poppy. 'He has driven away women far and near with his chivalry.'

'Do stop drivelling, Poppy,' he said, sharp enough to forestall any stories she might tell. 'Don't you think it a little unbecoming to trot out my failings to just anyone you bring home?'

The girl flushed and he knew he had stung her instead of his sister. He had not meant to. There was a tension in her, a thin crack that made her vulnerable. Yet she did not shrink from him. Instead she held her sharp chin in the air and looked him full in the face.

Sheltered in the old boys' bonhomie of the Flying Corps, he had been slow to realise how much more character was worth than pedigree. But rubbing up against all sorts and depending on the man next to you, he had come to see that competence, decency and grit were not the sole purview, or even the natural gifts, of the well-born. His mechanic, Jock Macintyre, for example, a former bicycle repairman, had kept him in the air, and his particular brand of profane wit had replayed in Harris's head in the midst of so many dogfights, focusing his mind and compelling him home. Jock, originally from Edinburgh, had kept a broad accent despite ten years or more in London. He had a great disdain for the higher-ups, and Harris had saved him on more than one occasion from the wrath of some titled buffoon of a Wing Commander who heard himself verbally castrated and damned by the burly mechanic. In return Jock had kept Harris's Sopwith Camel taped together and its engine inspected down to the last bolt and spark plug and had run to pull him from the burning wreckage of his machine after he flew home bullet-ridden and smoking from a dogfight over the Channel. People like Jock had made him swear that after the war he would choose his friends on merit, not just stick to the neighbours and schoolmates of his own narrow class. But between his melancholy and the sleepy society of Hazelbourne, he had quickly forgotten. And Jock, to whom he had roused himself from his stupor enough to write, had not replied to his several letters. Perhaps this hotel girl, who claimed to be a farmer's daughter but stared him down like a duchess, might prove him not a complete liar.

'I remember you too, Captain Wirrall,' she said. 'But I must hope the daylight has changed you completely, for I remember you were quite miserable.'

'You are too kind,' he said. A fresh breeze lifted a loose strand of her hair and fluttered the hem of her dress. For a moment he wanted to shake off the darkness and step over the sill into the sunny courtyard to join them. As a child and a youth he had always done so, disdaining a door where one of the tall open windows would do. But now the broad stone sill loomed as a geometry challenge. Would he have room to swing his left leg through? Would he spin and topple trying to compass the broadness of its ledge? In an instant he was defeated. 'I can't offer you tea,' he said to his sister, hearing himself sullen, petulant. 'There's no one in the kitchen.'

'We just popped up from the barn for a peek at the gardens,' she replied. 'I was giving Constance a quick lesson on the way over.'

'So I saw,' he drawled, and it was perhaps ungentlemanly but he enjoyed the pink blush in the girl's cheeks. 'I hope you'll show Miss Haverhill the laburnum walk,' he added. 'It's in peak bloom now and I'm not sure it will last until Mother's grand house-opening party.'

'Did you actually walk in the gardens, Harris?' asked Poppy. 'I'm astonished.'

'Shall I let you in the front door?' he asked.

'It's quicker if we just come through the library,' said Poppy. 'That way we can swear to Mother that we never crossed the threshold.' In an instant she was across the sill, ignoring his outstretched hand. Constance came more warily behind and Harris braced his back against the frame as she put a gloved hand in his and considered the sill. It was too broad for her to step across in her narrow walking skirt without hitching it to her knees. He was about to offer the front door again but she leaned on his hand and stepped both feet up, ducking under the sash and then stepping down. She passed close to him and he wondered if it was ever appropriate to warn a young lady that while she smelled deliciously of rose water and fresh air, it was overlaid with a strong essence of petroleum.

In the gardens, the girl walked the formal rose parterre, the grand border and the kitchen gardens with admiration and a confident eye for detail. It felt almost like an official inspection and Harris, who had agreed to accompany them with less reluctance than he himself had expected, grew increasingly amused as his small knowledge of plants became quickly exhausted.

'Are these Oriental poppies good self-seeders?' she asked, bending over to cup a lime green and apricot poppy in her palms as if it were the face of a baby. 'So many beautiful colours.'

'My father had all the poppies planted for me,' said Poppy. 'Of course I knew he hated my name, thought it was one of Mummy's little rebellions. So it was doubly nice of him, don't you think, to plant so many reminders?'

'I think the gardeners used to collect the heads and sort of redistribute them,' said Harris. He looked around for a gardener to advise on this, but there were few of them left since the war and today the gardens, dreaming under the shimmer of afternoon heat, were empty of man and beast.

'At Clivehill, I ordered sewing boxes with all the little compartments for pins and buttons to sort and keep seeds,' said Constance. 'They were perfect, except they arrived with various pictures of baby animals and ribbons printed on the lids.'

'I can't imagine our head gardener putting up with that,' said Harris.

'I thought the same,' said Constance. 'But it turned out it was easier to remember what seeds were in which box with all the different pictures. Tomatoes in the kitten box, gladioli in the baby bear and so on.'

'Quite the plan,' said Poppy.

'Of course, when Lord Mercer came home he preferred to have the boxes whitewashed and stamped with the family crest,' said Constance. 'Much smarter, I must admit, but as I left there were a few radishes coming up in the borders and some gladioli in the vegetable patch.'

'You seem to know your stuff,' said Harris.

'Well, it was the war, you know,' said the girl. 'The estate manager enlisted right away and Lady Mercer didn't really have the patience for dealing with the more mundane matters. I just started helping with the ledgers and the farmers all knew me of course – well, it grew from there. I really enjoyed running the estate and it felt like I was helping the war effort a little bit.' She sighed. 'I was sorry when it was over.'

'Lord Mercer took charge?' said Poppy.

'He was gracious enough to say I had held things together remarkably well for a girl,' she said. 'But he wanted to get a man in and run things properly.' She lowered her gaze and scuffed the toe of her shoe in the gravel. 'I was so busy trying to show him how well his estate was doing that I forgot men don't like women to be too competent. I should have been more circumspect.'

'Nonsense!' said Poppy. 'We wouldn't have won the war without competent women in the millions. Wouldn't you agree, Harris?'

'I wouldn't dare say otherwise, dear sister.' Two pairs of eyes looked at him sharply and he raised his hands in surrender. 'I would gladly have put the two of you in charge of the Western Front. You couldn't have made things worse, that's for sure.'

'Shall we get on to the laburnum?' said Poppy. 'The sun is affecting my poor brother's mind.'

Hidden beyond a wall of fat yews, the fifty-foot tunnel of weeping laburnum blossom glowed with yellow intensity under the filtered sun. Such magnificence commanded silence and the three walked without speaking amid the cool fragrance of the serried hanging flowers.

'It's like a cathedral.' Constance's voice was a whisper. The dappled light played across her face as she stretched on tiptoes to graze her fingertips against the blossom. A tiny drift of golden pollen shimmered down on her head. Harris was unexpectedly pleased that she shared his sense of awe. He had been coming every day to sit under the tunnel and allow his thoughts to be quieted by the beauty and peace. But of course one could not admit that to a girl one had just met.

'It's only transcendental like this for two or three weeks and the rest of the time, it's just green and acutely poisonous,' he said. She looked at him as if disappointed in his response.

'Harris pretends to care about nothing,' said Poppy. 'But when he was a boy he played here all the time.'

'Which is how I came to be aware that small boys planning to be Robinson Crusoe should not expect to survive on a diet of laburnum pods.' He could taste the bitter black seeds, so much like little peas. Fortunately, he had only chewed one or two. Still he remembered the vomiting and the fainting. He was told a gardener found him and carried him at a run to the house. He did not convulse they said, but slept for a full night and half the day. He remembered only waking up to his mother's loud weeping and his father, who never came to the nursery, gently wiping his forehead with a handkerchief and calling him 'my dearest boy'. It was worth the poisoning to hear the break in his father's voice.

'Perhaps the ephemeral nature of the bloom alongside the poison only makes it more poetic,' said the girl. 'We are forced to contemplate both the divine and the darkness.'

'The one is so fleeting,' he said. 'Perhaps it would be kinder to leave us to the dark, not tempt us with a beauty we cannot deserve.'

'Well, I just wish it bloomed pink,' said Poppy. 'All this yellow does make one's skin look slightly jaundiced.'

As Harris escorted the ladies back through the house and out into the sunny courtyard, he felt a strange combination of effects. On the one hand, his mood seemed to have lightened, just a thin crack in the gloom. On the other, he was suddenly anxious at their impending departure.

'If you don't mind, perhaps I could come back to town with you,' he said. 'I was going to call for a taxi later. Might as well save them the trouble of coming out here.'

'One more on the pillion!' sang out Poppy. 'It'll be heavy going up that last hill but we'll show Constance how the old bird can handle it.'

'I assume you're referring to the machine, not yourself?' said Harris.

'Oaf!' Poppy hit him hard above the right elbow and he leaned into the blow, feeling a sense of balance slightly better than expected. Perhaps some strength was returning, he thought, and another tiny sliver of light seemed to pierce his gloom.

'Actually, perhaps you'd permit me to drive?' The surprise, anxiety and delight all rushing across his sister's face together made him laugh. 'That is if Miss Haverhill would not be too terrified?' The girl gave a glance at Poppy that told him he had been discussed. Then she rewarded him with a grin.

'I'm fairly sure no one drives as fast as Poppy so I will be delighted to be returned to the hotel in perhaps a slightly less dishevelled manner.'

'I may take that as a challenge, Miss Haverhill. You might want to hold on tight to that pretty hat.'

He offered her his hand again as she climbed into the sidecar. From the corner of his eye he could see Poppy looking slightly nervous on his behalf. He was nervous himself, as he lifted his leg back and over the machine, releasing the button at his knee to allow his false leg to bend as he sat, and clipped the foot snugly into the foldout brace that Tilly had made. He passed his cane to Poppy and grasped the handlebars. He placed his right foot on the starter pedal and took a deep breath, hoping he would have the strength to kick the machine into life.

The vibration coursed through his body to join the pounding of his heart. He had been an invalid for too many months; his lassitude and weakness like a thick overcoat. As Poppy climbed behind him, and gripped him about the waist, Constance Haverhill took possession of his cane and stowed it by her feet. He couldn't see if she was smiling beneath the shawl snugged over her mouth and nose. He gave her a thumbs-up and she responded with a small wave. The machine was not an aeroplane, but it was good to feel power beneath him again. With another deep breath, he said a silent prayer that he would have the grip and strength to control the heavily laden machine. Then he slipped it into gear and rolled forward down the driveway.

Chapter 5

CONSTANCE GAVE HER ARM TO MRS FOG FOR A STROLL IN
the hotel's seafront garden after breakfast. The sun was shining and she
lifted her nose to catch a scent of honeysuckle and salt air on the light
breeze. A pleasant routine, established early, was the key to a restful holiday, according to Mrs Fog. Constance was grateful that their routine
seemed designed to allow her the maximum of free time. After an early
breakfast in bed, and a turn in the gardens, Mrs Fog would go to write a
few letters in her room and then join her set of elderly ladies on the Palm
Terrace for cards. Dismissed until luncheon, Constance was free to wander along the promenade or through the town's main street of shops,
looking at the dress fabrics, ribbons and hats at the haberdashery, fig-
urines and jars at the local pottery, and toys, buckets and spades, and
striped deckchairs at the seafront gift shops. She did not change for luncheon, only washed her face and hands and smoothed her hair. Mrs Fog
would add a small jacket and some jade beads to her shapeless morning
dress. Luncheon was taken in the dining room. Constance would have
preferred to eat on the wide outdoor balcony above the gardens, but Mrs
Fog was still waiting for a day without any breeze. She did not like to eat
with any draught strong enough to ruffle the lettuce in her salad. After
lunch, Constance was again free until teatime while Mrs Fog retired to
her room for an afternoon nap and reading. They would take tea on the
terrace and a scant hour or two later, Constance, having briefly lain

down herself in her room, would dress for an early dinner if Mrs Fog felt up to it.

This morning, as usual, they stopped at one of the wrought-iron benches dotted along the gravel paths that separated the beds of blue hydrangea and white lilies from the velvet green of the croquet lawn. Mrs Fog, despite her fierce independence, was still weak and often out of breath. She would not agree to the hire of a bath chair and so they had not been to church or even ventured as far as the pier. Her view of the sea had been all from the hotel's low front hedges or the Palm Terrace. Constance had suggested the hire of a taxi to the Municipal Gardens, but Mrs Fog detested the idea of being driven by a strange man.

'I suppose I shall have to have a taxi to church next Sunday,' Mrs Fog said, frowning at a large black car disgorging a family in front of the hotel. The taxi driver pocketed his fare and took off his cap to wipe his sweating forehead with a large chequered handkerchief. 'Such an expense and the drivers are so rude.'

'We could hire a chair for me to push you just as far as the lych-gate,' said Constance. 'We could park it under a tree and you could still walk into church on your own. I don't think you should worry about people seeing you.'

'I fear just the opposite,' said Mrs Fog. 'Once taking to a chair one becomes quite invisible to everyone.'

A motorcycle and sidecar pulled in as the taxi departed. It had been a few days, so Constance looked eagerly to see if it might be Poppy again, come to whisk her away to another adventure. But it was Tilly driving. The hotel doorman stepped to open the small door and Mrs Wirrall emerged, popping upright in a sudden blossoming of ruffles, petticoats and broad veiled hat, much like a bunch of paper flowers snapped from a magician's wand.

'That's Mrs Wirrall!' said Constance. 'I wonder what she's doing riding with Tilly?'

'More importantly, how on earth did she fit in that little thing?' said Mrs Fog.

'It's one of her daughter Poppy's sidecar taxis,' said Constance. 'I told you about them. Would you like to take a peek at it?'

'It would be polite to say good morning to your Mrs Wirrall,' said Mrs Fog. 'As she was so kind to host you at dinner the other night, without so much as an introduction, it's only proper that I thank her.' Constance took Mrs Fog's arm and manoeuvred her through a small gap in the low hedge. Mrs Wirrall was still shaking out her skirts and smoothing her jacket.

'Goodness me, I love my daughter, but riding in this thing is like being packed into a hatbox. I feel I should have myself steamed and ironed before lunch,' said Mrs Wirrall.

'You do not recommend such a conveyance?' asked Mrs Fog, shaking hands as Constance made introductions.

'Oh dear me, I forgot I'm supposed to be helping Poppy by being seen riding in it. It's not as bad as all that, Mrs Fog. In fact, it's quite exhilarating and the girls are very careful, aren't you, Tilly?'

'Yes, madam,' said Tilly. 'We know how to be careful. Believe me, you only have to drive a box full of eggs fast over a humpbacked bridge once to learn that lesson.'

'Yes, well, I think both Tilly and I have to perfect our diplomacy,' said Mrs Wirrall. 'But if you are in need of transportation, Mrs Fog, the girls only take ladies, so at least there is no chance your taxi will reek of some man's tobacco.'

'Would you care for a small turn around the hotel?' asked Tilly. 'Just a little ride compliments of Wirrall's?'

'I don't think so,' said Mrs Fog. 'I'm much too old for such novelty.'

'It's more fun than a bath chair and less ostentatious than a big taxi,' whispered Constance. 'Perhaps you'll like it enough that we can take one to church on Sunday.'

'That wouldn't be at all conspicuous, now, would it?' said Mrs Fog.

'Actually, it would be rather dashing, I think,' said Mrs Wirrall. 'Perhaps I'll take one myself.'

'Well, I suppose a turn around the corner wouldn't do me any harm.'

'Well done, Mrs Fog,' said Mrs Wirrall. 'I will want to hear all about it. I hear you are to be found on the Palm Terrace in the mornings?'

At this, Mrs Fog was persuaded and, arrangements having been made to have bouillon together later, she allowed herself to be carefully loaded into the small sidecar, her handbag on her lap and the door sealed.

'Very slow please,' said Constance.

'Like a box of baby rabbits,' said Tilly.

The motorcycle burst to life in a roar more ear-splitting than Constance remembered. She gave an encouraging wave and a smile, though her heart sank at the petrified look on Mrs Fog's face. Mrs Wirrall waved her gloves like a starting signal and Tilly pulled the machine slowly away from the kerb. The sidecar wobbled down the hotel's circular driveway and then Tilly took a hard left turn and popped out in front of a baker's van. Some horn blowing and a waved fist from the baker's man and Mrs Fog disappeared from view.

'Well, my work is done here,' said Mrs Wirrall. 'I can tell Poppy I gained a customer.'

'Let's hope my work is not done,' said Constance. 'If Mrs Fog survives the heart attack she'll probably send me home.'

'Or maybe she'll love it,' said Mrs Wirrall. 'It's rather like being a girl again on a fairground ride. But don't tell Poppy I said that. She'll only demand I support her further.'

As Mrs Wirrall went into the hotel, Constance hurried down to the end of the driveway. After several minutes of excruciating tension, she was rewarded with the sight of Mrs Fog, waving a handkerchief out the window as she was borne home in noisy triumph along the promenade.

Mrs Fog's qualified conversion to the joys of motorcycling did much to enliven their walk back through the hotel gardens.

'Of course, one could not venture far and heaven knows what would happen if it broke down. One can't expect a young woman to perform repairs, of course. It's a trifle noisy but some cotton in the ears. And Tilly informs me that the engine is much more economical than a great big taxi.'

'Tilly's also a mechanic, completely self-taught,' said Constance, as she held open the door and ushered Mrs Fog inside. 'She does indeed do repairs.' Mrs Fog seemed impressed but confused.

'Dear me,' she said. 'But as a librarian isn't she afraid of getting oil on the books?'

KLAUS WAS IN charge of service on the Palm Terrace in the mornings, when it was taken over by the more aged and infirm of the guests, a wrinkled horde who paid their upkeep but did nothing for a hotel's reputation for glamour. The town boasted no curative springwater or famous medical spas, but the wealthy and infirm still came for the convalescent power of the sea. Klaus thought the power might be greater outdoors than behind glass, but most of them were swift to claim their preferred chairs and tuck themselves into lap rugs to read the papers, work on mysteriously shaped knitting or play cards. One or two swore by a twice-daily constitutional: Klaus had just brought bouillon to old Colonel Smith, who always tottered across the road, any wind pushing at his frail body, so that some days he attained the desired pier entrance and some days he and his mutton-chop whiskers were carried sideways down into a stand of donkey carts, where he was often persuaded to an unwanted ride. Klaus would see him through the windows, being driven past the hotel with a look of pleading on his face.

Klaus now brought broth and cream crackers to the recently formed quartet of older ladies playing whist by a window. They were seasoned players, smoothly laying cards and sliding away winning tricks with the minimum of fuss, and all the while managing a steady stream of gossipy conversation.

'So I told him I was not going to be flimflammed in my own church and our usual Vicar would hear of it as soon as he was back from his retreat in Bournemouth – thank you, Klaus – and my sister Mary said she was not going to put a penny in the collection plate until I gave her the all-clear.' Mrs Howe, the granddaughter of an archbishop, spent a month every year playing whist and reminding everyone of her ecclesiastical pedigree.

'We had a bad locum too this year. I don't begrudge our Vicar his holiday but – Waiter, could I trouble you for a teaspoon of sherry for my bouillon – I find it so warming, have you ever tried it, ladies?' Mrs Midge was the widow of a local magistrate and for years had been coming in three times a week to masquerade as a hotel guest and drink complimentary bouillon. The hotel manager, Mr Smickle, had been treated preferentially by the magistrate over some question of an awkward financial situation and so this was allowed. Besides, Mrs Midge was a very friendly sort and made other widows and older women feel comfortable.

When Klaus returned with the small cut-glass jug of sherry and silver spoon usually used to garnish mock turtle soup, the conversation had moved on.

'Don't misunderstand me. I love my granddaughter and my money will all go to her – thank you, Waiter – Klaus, is it? Just another drop I think – but Constance nursed me through the worst of it and now, with her mother gone, the poor dear has nothing.' Klaus pricked up his ears at the mention of the young woman. He now placed this third woman, rather thin and austere, as Mrs Fog, to whom the girl, Constance, was the companion. Klaus had not yet heard enough gossip to fill in the story.

'Dear me, it's such a responsibility, all these family retainers. That's why I prefer hotels. One isn't responsible for anyone no matter how devoted they are – thank you, Klaus. What will the soup of the day be, I wonder?' The fourth in the quartet was Miss Jakes, a spinster of mysterious financial means who spent a month at the Meredith, another at a guest house in Gleneagles, Scotland, and passed the rest of the year in a ladies' residential hotel in London. She had spent much of the war hiding in the cellar and dining with WACS who had taken over the hotel.

'A chilled potato and leek, madam. Chef is preparing it now.' In the kitchen the chef was supervising the opening of several large tins of soup and chopping a disguise of fresh herbs with which to garnish the porcelain soup bowls.

'One wants to do something for her,' said the Fog woman.

'And yet one can't be responsible for them all,' said Mrs Midge, shaking her head as if she managed a mansion's worth of servants. 'I have an old nanny I love but I have three granddaughters who must come first.'

'One does so much and is so often met with ingratitude,' opined Mrs Howe. 'After what happened in Russia in 1917 – well, I could hardly look at my housekeeper after that. Twenty years of service and she tells me she isn't paid enough and wants mutton three times a week and twice the coal for her fire. In the middle of a war!'

'Constance isn't a servant though.'

'"Out you go, my girl," I said. "Not another night under my roof."'

'Perhaps you might find her a husband here. It's a busy town and there's a barracks two villages away.' Miss Jakes blushed at the word *husband*.

'That's why I make do with a daily girl. She makes my dinner midday and leaves me a plate of cold supper. It's all I need.'

'It's so hard to find them husbands these days. I thank the Lord my granddaughter, Rachel, has a fiancé.'

'So many of our poor dear boys gone. There was always someone in tears in the lobby. The girls bore up so well but I was often quite overcome.'

'And those who weren't lost are maimed or some of them quite mad. Poor Mrs Wirrall's son there with half his leg gone.'

'Poor indeed? With the husband dead and son an invalid, she controls all the purse strings, I hear. Did you hear how much she's spending to refurbish that house? And the country still reeling from the war?'

'She has a whole suite of rooms here.'

'She was a dancer they say and, well, the imminent divorce was an open secret . . .'

'She has promised us all an invitation to her house-opening party.'

The conversation sank to a whisper and Klaus lost the thread of it as he moved away down the long room. No matter, he would return for the empty cups and the talk would have circled around again. Gossip always reverted to the same topics: the suspicious woman, the origin of a man's money, the failings of government at all levels. It functioned like the ritual repetitions in church. The familiar points of the liturgy, the call and response, the amens. Only in between, a new story might spill out like a fresh sermon or an unexpected, less familiar hymn. As he pushed open the green baize door into the service area, he looked back along the length of the terrace and saw the young woman, Constance Haverhill, come in search of her companion. Klaus shook his head. A young woman with no dowry, in need of a husband? She was both a fresh new topic and a very old story, at once as unique as a snowflake and as common as a pebble on Hazelbourne beach.

THERE WAS A light rain this morning, and so Constance had decided against her usual walk and came to the Palm Terrace armed with her writing materials and the hotel's copies of *The Lady* and *Gentlewoman* magazines, and *The Times*, which she had seized by their oak spindles from the hanging rack of periodicals. Not wanting to interrupt Mrs Fog at her cards, she hovered only long enough to wish the ladies a good morning. The ladies gave her such frank stares up and down as to make it clear she was a subject of their conversation. She felt a faint flush of annoyance as she retired to a small table of her own several palms down the room. It was normal, she supposed, to wonder about people. People enjoyed a good gossip and she should not pretend to be above such things.

She pulled out her writing paper and a pen and set to completing a letter to her brother, Charles, that she had begun last night in her room. It was her intention to write him a brief and breezy letter every few days, not to force a repair of the rift between them, but to pretend it did not exist. She did this for her late mother's sake and because it was impossible to think of life with no family at all. Afterward, she began a much longer, and suitably gossipy, letter to Patricia Morton, a friend from school. Patricia lived in London, in a boarding house for young ladies, and worked as a secretary in a busy accounting office. It took two closely written pages of news, including stories of Mrs Fog, Mrs Wirrall, Poppy Wirrall and her friends, and the devoted waiter, Klaus, who brought her extra cream at breakfast, before she even attempted to broach the matter at hand. The matter was a position and whether her experience at Clivehill and her accounting and secretarial skills acquired by correspondence course during the war years might be qualifications for a job at Patricia's company.

After several minutes of chewing her pen, she wrote her request as lightly and as breezily as her amusing portraits, as if a position were no more than a fun idea, like sea bathing or perhaps motorcycle riding lessons. She had hoped Patricia would not see any note of desperation, but as she read over the letter she feared she might have erred too far in the other direction. Would Patricia see a request at all? To make sure, she added, 'I could be available as soon as required and hope you could also point me to suitable accommodation.' The letter sealed, she turned to the two magazines and, going straight to the back pages, she began to read the small advertisements for governesses, housekeepers, and, she hoped, perhaps a personal secretary or bookkeeper. She kept her pen poised to copy down addresses.

BEFORE RETURNING TO the Palm Terrace, Klaus brought a tea tray and an assortment of cakes to the Blue Salon where the Hazelbourne Victory Committee met on alternate Wednesdays at the invitation of Mr Smickle. He felt it his duty, he had let slip to Klaus, to offer such hospitality, and he hoped, as a humble manager, that it would do him no harm to be remembered for his generosity. And indeed, he had recently been made an alderman, and went about with great pride among the town's business and society leaders.

The question of the U-boat consumed the committee.

'After the recent difficulties with the towing, the navy tells me the safest recourse is to dismantle it piece by piece in a process that will take three months at least and be very noisy and unpleasant,' said Mrs Wirrall. She spoke evenly and with authority. She was effectively the committee's head, directing from her position as its secretary, the nominal chair, Mayor Harold Morris, being far too busy to attend.

'Well, we can't do that now,' said Mr Smickle. 'That would destroy our season.' He received nods of agreement from the other men of the committee. From what he had heard of their meetings, it seemed to Klaus that the gentlemen always returned to the subject of cost and how any funds disbursed might contribute directly to the economic uplift of the town. By town they seemed primarily to mean their own businesses. There were two other hoteliers, a brewery owner and the biggest operator of charabancs and private buses in the town.

'But how are we to celebrate Peace Day under the looming shadow of that ugly and monstrous machine?' asked one of the ladies, the head mistress of a local finishing school for young girls. 'It will blight all our pretty efforts.' The ladies of the committee understood that the centre piece of the Peace Day parade would be the returned soldiers from all the local regiments. While the gentlemen of the committee had made sure their businesses and civic organisations would be well represented with flag-draped buses, a salute from a squadron of seaplanes and free beer paid for by the town, the ladies of the committee were mostly interested in ensuring the parade route was engulfed in floral arrangements to show off their eligible girls, marching with their own schools, clubs and societies.

'I say, is the war still on?' The bluff voice belonged to the long-absent Mayor, Harold Morris, who strolled in as if it were nothing to arrive an hour and six months late to the committee. He bowed to the ladies.

'Sorry I'm tardy. Bit of a crisis with the Air Ministry. Had to sort them out as usual.' He came to a halt at Mrs Wirrall's chair at the head of the table and blinked at her, smiling. Silently, she rose and looked at Mr Smickle to the right. He rose, and all along the table everyone moved one seat down. 'Oh, I say, very kind,' added Mayor Morris as he sat down. 'Waiter, is there any more tea?' Klaus nodded and glided to the sideboard to refresh the pot from a tall silver samovar.

'We were discussing how to deal with the unfortunate relic on our beach,' said Mrs Wirrall. 'The only option is apparently to have the navy blow it in half with a ship's cannon, thus rendering it more able to be towed away.'

'A jest surely,' said Mr Smickle. 'You did not take it in earnest, my dear lady?'

'Well, we certainly can't have weeks of it being cut up,' said the owner of the next hotel along the promenade.

'I think it's a capital idea,' said Mayor Morris. 'It gets the job done and will provide quite a spectacle. We could sell tickets.'

'But will it be safe?' asked Mr Smickle. 'The proximity to the hotels?'

'I share your concern, Mr Smickle,' said Mrs Wirrall. 'I find it hard to believe, but they do insist it will be perfectly safe.'

'That's settled then,' said Mayor Morris. 'Let's arrange a date and get some handbills printed up.' He did not volunteer to design or see to the printing of any such flyer, Klaus noted. One of the other ladies was put in charge, as they always seemed to be, and the Mayor went away thoroughly satisfied with his own leadership.

Mrs Wirrall came to the Palm Terrace and was persuaded to have a cup of bouillon with Mrs Fog and her card-playing friends. That she did not play whist was declared a terrible disappointment by the ladies, whose voices tumbled over each other in their eagerness to engage in conversation. Mrs Fog seemed almost unable to make herself heard, but Mrs Wirrall took pains both to ask her direct questions and to compare their situations.

'Oh, Mrs Fog and I, who have a similar love of fresh air, I believe . . .'

'Mrs Fog and I, both having raised daughters . . .'

'Mrs Fog, I think you must have one or two very good recipes for jam to share with me?'

Constance was grateful to hear her kindness and admired how she seemed to fend off the ladies' more obvious flattery in a way that suggested Mrs Wirrall was not naïve about their opinion of her. When she left, sweeping away in her usual grand style, it was as if a lamp had been turned off. As the rain splattered heavy against the windows, Constance turned to the employments section of *The Times*, where her pen skipped over the openings for governesses and hovered longingly over paragraphs advertising 'Investment and managing position offered in Borneo rubber plantation' and 'Young Ladies and Gentlemen to join a European circus – no experience required'.

When Klaus returned to the Palm Terrace to sweep away the last of the bouillon cups, the card quartet were still at their gossip, but to his surprise the tenor had changed:

'I'm so glad she included you, dear Mrs Fog. Penneston is such a magnificent house.'

'And to think, dear Mrs Wirrall being inspired by my Albert's roses. You must come and see them, Mrs Fog.'

'I shall have to get my silk dress retrimmed. Nothing showy, but I think perhaps one or two silk carnations at the shoulder?'

'Dear Mrs Wirrall was so kind to suggest that no fuss be made.' This was Mrs Fog, and Klaus heard the genuine tone of her voice. 'One is so limited when travelling.'

'I'm sure you'll look perfectly wonderful, but there are some ladies I could name who will be very glad not to have to incur the expense of a new dress.' Mrs Howe looked around as if women in tattered rags might be hiding behind every potted palm.

'Mrs Wirrall is always dressed so finely, I'm wondering if my dressmaker would have time to run me up a new evening dress?'

Klaus refrained from shaking his head at how swiftly gossips can be turned under the firm hand of such an expert lady as Mrs Wirrall. He admired her ability to wage the endless war of social society. A twitch in his lips sent him hobbling quickly along the room and, as he passed a small wicker table where the girl, Constance, was bent over her newspaper, he detected a slight shake in her shoulders and understood her to be smothering her own laughter.

BEFORE LUNCHEON, CONSTANCE went to ask the front desk to post her letter to Patricia and was given in return a letter for Mrs Fog, from the local address in Cabbage Beach. Constance went up the lushly carpeted staircase from the lobby, enjoying the cool shine of the mahogany banister and the smell of peonies massed in a vase the size of a public fountain. Halfway along the bright, lofty corridor, where the smell of rain blew in from a tall window at the far end, she knocked at the double doors of Mrs Fog's room and went in.

Mrs Fog sat in front of her dressing table struggling to free her favourite blue pearl beads from where they had become entangled in her hair.

'You have a letter,' said Constance, coming over to hand it to her. 'Here, let me,' she added, trading the letter for the clump of knotted hair and beads. It would not do to tear at Mrs Fog's diminishing hair or break the fragile old beads. 'Hold still,' she admonished as Mrs Fog reached for her letter opener.

'It's very hard to stay still and open a letter,' said Mrs Fog, holding the envelope and small silver knife at an uncomfortable angle.

'The letter can wait,' said Constance. 'Put it down for one moment at least.'

'Depends who it's from,' said Mrs Fog. 'I don't have my glasses.'

'Someone in Cabbage Beach.' Mrs Fog was suddenly still. Her hands lay in her lap, her eyes stared unseeing at the mirror.

'Good,' said Constance, pulling gently on one or two pieces of hair caught in a loose silver link. 'I think we've done it. There.' She stepped back in triumph, laying the beads around Mrs Fog's neck. Mrs Fog remained still. 'Are you all right?'

'I had a letter among my things,' said Mrs Fog slowly. 'I haven't been able to find it for several days.'

'The letter to Cabbage Beach,' said Constance. 'I saw it on your desk the other night and I took the liberty of handing it in at the front desk for you.'

'It was only a draft,' said Mrs Fog, her voice low. 'It wasn't supposed to be sent.'

'I'm so sorry, but it was all sealed and addressed,' said Constance. 'I thought you had forgotten to post it.' Seeing Mrs Fog's white face and trembling hands, she added, 'Have I done something terribly wrong?'

'No, no, child, I'm just being a silly old woman.' Mrs Fog raised the envelope to peer hard at the handwriting. 'It's just an old school friend, but I was in two minds as to whether I would contact her after all these years.' She held the letter to her heart. 'People that were once so important, one can't be sure how they feel today.'

'But she has written back to you,' said Constance. 'And isn't Cabbage Beach nearby?'

'Mathilde de Champney,' said Mrs Fog slowly, as if testing the name's unfamiliarity in her mouth. 'All these years I've never been back to see her. I wonder what she must think of me.'

'You must open your letter at once and find out,' said Constance.

'Maybe after luncheon.'

'Did you not tell me we must live life to the fullest, Mrs Fog?' Constance put her hands on Mrs Fog's shoulders to still the tremor in her frail body. 'I think the waiting will just spoil your appetite.'

'Very well,' said Mrs Fog. She held the envelope up, a simple heavy linen envelope now freighted with all the suspense of an urgent diplomatic cable. 'So many years of letters unsent.' She sliced the envelope and read from the single sheet of paper inside. Then she closed her eyes as tears leaked down her cheekbones.

'Mrs Fog?' said Constance, appalled to think she had been the instrument of the old lady's unhappiness. 'Are you all right – what can I do?'

'Mathilde invites me to visit. She says she has never forgotten me.'

Mrs Fog blinked rapidly and wiped her eyes on her sleeve with all the finesse of a child. 'It is as if the years have fallen away.' Constance noticed she did not offer her the letter to read as she usually did with her correspondence. Discussion of her letters, and the parsing of paragraphs, was usually a great hobby of Mrs Fog's. Instead she tucked it into its envelope and pressed it to her heart before shutting it away in the dressing table drawer.

'I will go to her tomorrow afternoon,' said Mrs Fog, musing as if Constance was not in the room.

'Oh, but the next tea dance is tomorrow,' said Constance.

'Will you be very upset if we miss it?' asked Mrs Fog.

'No, of course not,' said Constance, quelling a surge of disappointment. Without Mrs Fog to chaperone, she would be unable to attend the dance. She had thought herself indifferent, but she had also dusted her silk shoes and hung her lilac skirt in her window to air. She had hoped to see Poppy and one or two others there, and Mr Newcombe, alone in his shyness and under the curious eye of every matron in the dining room, had risked crossing the floor at breakfast to ask her to keep him a dance.

'Only one's friends disappear and are lost with age,' Mrs Fog added. 'I'm afraid if I do not act I will hesitate and this chance too will disappear.'

'I hope you will permit me to go with you, then?' said Constance.

'Goodness me, I don't suppose you'd have much fun listening to two old ladies remembering our youth in the time of the old Queen,' said Mrs Fog. 'I'm sure she'll give me tea. So I won't be back before dinner.'

'I'm sure Lady Mercer will be so happy you have a friend nearby,' said Constance, resigned to spending the following afternoon hiding in her room.

'We will keep this to ourselves for now,' said Mrs Fog, her voice sharp. 'If you could do that for me?'

'Certainly,' said Constance. 'But what if it's still raining? In your weakened condition . . .'

'We should have the doorman call that young lady's motorcycle service,' said Mrs Fog, ignoring the weather as if she did not usually shrink from the merest hint of the damp. 'I'm sure they are discreet and will look after me. And they are probably a good deal cheaper than that nasty taxi?'

'I will telephone myself on our way to lunch,' said Constance. She hated the small, varnished mahogany booth under the main staircase, furnished with a red velvet bench and a heavy black guest telephone. With the glass door closed it became airless and Constance felt rather like a dead butterfly in a case. But she believed the lady telephone operators would be more discreet than the hotel doorman.

'I can't possibly manage any food,' said Mrs Fog. 'You go on. I think I'll lie down a little.'

'Are you sure?' asked Constance. 'Shall I have something sent up?'

'If you could tell them two o'clock sharp tomorrow?' said Mrs Fog. She waved a hand in dismissal. 'And I don't see the need to share all my business with the gossips here at the hotel, Constance. Please make that clear.'

Chapter 6

BY THE NEXT AFTERNOON, IN TIME FOR MRS FOG'S EX-
pedition to Cabbage Beach, the rain had stopped and the seafront appeared washed and radiant. The sun dazzled in reflections from countless
puddles and the hotel's awnings dripped as if edged with loose diamonds.
To Constance's surprise, it was Poppy at the helm of the Wirrall's taxi
standing in the hotel forecourt. Poppy was handing a Gladstone bag to
the doorman.

'Remembered my bag this time,' she said. 'After I run Mrs Fog over
to—' She stopped as Mrs Fog coughed loudly. 'Right. Well, after I return
from Mrs Fog's errands, Mother insists I attend this tepid tea dance. I do
hope you're going, Constance.'

'I should have thought of it sooner,' said Mrs Fog. 'Dear Mrs Wirrall
will I'm sure be happy to chaperone you too, would she not, Miss Wirrall?'

'Of course,' said Poppy slowly. 'Though the afternoon dances really
don't require chaperones and we girls just sort of make a gaggle and look
after each other.' From this, Constance understood that Mrs Wirrall's
presence was not at all confirmed. Fortunately, Mrs Fog did not seem to
notice.

'Splendid. You shall go to the ball, Cinderella.' Mrs Fog beamed and
patted Constance on the arm.

'I'm perfectly happy not to,' said Constance, feeling some irritation was warranted. To have a treat confirmed, then to have one's hopes dashed, then reinstated just when one had become resigned, and to be expected to be happy, resigned and thrilled again, all within the space of a few hours. Like a kitten tormented by small boys. Her pride suggested she should go lie on her bed and read, and try not to hear the strains of the violin washing down all the corridors from the lobby.

'Oh, please do come,' said Poppy. 'It would make it so much less abysmal for me.'

'Well, if it's that awful, I can hardly wait.' Irritation could not be maintained in the face of Poppy's encouraging smile. 'I'll see if I can find something to wear.'

The hotel's Grand Dining Room had been decorated with two additional large stands of pretty pastel silk flowers, and the low stage now featured a painted backdrop of a flowering riverbank. The musicians were dressed in boating attire complete with straw hats, while a pair of large wooden oars and a coxswain's megaphone lay at the foot of the stage, forming a sizeable tripping hazard, thought Constance, should the dancing become crowded. At the smaller tables around the dance floor, clusters of girls in pretty summer dresses and white gloves sipped fruit punch. There seemed a slight vibration of anxiety in the room and Constance wondered if it was because the number of young men gathered at two bar carts, and the small contingent of Canadian Army officers congregated in the entrance as if they had not meant to attend, was much too small to supply dance partners for all. To retreat rather than sit all afternoon with an empty dance card seemed suddenly desirable, but already Poppy Wirrall was waving a glove at her from across the room and the waiter, Klaus, was offering her his arm.

'I hope you will enjoy the orchestra, miss,' he said.

'Thank you,' she said. His arm was rigid and thin like an animal bone. She thought briefly that it should be she helping him across the room. 'Do you enjoy music, Klaus?'

'It is a balm to the soul, miss,' he said.

'Though it can't be perfect in the loudness of a ballroom,' she said. 'I'm sure we sound like a herd of elephants.'

'Music is life, miss,' he said, handing her to a chair. 'It is good to hear life dancing again.'

Mrs Wirrall was present, wincing at the taste of the fruit punch and loudly appraising the reticent band of men to Poppy and to the Morris twins, seated at an adjoining table. Iris was already dancing, her red hair loose in its coils as she swung by on Sam Newcombe's arm.

'Poppy didn't want me to come, but I heard that Mrs Fog commended you to my care, so here I am,' said Mrs Wirrall to Constance.

'We would have taken care of her, Mother,' said Poppy. 'But you are always welcome.'

'I should warn you that the Canadian officers are very pleasant and it is too bad they have not yet been able to go home,' said Mrs Wirrall. 'So we must entertain them. But if they ask you to dance be sure to ask them about their wives.' Guinevere Morris shook her head and her pearl drop earrings beat a tiny tattoo against her jaw.

'Oh, Mrs Wirrall, they can't all be married, can they?' she asked.

'Married men make perfect dance partners,' said Evangeline. 'So much more experience and so much less pawing about.'

'Anyone tries to paw me, I'll give them a good kick on the ankle,' said Poppy. 'Completely by accident of course.'

'If you glower like that no one will get close enough to be impertinent,' said her mother.

'Yes, do try to look approachable, Poppy,' said Evangeline. 'Or they'll all be too frightened to venture to this side of the room.'

'We are so happy you came, Constance,' said Mrs Wirrall. 'Do you suppose Mrs Fog would be upset if I asked Harris to order us a teeny bottle of champagne? I can't drink this fruity water. It will quite upset my digestion.'

'Harris is in the snug with my brother, who is ignoring his duty to us,' said Evangeline. 'If he doesn't come in soon, I shall have to order a cocktail myself.'

'Contain yourself at least through the mazurka,' said her sister. 'Last time we had to leave early and I had to practically carry you home.'

'It's so wonderful to be young and to be dancing,' said Mrs Wirrall. 'I envy you girls.'

Constance leaned over to Poppy to ask quietly, 'Where's Tilly? Doesn't she like to dance?'

'Between the library and working at the barn, Tilly doesn't have much time for the social round and I don't like to press her,' said Poppy. 'She and her mother must manage on quite a small income. We value our friendship of course. She's the absolute salt of the earth.' The Morris twins seemed amused and giggled behind their hands.

'Sorry, I didn't think,' said Constance, loud enough to include the twins in her response. 'I imagine I too will soon be managing on a small income. I should enjoy the dancing while it lasts.'

'Oh, a sort of tea dance Cinderella,' Evangeline said with a giggle as a pair of Canadian officers came to claim the twins. 'Now we shall all imagine you turning into a pumpkin at six o'clock.'

'Don't listen to her,' said Gwinny. 'A pretty girl with your connections will not want for admirers, so I have no doubt of you being able to keep up with us.' She too was swept away and Constance was left to hide her blushes, both at being called pretty and at the suggestion that she should seek to float along in society on the generosity of strange men.

'Idiots!' said Poppy. 'At least Gwinny is just a fool, but Evangeline knows how to twist the knife. I really shouldn't be friends with them but I've known them since the cradle so we are stuck with each other. It's like having a large goiter.'

As it turned out, there was no shortage of gentlemen asking Constance to dance, and while she was quick to refuse several offers of refreshment, it was a relief – and a quiet satisfaction – not to be a wallflower. But dancing was never quite as wonderful as one expected it to be, she thought, as she circled the room with a Canadian airman. He was not the first of the afternoon to step on her toes with his heavy boots, but he had an exhausting way of pumping her arm up and down as they turned, as if to power them along as he talked about himself over the noise of the orchestra.

'Got a little farm on forty acres in Manitoba. My mother and father are running it for me while I'm gone. Between you and me I think they're holding us here in case things don't work out in Paris, but I'm hoping to be home before the moose-hunting season.' After this summary of his prospects, he asked her if she didn't think it was important that men and women got along swimmingly, and after she nodded, he smiled so broadly she could only hope that she had not acquiesced to anything inappropriate.

As the orchestra arrived in a flourish at the end of the song, Constance saw Poppy wave across the room and she told the disappointed airman that she must rejoin her friend.

'I really don't enjoy being a slab of meat on a butcher's counter,' said Poppy, reaching under the table to massage a sore foot. 'Most of them can't dance and they are always trying to lean in and sniff one's hair.'

'Sam Newcombe dances competently,' said Constance. 'But he did nothing but talk about you all the way around the floor.' In his slight stammer, Sam had enlivened a fox-trot by answering many questions – 'Yes, Poppy insisted on the women, you know . . . the Brigadier had no use for them . . . she used to climb trees with us . . . impaled my leg once with an épée . . . crystalised ginger is her favourite . . .' – none of which had been asked.

'Harris and I have known Sam for years, of course,' said Poppy. 'His father expects him to find a wife who will finish his transformation from trade baron to landed gentleman.' She sighed. 'He insists he will marry only for love, but one can't help knowing one fits the father's description.'

'His devotion to you seems obvious,' said Constance, who found she liked the earnest young man.

'Poor Sam, I fear he will never pluck up the courage to tell me directly,' said Poppy. 'One hates a man to be overbearing, but at the same time one doesn't want to lead.'

'You could be kind,' said Constance.

'Yes, but instead I shall be selfish,' said Poppy as Tom Morris bore down on her with outstretched hand. 'Tom is the most overbearing and infuriating of flirts but I love a challenge, and when it comes to dancing he is a fabulous lead.' As Poppy was swept away in Tom's arms, their bodies bending together, Poppy throwing back her head in laughter as Tom leaned in to whisper in her ear, Constance wondered if Poppy could really be the only one who did not see the obvious spark between them.

The Canadian was hovering again and Constance looked around in desperation. Mrs Wirrall was engaged in talking with some of the other mothers at a nearby table and the other girls were all dancing. She was getting to her feet, determined to hide in the ladies' lounge, when someone tapped her on the elbow.

'Would you like to not dance with me, Miss Haverhill?' It was Harris Wirrall. 'You look tired and in need of refreshment.'

'It's not polite to tell a lady she looks tired, Captain Wirrall,' she said, but as the Canadian approached, she added: 'But I'd be very grateful.'

'Shall we go outdoors, where it's quiet?' he asked. 'Just give me your arm and look like you're helping the infirm.' He leaned more heavily than usual on his cane as she helped him out to the balcony and to a wrought-iron table overlooking the garden. The Canadian, watching them pass, gave a look of sudden comprehension and pity.

'Thank you for rescuing me,' she said. 'You didn't have to do that.'

'He looks the persistent type,' he said. 'Now they'll all see you are engaged in an act of charity and they won't ask to spirit you away.' He signalled a waiter and added, 'I can order you champagne, but I'd wager you are ready for some lemonade?'

'Champagne is such a wonderful idea of a drink, but it does make the afternoon a blur,' said Constance. 'I would be asleep before dinner.' It was cool and shady under the striped awning and through the open doors they still had a good view of the dancing. The music and noise were pleasantly muted, absorbed by the shrubberies and overarching trees of the garden.

'You dance very well, Miss Haverhill,' he said. 'Despite the best efforts of some of your partners.' His compliment caught her by surprise and she stumbled for a reply.

'Were you— Is it clumsy of me to ask if you enjoyed dancing, Captain Wirrall?'

'Shall we say I used to be an adequate partner,' he said. 'Now I stand in the corner. They really should hang coats on me.' He smiled, but she saw it grated on him. 'Do call me Harris. A captain with a peg leg sounds like a pirate.'

'Harris, then,' she said. 'Please call me Constance. Tom Morris already does so without invitation.'

'Ah, Morris. If we hadn't known him since our nursery days, Poppy would surely have killed him by now. His enthusiasm does get the better of him but he's not a bad sort.'

'His sisters are very beautiful.'

'Indeed,' Harris said, his tone dry. A waiter brought their drinks and he took up his glass. 'One must admire their frenetic dedication to every pleasure under the sun. They insist on forgetting the past and living only for today.'

'To live for today, one must be reasonably financially assured of tomorrow,' said Constance. Harris laughed, and for a moment his face lost its customary bleakness.

'It is true they are amply provided for,' he said. 'But even if they refuse to cry and rend their garments, they too have suffered. Gwinny lost her fiancé and Evangeline – well, she had certain expectations thoroughly dashed. Perhaps we should not fault them too much?' He frowned, though whether at the twins' misfortunes or at having to be generous to them, she could not tell.

'You are right,' said Constance. 'Hedonism is perhaps no worse a response to grief than misery.'

Poppy flounced through the open doors and plopped onto a seat, fanning her face.

'Evangeline told me she'd seen you two come out here. I told her a public terrace was hardly scandalous, but I think you succeeded in making her a little jealous, Harris.'

'Don't begin a game you don't want to play, Poppy,' said Harris, glaring.

'I just needed a moment to rest,' said Constance. 'Your brother was kind enough to accompany me.'

'Sorry, completely banal comment on my part. I think they're bred into us.' Poppy grinned. 'I apologise to you, Constance, and I promise to tease you, dear brother, in more inventive ways.'

'See that you do,' he said. 'If you're going to remain, I shall leave Miss Haverhill in your charge and go in to see who might be sheltering in the snug.' He got up and went away, and despite his frown, Constance was sorry to see him go.

'Touchy,' said Poppy.

'Are he and Evangeline close?' asked Constance. Suddenly Evangeline's quietly averted eyes, the way she and Harris did not talk or tease each other, seemed to make sense.

'They were engaged once,' said Poppy. 'A commitment which then quietly lapsed. No throwing over or anything for which she could appear at fault.' She sighed. 'I try to be kind but it wasn't fair. She just drifted so gently, no one even saw the ripples as her big fat webbed feet paddled away.'

'You love your brother very much,' said Constance. 'I can understand that.' Late afternoon and her own brother, Charles, would be cutting hay, or moving the small herd of beef cows to fresh pasture in the upper fields. She could see him, a small figure, walking down the hill to the farmhouse huddled in the valley; the smoke rising from the chimney, the dog running to meet him. A house with no children and his wife, Mary, struck almost dumb with grief. Perhaps she had been too quick to take offence when her sister-in-law lashed out, accusing her of bringing the influenza to them. Perhaps she had thought too much of her own grief and not enough of theirs.

'I'd do anything in the world for him,' said Poppy. 'Just please don't ever tell him that.'

In the Grand Dining Room, Constance and Poppy had barely returned to Mrs Wirrall when Iris and Sam Newcombe arrived at the table, out of breath from a rousing ragtime shuffle.

'Half the mothers in the room were scandalised,' said Iris.

'Lot of knees on display,' said Sam. 'One doesn't look, of course.'

'Sam has invited us all to a beach picnic on Saturday,' said Iris. 'Do say you'll both come because Gwinny and Evangeline should not have to endure me on their own. You know I can't restrain my tongue.'

'Just a jaunt over to Cuckmere Haven,' said Newcombe. 'Very rustic spot. Shan't be disturbed there. Have a fire and so on. Nothing like tea brewed over a wood fire.'

'If you make it sound too rustic, I doubt the twins will come,' said Iris. 'If I were you I'd emphasise the champagne and strawberries.'

'Sounds marvellous,' said Poppy. 'Count on us.'

'And the question of chaperonage?' said Mrs Wirrall. 'I am sitting right here, you know.'

'I think after all those months riding hundreds of miles between army bases I can behave myself on a daytime picnic, Mother,' said Poppy. 'But if it makes you more comfortable, you can insist that Harris chaperone us. It will do him good to get some sea air.'

'You are not wrong,' said Mrs Wirrall. 'And Constance can be relied upon to be sensible I'm sure, so if she accompanies you I have no objection.'

'I should ask Mrs Fog,' said Constance. 'She may need me.' She was not sure she was flattered to be considered almost a chaperone and thought that next time the orchestra struck up a racy ragtime, she might overcome her natural modesty and accept an invitation to try it.

Iris and Sam went away to secure the others for the outing and Harris appeared again from deeper within the hotel. He was accompanied by two Indian gentlemen whom Constance recalled having seen at breakfast once or twice. Their demeanour was always quiet, but their summer suits were well tailored and she had seen them drive away one morning in a small but gleaming car.

'Mother, Poppy, Miss Haverhill, may I introduce Captain Kumar Pendra, late of the Royal Flying Corps,' said Harris. 'We met briefly in Saint-Omer and he also knows Sam Newcombe.'

'A pilot from India? How marvellous,' said Mrs Wirrall. 'I am a true admirer of your country, Captain Pendra.'

'It's just Mr Pendra now,' said the young man. He did not seem to take offence but he raised an eyebrow and, in his slim face, brown eyes promised mischief. 'A lowly civil servant, making my way in the world.' Constance doubted his easy manner was at all suited to the work of government bureaucracy, but she took an instant liking to the young man and the way he shook her hand with as much care as he did Mrs Wirrall's.

'And his colleague, Mr Nag Basu,' said Harris. Mr Basu did not offer to shake hands with anyone. He hung back and gave a small bow.

'I think I have seen you in the dining room this past week,' said Mrs Wirrall.

'I would have introduced you earlier, Mother,' said Harris, 'but Pendra quite neglected to tell me he was here.'

'I did not wish to presume,' said Pendra. 'Basu and I are here for a few weeks, as part of a larger trade mission, to conduct a small survey of business opportunities. We thought to pass quite unremarked in the crowd.'

'Yet your list of acquaintances grows.' Harris laughed. 'In addition to Newcombe and myself, I see my mother's friend Colonel Smith is trying to engage your attention.' Indeed the elderly Colonel with mutton chops was beckoning imperiously with a teacake from a table on the Palm Terrace.

'Insufferable!' said Mr Basu, stiffening his back.

'No, no, he's quite amusing,' said Pendra. 'The man is delightfully torn between his desperation to talk all things India with me and his certainty that our being here is an utter violation of club rules. His confusion is quite disarming.'

'He's not all there, I'm afraid,' said Poppy. 'He confuses my mother with Queen Alexandra sometimes.'

'Well, others have noted some slight resemblance,' said Mrs Wirrall, patting her hair. 'When she was much younger of course.'

'I find the Colonel much more lucid after a strong brandy,' said Pendra.

'Hhh-hmmm.' The harrumphing sound was Mr Basu's only comment on the matter.

'As a fellow visitor, how do you find Hazelbourne, Miss Haverhill?' continued Pendra.

'I find it delightful,' said Constance. 'But I would not have thought of it as brimming with business opportunities?'

'You see through me so easily, Miss Haverhill. Perhaps you possess the psychic sensitivity claimed by so many fashionable ladies these days?' His gaze seemed to take her measure and she willed herself not to drop her eyes.

'No, indeed I despise all such pandering to superstition,' she said. 'I simply observe that Hazelbourne is not exactly the beating heart of British industry.'

'Don't let Tom Morris hear you say that,' Poppy said with a laugh. 'He and his father are sure Hazelbourne Aviation is at the leading edge of Britain's future.'

'Started by the Morris family just before the war,' explained Harris. 'Quite a big operation and several hangars, though the runway field is rented from Penneston.'

'I've been up there,' said Pendra. 'I hope I won't offend you if I observe that Hazelbourne Aviation, however large, is a rather quaint operation and a bit resistant to change?'

'Indeed,' said Poppy. 'You know they won't allow ladies to learn to fly?'

'They are not so welcoming to chaps from the colonies either,' said

Pendra. 'Quite scrutinised my flying credentials and were not able to provide me a machine to take up for a flip.'

'One-legged chaps are also frowned upon,' said Harris, his grin turning briefly into a grimace. 'But I'll have a word with Tom Morris myself, Pendra. Tell him about your war record.'

'Oh, that's quite all right,' said Pendra. 'We are too busy to fly, aren't we, Basu?'

'It was agreed that flying would not be on the agenda,' agreed Basu, his voice firm with disapproval.

'No, you are studying the business opportunities,' said Constance.

'Yes, but the lady detects an ulterior motive, and I must confess it. Before the war, the late Maharajah of Kochi Benar, our beloved state, convalesced here in Hazelbourne for many months,' said Pendra.

'What a small world!' said Mrs Wirrall. 'Why, I knew the Maharajah. We met over bridge and I entertained him at Penneston many times. He loved Hazelbourne-on-Sea.'

'His affection for Hazelbourne is well known in Kochi Benar,' said Pendra. 'When I met Captain Harris, it seemed so much like fate that I promised myself when the war was over, I too would visit this paradise of the English seashore.'

'The Maharajah was one of the few men I have met who was not afraid to take the advice of a woman, Mr Pendra,' said Mrs Wirrall. 'He and I had many discussions of politics and of the needs of the poor. He believed the prosperity of his state lay in the betterment of his people.'

'A man ahead of his time,' said Pendra. 'Our people mourn him still.'

'Yes, unfortunately, after a few months his health took a sudden turn for the worse and he died here,' Mrs Wirrall explained to Constance. 'His funeral in London was attended by the King himself.'

'I am so very sorry,' said Constance, for Mrs Wirrall's eyes had grown moist with unshed tears.

'Of course the gossips refused to comprehend such a friendship,' said Mrs Wirrall, dabbing her face with a handkerchief. 'But what is a little scandal against the opportunity to be consulted by such a great man.'

'To find such accomplishment and beauty in one must have contributed to the late Maharajah's fondness for Hazelbourne,' said Pendra, and Constance detected a suppressed smile.

'I remember, on one occasion, he was distracted from our bridge game by some trouble with the British agent in his state.' A brief pursing of the lips indicated Mrs Wirrall did not excuse even royalty from this cardinal sin of the bridge table. 'At the tea break, we discussed the benefits of a slightly more direct approach, and the next day, the Maharajah personally sent the King a pair of rare white peacocks. When I played Salomé, we had them stencilled on the theatre's backdrop, you know, and I always found them so beautiful.'

'Mother's direct approach resulted in the Maharajah's salute being raised from eleven to thirteen guns, I believe,' said Poppy, with a chuckle.

'An arcane but crucial difference in protocol that is no laughing matter, Miss Wirrall,' said Pendra, shaking his head gently. 'I believe the new Maharajah of Kochi Benar has been invited to join an Imperial council of the leading princes, so your mother's advice may have been of some import in enhancing the prestige of our state.'

'Oh, I'm sure it wasn't any of my doing,' said Mrs Wirrall, and Constance saw delight mingle with her modesty. 'But he was kind enough to say I had the instincts of a statesman.' She might have said more but Harris stepped in.

'Are you also charmed by Hazelbourne, Mr Basu?' he said.

'I cannot say that I am,' said the taciturn Basu. 'There are many English people who served in India who choose to live here, and even some Indian people. But it is quite puzzling to me as to why.'

'Sunny climate and one of the driest spots in England,' said Harris. 'Reminds them of the hill stations, I expect.'

'But it is as flat as a chapati and it rains every other day,' said Basu. 'In our country at least the monsoon sticks to its own season.'

'On the other hand the rain produces both ladies and flowers of the most delicate charm,' said Pendra, looking at the dance floor. 'A veritable bouquet of loveliness.'

'Do you dance, Mr Pendra?' asked Mrs Wirrall. 'All of England is in a craze for it.'

'I have been known to shake a leg in Paris and London,' said Pendra. 'But in such a genteel environment as Hazelbourne I do not desire to – shall we say – provoke any vexation among the older generation.' Constance stifled a chortle and the young man raised an eyebrow at her.

'I heard some old ladies muttering at me just for waltzing with a Canadian,' she explained and then halted, aware too late of a possible insult in the comparison. 'I'm sorry – I was just laughing at how awful they are.'

'I assure you most girls don't pay the old biddies any attention,' added Poppy.

'I'm sure our young ladies will welcome another competent dancer.' Harris looked at Constance as he spoke.

'Of course,' she said and then wondered if she had just asked to be invited to dance. She lowered her gaze in confusion.

'Yes, Hazelbourne can be genteel if you mean staid, parochial and judgemental,' said Mrs Wirrall. 'I swore off dancing in public myself for similar reasons. But I plan to dance again at the ball I am giving on Peace Day, and I invite you and Mr Basu to be my guests.'

'Oh, I couldn't presume,' began Mr Pendra. 'You are too kind.'

'Nonsense. Any subject of the dear Maharajah, not to mention one who has served in the war, is more than welcome,' she said. 'Others can come or not as they please. I have decided to be finished with worrying about them.'

'Unfortunately, Basu and I are expected in London, where we will join the Peace Parade as part of the Indian contingent. Were we not so engaged, we would have been humbly grateful to accept your kind invitation.'

'London. How exciting,' said Mrs Wirrall. 'You will see the King himself.'

'Indeed!' Basu's face lit up, but Pendra gave him the faintest of frowns.

'If only for a moment, ma'am,' Basu added. 'There are to be thousands in the parade.'

'If you ladies will excuse us,' said Pendra. 'We shall invite dear Colonel Smith to join us for a drink and try to persuade him that we are not at the Bombay Club. I can't resist seeing Basu get so upset when the Colonel mistakes him for a waiter.'

Constance was doubtful Mrs Fog would approve an afternoon excursion of young people to a secluded beach far from the prying eyes of the town, but when Mrs Fog returned, shortly before dinnertime, she seemed much too happy and distracted by her own plans to worry.

'Oh good, my dear, then I shan't have to worry about leaving you alone,' she said. She had stretched out on her bed, still in her afternoon dress and shoes, and declared herself too tired to do more than eat a soft-boiled egg and go to sleep. 'Only Mathilde and I are to visit the old people at the workhouse and then have tea with the master. Mathilde goes every Saturday afternoon and brings them little treats and teaches them to draw and paint.'

'Your visit went well?' asked Constance.

'She welcomed me with open arms and would not hear my pleas for forgiveness,' said Mrs Fog. 'I am just so sorry I did not pluck up my courage and write to her years ago.'

'I would love to meet her,' said Constance. 'I want to hear all about your youth together.'

'I'm sure you will in good time,' said Mrs Fog, considering Constance from beneath lowered eyelids. 'But here we are in such a comfortable arrangement where each of us may follow our own wishes. You are such a sensible girl, Constance, that I do not hesitate to free you from being chained to my side.'

Chapter 7

THE SUN TURNED THE INSIDES OF CONSTANCE'S EYELIDS
red and burned against her bare forearms and the tops of her feet. Still
and drowsy, she lay pressed against the pebbled beach, the taste of salt
on her lips and her hair gritty with sand. Her short bathing costume was
still damp around the neck and knees. She had felt exposed at first, dropping her towel and running into the sea, always swimming behind Poppy
and away from the young men, who maintained a respectful distance,
but whose eyesight was no doubt sharp enough. Now, stretched prone
beside Poppy, she felt as limp as seaweed. She pointed and flexed one
lazy foot, admiring the rim of sand on her toes. Poppy stretched her
arms overhead.

'Oh, to be this free and unencumbered the rest of my life,' said Poppy.
'No shoes, no stays, no one caring if your hair is perfectly pinned. I could
spend the whole summer camped on a beach, grilling mussels over a
fire.'

'Are we collecting the mussels or are we dashing into the fishmongers
in our bathing suits?' asked Constance.

'I haven't planned all the logistics,' said Poppy. 'I assumed the mussels
would just appear, but whether by magic or servant I have not yet
decided.'

'It is wonderful, just for a moment, to act like a child, but it isn't a very practical solution to one's problems.' As Constance propped herself on her elbows, she too felt the enchantment of this remote valley, hidden between two chalk hills, its small river carving lazy oxbows through pasture and marsh to empty into the sea on the deserted beach. A few lonely coast guard cottages on the western cliff were the only signs of civilisation. It was so different from the organised and public nature of holidaying in Hazelbourne that she also wished they might hide away here, not just for a Saturday afternoon, but for all summer.

Down the beach a little ways Tom Morris and Sam Newcombe, still in their long striped bathing costumes, were playing about with a ball and cricket bat. The slow, exaggerated bowling, the careful stepping to knock the ball away, the loping up and down the narrow, wet strip of sand, seemed like a ballet. The audience for this performance, sitting in deckchairs, consisted of Evangeline and Guinevere Morris, who had declined to swim, and Iris Brenner, who was wrapped in a large towel, drying her long red mermaid hair. Harris, in summer flannels and a battered panama hat, was reading a book, enigmatic behind dark glasses.

'I suppose we should go over there?' Constance said.

'Oh, please let's stay here a little longer,' said Poppy. 'Is Tom still showing off?'

'He is,' said Constance. 'He keeps looking over.'

'Make sure you refuse to notice,' said Poppy.

'Is there some understanding between you?' asked Constance. 'He seems very enamoured.'

'He believes so but I am not being cooperative,' Poppy said. 'I shoo him away, but he's as persistent as a spoiled dog. And about as reliable.'

Constance laughed. 'I haven't known you long,' she said. 'But I can't see you choosing a man because he's reliable!'

'Let's not spoil the day focusing on Tom,' said Poppy. 'He can do that all by himself.'

'Is Harris a sportsman?' asked Constance, changing the subject. 'I mean it must be hard for him now.'

'He was a sculler up at Oxford and played some cricket,' said Poppy. 'He was also a great swimmer, but now I can't persuade him into the water.' She sighed. 'Stubborn, stubborn, stubborn.'

'Such a terrible thing, the war,' said Constance. She knew Harris would rather die than be pitied but her heart felt for him, so pale and stiff, under the protective shadow of his hat brim.

'Oh, I don't know,' said Poppy. 'I'm rather sorry it's over.'

'Poppy!'

'I know. It's a despicable thing to say.' Poppy sighed and sat up, hugging her knees to her chest. 'But think about it for a minute. If the war were still going, I'm pretty sure the new Royal Air Force would have found something for Harris to do – flying support, a training position? And I loved being a despatch rider and running the group. All the girls loved it. It was hard work, to be sure. So many late nights in the cold. Once I rode all the way to Plymouth in a sleet storm and had to sleep on a cot in the signals office. The lieutenant in charge offered to marry me on the spot and his men made me a cooked breakfast and sent me away with two extra cans of petrol and half their chocolate ration. We were reviled in the beginning – I'm not sure if they were more afraid we were incompetent or unwomanly – but when they got used to us, we earned their respect.' She palmed a few pebbles and lobbed her artillery towards a patch of dry sand where they each made a tiny crater on impact. 'I guess I got used to feeling life was urgent and I was doing something important. Now we are all expected to go home to the kitchen or drawing room.'

'Somehow it is less exhausting to work twelve hours a day than to sit around waiting for the tea bell to ring,' agreed Constance. 'I miss going to the estate office early in the morning and making my tea on a gas ring. I miss keeping a tidy ledger. I even miss the muddy farmers coming in, not scraping their boots enough and shaking the rain from their coats all over my floor.'

'Do you think they miss it too, despite the horrors?' Poppy nodded down the beach. Harris was now walking slowly along the shore, just out of reach of the lacy flapping of the small waves, his face lifted to the horizon. Tom Morris was wrestling Newcombe for the cricket ball; still upright, kicking up sand and pebbles, now leg hooking over leg, now arms thrusting through arms, the sheen of sweat on a bare forearm, thigh muscles carved in steep relief. 'I sometimes wonder which life seems more real to them,' she added.

'I think most men seem determined not to think about it at all,' said Constance. 'They just want to get on with things.'

'Maybe that's the problem with Harris,' said Poppy. 'If only he had something to get on with.' She sighed. 'All he seems to do is think and brood. I worry for his sanity sometimes.'

'I don't know your brother at all well,' said Constance. 'But I think he's entirely too sharp-tongued to be in danger of a breakdown. When he lapses into mute disinterest, then you should worry.'

'A small period of muteness would not go entirely amiss,' said Poppy. 'Shall we dress ourselves and pounce on that picnic hamper?'

The gentlemen joined Harris in a stroll down the beach to give the young women a measure of privacy while they dressed again. With clothes scrambled into behind a towel and imperfectly buttoned, Constance noticed the others did not bother getting into stays and left their stockings and shoes abandoned. Shyly, she followed suit, listening to their blunt conversation.

'But will there be anyone to dance with at your mother's ball?' Gwinny asked Poppy.

'There were so many men to dance with in Bath,' said Evangeline. The twins had spent most of the war living with an aunt. 'Not that I wish the war were still on but there just aren't the new men to dance with now.'

'Not that they were all or even mostly available.' Gwinny looked at her sister in mock severity and Evangeline giggled.

'True. One had to dance with a lot of frogs to find the rare prince,' she said. 'But now the tide has really gone out.'

'You're off to London in the autumn, I hear,' said Iris. 'No doubt you'll have your pick of men there.'

'No, it's the same there.' Evangeline looked down the beach where the young men could be observed in the distance collecting large pieces of driftwood for an entirely unnecessary bonfire. 'The lame, the halt, the malingerers and the foreign.' She sighed. 'The cream of the English aristocracy has been lost.'

'Evangeline!' Even her sister, Gwinny, had the grace to look scandalised.

'Evie likes her men landed and liquid,' explained Poppy. Dressed, and perhaps disgusted, she walked down to the water, where she began to skim stones with a practised expertise. Constance felt an urge to walk away too. Somehow when the twins were present, the women's freedom and ease, even the wit of Poppy and Iris, edged across some invisible pale into a cruelty that gave her pause. The Morris girls might have position and wealth, but they had not one ounce the sense or character of a Tilly, who, once again, had not been invited.

'Well, a girl has to look out for herself,' said Evangeline, pouting. 'We don't get handed everything like Tom or Harris.'

'I hear you were very fond of Harris.' The words were out before Constance could stop herself. There was a silence and she feared that in her urge to challenge Evangeline's vulgarity, she had overstepped.

'Of course we were both fond,' said Gwinny. 'Such a terrible thing. Poppy knows how devastated we were.'

'He was such a wonderful dancer too.' Evangeline shivered then lowered her voice. 'But can you imagine the wooden leg hanging on the bedpost at night?'

Iris snorted in disgust. 'You are the giddy limit, Evangeline. Face like an angel but all the tact of a bedpost yourself.'

'Evangeline is very delicate,' said Gwinny. 'Harris understands.'

'What about Sam?' asked Constance. 'He seems very kind and generous.'

'It's good to have a brother with generous friends,' said Evangeline. 'Of course Sam would like to propose, only he can't tell us apart.'

'Evangeline is just jealous because Sam is quite devoted to Poppy,' said Gwinny. 'Don't tell Tom.'

'Our grandmother, being an earl's daughter, would have made him come in the back door you know,' added Evangeline. 'Being in trade.'

'Isn't he in the same business as your father?' asked Constance, feigning puzzlement. 'I thought you were one of his biggest customers?' Evangeline bristled like an angry chicken.

'Sam's grandfather was a blacksmith while our family is ten generations of gentlemen in this county,' she said. 'Flying is considered a gentleman's pursuit, you know, and then in the war my father felt he must do his part.'

'Evie is a dreadful snob,' said Gwinny. 'She won't even visit the workshops.'

'Shut up, Gwinny!' An ugly frown marred Evangeline's porcelain brow. 'I wouldn't care about Sam's background, of course, but then he also didn't serve so there is the tiniest hint of the white feather.'

'But I thought he wasn't allowed to serve,' said Constance. 'He was essential like my brother, the farmer.'

'Of course, but he could have run away and signed up under an assumed name,' said Evangeline. 'By no means am I calling him a coward, but what would one tell the children?'

'Better snag a Canadian if the home boys don't measure up,' said Iris.

'Ugh, and end up on some beaver farm in the wilderness?' said Evangeline. 'I'd rather marry that Indian chap Harris and Sam are so fond of and be a memsahib.'

'You really are pitiless, Evangeline,' said Iris. She looked angry now and Gwinny laughed to divert the conversation.

'So you see, Constance, it is a very small pool in which to fish. Our brother, on the other hand, is pressed about with female attention.'

'He seems to enjoy it well enough.' Constance could not keep a note of sarcasm from her voice.

'Oh, the new girl fires a shot across the bow,' said Gwinny.

'Tom's fixed on Poppy,' said Evangeline. 'I don't understand it myself. We've grown up together and I love her too, but she's always been so abrasive. She used to pull my hair all the time.'

'You deserved it then and now,' murmured Iris.

'War really makes you think,' said Gwinny. 'I believe he's looking to settle down. I wish she would accept him because then he would be sure to stay here and demobilise.'

'War makes me think life is far too short to settle or be sensible,' said Evangeline. 'I plan to devote myself to parties and dancing.'

'I can't bear him to go to Russia again,' said Gwinny, and Constance saw fear in her face. She would have liked to say something comforting, but Gwinny turned away and Iris was already signalling to the men, and Poppy, that it was safe to rejoin the picnic party.

Soon Tom Morris was setting a match to a pile of driftwood, set in a ring of beach stones, and Sam Newcombe was fussing over the large hamper he had somehow acquired, which contained cucumber sandwiches, cold chicken legs and a large pork pie with a glistening, salty crust.

'I have a box of cherries and some sort of cake too,' he said. 'Champagne, ladies? It will take a while to boil a kettle for tea.'

'However did you come by such a feast?' asked Evangeline.

'Best not to ask him,' said Iris. 'It's not polite to force a man to lie.'

'Nothing underhanded,' said Newcombe, slightly huffy. 'Some sacrifice of ration coupons. Bottle or two of good whisky to the hotel chef. All about connections, you see.' This was a long speech for the man and he blushed as he busied himself pouring champagne into tin mugs.

'Well, it's heavenly,' said Poppy, biting into a sandwich. 'Oh my goodness, this is real butter.'

'Someone please slice up the pie,' said Iris. 'I would do it myself but I can't see for my mouth watering.'

'Well, maybe just a small sandwich and some cherries,' said Evangeline. 'Harris, can I bring you something?'

He looked up from his book and seemed to Constance to be surprised by the direct address.

'Don't encourage him to be lazy,' said Poppy. 'He spends far too much time being waited on hand and foot.'

'In a moment you will encourage me out of this deckchair to push you into the sea, dear sister,' said Harris. 'Thank you, Evangeline. I will be happy to accept your offer.'

She arranged chicken, sandwiches and a fat slice of pie on a second plate and picked her way over the pebbles to his side, where she sank to the ground to join him. Constance took her own food and sat with Iris, who was winding her hair into a long plait.

'Aren't you tempted to cut your hair?' said Gwinny, bringing Iris a slice of pork pie. 'It's beautiful but I can't imagine how you even squash it under your helmet.'

'I didn't cut it during the war because I wasn't going to let the Kaiser dictate my life,' said Iris. 'And if I didn't cut it in the face of the enemy, I'm not about to do so to submit to fashion.'

'And what about you, Constance,' said Evangeline. She smiled but Constance felt the hint of malice. 'Are you not tempted by the freedom of the modern style?'

'I imagine it requires care and attention to keep one's hair as lovely as yours,' she replied. 'I'm so used to my hair that it takes me no time at all.'

'I don't envy you all trying to get the salt out,' said Evangeline. 'Our maid would have a fit if we came home with salty hair.'

'So where's the freedom if you can't swim?' said Poppy. 'Really, Evangeline, you do talk absolute rot sometimes.'

'Your hair is also very nice,' said Sam to Poppy, whose face was stuck about with drying tendrils.

'Why does no one fuss over men's hair?' she replied. 'Perhaps we women should consider the benefits of a strong pomade.'

'Let's not argue on such a beautiful day,' said Evangeline. 'On a day like this we should all appreciate that we are friends.'

'This is what we fought for,' said Tom, coming over and plopping on the pebbles at Constance's side without an invitation. She stiffened as he leaned in, brushing against her arm as he raised his mug in Poppy's direction. 'Days of leisure in the sun with champagne and beautiful girls.'

'Some of us don't want to be idle,' said Poppy, rolling her eyes at him. 'Some of us want nothing better than to roll up our sleeves and contribute to the industry of the nation.'

'Not me,' said Evangeline. 'I've done my bit. Now I want to laze about and have many admirers.'

'We all appreciate it,' said Sam to Poppy. 'Your contributions. War effort won at home and all that.'

'Working is still novel for you women, is it not, Constance?' said Tom. 'But if you tire of it you can always marry. If Poppy won't have me, I could be persuaded to take you on, perhaps?' This offer was too unexpected for Constance to think of a suitably curt response. She could only try not to visibly shrink from the leer of his smile.

'Don't bother, Constance,' said Poppy. 'Unlike those of us who have suffered for years, Tom, she isn't used to your abominable sense of humour.'

'Miss Haverhill is hardly a shrinking violet or you wouldn't have made her your protégée,' he replied. 'I just meant to explain that poor chaps like me and Sam may never be free from the burden of working. What do you say, Sam? Or has the old pater made enough in the strife for you to retire to the country?'

'My father? Determined to see me settled in the country,' Sam said. 'But also manage the business. Not consistent, you see.' He blew out his cheeks. 'Your father expects the same, I imagine.'

'Yes, he's very persistent that I work my lazy bones,' said Tom. 'We are not like Harris, master of his own estate at twenty-seven.'

'Perhaps you haven't met my mother?' asked Harris. 'Regardless of the niceties of inheritance, she shows no sign of handing over the reins.' He sighed. 'Not that I want them particularly. My father was happy to exchange banking for the country baronet's life of the hunting saddle and his London club, but I can't imagine anything more boring. You are the lucky one, Tom.'

'Not that Tom does anything but fly silly aeroplanes,' said Gwinny. 'I know more than him about how the business runs, but of course Daddy isn't giving me a job.'

'Nor me,' said Harris and Constance noted the thinning of his smile.

'If it were up to me, of course,' said Tom and looked away across the sea. A small pause opened up, as happens, Constance thought, when no one is quite sure the thrust of the conversation but understands an awkwardness is implied. Harris seemed to gather himself and gave a small laugh.

'Someone recently pointed out to me that lying about in despair is reserved only for the truly wealthy.' He raised an eyebrow at Constance. 'So in the interest of my own sanity, and because my mother may run us into the ground with her renovations at Penneston, I'm actually thinking of following my father into the bank.'

'That's wonderful!' said Poppy, her face momentarily alight. She quickly recovered to add, 'I don't suppose the bank will have a post for me too?'

'I believe your complete disdain for numbers might be a greater barrier than your sex,' said Harris. 'Not that you don't understand them perfectly – you just refuse to be limited by them.'

'Living within your means is a fiction men impose upon women,' said Poppy. 'You run up debt as if it's a part of being a gentleman, and meanwhile I am to watch the pennies in my purse even though I have women depending on my business.'

'Well, I don't want to work or have any part in any stuffy old business,' said Evangeline. 'I'd rather be famous.'

'I don't think people like us understand how many women must work to support themselves,' said Iris. 'And now the government seeks to push them out of so many industries and yet it does not provide husbands down at the Labour Exchange.'

'My goodness,' said Poppy. 'Can you imagine if they offered the choice: parlourmaid at a pound a week or a nice portly chap with a green tweed suit and a smallholding.'

'I'll take the chap,' said Iris. 'The green suit will go with my hair.' Constance joined in the general laughter but felt a shiver down her back. Perhaps it was just a wisp of breeze down the valley, but perhaps it was all the advertisements for parlourmaids that she had skimmed over in the newspapers. Her new friends could laugh, as Sam poured more champagne, for summer seemed endless and it was all a joke to them. They could not know how close a girl like Constance, with no money and few prospects, might be to being grateful for such a position come September.

Chapter 8

TUESDAYS WERE KLAUS'S DAY OFF. SUNDAYS WERE NOT permitted to the professional waiter as being a day of rest for others meant the hotel was always busy. Klaus had long accustomed himself to welcoming the faithful back from church to an ample luncheon. And he tried to keep a suitable Christian forgiveness in his heart as those who enjoyed the freedom to attend services also complained about them freely and with great enthusiasm over their roast potatoes. Tuesdays were when he could be spared, and still he trembled lest there be the knock on the door asking him to work. Today he dressed quickly and slipped out without breakfast, gaining the street with his breath held and his hands clutching his coat around him. His shoes, the soles nailed so many times, struck loudly against the pavement as he hurried away.

In a back street behind the large hotels, he passed the plain cement Baptist chapel where, before the war, a small group of German Lutherans were allowed to meet on a Tuesday. Of course, the Germans – one or two shopkeepers, other waiters, a Hanoverian governess – were all gone now. Shortly after his return to Hazelbourne, Klaus had ventured in again and the minister, who had lost a son to poison gas at Ypres, had welcomed him effusively. But the grip of the minister's hand was painful, and his eyes searched Klaus's face as if the waiter were a personal test of faith that he must endure. Klaus went away sadly, denied the sanctuary of a quiet pew.

He turned inland now, and by degrees the streets grew steeper as he reached the old town. Here the shops and houses of five centuries huddled down together; the smug, flat-fronted Regency rubbing against the jutting black-and-white timbers of the medieval. The streets bent to accommodate ancient trees and met in awkward numbers at crossroads older than any settlement. Far from the illusions of the seafront, ordinary English shopkeepers and tradespeople plied their trades and rubbed along with a smattering of Europeans.

The cobbler from Poland still had his shop. He claimed to talk to the dead and to heal people with the very hands that had, several times, resurrected Klaus's one good pair of shoes from a dry, split, leathery death. On a narrow alley Klaus looked in vain for the ironmongers from where he hoped to buy some clothes pegs. The shop was gone, the building empty, and the sign ripped from above the broken windows. Klaus was surprised. The ironmonger and his wife were from Stuttgart, so his business had no doubt been confiscated by the government when he was interned and later, probably, deported. But such a profitable business – Klaus was sure some local Englishman would have snapped it up cheaply. Two doors down, above a greengrocer, the Romanian music teacher was also gone; a small Studio to Let sign on the greengrocer's door. A musician by passion and teacher by necessity, the Romanian seemed to teach mostly by performing, and violin music would pour from his open windows until housewives forgot their errands and paused on lightened feet as if about to dance. He was not German, but perhaps the people and the pupils had not differentiated their hostility.

Under a gnarled oak, by an old water pump where horses still paused to drink from the mossy trough, Klaus sat on an iron bench in the shadows. Across a triangle of streets, in the full blaze of the sun, he watched the large Georgian shopfront of the bakery that used to be *Otto Kuchner, Master Baker*. The open door still emitted the same scent of burnt sugar and almonds, but the shop was now called *Wilson and Sons, British Bakery*. On tiered glass shelves in the window there lay a single strudel, now labelled 'apple sugar turnover'. It was flanked by three sticky currant buns, a lopsided brown loaf and the pale Gibraltars of a half dozen English scones. The rest of the marble counter was empty; the war might be over, but all the bread was still gone before the end of the morning.

Klaus remembered old Otto, as bent as a shepherd's crook, his hands with knuckles knotted like wooden beads, always up at four in the morning to put the risen bread in the oven. His wife, and daughter, Odile, used to beg him to rest. Odile. Her name was like a melting lemon drop in Klaus's mouth. Odile with the plain face, the strong back and muscled arms from years at the heavy wooden bread trays. Odile, with fingers as swift and nimble as a child's, piping fragile dough into cups and flowers, braiding strudels like hair, painting in the air with tendrils of burnt sugar. Odile, a spinster past her thirtieth year who frowned and crossed her arms behind her rolling pin, as adamant as a princess in a Grimm's tale, and declared herself too busy to marry. Her parents could only shrug their shoulders in despair and offer each of her many rejected suitors a kuchen in a twist of paper as they left. But behind her bluster and her hair braided so tight it hurt to look at it, Klaus could see the shyness of a woodland creature. Behind the practised smile of the shop counter, he could see instinct had set her against man. Some trauma in her childhood perhaps; the difficult journey to life in England of which her parents would never speak. Klaus, older by a decade and broken around the edges himself, had felt his mute soul go out to meet hers as she handed him a soft bread roll in a paper bag.

He became a regular customer, and even a friend as he helped Otto secure a contract at the hotel to supply fancy German pastries for afternoon teas. On slow Tuesdays he might be asked to step into the rear parlour for a cup of tea. He was polite to Odile and listened gravely to her mother bemoan this or that gentleman whom her unmanageable daughter had sent away.

'But you would be lost without her,' Klaus would say, and the mother would wipe her eyes and nod and be comforted until the next time. Klaus never put himself forward. His worship of Odile was his own secret. She was like a hot flame that burned in him. She made his work pleasant, his room a castle, his back as straight as a duke's. When he brushed his best suit, it was in case he might walk with her one day. When he faced an angry hotel guest with quiet authority, it was in the hope she might one day appear in the lobby and catch sight of him. When he put aside money under a loose floorboard, it was with dreams of a small cottage and Odile singing at the hearth.

And then the troubles in Europe grew and there was awkwardness in the air. A rumour that the English might expel Germans; a whisper of friends leaving while the ports were still open. It became hard to gauge how to pitch one's opinion on the situation and impolite to speculate where others' loyalties lay. Klaus, waiting on tables of Englishmen who snapped their newspapers and made increasingly loud suggestions about the innate aggression of the German race, was embarrassed by Briton and German alike. When war was announced, he could only pray the unpleasantness would indeed be over by Christmas. He did not blame the English for being wary. He only tried to be as invisible as possible.

One day the police were in the lobby asking about him and the three German chambermaids. The same day Mr Smickle told him he should go home and stay out of sight for a while. It did no good to protest that he was naturalised. Mr Smickle handed him an envelope with a month's wages and told him he was sorry.

'If it were up to me?' He raised his hands, helpless. 'And perhaps go stay with someone away from the coast. They are worried about spies.'

Back then, Klaus had a nice attic room in a boarding house by the park. His landlady had always had a soft spot for him, tut-tutting over his thin shoulders and feeding him an extra egg, a second slice of roast beef. The travelling salesman who kept a large room on the first floor joked that she was fattening Klaus up for marriage. As the fever of war grew – parades of recruits, posters on the promenade, young women collecting for war bonds – the landlady began to feed him the gristle end of the roast, eggs fried hard and leathery, and to forget his sheets on washday.

In the town, where he walked with his head down, the Romanian suffered a brick through his window that damaged his violin, and the Polish cobbler took to keeping a cricket bat at his counter and to displaying a Union Jack in his window. When the ironmonger and his wife left, closing the store on market day, rumours swirled that they had been bundled off in a police van. Klaus hurried to the bakery, fearful and sorry he had stayed away, humiliated by his own unemployment. At the bakery a new sign was being painted, the curling W of a stencilled *Wilson* already filled in with red, white and blue stripes.

'How are you all?' Klaus asked old Otto, who was sitting on a chair they kept for elderly customers. Klaus had never seen him sit before. 'Who is this Wilson?'

'My daughter, she is to be married this afternoon,' said Otto. 'The man who brings the flour will be my new son-in-law.'

'Married?' said Klaus; he balanced on knees that felt boneless. 'I had no idea she had a sweetheart.' The baker shrugged.

'She will be English. It will be an English bakery.' A tear rolled down the baker's cheek and he dashed it away with his hand. 'It is for the best. They can't take it from us now.'

'The ironmongers?' Klaus asked.

'Taken away and their shop is confiscated.'

'I am so sorry,' said Klaus.

'Forty years of struggle and all is gone,' said the baker. He shook his head. 'At least my daughter will be safe now.' Odile emerged from the back room with a tray of hot bread and, though she smiled at Klaus, her eyes were red-rimmed and flickered with fear. Fear of marrying or of the arrival of the police he could not tell. Perhaps he made her afraid – made them more vulnerable just by his presence?

'I wish you congratulations,' he said, bowing to her. 'I hope you will be very happy.'

'Happiness is for silly girls,' she said, raising her chin. 'As a woman I hope to be a good wife to my husband.'

'If I can be of service to your family,' he said, but he was too late. Her careful smile made his heart ache in his chest. 'I am also English by naturalisation,' he blurted out.

'Yes, but your name is Zieger,' said Otto. 'I don't think you are safe either. As I told my wife, Wilson is many things – some good, some bad – but there is no doubt he is a real Englishman and his name may save us all.' By this admission, Klaus understood he had been considered, though he had never spoken. A wash of shame came over him that he had been a coward in his heart and all of them had seen his cowardice.

'May the name of Wilson be the largest of umbrellas and these troubles the smallest of rainstorms,' said Klaus. 'May it all indeed be over by Christmas.'

'I pray to God it is,' said Odile, her face white. Then she laughed without mirth. 'Though if it is, we will have made a poor bargain.'

He heard the parents were taken away to internment shortly before himself. This being England, there was a civilised air to the destruction of lives. First an appointment at the police station. Then the letter from London giving a few days' notice of one's removal. A list of what to bring and not bring as if one were leaving for Scout camp. In vain Klaus had gone again to the police station with his papers and a letter attesting to his good character from Mr Smickle. The sergeant on duty had shrugged and suggested he write to London with any objections. He had spent a whole winter in an internment camp on the Isle of Man, where every day he brushed his clothes and washed in a cold-water basin and tidied his narrow bunk as if at home. Everyone was civil, even the guards, and some small clubs were arranged and some basic lessons continued for the puzzled children in the women's camp. And everyone did their best to pretend they were not housed in freezing wooden huts behind barbed wire, like animals, with no promise of a future. It was six months before his case was reviewed and he was released, with a train ticket to London and instructions not to go near the coast.

Now, as he sat on the bench, lost in the flicker of old memories, Odile came to the door with a broom in her hand and began to shake out the doormat. She looked older, of course, perhaps more than four years of worry in her face. Her hair was loose in its braids, frizzy around her forehead. She swept with short strokes, attacking the dirt. Her apron was stained and frayed at the bottom. A man came out, her husband, Wilson, judging by the way he gripped her arm and patted her bottom as he left. He was thick-bodied, with rusty hair and the lazy swagger of a man who lived by the work of others. He lit a pipe, tugged at the lapels of his coat and strolled away down the street as if it were already afternoon and the shop shut up for Tuesday's half-day early closing. Sitting in the shade, Klaus trembled and wondered if now, after avoiding this street for several weeks, he had the strength to go to her.

At her door, she swept the dust right over his shoes and when she raised her eyes to apologise, she looked confused, blinking into the sun.

'Herr Zieger? Is it you?'

'It is the very same, Mrs Wilson. You remember . . .' But she stopped his speaking by dropping her broom, throwing her arms around him and burying her face in his chest, weeping.

'Oh, oh, oh' was all she could manage between sobs and Klaus, at the same time stiff with embarrassment and weak with compassion, could only do his best to hold her upright and pat her back in, he hoped, not too forward a manner.

'There there, my dear, would you like to sit down?' he said as she finally pulled away, hiccupping.

'No, no, I'm so sorry, Herr Zieger. I don't know what came over me.' She wiped her eyes on her grubby apron and laughed. 'It was almost as if my parents had returned; as if the last years were just a bad dream.' Her eyes sparkled with tears and her nose was red. He thought her beautiful.

'Come in, come in. I was just closing anyway. Come into the garden and have some tea and some food.'

'I shouldn't impose,' he said.

'After you desert us for so many years, I think you owe me this,' she said. She had hold of his hand and it blazed warm in hers.

'Your husband?'

'It is Tuesday. He is gone for the afternoon,' she said. 'Besides, he cannot object to an old friend of my parents.' She led him into the shop, dark after the bright outdoors, and barred the door. 'Go through the passage,' she added. 'The children are in the garden.'

The garden behind the bakery was no more than a sunny courtyard, edged with some carefully tended flower boxes. Three chickens scratched in a small coop in one corner and washing hung on a line along the sunniest wall. Under a sunshade, a rough home-made crib contained a baby, who had hauled herself upright on the bars and now bounced as in a drunken dance. A toddler boy sat on the flagstones playing quietly with a wooden car and a stick of chalk.

'You have children,' he said, a redundancy standing in for the more nuanced small talk that escaped him. His throat felt choked and his mind empty. He could only look at her as she swept a peg basket from a wire chair and folded laundry from a metal table.

'James and Alice,' she said. 'Very English names. Please sit down. I will bring tea and strudel.'

Klaus sat cautiously on the thin chair and withstood the stares of both small children. He nodded to them. They continued to look at him and the baby's lip began to tremble.

'What do you draw with your chalk?' said Klaus to the boy, who shrugged and scraped the chalk on the ground. 'Do you draw roads for your car?'

When Odile came out with a heavy tray, Klaus was crouched on the ground and had already drawn a network of chalk-outlined roadways from the chicken coop to the side gate and around the table to the flower boxes. He was trying to draw a major crossroads in the centre but was hindered by the boy, who could not wait for it to be finished and was already loudly motoring his car over Klaus's knuckles. The baby was bouncing and chortling, watching her brother's play.

'Oh my, you are good with them,' said Odile.

'Not really,' said Klaus, getting painfully to his feet, too slow to help her set the tray on the table. 'I have a passing interest in civil engineering.

I have definite ideas about road design in the modern town, but unfortunately I am only a waiter and my ideas are therefore moot. Your son is the first to listen to me.' Odile laughed, the lines on her face softening.

'You always were so funny, Klaus.'

Over tea they sketched faint pictures of their lives since the war, softening the edges, leaving white space between the lines of pain. Her parents were in Germany, she said, eliding over the misery of deportation and absence.

'I try to send a little money but my husband— Business has not been easy.' The husband had seemed adequately fat and Klaus had noted a new coat. But it was not his place to contradict or to probe her faint blush. He, in turn, embroidered a story of his own exile in London, mentioning the green refuge of the parks and the excitement of the crowds. He had once made an expedition to the centre and spent a day looking in at the plate-glass windows of department stores. This he managed to extend until it seemed as if he had not only summoned the courage to enter the gilded interiors but that he took tea in a fountain-cooled atrium often. She did not know that Earl's Court was impossibly far from Harrods for him or that, after the indignity of the hostel and the asylum, he had been grateful to work six and a half days a week in a quiet boarding house for travelling salesmen and sleep on a pallet in the cellar. After room and board, and given his German accent, he was paid a pittance, so on his half days and at night on Saturdays, he washed dishes in a Chinese-owned nightclub in Limehouse. The money was good, but the boss would bring other Chinese businessmen to gape at him, sweating in his uniform and up to his elbows in soapy water. At first he had been afraid – thinking they came to stare at the enemy German. But they were always animated, laughing, giving him little bows. He understood the boss found it a matter of pride to employ a European in this servile position – and that part of that pride was to display how well he was treated. His humiliation was tempered by his appreciation of their humour in the reversal of the usual colonial roles, and by the little gifts and coins his boss's friends bowed over and left for him on his draining board. But all he told Odile of the nightclub were the silk lanterns and the women in embroidered Chinese dress serving champagne and selling red roses; and food such as the entire carp, roasted, glazed and set on a varnished model teak boat, swimming in a sea of flower petals. As he spoke he could smell the vintage champagne, from bottles priced higher than a month's wages, which sometimes came back to the kitchen half full at the end of a night. The taciturn cook and his helpers would drink, and then they would grow merry, slapping him on the back and gently abusing him in Mandarin. He would be invited to drink, and to eat a bowl of rice flecked with leftovers, as the dawn rose over a grimy London.

'It is all behind us now.' His stories, one small lie stacked on top of another like a house of cards, seemed to peter out in the telling.

'We can't go back and we can't go forward,' she said, and he was simultaneously wounded that she saw his condition so easily, and happy that she offered to share this paltry limbo. But he urged her to hope as a drowning man might push a woman into a lifeboat.

'You have your children,' he said. 'Your future will grow.'

'They are my joy,' she said. She held out her arms to the toddler and he came to her, presenting the top of his head for a kiss. She laughed. 'He is impatient with my boundless affection.'

'*Er ist ein männlicher mann,*' he said, smiling.

'We don't speak German,' she said. If the slight pinching of her face betrayed unhappiness, she would never speak of it. 'It's better for them, my husband says.'

'I should be going,' he said. He did not think he should shake her hand. He rose and clicked his heels as he made a small bow.

'I write to them, you know – my parents – but I know I shall probably never see them again,' she said. She rose from the table, twisting her hands in her apron. 'I shall tell them about you, Herr Zieger.'

'It was good to see you again, Mrs Wilson,' he said, and in her wet eyes he could see himself, very small, putting on his hat.

Chapter 9

HARRIS WENT UP TO LONDON ON TUESDAY NIGHT, AND stayed overnight at his Officers' Club in Mayfair. He had hoped a good night's sleep and a hot breakfast might set him up properly to meet Mr Llewellyn, the senior partner at his father's bank. Insisting on taking the train had been a mistake. So many stairs just to get up and over to the London-bound platform and then the train creeping along, stopping at every hamlet. Even in the first-class carriage, he felt the eyes looking at him sideways. And the newspapers he had bought to pass the time, full of Alcock and Brown's historic first flight across the Atlantic, only made the day more bitter.

Upon reaching Charing Cross, he had almost twisted his good ankle misjudging the train's high step and the platform. For an instant he saw himself spreadeagled on the ground, undone by his own vanity and a flimsy ebony cane. A few hobbling dance steps and he remained upright to begin the long march to a taxi stand. Even the club had a flight of marble steps to the oak door. He had waved off the doorman who hurried to help him and had climbed slowly, painfully up each step, arriving sweaty and angry at the portico.

A good dinner and two large glasses of Scotch whisky had mellowed his temper but sleep proved elusive as he lay in the rough sheets of an unfamiliar bed and watched the moon sail over London. Thoughts drifted in and out of his head like guests at an infernal party. He worked over tomorrow's meeting in his head, playing both himself and Mr Llewellyn, and was surprised at how Mr Llewellyn got the upper hand more than he liked. And then he sank, struggling, into a dream in which Mr Llewellyn ranted about the Flying Corps boys; how he thought them arrogant and bloodless playboys. Mr Llewellyn wanted the details of his amputation – the duration and how much blood had spilled on the operating room's tiled floor and the name of the nurse with the red hair; the one whose hand he gripped as he cried like a child before they gassed him with ether and took his left leg off below the knee. Harris couldn't remember her name. Only her porcelain face, and hazel eyes brimming with tears over a surgical mask. Somehow she was there now, still in her mask. She gripped his hand and murmured something kind. Mr Llewellyn wasn't impressed. He puffed up his chest, continuing to inflate in size until he assumed the shape of a zeppelin and rose to lie against the ceiling, still puffing a large pipe. Harris woke sweating and gasping for breath in the dawn. A chorus of birds sang in the treetops, unconcerned with the plight of humanity.

Breakfast made him nauseous. He nibbled toast and poked at a boiled egg with all the appetite of the invalid he was supposed to be. He drank two pots of tea, which made him jittery. Afterward, he was too tired to take the creaking lift and the long corridor to his room, so he wiped his face with a fresh towel in the gentlemen's lounge on the ground floor, called for a taxi and began the treacherous stepping down the marble stairs to the kerb.

The bank, on a side street near the Exchange, was an imposing stone building with a liveried doorman, and several acres of slippery black-and-white marble tile between the door and the oak desks of the clerks. It smelled like church – and why would it not, Harris thought, thinking of the money lying at rest in stone vaults beneath their feet. He girded himself for the trek across the banking hall, but a young man materialised from a side door and escorted him through a thickly carpeted corridor and into a brass lift.

Mr Llewellyn's office was plusher than a bishop's, with dark panelled walls, a large fox-hunt painting above the vast polished desk. Two leather chairs stood in front of the desk and two wing chairs in front of a carved fireplace. Though the summer sun shone outside, thick drapes and linen sheers kept most of it out and there was a small coal fire to ward off the chill.

'So pleased to see you, young man,' said Mr Llewellyn. Harris was relieved to see he was not smoking a pipe. 'Let us sit comfortably and we'll have some tea.' He signalled the young man and led the way to the wing chairs. 'Your father was a valued partner and shareholder of this institution, as was his father, and it has been our privilege to manage your family's finances these many years.' He cleared his throat. 'Our condolences.'

'Thank you,' said Harris. 'I know my mother has been very grateful for your support while I've been away.'

'A terrible few years,' added Llewellyn. 'I fear none of us has come through unscathed.'

'You have lost family?' asked Harris.

'Not directly, no,' said Llewellyn. 'Mrs Llewellyn and I do not have children. But we have lost many young men from the bank itself. And for all of us, the halls of our alma maters are draped in black bunting for the young boys gone to glory.' Here he took a large handkerchief from his pocket and dabbed the corner of his eye. 'I am on a committee at my club to get up a memorial wall. Quite wrenching the number of names. We are considering whether to order them by name or by year of initiation. And then of course it's rather unpleasant having to verify that they died in action and not of this damned influenza.'

'A grim task,' said Harris.

'One I take on with all sense of duty,' said Llewellyn. 'Of course, it is terrible the life lost to illness, like your father. But a wall of heroes must be about death in the line of fire, don't you think?' Harris had not considered his opinion on the matter, but a vague sense of rage set a pulse racing in his wrists. Fortunately, he was not required to answer, firstly because Llewellyn seemed to consider his own question entirely rhetorical, and secondly the young clerk had returned with a handful of large ledgers and a steward in a dark uniform and white gloves carrying two cups of tea on a silver tray.

'The Penneston files, sir,' said the clerk.

'Thank you, Moresby.' He did not acknowledge the steward, whose hand wobbled slightly as he set the cups on convenient side tables. Fortunately, the tea did not slop into the saucers. The steward silently offered a sugar caddy.

'No, thank you,' said Harris. He noticed the small silver pin on the man's right breast pocket and nodded. 'You were wounded too, I see?'

'Got in a bit of trouble at Gallipoli, sir.' He hesitated, his eyes flickering to the clerk. 'Eighty-sixth Brigade, Second Royal Fusiliers.'

'You chaps had a very rough time of it,' said Harris.

'Yes, sir, thank you, sir.' There seemed no more to say. The man drew himself up, gave a brief bow to Mr Llewellyn and withdrew with the clerk behind him.

'Good chap that,' said Llewellyn. 'Got a name like a fish, Haddon? Haddock? Batman to a colonel who got himself blown to smithereens. He took a piece of shrapnel to the chest. Any more than two cups of tea and he has to bring it on a trolley. But we go above and beyond here to hire our men wherever we can. Got a man working in the vaults who can't work in daylight, you know. Only one eye left, so sensitive to light he wears dark glasses even in his own house. Of course you can't put a man like that in the banking hall where the customers might see him.'

'No, of course not,' said Harris.

'And we don't expect them to advance much. I have to say it's not just the physical damage, you know. There's something not quite right in the mind with most of them. Dreadful business. We all do what we can, but what can we do?'

'I feel very privileged to have been in the Flying Corps and not subjected to the trenches,' said Harris. 'In the hospital I saw some of the horrors. I don't think the public knows half of what our troops suffered.'

'Well, victory is ours now,' said Llewellyn, sucking at his tea. 'Time to settle our accounts with Germany so we can all get back to making money.' He put down his teacup and picked up a fat brown ledger, adding, 'Your father and I agreed at the start of the war that we would hang on to several German stocks, and I have high hopes both sides will come to terms shortly and we'll be able to see them redeemed.'

'German stocks?'

'Only the most secure. Very good manufacturing companies. We saw no need to let the political unpleasantness derail our investment strategy.' He ran his fingers down a column of figures. 'I'm afraid there continue to be difficulties with the Russian bonds. Our government is paying the interest until the Russians come to their senses and oust these dreadful Bolsheviks, but I'm afraid, as I told your mother, they are trading today at half their value.'

'So if we need money, we can't sell them?'

'I would not advise it,' said Mr Llewellyn. 'But I am confident that this will be resolved in the near future. Meanwhile the bulk of the portfolio remains solid as houses in our own stock, though when we converted some to war bonds, we did rather sacrifice our interest rate to our patriotism.' He stopped to chuckle at his own humour before continuing. 'However, the government has paid a nice rent for Penneston house these last four years, which has offset some of your other agricultural losses. And there is a claim for rent still due on the airfield. Yes, I am pleased to say that overall, under almost impossible conditions, I believe we managed to come through well enough for you.'

'I am relieved to hear it,' said Harris.

'Yes, in terms of the management of the assets, I believe we have done very well all things considering.' He paused to sip his tea. 'But there is the very real issue of liquidity.'

'We don't have enough funds?' As if the clouds had briefly parted to let a ray of sun slice through, Harris saw the hard truth hiding inside Mr Llewellyn's circumlocutions.

'With such a rise in the price of everything, your parents had to draw down more each quarter, and with taxes, and of course the recent blow of death duties, outgoing expenditures have rather drained the cash re-serve,' said Llewellyn. 'I think with some economies here and there – nothing drastic – you would be fine while we wait for times to improve. But your mother's renovation of Penneston has been costly. And while we were happy to tide things over mid quarter with bank funds – at a very modest rate of interest—'

'My mother didn't mention any difficulties,' said Harris, reeling as if from a blow.

'Ah well, the ladies are not always able to grasp the niceties of high finance,' said Mr Llewellyn.

'How bad is it?' asked Harris. It was his fault, of course, he thought. His mother had assured him all was well, but what sort of grown man leaves such matters to his mother? Wallowing about feeling sorry for himself, while Penneston fell into debt, he was like some sort of oblivious Nero, minus a leg and the fiddle.

'As your mother seems to find hotel living agreeable, you might consider leasing Penneston for a few more years?' Mr Llewellyn droned on. 'Or perhaps, as agricultural land is at a premium right now, you might consider selling some acreage? If not, serious economies will have to be taken, to which I fear your dear mother is not so much opposed as in a state of disbelief.'

'I see now that it is more urgent than I thought to buckle down and set to my profession.' Harris drew himself upright, like the officer he had forgotten he was, and set his jaw in a new resolution. 'I did not expect to inherit these responsibilities so soon,' he said. 'Before the war I thought only of flying and ignored my father's suggestions that it was time to come into the bank. I believe I must do my duty now.' Even as he said it, a wave of grief washed through him, and whether love for his father or love for flying was uppermost, it almost overcame him. He looked away to hide the sudden emotion.

'But you are a gentleman now,' said Llewellyn, a hesitation in his voice. 'Your father, as his father before him, was proud to serve Queen and Empire as a banker, but with his elevation to baronet, his role as a gentleman became primary.' Llewellyn gave an oleaginous smile and nodded as if satisfied with his own advice. 'Be assured we can simply sell a few acres – perhaps the airfield land – or as I say, since you have no wife yet, you might go abroad and enjoy yourself for a few years on the proceeds of letting the house.'

'I came here today to ask you for a position,' asked Harris. 'My father indicated that one would be held for me while I served my country?'

'Ah, an old courtesy to our partners, and dear to my heart, that our eldest sons should follow in our footsteps – but I'm afraid the old traditions have been changed by this war and we have had to make our own strict economies.' Llewellyn shook his head as if some obscure government department had legislated all power from his hands. 'And besides you have sacrificed enough, dear boy. You should rest and recover. The country is so beneficial to the health.' He shifted in his seat and looked around as if to find support in the draperies or the heavy furniture.

'With respect, I have lost part of my leg, not part of my brain, sir,' said Harris. He did not wish to beg, but it was clear to him now that Penneston was in dire need. He would look Llewellyn in the eye and, with absolute frankness, ask his help. 'I need the post, sir. I do not ask for any favours, only to start at the bottom and prove myself.'

'And so I would counsel you to wait a while – a year or so perhaps – and see how you feel then,' said Llewellyn. 'In the meantime, the world will change again and our clients will no doubt become perfectly comfortable with those returning heroes who must carry the scars of their service. Yes, it will all be so much easier in a year or two . . .'

Seeing no way to penetrate the thick walls of Mr Llewellyn's bland evasions, Harris was forced to accept defeat. 'I would like to take home a full accounting of our holdings,' he said. 'Can such a ledger be prepared?'

'Of course, of course!' Mr Llewellyn seemed relieved and delighted to steer into this safer course and leaned in to extend himself fully. 'And what say I roll your mother's current loan into a new and larger loan to tide things over for a few months? I would think a thousand pounds ought to do it?' Harris was tempted to tell him no and give him a sharp lesson in

the history of the bank; his father famously being a successful senior partner and Mr Llewellyn the grateful lieutenant clinging to his coat-tails. But
a cursory view of the Penneston holdings had already shown him that Mr
Llewellyn was correct. There was a shortage of ready cash.

'Thank you,' he said. 'If you would please release funds to any out-
standing tradesmen's bills for which my mother has written a cheque, I
would not like her to suffer any mark on her reputation.'

'And why don't I send for a couple of hundred pounds in cash for you
now?' said Llewellyn. 'A young man will have his expenses.' He seemed
to find this very amusing and gave Harris a broad wink. 'And it may be
easier to guide your mother to new economies if you sweeten the news
with a gift. I find a new hat often agrees with my wife.'

PENNESTON LODGE, THE estate's dower house, was one of the large
villas set above the prosperous west end of the town. Behind a tall brick
wall and gates, a short gravel driveway bent sufficiently around a large
yew hedge as to make the front of the house invisible to the street.

'It gives the poor patients privacy, because some of their injuries are
terrible and we all know people either stare or don't want to look at
them,' said Poppy, as she pulled off her helmet and gloves. Around them
six other ladies of the Hazelbourne Ladies Motorcycle Club were also
dismounting in the golden sunlight of a late Wednesday afternoon. 'We
took them to the beach once and I saw a mother grab her child and run
– which was very funny because it left a very confused nanny who, I
swear, had never seen the mother pick up the baby before.'

'What if I flinch?' said Constance. 'What if I do something wrong?' She
had been excited to be included in the club's twice monthly outing to the
convalescent home but she was starting to become anxious. She was
used to illness but not to disfigurement. She had performed adequately,
she hoped, in proving supportive of Harris, but an amputation well disguised under clothing might be no test, she feared, for her response to
some of the injuries within the villa walls.

'You are incredibly kind,' said Poppy. 'So when you do flinch, and you will because you are human, you'll press on and the men will forgive you.'

'They only pretend to bite,' said Iris, overhearing them as she removed a box of scones from her saddlebag. 'But watch out for Tubby Jones. If he thinks you're staring at him as if he's a monster, he's not above growling like a dog to prove you right.'

'You don't have a sidecar?' asked Constance. Poppy had described how the club usually came to the convalescent home two ladies to a machine; the riders giving rides while the sidecar passengers hosted tea on the lawn.

'Some of the chaps appreciate a real ride,' said Iris. 'I take them up on the Downs and really let the machine out. It's good practice for me to ride with the extra weight.'

'And some of those chaps appreciate they get to hug Iris hard for a quarter of an hour,' Poppy added.

'Doesn't bother me,' said Iris. 'After what they've given, let them squeeze a little. But they've all been perfect gentlemen.'

'Because they know if they get out of hand, she'll scrape them off on a blind curve,' said Poppy.

'I may have made that clear.' Iris grinned and shook out her hair. 'Shall we go in?'

The villa was painted in light cream and greens and, with its high ceilings and waxed floors, looked little different from one of the high-quality boarding houses in town. Through doorways, small wards of metal beds could be glimpsed, and nurses came and went, bobbing their starched caps in welcome. Coming from a side hall, a bent old man with no hair stopped in his tracks and turned away. Constance was already past when she remembered there were no old men here, only recovering soldiers. She glanced back to see the ruined face of a boy peering at her: a puckered cheek, an eyelid drawn down, a hand burned and scarred, gripping a cane. She had already failed.

In the gardens, small groups of men, wearing the standard baggy blue cotton uniform of the convalescent soldier, were seated on the vine-covered terrace or under picturesque white umbrellas on the green lawn. Some were in wheelchairs; some had crutches leaning against their seats. Many were smoking a cigarette or pipe. One nearby was cheerfully blowing smoke out of a cauliflower-shaped hole that should have been a nose. Constance's throat threatened to close and Poppy, already smiling and waving, squeezed her hand hard enough to make her gasp.

'Smile. You'll be fine.' She was stern and Constance smiled because to let Poppy down would be unthinkable. As she went forward to be introduced as a new member of the club, she hoped no one would detect that behind her grin she was speaking sternly to herself all the while.

The first rides were off. A dressmaker, introduced as Jenny, was supervising tea from a table of hot-water samovars and teapots the size of small dogs. With a reassuring smile, she commandeered Constance's help to pass trays of teacups and cakes; this being a beginner's job, she said, easier than having to sit and make small talk. She made Constance drink a cup of sugared tea first. Steadied by the tea, Constance was grateful for the chance to keep moving about with a smile and a nod, and it grew easier with each new pass of the tray. Behind the disfigured faces, she found ordinary men, some of whom cried to be offered a cup of tea and a cake from her hand. Some kept apologising, as if their appearance were a bad suit of clothes they had worn to the wrong occasion. Some had to have their teacup taken for them by a nurse who held the cup or pushed a straw through ruined lips.

When the riders returned, Constance went to the front steps with a tray of tea and buns for the women and to watch as two orderlies and a nurse helped the next group mount. She saw them lift a man with no legs and only one arm into a sidecar and strap him with extra leather straps:

'Look at me, I'm a bloody picnic basket,' said the man.

'Language, please!' said the nurse, helping to fasten a scarf about the face of the man with no nose.

'No one notices their faces under goggles and a scarf,' said Tilly, taking a currant bun and swallowing some tea before going out again. 'Just like no one knows you're a woman at fifty miles an hour. It's a bit of freedom.'

Iris and Poppy were arguing with a nurse about whether a young man with one arm in a sling and a splinted leg was safe to go out on the pillion he was already straddling. He feigned amused indifference while a cigarette trembled in his good hand.

'He's not going to fall off,' said Iris. 'I'll keep a hand on him.' She gave the young man a broad wink and Tilly laughed.

'That's Sergeant Arthur Woodridge,' said Tilly. 'Rode fifty miles from the Front with that shattered arm, and a critically wounded comrade tied behind him, and now they want to put him in a sidecar.'

'That's terrible,' said Constance. 'I suppose they want to keep him safe.'

'Of course Iris lets him switch places when they're up on the cliffs,' said Tilly. 'And I'm working on a clutch extender, because it looks like they'll have to take the leg after all.'

'How do they bear it?' asked Constance. The young man hooked his good arm around Iris's waist as she started the motorcycle, and closed his eyes as he lifted his face to the wind.

'Some of them don't,' said Tilly. 'That's why we come. Not that we expect to save them, that would be hubris. But if a cup of tea, and a smile from a girl, makes them put off the darkness another day, we've done our part.'

'You are right,' said Constance. 'I need to be less of a coward.' For the rest of the afternoon, she sat wherever she was asked, and talked to the garrulous and coaxed the shy into words. She made sure to look into the eyes of those expecting her to turn away, and to look away at the view of town and sea below with those who did not want to be stared at. At the end of the tea she had even been introduced to Tubby Jones, a painfully thin man, almost concave, with a badly rebuilt jaw and cheek. He greeted her not with a growl but only a mildly cantankerous, 'Where are the pretty twins? Are we too much for the beauties?'

'You have done your best to personally drive them away,' said Poppy, who had finally agreed to accept a cup of tea herself. 'But I'm happy to say you have not succeeded and they will come another time.'

'The twins send their love,' called out Iris. 'And they sent you Constance, who is a much better conversationalist.' Tubby waved as he went in.

'And twice as useful,' said Jenny, refilling teacups for the ladies. Constance smiled, but wondered why usefulness and beauty always seemed to be presented as mutually exclusive; for as a girl she would have liked to be called pretty too.

The machines had disgorged their last passengers and the ladies were mingling to say goodbye; the leathers and driving coats amid the white dresses as the patients, in their blue hospital uniforms, walked, shuffled or were wheeled into the villa to rest before the early dinner gong.

'I can't tell you how much they look forward to your visits.' The crisply uniformed young nurse spoke shyly, from which Constance understood she found the group slightly intimidating. 'They talk about you all the time.'

It was a pleasant shock to be part of a group held in such high respect. Since her mother's death, Constance had moved in a fog of grief and had accepted, without thinking or complaint, her demotion from estate manager to nurse and companion. Being alone, she had had no one with whom to talk and spar; no one to reflect back her own worth. She realised now how far she had sunk in her own imagination.

'I bet they talk,' said Iris. 'Scoundrels!'

'Only in the most respectful of terms,' said the nurse. She turned to Poppy. 'How is Captain Wirrall? We hoped he might accompany your mother to visit the men one of these days. It is always inspiring to see people who have gone on to thrive.'

'He's improving,' said Poppy. 'I'm afraid it would be rather painful for him to visit just yet. I'm sure you understand.'

'Of course,' said the nurse, but her face was disappointed as she wished the ladies well and went away.

'Last time he came he fell into a melancholy crisis for close to a month,' Poppy whispered crossly to Constance. 'I don't know why people don't understand he's trying to get away from all this.'

'Some of these men will never get away from their injuries,' said Constance. 'I never imagined the suffering.'

'Well, the newspapers don't like to spoil the victory with a full display of the cost,' said Iris, leaning in to join the conversation. 'Two million disabled and over forty thousand amputees. Sometimes it seems as if the dead are more convenient than the wounded.'

'My mother and I are committed to doing as much as we can for the poor devils,' said Poppy. 'But it's not fair to burden my brother.' For the first time, Constance felt the surprise of a slight difference of opinion between her and Poppy. Of course Harris's melancholy must be a concern, but it seemed as if Poppy sought to keep him away from the convalescent home more to separate him from the stigma of disablement. Constance hoped she was wrong, for such a plan would not be a credit to her new friend.

'When he feels stronger, perhaps your brother will find it less of a burden,' said Constance. 'It will take men of position and influence, such as Harris, to make sure these men are cared for and not shunned.'

'You're right, of course,' said Poppy, and Constance was relieved to hear it.

'The nurses here try to keep them as long as they can,' said Iris. 'But then it falls to their families to take them in because they are practically unemployable.'

'The pensions are much too small to live on,' added Poppy. 'Wouldn't keep me in petrol.'

'Perhaps in the next election we'll vote in more than just one woman as an MP and then we can address all the rank injustices in this country,' said Iris.

'Have you been going to those socialist meetings again, Iris?' asked Tilly. 'I don't know how you expect to get sponsorship for your racing if you're going to fly the red flag.'

'It's not socialist to care for the poor and sick,' said Iris. 'My uncle is a vicar.'

'I'm sure they don't wish to be paraded about but perhaps more people would care if they got to meet them,' said Constance.

'Paraded about – that's exactly the answer,' said Poppy. 'I must make sure Mother's committee includes them in the Peace Parade. After all, they are the reason we have the peace.'

'Not sure how well that will be received,' said Iris. 'I think the parade is to be all flowers and fireworks. Nothing to mar the fun.'

'Nonsense!' said Poppy. 'I'm sure they can stand a couple of charabancs of the wounded heroes in among the schoolchildren and the town council.'

'They may not want to be stared at,' said Constance.

'Best to appear where others will be forced to give you the respect you deserve,' said Poppy. 'I'm sure all the applause will do wonders for them.'

Constance could not fault Poppy's intention but she wondered if Poppy knew that not all people could hold on with such bracing optimism and stubbornness.

'It's just like Poppy insisting on our coming out in public as the Hazelbourne Ladies Motorcycle Club,' said Tilly. 'Whether we like it or not.'

'I suppose we could corner Sam Newcombe at the races this Saturday and get him to underwrite lunch tickets for the men,' said Iris. 'Get him to do some real good in exchange for a little publicity?'

'Terrific,' said Poppy. 'Constance, you should help me talk to Mother as soon as we get home.' As she pulled on her driving gloves, she paused to deliver a compliment of which Constance found herself growing tired. 'She thinks you are sensible, so she'll listen to you.'

Chapter 10

❧

A TENTED VILLAGE HAD SPRUNG UP IN A SERIES OF FIELDS outside the rural village of Polegate, the canvas white like mushrooms against the dark hedges and colourful pennants streaming from every pole and guy rope. Official marquees for the races were interspersed with others from companies hawking motor-related items. In the largest field, an oval racetrack had been picked out in white paint and red-and-white temporary fencing. A pair of horses were still mowing the grass. On a dirt track at the base of a steep curving hill, barriers and a banner marked the start of the hill climb course. In a separate field, a military surplus auction struck a sombre note with its encampment of dull green tents, lorries and trailers. An unwelcome reminder of the war.

Makeshift camps of motorcycle clubs were strung out along paths already well marked by tyre tracks in the grass. Each camp had its gleaming machines drawn up for inspection along the front with all the crispness of a military drill, while in the back most of them were jumbles of tools, supplies, chairs, tables, picnic hampers, hastily strung sunshades and the occasional washing line. Constance, who had hurried through an early breakfast with Mrs Fog to meet Poppy and her motorcycle at the hotel's front door, was as thrilled as a child at the circus, dazzled by the colours and the crowds. She lifted her face to smell the smoke from cooking fires and a dozen kinds of breakfast mingled with the strong scent of petrol and oil.

The members of the Hazelbourne Ladies Motorcycle Club were gathered under a tall oak in the corner of a field drinking hot tea from an enormous battered tin urn and eating bacon sandwiches and plums. On this fine Saturday morning, it made a festive picture: the intense green of the grass, trees still exhaling a fog of dew, the young women in knee-length coats over knickers and boots, or muslin dresses and picture hats, milling among the shining motorcycles. They drew some attention from men who found reason to pass along the road from other camps, nudging each other and mumbling comments, but the young women ignored them. To the front, two women were busy unfurling and staking out the club banner. In the rear, Tilly was tending a blackened frying pan so large it sat on legs over the campfire. She wore gauntlets and a leather work apron against the aggressive spitting of the bacon. Behind her, a small builder's lorry stood somewhat dirty and incongruous.

'Good, Tilly's arrived with the lorry,' said Poppy as she climbed off the machine. 'She's brought my racing rig and I promised to buy the barn a drill press and a bigger lathe from the army surplus auction this afternoon. With those we should finally be able to accept enough work to employ her full-time.'

Constance stepped from the sidecar with what she hoped was the experienced air of a real lady motorcyclist and took off her goggles and the large scarf securing her straw hat. The club members were already surging forward and she felt the long anxious moment when one is alone and unrecognised in a crowd. Then Poppy was dragging her forward, announcing her name loudly, and she was pressed on all sides with handshakes and greetings. Some of the women she had already met at the convalescent home, but she could not hope to remember all the names. She was happy to recognise the Morris sisters, whose motorcycle of robin's-egg blue sported an elegant lightweight sidecar made of wicker, and Iris, who was in charge of a fearsome-looking motorcycle of utilitarian black and dark green. It seemed stripped for action with only a narrow saddle over the large engine; its sole decoration was a small painting of a diving eagle on the petrol tank. Poppy's racing motorcycle looked diminutive by comparison.

'We call Iris the "Mantis",' said Poppy. 'On account of that's how she looks with her limbs folded over the machine.'

'I call Poppy the "Trollop"' on account of how she's so eager to fold her limbs over anything,' said Iris, her face stern but her eyes laughing.

'Don't be shocked,' said Poppy. 'We're frightfully fierce competitors with each other and that includes the insults.'

'We're forced to be as there are no other women to compete with,' said Iris. 'We will have to get you racing, Constance.'

'I'm only just learning how to be a good sidecar passenger,' said Constance.

'Oh, you won't want to be a "Muffet" for long,' said Iris, looking her up and down appraisingly. 'At least you're a very decorative one.' Constance blushed. Her glazed straw hat and her white dress, with its flounce of lace and two rows of turquoise buttons down the front, had looked so charming at the hotel that she had been quite pleased with her appearance. Mrs Fog, who had been eager to release her for the entire day, so she might spend it with her old school friend again, had kissed her cheek and pronounced her to be quite the blooming flower. Now she wished she were wearing a leather coat and trousers like Poppy and Iris.

'Can we interest you ladies in a bacon sandwich?' Constance recognised Jenny the dressmaker, now wearing brown coveralls and a jaunty headscarf. She held out a tin plate with several thick sandwiches lavish with bacon and grease. 'Better take those lovely white gloves off for this.'

'Jenny is going to ride for Wirrall's now,' said Poppy. 'She used to manage Hazelbourne Aviation's sewing and doping shops as well as the dressmaking.' She took a sandwich from the plate. 'I'm hoping we can give her more hours as Tilly takes on more repair work.'

'I'm very grateful for the hours you've given me,' said Jenny. 'With the airfield job gone I didn't know how we would manage. I didn't want to go back into service. Not with the baby at home.'

'She lost her husband at the Somme,' added Iris, as Jenny moved away to dispense her wares to others. 'She has to support her mother and the baby, and the war pension and sewing hardly keep food on the table.'

'Of course my mother is desperate to find domestic help now the house will be open again,' said Poppy. She lowered her voice and leaned in to whisper to Constance. 'My loyalties are quite torn, but there are limits. I can't have fellow motorcycle riders and club members blacking our grates and serving our breakfast.'

'But you can't keep taking on girls if you don't have income to support them,' said Iris, folding her arms. 'For their sake and for Tilly, you better get us a lathe at the auction today.'

'The lathe, a drill press and – if you please – a portable foundry, just for casting a few bits and bobs.' Poppy laughed. 'Tilly gave me an entire list, but can we worry about that after the racing?'

'I've already been over to look at the hill climb course,' said Iris. 'The officials came by and tried to persuade us to withdraw based on the conditions, but I told them it was all fine and dandy.'

'Anytime it's a bit muddy, or a bit icy, or even a bit too dry and perfect they become convinced that it's too dangerous for us,' said Poppy.

'At least today they tried to persuade us to give up,' said Iris. 'Sometimes they just forbid.'

'That's because I persuaded Sam and the Morris twins that Newcombe Foundries and Hazelbourne Aviation should sponsor the Rig and Rider Parade of Elegance prize,' said Poppy. 'A little greasing of the wheels of progress never hurt.'

'Is Sam here?' asked Constance. 'And Tom?' For some reason she felt too shy to ask after Harris.

'Sam is here promoting his motorcycles and parts,' said Poppy. 'Tom is too much the snob for motorcycling, and Harris is in some awful fug after his trip to London so I left him to his dark mood.' She waved as if to dismiss her brother but Constance felt her disappointment.

'If the twins are sponsors does that mean they are ineligible to compete?' asked Constance. 'They look so impeccable I was sure they would win.'

'Oh, they'll have all the limelight,' said Tilly, arriving with a teapot and a fistful of tin mugs. 'They are to lead the parade of riders and judge the event. Not to mention Newcombe has a poster of the Morris girls that's as tall as his company's tent.'

'And to think they are the same girls who look down on the likes of Jenny being in the club because she works for a living,' said Iris. 'Then they sell themselves all over just for the fame.'

'Not just the fame,' said Tilly to Constance. 'The blue baby carriage they call a motorcycle was a custom gift from Newcombes.'

'I wouldn't ride that thing if it were the last transportation out of hell,' said Iris, accepting a steaming mug of tea as black as dirt.

'Come, come, Iris,' said Poppy. 'We welcome all to the Hazelbourne Ladies Motorcycle Club. That alone drives the Morris girls to distraction.'

The day became a hot blur of loud machines and clouds of dust drifting over the dry fields. Constance could not keep straight the various circuits and number of heats that marked each race on the oval track, but she was drawn in by the enthusiasm of the crowd and the way it moved, in a dark tide of men's hats, from track to hill course to the festive beer tents and exhibits. She missed the light and colour of women and girls. She and the club members were most of the few women present. There were also some boys, grey kneesocks and flat caps, minnowing in and out among the men.

She did her best to understand the timed hill climb, consulting her printed programme closely to watch for Iris and Poppy. She and Tilly positioned themselves on a knobby cliff halfway up the hill, where a stand of oaks gave some shelter from the sun. When Poppy's name was finally called, garbled through a giant megaphone and alternately cheered and jeered by the men, who nonetheless all pressed forward for a better look,

Constance could barely breathe for fear and excitement. Tilly produced a steel-cased stopwatch from her coat pocket and tensed her thumb over the button.

Constance was not sure what she expected, but in a fierce growl and scream of the engine, Poppy appeared up the track, sank low into a turn, one leg jutting out as if to brace against the ground, popped up and airborne over a nasty hump, and was gone past in an arcing cloud of dust.

'Did you see the height on that jump?' asked Tilly, her eyes alive with excitement. She consulted the stopwatch. 'And she was fast through the turn. If she can stay upright and plough the mud on the last ramp, she'll be in the top five!'

'I thought she might fall,' said Constance. 'She leaned so far over.'

'Here comes Iris,' said Tilly. The megaphone barked, unintelligible over the roar of another engine grinding up the hill. Constance recognised Iris's dark, plain motorcycle; the rider, almost flat against the handlebars, spun through the corner in a cloud of dust and pushed the machine harder as it soared over the hump and away.

'Faster through here than the last meet by three seconds,' said Tilly. 'At this pace she may win.'

'I couldn't tell it was her at all,' said Constance. With her flaming long hair concealed beneath her leather cap, goggles pressed against her eyes, cheeks coated with dust, and no hint of feminine flourish, Iris had looked, to Constance's surprise, exactly like Poppy and the three or four men who had gone before. 'I only knew Poppy by the navy trim on her coat.'

'They'll both be very happy to hear that,' said Tilly. 'Another half an hour in this dust and we can say the same about ourselves. 'We'd better find you a pinafore to put over that outfit or you'll be no good to us in the Rig and Rider Parade.'

'Oh, I can't be in a parade,' said Constance. 'Don't you have members who want to participate?'

'Look, it's a silly competition most of us despise, but as a club of women we need to make a good showing to counteract the notion that we are all would-be men in skirts,' said Tilly. 'Of our two entries, Iris will be one, assuming her machine is undented and we can get it cleaned up in time. Poppy will take the other spot with the sidecar to publicise the taxi service.'

'But I assume there are other girls who'd like to ride with her?'

'Yes, but many of us are more competent than decorative,' said Tilly. 'And we're liable to bite off the judges' heads if they say something stupid.'

'I'm not sure that's a compliment to me,' said Constance. 'Am I such a mouse?'

'No, you're pretty and a diplomat,' said Tilly. 'Poppy says you know how to handle authority. She thinks you'll be perfect and I have every faith in you.'

'Thank you.' Constance thought it strange that she had so recently longed to be called pretty, but today, among these women, she would have given anything to join the ranks of the competent. Still, to have Tilly's faith was mollifying. 'I shall do my best,' she said.

'Let's go to the finish line and see the results,' said Tilly. 'Then Poppy is off to the auction in the other field. In addition to the equipment, there are half a dozen motorcycles for sale and one or two stretcher-bearing sidecars that would make great delivery boxes.'

The lorry would not be large enough to accommodate Poppy's auction purchases, thought Constance. She had bid aggressively to secure two motorcycles and she was now bidding on a trailer that held what might or might not be all the parts of a dual-control trainer biplane. In the crowded tent there were only a couple of other bidders and the auctioneer was going slowly, prodding the crowd.

'In need of one or two repairs obviously,' he said, as if it were an automobile with a dent on a wheel hub instead of a fuselage roped inside a wooden trailer with the wings detached and roped alongside. One wing trailed broken struts and a ragged edge of torn linen. 'Engine included and no damage to the propeller, I'm told,' he continued. 'Two seats and dual controls perfect for flying lessons or taking your lady friend on a picnic. A nice project, gentlemen. Are you really going to let the lady have it for two hundred guineas?' There was a murmur of laughter from the crowd, and a red-faced man, scowling under a cap, waved his newspaper sharply.

'Two hundred and ten guineas,' said the auctioneer. 'You do know the trailer comes with it, gentlemen?' Poppy's hand was in the air but the auctioneer was scanning the crowd, deliberately oblivious.

'Are you sure you want it?' asked Constance. 'There's no guarantee it will ever fly. I thought you needed to buy machinery?'

'My brother will get it flying,' said Poppy, keeping her eyes on the auctioneer. 'I don't know why I didn't think of it before. Harris has been so silent and abjectly low these past few days; I've been so worried. But this is just the project he needs – if I can get this damn man to acknowledge my bid.' She poked her hand higher into the air, a frown on her face and no attempt at the nonchalance of the other auction bidders. She was still angry, Constance thought, from the hill climb results. Iris had won on speed but been marked down three points by the judges for arriving particularly mud-splattered at the finish line. As club secretary, Poppy had exchanged some terse words with the judges on Iris's behalf and had had to be pulled away before the judges disqualified her own fifth-place run.

'Over here!' The voice at Constance's shoulder made her jump. It was Sam Newcombe pointing at Poppy.

'Two hundred and twenty guineas, please,' said Poppy. The auctioneer frowned and nodded as Poppy turned to hiss, 'I don't need your assistance, Mr Newcombe. I'm quite capable of bidding for myself.'

'Of course, no doubt, Miss Wirrall,' stammered Sam as he raised his hat. 'But the fellow in the cap? Bit friendly with the auction house. Bids for some big operation in Brighton.'

'Do you mean it's rigged?' whispered Constance.

'No, no. All very gentlemanly. Just sort of a friendly bias. Bit of a wink now and then.'

The fellow in the cap was now consulting a colleague and the other bidder, a man too broad in the girth to fit in any cockpit, was shaking his head under his large black bowler hat. 'He's a scrap dealer. Too rich for him at this price,' added Sam. 'Hope you wanted the thing because I think you're going to get it.' Poppy turned pale but she nodded.

'I must have it.'

'Two hundred and twenty guineas to the little lady,' said the auctioneer. 'No doubt she can knit it a new fuselage cover. Are we all done, gentlemen? I'd take ten guineas more?' The man in the cap shook his head, and the auctioneer took a long, slow look around the chuckling crowd. Then, disappointed, he sighed and brought down the gavel. 'Sold.'

'Congratulations,' said Constance. 'I think?' Poppy grinned and began to push her way through the crowd to the auctioneer's associates to pay for her purchases.

'Would she be offended if I sent a couple of men over? Help with loading and hitching. That sort of thing?' said Sam.

'I think that would be lovely, Sam,' said Constance. 'Did you see Poppy race? She was wonderful.'

'As fiery on the track as in front of the judges,' said Sam. 'Quite the Valkyrie. Not that one admits to Wagner now.'

'Can't you do something about the judges, Sam? They seemed so unfair to Iris and you are an important sponsor of the event.'

'Ah,' he said and pursed his lips. After a moment he sighed. 'Making waves is not part of the drill, you see? Defeats the purpose.'

'Chivalry must kneel to commerce?'

'Quite. Very uncomfortable of course. If it were up to me . . .'

Poppy returned clutching a sheaf of papers and shaking a very floppy slim purse.

'That's me all cleaned out for the quarter,' she said. 'I'll be eating bread and jam until September but the machine is ours.'

'Quite a project,' said Sam. 'Bit out of your usual line, Poppy?'

'I'm branching out,' she said. 'I'm sure Tilly and Harris can get her flying again. What do you think, Sam? Maybe you can look it over with Harris. Let me know what she needs?'

'Delighted,' said Sam. 'Might be able to contribute a few parts.'

'Maybe we'll start a whole air fleet,' said Poppy. 'Give Tom Morris a run for his money.'

'Maybe no need to tell Tom?' said Sam. 'Hazelbourne Aviation is my biggest customer in the South, you know.'

'We'll keep it just between us two then,' said Poppy, taking his arm. 'You really are a friend, Sam.' He blushed a bright red at her use of his first name.

'Delighted, delighted,' he mumbled. Constance felt bad for him. Harris would never have swallowed such an obvious buttering-up. Poppy took her arm on the other side and gave her a broad wink as the three of them walked away.

Tilly was busy tapping out a small dent on Iris's motorcycle as a bevy of other women put the finishing polish to Poppy's sidecar rig and tied garlands of flowers to the handlebars. A second garland surrounded the sidecar itself with light blue ribbons woven in between.

'Let me help you,' said Jenny, who began brushing dried mud off the hem of Constance's dress as she was attempting to smooth her hair, peering into the side mirror on Tilly's lorry. On one arm, Jenny carried three starched and ironed blue silk sashes, each embroidered with the club insignia. In her hand were three floral corsages with pins.

'Those are exquisitely done,' said Constance.

'Well, it makes a change from running up blouses and altering old ladies' summer coats for the umpteenth time,' said Jenny.

'I feel like the prize pig at the village fete,' said Iris, stepping down from the lorry where she and Poppy had gone to dress. She had changed into a short embroidered grey silk jacket and knee-length white cotton tea dress over full-length Arabian trousers with embroidered grey silk ankle cuffs. Her hair was twisted into a simple chignon but was so ample and long that a plait still fell over one shoulder. She wore boots of light blue with silver laces.

'You look wonderful,' said Constance. She said it automatically and meant it, but even as she spoke, she was forced to admit the outfit was so unconventional that she would find it impossible to wear herself. Constance hoped it was not a failing to acknowledge that she would never have the courage to live so openly in defiance of convention.

'I don't ever wear a dress to ride so I hope this will do?' said Iris. 'And I'll wear the sash but I'm not wearing the flowers, so don't even ask me, Jenny.'

'Can I please pin some ribbon on your handlebars, then?' asked Jenny. 'Just a small ribbon so you look part of a team?'

'Very well,' said Iris. 'But please remember I am not a Christmas present. I'm a serious racer.'

'Is Iris being difficult again?' asked Poppy, jumping down from the lorry. Her own outfit resembled old-fashioned horse-riding attire, with a long white skirt looped up at one side over slim jodhpurs and polished riding boots. A flounced white blouse was paired with a slim blue jacket and the whole topped with a simple straw boater whose ribbon matched the club sash.

'At least Constance looks the part,' said Jenny, as she placed sashes over each of their heads and fastened two of them with flowers on the shoulder. For Iris she merely jabbed in a small pin, making Iris swear. 'I shall pin the extra corsage to Constance's hat,' she added. 'It will be perfect against the straw and your dark hair.'

'Sashes and flowers for all,' said Tilly, producing blank blue sashes and a box of small floral buttonholes. 'We didn't have time to embroider them all. We'll give you all the patterns and the colours and you can do them in your own time.'

'Now we'll look like a club,' said Poppy, smiling at all the women gathered around her. 'I know it's silly and Iris hates it, but it's important that we remind the men we are fully feminine and therefore nothing to be afraid of.' Iris snorted and Poppy gave her a mock glare. 'Let's be as charming as we are competitive and hopefully they'll let us compete at more meets.'

In a round of enthusiastic applause, Poppy and Iris took to their motorcycles and Constance climbed into the sidecar. She was nervous in her excitement. She had become so accustomed to solitude at Clivehill that she was suddenly afraid to be so visible in the crowd. She had almost forgotten what it was to have friends. For a moment she was back on the school playing fields, surrounded by chanting girls, muddy, bedraggled, and waving their hockey sticks. Something stirred inside and tears threatened her as she felt, like a blow, the emptiness of the war years and all the companionship lost. But here were new friends, coming forward to pat her on the shoulder, to smile, to shout words of encouragement.

Poppy kicked the motorcycle into life and led the two machines out onto the path, where they merged into the slow parade of vehicles. The rest of the club streamed across the field, towards the central racetrack and the viewing stands, an ethereal wave of white dresses and blue sashes.

There was music from a small brass band, cheering from the rails and the mingled smells of grass, flowers and exhaust as the Rig and Rider competitors made their two slow parade circles around the track. Constance waved and smiled until her arm ached and her lips froze into place. Poppy waved too, guiding her machine with one relaxed hand in clean kid gloves. Iris nodded her head and saluted from time to time, concentrating on keeping her motorcycle upright at such slow speed without having to put her foot to the ground. Past the viewing stand they went, and Constance could see the Morris sisters and Sam Newcombe nodding their heads and making notes with the other competition judges.

As they turned from the final circuit to finish lined up on the centre grass, Constance told herself she did not care who won prizes, but she remembered how important Tilly thought a good showing to be, and she sat straight in the sidecar and waved as enthusiastically as a schoolgirl. Then, while the judges huddled on the stage, she held her breath as the crowd clapped and whistled and roared for the results.

Third place! A yellow rosette and certificate were presented to the Hazelbourne Ladies Motorcycle Club, and Poppy ran up to the dais to receive them from Evangeline Morris. In second place was a newly married couple who rode a Newcombe machine with a wicker sidecar, just like the Morris sisters' outfit. The winners of the Rig and Rider Parade of Elegance competition were a man with a scarlet motorcycle and sidecar, wearing the full dress uniform of a navy captain, and his youthful female passenger, riding in a white gown draped with the Union Jack. Other prizes were then presented. Iris received a bronze medal for the hill climb and strode across the dais like a queen, her chin held high. The winner was presented with a large cup, and as he shook hands with Iris, Constance could see, even from her position on the field, that he could not look Iris in the eye.

The laughter and the congratulations as the women packed up their camp made Constance wish the day did not have to end. As the evening chill began to conjure mist from the grass, the last of the boxes were packed, and the women began to drive away in convoy. The lorry with the broken aeroplane and its trailer hitched behind took its place in the middle of the pack. Poppy and Constance waited to take up the rear.

'I hope you enjoyed yourself?' said Poppy. 'I hope you forgive me for throwing you into the parade?'

'It was a wonderful day,' said Constance. 'I'm so happy to have been included.'

'Be careful,' said Poppy. 'Next thing you know, you'll be taking more riding lessons.'

'I think I just might,' said Constance. 'I've decided that a woman should always aim to be competent rather than decorative.'

Chapter 11

HE UNDERSTOOD THAT PICKING THROUGH THE PHOTO-
graphs was an intentional infliction of pain, like pressing a thumb against
a drawing tack until the skin splits, and feeling the release of a tiny swell-
ing bead of blood. But Harris was compelled to look at each smiling face.
His closest friends, Jeffries and Matheson, grinning by their Curtiss Jen-
nies, holding their prize medals for graduating flight school first and
second. Jeffries trying to grow the mustache that never would come in –
they teased him mercilessly about it – and Matheson with a pirate's grin
and the shock of dark hair that defied all attempts to keep it brilliantined.
The whole squadron lined up on the King's birthday in front of the hangar. Probably should have taken the photograph before the dinner. He
himself was just one of many leaning discreetly on the next man. In his
case, bracing a knee against Jock, his mechanic, who knelt in the front
row, swearing under his breath. Their commanding officer was in the
middle trying so hard to look severe that his eyes were crossed. A
difficult-to-capture photograph of them coming home from a night raid,
a line of Sopwith Camels approaching over a hill next to a blasted tree,
the lead aircraft trailing a thick plume of smoke. The pilot survived that
landing, coming in on fumes and a broken rudder, but weeks later he was
shot down over the Channel. Matheson was brought down by the archies
over the German lines at Verdun. Jeffries, first in class, and then never
making it out of the country, his plane malfunctioning after takeoff

and diving into a wheat field. The CO was still with them at the forward base in Saint-Omer. By the time he disappeared during the Third Battle of Ypres, the numbers of dead had become numbing, the grief briefer.

Brief grief: always there was the moment of turning away, of giving up on straining to hear another engine coming home behind the hill. A sandwich or a hot pie chewed in silence and a cup of strong tea burning the throat. Then a quick wash and maybe a sleep. Because in the Flying Corps, the ritual was clear. To honour the men who did not come home in the evening, the dawn flight would go out uninterrupted.

In the pictures Harris kept, the battered envelope made soft by constant handling, the sun was always shining, the wind catching hair, flags, trouser legs. What he remembered keenly from the war was the freezing rain, the mud; wind across dark runways; chilblains; red, dripping noses; shivering even in a thick sheepskin coat. He could not remember the thought of dying ever crossing his mind as the camera flashed, but in the pictures they all smiled as if saying goodbye. Sometimes a stray thought whispered through his brain that it was unfair they had all gone on without him. Left him behind with nothing but the pulsing ache of his leg, the pain, the sores, the stares of others. Like the crippled boy left behind, still hearing the laughter and the faint piercing whistle of the Pied Piper, deep in the mountain.

Today the pictures had been a distraction from his more pressing difficulties. The closed door to any lucrative banking partnership, and the unexpected lack of ready funds in the estate, threatened to overwhelm him. The Penneston ledgers lay strewn on the library table, where he had attempted to penetrate the mysteries of the estate's income and rents and the many large withdrawals his mother had made. He paled at the thought of confronting her. What sort of son was he to demand her receipts while informing her that he could neither grow the family fortunes through his own labour nor continue to support her expenditures? The task loomed impossible, and the remediating options suggested by Llewellyn might be sound, but they seemed to Harris to be untidy, and to risk publicly undermining his father's good name. With a grim humour

he noted that a son who felt closer to his dead comrades in old photographs than to most of the living around him might be ill-equipped to
pilot his father's legacy into the future.

Mired in his thoughts, he tried to ignore the deep booming knock at
the front door. But it was persistent, almost rhythmic. He rose, stiff from
sitting in the dark library, and limped, halting, to the front hall. On the
step was Iris Brenner, in dusty motorcycle gear, with dirt and leaves in
the sweep of her red hair.

'Halloo,' she said, confident as a brigadier. She waved at the Wirrall's
motorcycle taxi on the forecourt. It too was dusty, and it bore the wilted
remnants of flower garlands. 'Poppy asked me to collect you. Your immediate presence is required at the barn.'

'What on earth?' he began.

'I am not authorised to offer any details,' she said, putting up a hand. 'I
am merely to impress upon you that it is imperative you come with me.
If necessary, I am to express that it is by way of an emergency.'

'Well, obviously it isn't,' he said. 'I fail to see why I should jump when
Poppy asks.'

'Well, obviously it wouldn't do to seize you by the collar and drag
you,' said Iris. She cracked her knuckles like a boxer. 'If you insist, I will
flutter my eyelashes and beg you to accept a young woman's plea?' She
drew herself up to her full height and gave him a smile with only the
slightest touch of menace.

'I'm not sure such coquetry works with quite the amount of dirt you
have on your face right now, Iris,' he said. 'But in the interest of gallantry,
I will submit.' She laughed out loud, slapping her gloves against her trousers.

'Good man,' she said. 'I would shake your hand but my hands are filth-
ier than my face. Always the sign of a good day out.' As he climbed into
the sidecar, she handed him a green floral silk scarf.

'A bit too jaunty for my taste,' he said. 'I draw the line at fancy dress.'

'It's a blindfold,' she said. 'Put it on and no cheating. This is a surprise.'

'Quite unnecessary,' he said, tying it around his eyes. 'When being driven by a woman I always keep my eyes closed.' He didn't see the punch coming. As they drove away he nursed an arm now numb from shoulder to elbow.

CONSTANCE WAS EXHAUSTED. It was a good sort of exhausted. She was happy even though her cheeks burned, her hands were rimed with dirt and her dress was smeared about the hem. She feared her summer boots were ruined from all the dust lodged in the fabric and laces. As she stood on the road at the corner of the barn, she marvelled at how energetic Poppy seemed to be. She was guiding the last of the purchased motorcycles down a makeshift ramp from the borrowed lorry. Tilly, stacking picnic hampers, toolboxes and the rest of the detritus of the day in neat heaps inside the barn, looked tired and a little drawn. Poppy seemed not to notice and kept up a stream of enthusiastic chattering.

In pride of place in front of the barn, glowing in the low slabs of evening sunlight, was an aeroplane in rather sorry condition. It had been wheeled off the trailer, the fuselage sagging to one side, the wheel strut bent at a strange angle. The wings, surprisingly light but bulky and fragile, had been carefully laid on the grass to each side. A small heap of extra cables lay in a tangle to the rear. It looked like a bird of prey with its wings torn off. Still, it was impressive to see up close, thought Constance, taller than she expected, the varnished wood and linen smelling rather like a sailboat; and solid enough to make it seem impossible that it could take to the sky even if they reattached the wings.

Constance's only job now was to stand in the lane and warn the others when Iris arrived with Harris. Poppy was adamant that he be surprised. She had a determined optimism that the shock would jolt her brother from his moodiness. Constance hoped she was right but could not altogether suppress the thought he might be naturally peevish. Perhaps it was only the tiredness that made her feel so unkind. She leaned against the barn and yawned. It was still warm in the low evening sun, and she closed her eyes momentarily, the day a sleepy, happy blur.

She almost missed them. After a day of roaring engines her brain might have ignored one more if Iris had not tooted her horn. Springing awake, Constance waved, first at Iris and then, dashing around the corner, she waved and shouted at Poppy, running, panting, to join her and Tilly in front of the aeroplane, a small honour guard, albeit one that would not pass close inspection. Iris helped Harris from the sidecar and led him by the arm.

'On a count of three—' said Poppy.

Constance wondered if Poppy had expected uncomplicated surprise and gratitude, perhaps loud exclamations and thanks as Iris removed Harris's blindfold. Or should she have known better than to expose her brother to the happy smiles and clapping of their little audience? Harris's face darkened and Constance was moved to see pain, joy and anguish chase each other across his eyes. He walked over slowly, leaning on his cane, as stiff as if on parade. He stood by the Sopwith Camel and Constance saw the reverence with which he placed a palm against the cockpit wall, letting out a breath between his teeth.

'Maybe we should just dash off and check things in the barn,' whispered Tilly, and Constance nodded, but hesitated, unwilling to leave a stricken-looking Poppy.

'Don't leave on my account,' said Harris, clearing his throat. He looked around, blinking. 'Sorry, I was a bit overcome to see the old girl.' He patted the fuselage. 'One of ours, you know. Just a trainer, of course, but when the Camels came in in 'seventeen, she taught us how to handle them. He walked to the tail end and ran his hand over a faded number stencilled on the side. 'We banged her up a bit before we left but nothing this bad.'

'Looks like they were breaking her down for parts,' said Tilly. 'The rudder is dismantled and wrapped up in oilcloth and there's bits of the engine in a box but they're all individually wrapped and numbered. I hope it's all there.'

'The war ended,' said Harris. 'I guess they closed half the flight schools.'

'Did I do the right thing?' asked Poppy. 'When I saw it at the auction, I thought of you.'

'Because she's as damaged as I am?' he asked. Poppy looked as if she might cry and Constance frowned at Harris, who seemed to realise his rudeness. 'I'm sorry, ladies,' he said. 'Silly of me to be affected by seeing the old girl, but in extremity, one did get attached.'

'Will she fly?' asked Poppy.

'I'd say it's quite a project to put her back together,' said Harris. Constance watched his face crease into worry. 'I'm not sure we can take on such an expense just now.'

'I'd love to work on it,' said Tilly. 'But it's a bit beyond my skills. I'd need help, and the proper machines, of course. That drill press would have been just the thing.'

'I'm sorry, Tilly. I promise I'll get you one next quarter,' said Poppy, pleading. 'I just couldn't pass up this opportunity.' Constance now began to understand Tilly's tired face. It was disappointment, not exhaustion.

'Of course,' said Tilly. 'Family comes first.'

'Wait, you didn't get either machine?' asked Iris. 'I gave you twenty pounds for the lathe.'

'I'm sorry, Iris. As I told Tilly, I just jumped at the chance,' said Poppy. 'I'll pay you back. Don't be angry with me.'

Iris glared. 'That's hardly the point,' she said. 'Those machines were going to bring in enough business that Tilly could work here full-time. You made a promise, Poppy.'

'Oh, it's perfectly all right,' said Tilly, turning her face away to hide a trembling lip. 'Let's not fight about it. Not after all we've been through.'

'And what about the other new girls?' Iris's face was a red that clashed particularly with her hair. 'You promised them increased hours and now you've bought an aeroplane that'll cost hundreds to fix. Where is the money going to come from?'

'She's not wrong, Poppy,' said Harris. He was leaning down now, running his hand over a tear in the linen belly, tugging on the bent wheel strut. He was careful, solicitous even. To Constance, he looked like a farmer inspecting a sick cow. 'I'm not sure we have the funds,' he added. 'But maybe Tom Morris can loan us a mechanic and machinery.'

'Not really the point, Harris,' said Iris, exasperated. 'Even if you fix up the aeroplane, flying lessons taught by you do not exactly create employment for the girls, do they?'

'But it can be the future of the club, Iris,' said Poppy. 'Think of it. Women learning to fly. We'll have wealthier members lining up to join and they'll need repairs and lessons, and I'm sure they'll use our taxi service.'

'You want me to teach women to fly?' Harris looked puzzled, but whether at the concept of ladies in flight, or at the idea of himself being able to fly again, Constance could not tell.

'And no doubt, like the Morris twins, the wealthy girls will also object to letting poorer girls join,' said Iris. 'You can't mix democracy and wealth, Poppy.'

'Let's not fight about it now, Iris,' begged Poppy. 'I'll make it right, I promise you.'

'Do you really think Tom Morris will help us?' asked Tilly. 'He has all the machinery we would need.'

'Speak of the devil,' said Iris. She lit a cigarette and pointed her spent match to where a man was walking swiftly across the fields towards them. As they looked, he waved his hat. 'Man the cannons. Enemy approaching.'

'Iris doesn't like that he keeps pressuring me to sell him my business and machines,' said Poppy to Constance.

'I thought he was just joking,' said Constance. 'Why does he want a motorcycle business?'

'He doesn't, but like so many other men, he doesn't like to see women running things,' said Iris. 'I tell Poppy he is not to be trusted.'

'He believes that when I give up motorcycles, I'll be ready to settle for marriage,' said Poppy. 'Iris is very protective of me.'

'I was protective,' said Iris. 'Now I'm mad at you for Tilly's sake.'

'Tom doesn't mean anything by it,' said Harris. 'He's always just been a bit overbearing.'

'I'd love to be overbearing and have people agree I don't mean anything by it,' said Iris. 'Unfortunately I know perfectly well that when I am overbearing, which I often like to be, they call me an absolute shrew.'

'I wonder if Newcombe told him?' said Tilly, returning to the topic of Tom Morris.

'That would prove my theory that men are much bigger gossips than women,' said Iris. 'What do you think, Harris?'

'About men being gossips or about you being an absolute shrew?' said Harris. 'Because personally I find you incorrigible but perfectly charming.'

'I just hope he hasn't come to gloat,' said Poppy. 'It does look a bit sorry all laid out in bits.' It was as if a small cloud had briefly crossed the sun, thought Constance, the way the atmosphere shifted. A subtle tension passed invisibly from one to another like electric current.

'Well, he wasn't invited so he has no right to comment on the slightly dishevelled state of the machine or us,' said Iris. She turned to Tilly, who was brushing at her stained shirt and tucking stray hair into pins. 'For goodness' sake, we are not his sisters, Tilly. Stop fixing your hair immediately.'

TOM MORRIS SLAPPED Harris on the back, shook hands vigorously all around and loudly congratulated Iris, Poppy and Constance on their success at the races.

'I just sat and waved, I didn't actually do anything,' said Constance.

'My sisters tell me you were fresh and charming,' said Tom. 'They were frankly a little jealous the club could put on such a passable show at elegance without them.'

'So did Evangeline and Gwinny tell you about our aeroplane?' said Poppy. 'I bought it for Harris.'

'We're glad you came up,' said Harris. His face was now composed to look slightly bored, which Constance recognised as the usual demeanour of a man who wouldn't dream of openly asking another man for help. 'Poppy wants to know if I can get it to fly and I said we should ask your advice.'

'I heard about it from my agent who failed to get it for me at the auction,' said Tom. He was smiling as widely as a carnival barker. 'We've been looking for a different trainer for some time. Something for students to move on to from the Avro.'

'I wish I'd known,' said Poppy. 'I would have bid more aggressively.'

'Of course I didn't know it was in quite such terrible shape,' said Tom. He wandered up to the damaged wing and twisted off a small dangling strut. 'You'll need a professional shop to patch this up. I expect the engine is a nightmare.'

'We were just saying that maybe you might help us,' said Harris. 'I'd love to see the old girl fly again. It would be a reminder of all the men, you know.' He stopped, clearing his throat and poking at the grass with the tip of his cane.

'I'll do better than that. What I'd like to do is take it off your hands,' said Tom. 'I'll give you and Poppy a fair premium over your auction price and drag this sorry lot out of here for you. If you really want to see it flying again, I think you need someone who can afford to give it the proper attention and a long-term future.'

'It's not for sale,' said Poppy.

'I thought you said it was for Harris?' said Tom. 'Look, I'll throw in that you can come over anytime, Harris, and I'll take you up myself.'

'You don't think I'll ever be fit to fly, do you?' said Harris slowly, and whether because of their friendship, or because Tom was also a pilot, Constance saw this strike him as a particular betrayal.

'Not at all. I think you've done remarkably well, old chap,' said Tom. 'But you know better than anyone that the Sopwith Camel is a temperamental beast to control. Skittish as a wild horse.'

'Well, she's a long way from flying. Possibly time to grow a whole new leg,' said Harris, his voice grim. 'Besides which, Tom, she was a gift from my sister, so I'm rather obliged to keep it at least until she stops caring about it.'

'We're going to start a flying school,' said Poppy. 'Lessons for ladies. Harris is going to run it.'

'Joining Poppy's merry coven, are you, old chap?' said Tom. He was still smiling, but Constance noticed the slight sneer underneath.

'It's all a bit new to say, Tom,' said Harris, deliberately jovial again. Underneath the friendly exchange, the two men seemed to circle each other like two wary bulls. 'But what do you think about fixing her up?'

'I say it'll be expensive,' said Tom. 'I can send one of our mechanics over to give you some advice. But if you're wanting me to fix her for you, we're very busy right now. I have to give our own machines priority. It might be a few months.'

'We can't wait that long,' said Poppy. 'No one wants to learn to fly in November.'

'Well, first things first,' said Harris. 'Thank you, my darling sister, for the most incredible of gifts, even if it is in slightly used condition. And thank you, Tom, for the offer of your mechanic's advice. Can I offer you a drink back at the house?'

'No thanks,' said Tom. 'I must get home. But listen – if you change your mind about selling it . . . Just think about it for a while.'

He strode away across the field towards his own lands and Poppy managed to keep her lips pressed shut until he was almost out of earshot.

'Infuriating!'

'He is,' agreed Harris. 'Sometimes I actually understand why you insist on tormenting him. On the other hand, you might have made a decent profit today and instead— Well, we must hope she turns out to be a functioning aeroplane and not a white whale.' He patted the fuselage, and Constance saw a light in his face she hadn't seen before. 'We'll find the money somehow, Poppy.'

'Oh, thank you, Harris!' Poppy said and crushed her brother in a hug that threatened to topple them both onto the grass.

'We should get her put away before the dew gets to her,' said Tilly, her voice low. 'I'll bring some tarpaulins from the barn and we'll wrap her up.'

'Good old Tilly,' said Iris as Tilly disappeared into the barn. 'You can always rely on her, can't you, Poppy? If only she could expect the same in return.'

'That's uncalled for,' said Poppy.

'No, I think it deserved to be said.' Iris buttoned her jacket and pulled on her riding gloves. 'I'll go now before I say something more that might be overdue, my friend. I'll stay at my aunt's for the time being.' She threw a mock salute at Harris and Constance and added, 'Complete shrew and proud of it.'

When Tilly returned with the tarpaulins, they all ignored Iris's departure, but her absence hung between them. For the first time, thought Constance, the atmosphere at the barn seemed spoiled. In silence, they managed to lay the wings on trestles and cover both wings and fuselage with tarpaulins and sacking. As Constance tucked the last piece of rough burlap around an exposed strut, the tiredness made her fingers weak. She shook out her hands, leaned back against the aeroplane and closed her eyes.

'Tilly, get some water.' She heard Harris's call. 'I fear we may have overtaxed the new girl.' His voice held concern.

'I'm perfectly fine,' said Constance, taking a few deep breaths. 'Just a bit tired.' A firm hand supported her by the arm. She blinked her eyes open to see it was Harris, his worried face close to hers.

'Wait a few moments,' he said. 'They're bringing you a glass.' Tilly arrived at a jog with a tin mug of cold water and a wet handkerchief. Constance drank and then dabbed at her forehead and cheeks with the cool fabric.

'It was such a wonderful day,' she said.

'Are you sure you're all right?' asked Harris. When she nodded he dropped her arm and she rather wished she had not been so quick to agree.

TILLY OFFERED TO drop her at the hotel. It was a loud, rattling ride in the borrowed lorry and hard to talk over the noise.

'I'm so sorry you were in the dark about the aeroplane,' Constance shouted in a vague attempt to comfort Tilly.

'Not my money, not my barn,' said Tilly. 'I'll just have to stay at the library a little longer, that's all.' She shrugged. 'It's not as if I don't enjoy the books. I just don't really love being around all the people and I'd rather rebuild engines.' Her face did not look any less mutinous and Constance felt it best to keep quiet and let Tilly take out her frustrations on the pedals and gearstick of the lorry as she sent it careening around the bends. She was glad to reach the hotel in one piece, though it was a little discomfiting to have to descend from such a vehicle in full view of the doorman. Fortunately, she did not have to suffer any interrogation from Mrs Fog on her late return. The undermanager, Dudley, accosted her in the lobby with a barely disguised sneer at her dusty dress and a small folded note from Mrs Fog, who, she said in a rushed and badly blotted hand, had been invited to stay the night in Cabbage Beach and would be back tomorrow in time for church.

'May I have dinner brought to your room?' asked Dudley, by which Constance was forced to deduce that he had surreptitiously opened and read the note.

'Yes, and please bring me extra custard with my pudding,' she said. She had meant to sound haughty and imperious but instead, as she swept away, she feared her request had only made her sound like a ravenous child.

Chapter 12

⌒

IN A SHARP REVERSAL OF THEIR USUAL PATTERN, THE NEXT morning saw Constance installed on the Palm Terrace and Mrs Fog still out. At first it was amusing that she might not return in time for church. Constance, dressed and ready, with her gloves in her hand, had wondered whether her duty lay in worship or in waiting. A lingering tiredness from the prior day's adventure had weighted her decision and she was presently installed in a comfortable chair with a newspaper on her lap and a good view of the hotel lobby. Her drowsy gaze wandered often to the sunny seafront, beyond the window, where people, all tidied into their Sunday best, strolled with a Sabbath dignity, and even the waves seemed restrained and well behaved. She welcomed the quietude. Her mind was pleasantly full of motorcycles and aeroplanes, of her new friends here in Hazelbourne and her old friend, Patricia, in London.

Patricia's letter had been at the front desk this morning, and amid the sprawling, much ink-blotted lines of news, her friend had let her know of a position available in the accounting office where she worked. She had urged Constance to send her a list of her qualifications and confirm a date she might come up to London to interview. In daydreaming, there is no need to pick among delights, and so imagining a future of responsible work and shared rooms in London did not diminish Constance's pleasure in Hazelbourne but only caused her to design elaborate plans for how she would visit after her move. She would stay with Poppy at the barn, or possibly Tilly's mother had a box room?

The luncheon gong roused her, and now a small anxiety crept in. It occurred to her to telephone Poppy's barn and see if a taxi to the hotel had been booked. In the cubby under the stairs, she lifted the heavy receiver and asked the hotel operator to put her through.

'Wirrall's Ladies Conveyance.' Poppy's voice was bolstering in its confidence and cheer. After profuse thanks for the previous day's adventure, Constance asked after Mrs Fog's plans and Poppy consulted the thick black ledger in which she kept the schedule. 'Originally nine o'clock,' said Poppy. 'But someone called back and changed it to three o'clock. Don't worry. I'm picking her up myself. Tilly's on call but there was some meeting at the library.'

'How is Tilly?' asked Constance.

'She's perfectly fine and has that aeroplane engine in pieces,' said Poppy. 'Iris, on the other hand, is not speaking to me, but that's also perfectly normal. I am a horrendous friend but a long-standing one. It will blow over like a summer storm.' She laughed. 'Are you checking up on Mrs Fog or me?'

'As it happens, I would like to go to Cabbage Beach this afternoon,' said Constance. Perhaps you could pick me up and take me over there a little earlier?'

'Would Wirrall's Conveyance be dropping you at the same address perchance?' asked Poppy. 'Not that we would give out any addresses.'

'I believe it's an old vicarage,' said Constance. 'It's a small place, so I should be able to find it.'

'So you're now chaperoning Mrs Fog?' asked Poppy. 'Shouldn't it be the other way around?'

'She hasn't been well and now she's staying out all night,' said Constance. 'Surely she can't object to me popping along for a brief introduction to these friends of hers?'

'Well, you're probably going to lose me a customer, but all right. You'll be riding pillion on the way home, so dress accordingly.'

CABBAGE BEACH WAS a small collection of mostly new villas set in tidy flower gardens along a dirt road, next to a broad shingle beach. Some older farmhouses and cottages were scattered in the broad marshes behind, their age shown in the larger hedges and trees that protected them from the wind. An ancient pub anchored one end of the village, and there was the obligatory shop and village hall. Poppy stopped on a humpback bridge to point out a sprawling golf course and, behind that, the wooden huts remaining from a recently shuttered military camp and hospital.

'Only a few Canadians still there waiting to be repatriated,' she said. 'In the last couple of years it was their hospital. They were hard hit by the influenza last winter. You can imagine being on the marsh in a wooden hut didn't help much.'

At the far end of the village was another cluster of older, larger trees. And behind a thickly woven hawthorn hedge some eight feet high stood a house of warm old brick and tile under a tall, red-tiled roof. The east-facing front looked to have been improved in Regency times with large, thin-framed windows painted a creamy yellow. The rest of the house seemed much older, the roof low in the back to ward off the prevailing westerly winds. A profusion of flowers almost submerged the front garden, and to the side a south-facing terrace and long lawn could be glimpsed sweeping to the sea. Poppy parked where a spreading beech tree hung over into the road.

'It's called the Old Vicarage,' said Poppy. 'But there's no church. People go into Bexhill on a Sunday.'

'I shouldn't have come,' said Constance. 'I feel foolish now.' In the sunshine, and amid the fat shrubberies, it seemed silly to have imagined danger or illness afflicting Mrs Fog, however frail she might be.

'Just because they live in a nice old house doesn't mean they can't be awful people,' said Poppy. 'Penneston is nice and we're a hideous family.'

'Don't be silly,' said Constance. 'You and your family are the kindest people.'

'I'll wait right here,' said Poppy. 'You march up there and demand Mrs Fog's release.'

'You should come with me,' said Constance. 'I can't leave you here like a servant.'

'That's my job, miss.' Poppy touched her imaginary cap and grinned.

The front door was faded grey oak with a weathered lion's-head door knocker. The doorstep was red quarry tile, well scrubbed and dusted. In the eaves above, swallows darted in and out of nests made of mud, and in the tall flowers, an orange cat was sleeping in a patch of sun. The sound of the sea tumbling against the shingle bank came faintly on the breeze.

Constance knocked tentatively at first and then louder. She heard feet on a stone passageway and the door opened to reveal an older gentleman dressed in a dapper navy linen jacket over cream linen pants and a yellow silk cravat with an embroidered pattern of honeybees. His hair was grey, still thick and wavy, and his eyes a piercing blue in a complexion as dark as that of an old farmer at the end of a long summer. In his hand he held a book, his index finger keeping his place, as if she had just disturbed him in his library.

'I'm sorry to trouble you, I'm looking for Mrs Fog,' said Constance. 'I was told she might be here?'

'To be sure, come in,' said the man. 'Would you happen to be Constance by any chance?' He gave her a generous smile and waved her in as if she were a friend of the family.

'I am. Very pleased to make your acquaintance?' She phrased it as a question, caught in the awkwardness of having to ask a man his name in his own home.

'Simon de Champney,' he said. 'My sister, Mathilde, and Eleanor are childhood school friends.' It took one or two heartbeats for Constance's brain to connect the name Eleanor. She was so used to thinking of

Mrs Fog by her married surname. She had always seemed like an old lady. It was hard to imagine her as ever having been a schoolgirl with playmates and pigtails. 'They're in the garden,' the man, Simon, added. 'Do come through.'

Constance caught only the briefest impression of the house. The old flagstone hallway held a mirrored hallstand and an almost ceiling-high portrait of a dark-haired lady in full Spanish dress, complete with fan and black lace mantilla. She had the same watchful blue eyes as Mr de Champney, and Constance wondered if Spanish ancestry might explain his complexion. There was a snug library to the left and a small dining room to the right, with carved oak chairs and a cabinet piano. Beyond the library, glass doors led to a sunny drawing room and conservatory, giving way to the garden.

Perhaps *drawing room* was the wrong term? It was more like an artist's studio. Books and periodicals spilled out of low shelves, and watercolours and inks were arrayed on a table stacked with finished paintings and sketches. One wall was covered floor to ceiling in pictures, no two framed alike and yet the whole effect as harmonious as a poem; a sewing basket and a leather box of knitting supplies were tucked to one side of a large comfortable settee. Under a window, a weaving in shades of lavender and blue wool sat almost finished on a large polished oak loom. Above the fireplace, an oil painting showed a small white house on a hilltop with a large veranda and a palm-fringed lawn leading to the sea.

Beside the fireplace, someone had been whittling a walking stick. The raw wood stick, leaning against the mantel, already revealed a pattern of leaves and an acorn finial. The curled shavings had been neatly swept up and dropped into the grate. Constance felt a sweet piercing of the heart as she remembered her own father whittling wood into the kitchen stove, her mother shaking her head at the mess but smiling as he offered his children small rough carvings of birds and sheep. Where were they now, those simple offerings? So delightedly received, so carelessly abandoned. Perhaps one or two lingered in an old kitchen drawer in the farmhouse? How Constance wished she had known as a child to preserve them.

'What a lovely room,' she said, an inadequate expression of her admiration.

'We wage constant war against our housekeeper,' Simon de Champney said. 'She is forever popping in and cleaning everything away. She means well, but she would destroy every last vestige of creativity in search of a tidy parlour.'

'It's just the right amount of creative effusion,' said Constance.

He pushed his eyeglasses up his nose and peered around. 'We don't receive many visitors,' he said. 'Perhaps it is a bit dusty? At our age one doesn't notice as much. If Eleanor's presence is going to unleash a tidal wave of guests upon us, I suppose we shall have to let Mrs Hobart in more often to mop about a bit.'

In the conservatory, green blinds were drawn cool against the pitching sun. A tall fig tree in a brass pot leaned over a collection of succulents and ferns set about on the stone floor. In one corner a birdcage in the Chinese style held three yellow canaries, and below them, in an area penned about by short wooden palings, two tortoises sunned themselves and nibbled at half a head of dark green lettuce.

'Mathilde's Zoo,' he said, by way of explanation. 'We have six chickens in the garden and two cats in the stable. I'm holding the line at her getting a goat.'

The lawn beyond the conservatory led directly to the shingle beach. A low gorse hedge provided a short windbreak and, tucked in its lee, Mrs Fog reclined in a deckchair, listening to her companion read to her from the confines of a large Moroccan hammock. A snippet of Emily Dickinson floated on the breeze before both women took notice of Constance's arrival and sat up.

'Is everything all right?' said Mrs Fog. 'Why are you here?' Constance was not quite sure what to say. To admit that she had been worried would be to insult these seemingly worthy people, and in their own lovely home. The woman, Mathilde de Champney, was smiling at her in the friendliest of manners. She had the same thick grey hair as her brother, pulled back tight into a large bun at the nape of her neck. Set against Mrs Fog's convalescent paleness, her complexion was also dark but, unlike her brother's, her eyes were a warm brown. She wore a loose summer dress of embroidered cream linen, and her bare brown feet peeked out from under its long hem.

'Well, we've kept you far too long, Eleanor,' said Mathilde. 'No doubt your young friend worried you had been kidnapped.'

'It's just that she's been unwell,' said Constance. 'I thought you might need me.'

'Well, as you can see I'm perfectly fine,' said Mrs Fog. She did indeed look fine. The sun had pinked her nose and cheeks. Her feet also poked out bare in the rather long grass. And Constance could not be sure, but Mrs Fog's clothes also looked loose, as if she might have taken off her stays. Her face wore a small frown like that of a petulant child. 'And I didn't order the taxi for another half an hour.'

'I didn't mean to disturb you all,' said Constance. 'I can wait outside with Poppy Wirrall.'

'You left Miss Wirrall waiting in the street?' said Mrs Fog.

'She insisted. In her capacity as a taxi driver.'

'The late Sir John Wirrall's daughter,' explained Mrs Fog.

'Well, she must come in and have some tea,' said Mathilde, laughing. 'Would you fetch her, Miss Haverhill? I would send Simon, but he might frighten her in that disreputable coat.'

Poppy was induced to join them, and the much-maligned house-keeper, Mrs Hobart, kept a neutral face as she brought out a large tea tray to set up on a folding rattan table under a pear tree.

'It's been such a lovely visit,' said Mrs Fog. 'I can't remember when I've laughed so much. Your piano playing is still so exquisite, Mathilde.'

'It's been too short again,' said Mathilde. 'I'm so happy you still love poetry.'

'So you two knew each other fifty years ago?' asked Poppy. 'What happened?'

'It hardly matters.' Mathilde reached out and patted Mrs Fog's hand.

'It was another lifetime and we are determined to waste not a minute of the one we have left.'

Simon cleared his throat and said, 'It's as if the years have been stripped away. I see you now as I first saw you sitting in that ridiculous rowing boat on the river Thames. You wore a hat the size of a carriage wheel.'

'And red boots. I remember the fashion was for red kid boots. They were quite the rage,' said Mrs Fog. 'And the young man squiring us insisted on standing up to hail one of his fellows and he fell in and I was quite in hysterics and Mathilde had to row us to the shore.'

'Some girls wear pretty hats and some girls can row,' said Mathilde. 'I remember being quite upset at the time. You got all the attention.'

'I might have insisted on my own fragility a bit too much,' said Mrs Fog. 'Your brother and his friends were all so dashing I couldn't help myself.'

'Well, you'll be pleased to know nothing changes,' said Poppy. 'We are still expected to simper and faint and hide our abilities in all things worldly. I find it exhausting, myself.' She accepted a cup of tea and brushed dust from the knees of her driving trousers.

'But I believe you are running your own business, Miss Wirrall,' said Mathilde. 'Surely times must have changed for the better.' They fell to discussing the business, the motorcycle club and Poppy's most recent venture.

'I may have overextended myself on the aeroplane,' Poppy said.

'And is it your intent that your motorcycle ladies should also become pilots?' asked Mathilde. 'I imagine that would raise some eyebrows.'

'Surely it's much too dangerous for women?' asked Mrs Fog.

'I don't see why it would be,' said Poppy. 'My brother is a first-rate pilot and flying lessons for ladies might be just the thing for us to finally turn a profit.'

'And will you be the first student, Miss Haverhill?' asked Mathilde.

'I shudder to think of such a thing,' said Mrs Fog. 'Constance is much too sensible.'

'It would be much too expensive, I fear,' said Constance. 'I must make my way in the world, Miss de Champney.'

'Yes, we ought to have some sort of scholarship programme.' Poppy drifted away for a moment, lost in plans for a ladies' flying school.

'Do you have exciting plans for the future, Miss Haverhill?' asked Simon. 'Eleanor tells us you are the most capable and intelligent of young women.'

'Thank you,' said Constance, more to Mrs Fog than to Simon. Mrs Fog only drank her tea and Constance also looked away. Both of them were unused to effusiveness. 'Mrs Fog has been very kind to bring me with her here, but I must look to my future. An old school friend is arranging an interview for me in London.'

'An interview?' asked Poppy. 'But we can't afford to lose you. Surely, Mrs Fog, you and Constance will be here through the summer at least?'

'Perhaps,' said Mrs Fog. She shifted in her seat, uncomfortable. 'But one wouldn't want to stand in Constance's way.'

'We are only here a few weeks,' said Constance. 'It's a lovely holiday. But of course, holidays can't last forever.'

'Perhaps I could find you something locally,' said Poppy. 'As you know, it's my mission to employ women.'

'We count ourselves very fortunate to have made a permanent home here by the sea,' said Mathilde. 'But it is very quiet for young people, especially out of season.'

'I'm perfectly busy,' said Poppy. 'I think the city is for those who have nothing to do. They hide their sloth with a round of parties.'

'I think you're being a little unfair,' said Constance. 'Not that I know anything of city life. Surrey can be even quieter, I think.'

'Deadly quiet,' agreed Mrs Fog. 'Pity an old lady like me buried in a corner of the drawing room. Nothing to see from the windows but grass and cows. Having to call the chauffeur just to go down to the village.'

'But you have your whole family around you, Mrs Fog,' said Constance.

'Family is wonderful, but not a one of them plays whist or canasta,' said Mrs Fog. 'But perhaps you will return to live with your brother, dear Constance, and then you could come over and play a hand or two twice a week?'

'Are you really convalescing, Eleanor, or have you both just run away from home?' asked Simon.

In the laughter that followed, Poppy asked, 'Given how quiet our town is, I'm very surprised that we have not been introduced before. Do you by chance know my mother, Mrs Wirrall?'

'We live a somewhat retired life,' said Mathilde. 'We are an island unto ourselves.'

'You have made a small creative utopia,' said Mrs Fog. 'What more could one ask for?'

'Well, apparently a robust programme of canasta for a start,' said Simon.

'Your mother is well known in the area, Miss Wirrall,' Mathilde added. 'We have met her in the course of her good work for the widows and orphans fund, and she was most generous at the auction we held in the spring. But we would not presume to claim a social acquaintance.'

'She bought one of Mathilde's woven blankets and a set of water-colours of the lighthouse and seafront,' said Simon.

'You are artists,' said Poppy. 'My mother loves artists.'

'Mathilde is the artist. I'm just a hobbyist,' said Simon. 'I run a small printing press and generally potter around. Mathilde's talents elevate the atmosphere and imbue my own pottering with greater spirit.' He sighed. 'It is the goal of all Englishmen to retire to a gentlemanly existence in the country. And then we do and find we have nothing with which to keep ourselves occupied. My dear sister rescued me some time ago from a slough of despond and inactivity and for that I will always be supremely grateful.'

'Nonsense! You were always busy,' said Mathilde. 'A dizzying array of projects with no time to finish any. I merely suggested a more directed approach. And here we are adequately occupied and, I hope, pleasantly fulfilled.'

'A man could not reasonably expect more happiness,' said Simon.

'And yet one remains humbly open to additional gifts of fate.' Constance could not be sure, but Mrs Fog, busying herself at the tea urn, seemed to flush a little about the cheeks.

'The artistic life is not for me, I'm afraid,' said Poppy. 'I can't draw or paint to save my life. Also, I'm a disaster on the piano. So much so that people hesitate to invite me to dinner parties.' She paused and considered. 'I suppose I have too many projects. I do wonder sometimes if I am more restless than busy.'

'Art and happiness are wasted on the young,' said Mrs Fog. 'An excess of energy and ambition make it impossible for them to alight on anything long enough to appreciate it.'

'Were you unappreciative as a young woman, Mrs Fog?' asked Constance. It was her observation that older people conveniently did not remember having suffered any errors of judgement and lectured from an invincible high moral podium. One wondered how wars had ever begun or the price of coal inflated, given the impeccable record of wise decisions by all those over thirty.

'In my day one did as one was expected to do. One did not have the luxury of choosing one's own happiness.'

'I'm not sure there is much choosing now, Mrs Fog,' said Poppy. 'If I may speak frankly, we are being summarily ejected from our wartime jobs, our mothers still push us to get married and we can't even vote until we're thirty!'

'Miss Wirrall, I have a feeling you will succeed,' said Mathilde. 'Your passion is obvious.'

'Thank you, ma'am, you are very kind,' said Poppy. Her face shone with the pleasure one gets when the compliment is real and the giver a person one admires. Strange that although Constance and Poppy had only just met them, Mathilde de Champney and her brother were already such people. Their warmth, their friendly confidence, was like a balm. Somehow, all of them, including Mrs Fog, were seduced. It was less of a mystery now, thought Constance, that Mrs Fog should have extended her stay with them as much as possible.

Chapter 13

POPPY WIRRALL APPEARED ON THE PALM TERRACE TWO
days later and slumped into a chair, in a way guaranteed to rumple the
smart blue suit she wore. With a rosy cameo on the sailor collar, a pink
felt camellia on her white silk headband and beige suede shoes, she was
as well dressed and feminine as her mother could ever wish, thought
Constance.

'Do you mind if I join you?'

'Not at all,' said Mrs Fog, who was taking a break from playing cards
to discuss the possibility of Constance making a trip to London to interview for the accounting position. 'Shall I call for an extra cup
of broth?'

'No, I'm on my way to see my mother and brother upstairs.'

'There must be some occasion?' asked Constance, rubbing the sleeve
of Poppy's jacket with her fingertips. A light wool. Very good quality.
'Small family wedding? Sudden engagement?'

'On Harris's behalf, Mother has called a business meeting about the
family finances.' She grinned at Constance. 'Thought it might do some
good to send the sort of presentable daughter she always wanted to discuss my aeroplane expansion plans.'

'How is the restoration going?' asked Constance.

'Tom Morris was unable or unwilling to lend us any help,' said Poppy.
'Tilly is overwhelmed, and Harris is ready to give up. Flying, not

mechanics, being his specialty. I need to find a mechanic and I need Sam Newcombe to sell me a whole list of parts. Also I need money.'

'I think Sam would give you whatever you need,' said Constance.

'Yes, but I won't be bought and I won't lead a man on.' Poppy gave a loud sigh. 'And of course, I already owe Iris money. Harris is hinting at retrenchment, but I'm hoping to persuade Mother to make a further investment.'

'I hope she agrees,' said Mrs Fog. 'I have become partial to your little taxi service.'

'We are wearing quite a deep rut in the road to Cabbage Beach,' said Poppy. 'How are the de Champneys?'

'Very well,' said Mrs Fog. 'How is your brother?' And just like that she turned the conversation away, as she had done the several times Constance had tried to ask her more about them. She had responded only vaguely to all questions about their family and connections and become sharp at any persistent questioning. As Mrs Fog did not enquire too forcefully into Constance's own new friends in the motorcycle club, Constance felt it prudent to allow Mrs Fog her reticence.

After chatting for a few moments more about Harris and about motorcycles, Constance rose to her feet.

'If you'll excuse me. I really must write to Patricia before the last post.'

'Is that your friend in London?' asked Poppy. 'When do you go up?' Mrs Fog launched into a description of the difficulties with the unreliable train schedule, and Constance wished she would not, for it was not pleasant to hear one's limited financial circumstances hinted at in the repetition of the expense of the fare and the difficulties of remaining overnight. Poppy nodded several times and then, struck by a thought, her face lit up.

'And of course it is unpleasant to travel by train alone and one is likely to have to fend off unwanted attentions, especially from soldiers, and one can always ask the conductor to keep an eye but then one feels like a child.'

'Not helpful,' said Constance. 'I must get to London.'

'The lack of a chaperone is of great concern,' said Mrs Fog. 'My daughter, Lady Mercer, would be appalled to know I am failing in my duty. But Constance insists my health will not permit such a strenuous day, and I fear she is right.'

'Which is why she shall go to London with me,' said Poppy. 'We shall motor up together. I can deliver her to her interview and wait and then she can accompany me, as I have some business to attend to in the East End and, to be quite honest, I am nervous to go alone. We will chaperone each other and share the cost of the petrol and I'm sure it will be the same or less expensive than the train.'

'All the way to London in that little box?' said Mrs Fog, her voice doubtful. 'What if you break down?' Constance could see in her frown, visions of ravaging highwaymen and crashed vehicles upside down in muddy ditches.

'Not to worry, Mrs Fog, I'm an excellent mechanic and I carry a full toolbox,' said Poppy. 'I've made the trip before and I will be able to drop Constance right at her destination. No need to take taxis or buses across London from the train station.' She turned to Constance. 'There's a delightful café in Redhill where we can stop for breakfast if you have the time.'

'I can't ask you to do that for me,' said Constance, though she thought nothing could sound more exciting than such an expedition, to which the job interview itself would be almost an interruption.

'If Wirrall's Ladies Conveyance takes you to London, I'll be able to claim business petrol rations,' said Poppy. 'Would Friday be possible?'

'What do you think, Mrs Fog?' Constance asked. 'May I go?'

'You know I would wish to treat you just like my own granddaughter and refuse to allow it. But your circumstances are different, my dear, however much we would wish it otherwise.' She sighed. 'I suppose the journey can be completed in absolute daylight?'

It stung a little to have her position so carefully calibrated and articulated, however kind and carefully parsed the manner, but Constance took heart from Poppy turning aside to roll her eyes at her.

'Certainly,' said Poppy to Mrs Fog, with a hand to her heart. 'We shall be up with the dawn and home before dusk.'

'Then I give my permission,' said Mrs Fog. 'And if we keep it to ourselves, the question of propriety need not, perhaps, be addressed too closely.' She seemed very cheerful at this decision, and as Constance went to write immediately to Patricia, she reflected that Mrs Fog would no doubt find her absence another excuse to spend a day with Mathilde de Champney.

ON FRIDAY, CONSTANCE found herself on the road with Poppy. They stopped, as promised, at the small café in Redhill, which appeared to be nothing more than the front parlour of a cottage attached to a small roadside barn that offered motor repair and petrol. The wife of the owner served strong tea, porridge and eggs to travellers while her husband filled their tanks and mended their tyres. Poppy was known to the proprietress and, from their conversation, Constance learned that she knew Iris too. There were three men in the front room already, the acrid smell of their pipes and cigarettes mixing with the smell of frying, so the woman invited Poppy and Constance into her kitchen.

'As a woman you have to know where to stop for petrol and help,' said Poppy. 'I've had some places refuse to serve me. One time I had to flag down a complete stranger on the road and ask him to wheel my machine in and get it filled up. This place is a godsend.'

They sat at the rough wooden kitchen table and Poppy ate a plate of eggs and fried bread. Constance, worried about her interview and concerned to keep her clothes pristine, asked only for toast. There was no butter, but the bread came white and thickly sliced, and after the crumbly grey bread of the last few years, it tasted like childhood. The tea was strong and the colour of an old floor. It was poured from the largest brown pot Constance had ever seen, which was kept filled from a kettle always steaming on the edge of the stove.

'There's a bridge out after Waverley,' said the woman, refilling their teacups again, the giant teapot radiating a fierce heat as it swung by Constance's ear. 'If you turn at the postbox and take the lane past the church, there's a ford at the edge of the wood.'

'Our gracious proprietress knows all the roads,' said Poppy. 'And she knows all the problems.'

'My father worked the stagecoaches when I was a child,' said the woman. 'It's in me blood.' She went into the front parlour to threaten the other customers with the boiling teapot.

'And goodness knows what her mother did,' said Poppy. 'Because she ran quite the black market through here the last couple of years. I bought six yards of good Harris tweed and a bottle of real champagne last year.'

'Poppy!' said Constance.

'Oh, it's just a little commerce,' said Poppy. 'What's the harm?' Constance could have discoursed at length on the ills of the underground economy in wartime, but it was hard to resent the woman when she returned and asked if they would like a little of her damson jam with their bread.

The journey had begun in the dawn with the birds flinging themselves about in the trees for the joy of being alive and the sun just beginning to gild the shingle beach. Now, with breakfast done, the sun was quite hot and the countryside was becoming dusty and more thickly punctuated with villages and small towns. Poppy had suggested Constance travel with the top up so as not to arrive for her interview with goggle marks slashed across her face, but it was noisy and dark inside. As she bounced over the rutted roads, the countryside unfurled like a moving picture in the small square of the side window. Soon the towns began to blur one into the next and she knew they were moving through the southern suburbs of London. When villas and tenements gave way to townhouses and mansion blocks, she knew they were close. She checked her watch in the dim light. The time for her interview was drawing near.

∿

DRAPER AND WOODLEY, Chartered Accountants, occupied two floors of a brick building near Waterloo Station. The front was smartly painted in a deep red with a small, gilded sign near the door and large frosted windows concealing the busy practice within. Constance smoothed her dress, the serviceable brown wool that was her own, not handed down from Lady Mercer, and reached a hand to see if her hair was still in place.

'I'm not sure I can do this,' she said, feeling her breath flutter. Who was she, after all, to think she might work in such an impressive office? A few correspondence courses and the simple books of a country estate were a far call indeed from the high-flying commerce of London.

'Nonsense!' said Poppy, slapping her on the forearm with her driving gloves. 'You are an honorary member of the Hazelbourne Ladies Motorcycle Club. Hold your head up and think how Tilly would scold you if you wavered.'

'Very reassuring,' said Constance, her sarcasm hiding the fact that Poppy's words had indeed had the required bracing effect. She would walk into Draper and Woodley as if the whole club were lined up behind her.

'I'll wait in the little square we just passed,' said Poppy, still astride the machine. 'Come and find me when you are finished.'

The young woman at the front desk seemed flustered by Constance's arrival. 'You're Patricia Morton's friend,' she said, her eyes widening. 'To see Mr Draper?'

'Is Patricia available?' asked Constance. 'She said to ask for her and she would introduce me personally.'

'No, she's not,' said the receptionist. 'Please have a seat. I'll ring through.' After a muffled conversation on a large black telephone, a young man appeared, very thin with large hands, and led her through the open office. Rows of desks, occupied by young men, were silent except for the tapping of heavy adding machines and the scratching of pens on ledgers. To one side, a number of women secretaries rattled away on typewriters.

Mr Draper was polite enough to meet them at the door to his office.

He was a short man with a thinning hairline and a small paunch under his waistcoat, yet he had the broad smile and firm handshake of a man who thought himself attractive. He had not put on his jacket and wore his sleeves rolled up.

'Oh yes, you are Patricia's friend. Do come through.' He began to roll down his sleeves and put on his jacket, smiling all the while and waving to the many ledgers on his desk. 'You will forgive me, Miss Haverhill. We are in the middle of a most difficult audit for a very important customer and— You see, I treat you with the informality of a colleague already.' He waved her to a seat. 'May I order you some tea?' She declined, and he sat down at his desk, rubbing his hands together. 'Good, we shall forget the niceties and get right down to business. As you can see, we are a very busy practice.'

His office was smart and new, trimmed in light oak with a simple desk and a long row of matching filing cabinets set under a broad glass window through which the rest of the office could be seen.

'Patricia said you were wonderfully modern,' said Constance. By this she meant to indicate and confirm that he was willing to hire women.

'Oh yes, the lovely Patricia. She was equally admiring of you. We should assume she is a very good judge of character.' He smiled conspiratorially. He produced from a file the letter Constance had sent detailing her experience as well as the qualifications she had earned by correspondence school.

Mr Draper appeared to take only a cursory interest in her papers and seemed focused on more personal details, as if the job were already hers and they were now chatting as friends. He wanted to know where she had come from. Did she have family? Would this be her first time living in London and did she have friends here? It was, he said, important to him that she be happy.

'We often have very exciting, complicated work to do, Miss Haverhill. We do accounting for some of the best companies, not to mention one or two people whose names I dare not utter. You would be surprised how retiring important people can be, Miss Haverhill. We must be as discreet as priests. Sometimes Patricia and I would be forced to work late hours and even Sundays. It's important to me to find people with a passion for the work and with whom I – well, really all of us – hit it off, so to speak. We are like a happy family. A happy but very busy family.' He got up and came around the desk to sit in the chair next to her and hold out his hand as if to shake hers. When she offered her hand he held on to it and she battled a fierce desire to pull away. 'I'm so sorry to hear about your poor mother. Do you think you can be happy here, my dear?'

Constance could not help a fierce blush. She looked at her shoes, deeply conscious of all the office workers beyond the glass. Surely they had a full view of Mr Draper sitting too close, even if they could not see him holding her hand. She was not some naïve schoolgirl and she understood he was being impossibly forward, but she could not immediately think of a polite way to extricate herself.

'I could see my way to starting you at seventeen shillings?' He pressed her fingers. 'And I will promise to train you up myself. You will have all my support.' Her conscience suggested that the substantial offer was more than she could reasonably expect. Under the sinking weight of her confusion, she felt powerless until a vision of Poppy, sitting outside on her motorcycle, probably eating a sandwich in public, made her sit up straight and firmly withdraw her hand.

'Patricia said you have been wonderfully kind to her,' she replied, her voice steady and her chin high. 'Is she here? I would like to talk things over with her before deciding.' It was her last faint hope. If Patricia was happy here, perhaps she was wrong to see fault in Mr Draper's kind attention. After all, what did she know of men? Perhaps she was being a baby.

'Unfortunately, Patricia has left us,' said Mr Draper, making a long, sad face like a clown. 'A very great loss, I assure you. But of course that means I am more anxious than ever to acquire the services of a suitable girl. I hope Patricia mentioned that I like to be generous?'

'That can't be! I heard from her by the first post yesterday,' said Constance, the blood rushing in her ears. 'She didn't mention leaving.' She wondered why Patricia would ask her to come to work for a man who was even now sitting with his knees pressed towards her and his fingers tented to his lips. She could not imagine Patricia would knowingly betray her, and so she worried desperately for Patricia herself.

'Well, it's not for me to say,' said Mr Draper. He looked like a large toad about to leap on her from a lily pad. 'But I believe she is to be married? Lovely girl. I do hope it is so.' The room swam a little and Constance pressed her fingernails deep into the palms of her hands as she summoned the faces of Poppy and Tilly and Iris. All were scowling at the man, of course. She drew a deep breath. She was about to tell Mr Draper what she thought of him when a disturbance in the outer office drew their attention. A large woman was billowing down the room, hat bobbing as furiously as a seagull attacking an abandoned fish and chip bag. Mr Draper jumped to his feet and seemed torn between going to the office door and retreating behind his desk. The protection of the desk won and he leaped behind it as the door banged open.

'Mr Roderick Nigel Draper. I do hope I'm not disturbing you?' She spoke with all the quiet compression of a lit fuse disappearing into a firework.

'Sybil, I was not expecting you.'

'An obvious truth that does nothing to move along the current conversation.'

'Sybil, do shut the door. The staff will hear you.' She clicked the door shut with her heel, her face never leaving his. He continued, red about the cheeks, a look of mute appeal in his eyes. 'This is Miss Haverhill, come up all the way from Sussex this morning. Miss Haverhill, may I present my wife, the lovely Sybil Draper.' His wife had the doughy face of an undercooked currant bun, and Constance wondered anew at the apparent transforming powers of love.

'I don't care if she's come from Inverness, Roddy,' said the woman, pulsating with anger. 'The last one not out the door two minutes and you are backsliding.'

'It's not the same,' he said. 'Miss Haverhill is for accounts, not secretarial.' Mrs Draper turned to Constance and stared her up and down. She seemed to calm somewhat and, as she offered a grim smile, Constance was forced to wonder if her appearance had been deemed adequately respectable or simply dowdy.

'I'm sorry for your wasted journey, miss,' the woman said in a mollified tone. 'You are, I'm sure, an irreproachable young woman, but I'm afraid my husband and I have agreed that it is too difficult to manage any more women in the office.'

'Sybil, really.'

'Such a distraction to the men. And then they either leave to get married or they don't – and those are the worst,' she said. 'Besides, very soon the law will require us to employ our boys coming home. They do have families to support after all.' She spoke now as if she were sure of Constance being in complete agreement.

'I also need to support myself, madam,' Constance said, getting to her feet. 'But I can see there is no position here so I will not beg for one.'

'Yes, we women must look to our families and our husbands these days, I'm afraid,' said Mrs Draper. 'And those who can summon neither— Well, one hopes it is circumstances and not character, but one can't be too careful.'

'I'm so very sorry for the misunderstanding, Miss Haverhill,' said Mr Draper. 'Completely our fault of course. The new policy being so – well – new. My secretary should have thought to telephone you.' His wife suppressed a snort and opened the door with a grim smile.

'I do hope you have a pleasant trip home. The trains can be such a horrible crush.'

'Goodbye,' said Constance, determined not to sag under her hot humiliation. She held her chin up as she left, walking at a deliberate pace down the long room of the office, where everyone continued to work silently while pretending their eyes were not burning into her back.

It was far too short a walk to the square at the end of the street, and Constance had not had time to perfect a nonchalant response to Poppy's excited questioning. It was too humiliating to describe what had happened. Instead she put all her energy into controlling the awkward tremble in her chin as she told Poppy briefly that the job was to go to a man.

'It's appalling,' said Poppy. 'Are we to starve in the streets?' As the financial straits from which Poppy was currently suffering were the result of buying an aeroplane, Constance was not prepared to be as cheered by this support as Poppy might hope.

'Technically some of us are more likely to starve than you,' she said. 'But I appreciate the sentiment.'

'Insufferable of me, sorry,' said Poppy cheerfully. 'I never know what to say. But tell me what I can do.'

'There will be other jobs, I hope,' said Constance. 'But I'm worried about my friend Patricia.' She hesitated and added, 'I met the owner's wife. I rather fear Patricia has been unfairly treated.'

'It's like that, is it?' said Poppy. 'Then let's go and find Patricia. Where does she live?'

HAVING FLAGGED DOWN a passing cabbie to get directions, they set off again. This time Poppy lowered the sidecar's top and Constance, in goggles and scarf, happily put up with the stares of people they passed in order to enjoy an uninterrupted view of the bustling London streets.

Patricia had described a respectable boarding house for young ladies. As the motorcycle pulled up in front of a row of soot-blackened homes and cheap hotels, in a back street on the border of Kensington, the smells of liver and cabbage wafted from a basement-area kitchen. At Patricia's address, an attempt had been made to grow marigolds in window boxes, but they struggled in the north-facing shade and their brilliance too was dimmed by a light powdering of soot. The front door was propped open and two small suitcases sat on top of the steps. In an open wooden box alongside could be seen a kettle, teapot, books, hairbrushes and a single shoe. As Constance got out of the sidecar, a young woman appeared at the door with a rolled blanket and a bird in a small cage and Constance recognised Patricia.

That 'the Haverhill girl' had become friends with 'the Morton girl', as they were known at school, was perhaps made inevitable not so much by any shared interests as by dint of both being scholarship students. Children are swift and brutal in the arrangement of their societies and the confines of a boarding school only exacerbate the cruelty. A week after their arrival, two older girls led the whole common room in a game of choosing who was ugliest among the new girls. Constance could still hear their cruel laughter, smell the mingled soap and girl sweat, and feel the heat of her neighbour's shoulder against her own. When someone pointed to Patricia, saying her hair was filled with lice, the chant went around that she was a dirty grocer's daughter. One of the older girls pushed a heavy, cold pair of scissors into Constance's hand. 'Cut it,' she whispered. Did Matron come in while she hesitated, or did she bravely refuse? Enough of the girls seemed to think the former that they gave her some respect and eyed her sideways in sewing class whenever she picked up the pinking shears. Patricia thought the latter and became devoted to her. Constance could never be sure either way, and perhaps it was her uneasy conscience that made them friends.

Now Patricia squealed in delight at seeing Constance on the pavement and put down her belongings to fly into the street to embrace her.

'I'm so happy to see you. I couldn't write to you in time. Did you see Mr Draper? Did he hire you?'

'No, he did not,' she said, trying not to be short. 'Mr Draper let you go?'

'Oh no, I resigned.' She appeared to deflate a little but recovered. 'Mr Draper said I was his best girl ever and it was just a misunderstanding, but it was for the best because now I'm getting married tomorrow.' Breathless, she displayed a silver ring with a small opal. 'Derek's an engineer with the railways. Oh hello, I say, is that really your motorcycle? How smashing.'

'How do you do,' said Poppy.

'Well, let's not stand gossiping in the street like washerwomen,' said Patricia. 'Will you step into the front parlour? I can keep an eye out for

Derek from the window.' They entered the dark, narrow hall and then a front parlour flocked with green wallpaper and sprouting heavy mahogany furniture from a mossy carpet. It was like being submerged in a pond, thought Constance. They sat on the stiff horsehair-upholstered chairs. 'I'm sorry I can't give you tea, but I've packed up my kettle and I daren't ask the landlady.' Patricia spoke cheerfully but she eyed the door as if nervous.

'You are leaving?' asked Constance.

'Oh, I'm just going to stay with my Derek's mother until the wedding. I called him right away after I resigned. I was upset, I suppose. And that's when he proposed and it was so romantic of him to rescue me. He's coming to pick me up any minute now.' While they were speaking a thin woman in a turban and a long striped apron over a black silk dress came to the door, her arms folded.

'That room is going to need sweeping or I'll have to charge you for cleaning,' she said. 'I don't have all day to chase about.' Patricia's smile faltered but she replied with a wave.

'Mrs Rose, this is my friend, Constance, who was interested in sharing my room.'

'Oh, if you're leaving I don't think I could manage a whole room,' said Constance, more alarmed by the landlady than the prospect of being responsible for twice as much rent. The landlady looked both Constance and Poppy up and down, lip curled, eyes narrowed.

'Sorry, I'm keeping the room for a niece of mine,' she said. Her tone was respectful, and Constance wondered if they had passed muster or if the landlady merely felt outnumbered. 'I'm sure you're a very nice young lady, miss,' she added. 'But then again, unmarried girls can be trouble. I've recently learned my lesson, you might say.' Patricia went pink about the ears.

'There's no need to be coarse, Mrs Rose,' she said. 'My fiancé will be here any minute.'

'Fiancé?' Mrs Rose seemed to snort the word. 'The parlour is for residents, so please don't be long.'

'She seems to have developed ideas about me,' said Patricia, growing red.

'Whatever happened?' asked Constance. Patricia patted her hair uncertainly and her lip began to quiver.

'It's silly really,' she said. 'I'm allowed gentlemen callers on Sundays, but she made a fuss just because Mr Draper called a few times as well as Derek. I told her Mr Draper and I were working. But then Mr Draper also brought me home after work the other night and he was a bit overwrought telling me about his difficulties at home and – well, he sort of pinned me down and kissed me.'

'Oh my goodness, were you hurt?' asked Constance.

'No, of course not. Only the landlady came in and Mr Draper told her it was all a misunderstanding, but she started screaming at me to clear out my room as if it were my fault.'

'The man is a monster,' said Poppy.

'Oh no, he's very respectable,' said Patricia. 'He said I wasn't to think for a moment that I had deliberately led him on and that he would help me find a flat of my own nearer to the office.' She sighed. 'But then he couldn't help. I think his wife doesn't like me.'

'But you surely would not accept such help,' said Constance.

'As I told Derek, at least Mr Draper offered,' said Patricia. 'If you're not going to live alone, you might as well stay at home. What with all the spying and lecturing and "be home by dark", and on top of that, you have to pay them for the privilege.'

'And Derek stuck by you?' asked Poppy. 'He sounds like a fine young man.' Her face was studiously serious but for the raised eyebrows.

'Derek said I had better resign and we would get married right away; and then I wouldn't have to work at all,' said Patricia. She smiled. 'Derek says that marriage is the only really respectable job for a woman.'

Constance couldn't look at her friend. She studied an arrangement of painted china plates on the wall: commemorative keepsakes from the old Queen's diamond jubilee and the current King's coronation; pastoral shepherds and shepherdesses; and a number of soulful-eyed dogs. She wondered briefly how one got a dog to sit still long enough to paint its portrait. There was a smallness to the room and for a long, suspended moment, she hung drowning in its narrow respectability. Then she dragged her gaze away and went over to embrace her friend.

'I'm happy for you,' she said. 'You'll be such a beautiful bride.' Patricia raised her head, blinked a smile at both of them and burst into tears.

Chapter 14

Poppy and Constance were seated in a Lyons' tea rooms in Kensington and had ordered sixpenny afternoon tea specials with egg sandwiches and fruitcake. A uniformed waitress had brought the strong dark tea for which the shops were known.

'Hope this is all right,' said Poppy. 'I didn't think we were properly dressed for Harrods.'

'I'm surprised that stopped you,' said Constance. 'But after this morning, I can barely keep my chin up in here. Do you think I might get a job as a waitress?'

'Lyons's girls are like the army,' said Poppy. 'I fear I would never pass the deportment requirements.'

Poppy had ordered them a side dish of anchovy toast, some braised kidneys, which were as expensive as the teas, and a sliced pear. Constance mentally counted again the coins in her purse and worried. While Poppy was a generous soul, the gulf between them, which would be made deeper when Constance moved into the employed classes, was already visible in the many little expenditures to which Poppy, like her mother, paid no attention. To claim poverty when one was rich was very different than to be actually poor. When the waitress asked them if they would like more hot water, in a voice carefully modulated to hide her cockney accent, Constance blushed to acknowledge that all was relative. Even her own circumstances, though straitened, might be considered affluent by this young woman who had to make a living as a waitress rather than just joke about it.

Poppy had been coy about the afternoon's business for which she required a chaperone. It wasn't until they had finished their food and were pouring the last of the tea that she revealed their destination.

'We are going to visit Harris's mechanic, Jock Macintyre,' she said. 'He's a Scotsman, but he married a woman from the East End. He hasn't responded to my brother's letters and Harris is deeply upset, though his pride won't let him admit it.'

'If Mrs Rose, the landlady, could hear us, her view of unmarried women would be further dimmed,' said Constance.

'I knew I could trust you not to stand on the proprieties,' said Poppy, as the waitress arrived with a little silver basket containing their bill. 'Your support for my outrageous caper will earn you a permanent place in our barn.' The pleasure of Poppy's approval was slightly blunted by the flicker of disapproval on the waitress's face and the lingering thought that they might be the subject of gossip in the tea room kitchen.

'Why would the man not write?' asked Constance. 'I thought he and Harris were the greatest of friends?'

'That's what I intend to ask him,' said Poppy. She hesitated. 'I've seen some of Harris's friends quail at his injury. They don't know what to say. They bluff about and are as hearty as Falstaff and then they telephone less often; become very occupied with careers or sick mothers. You see how Tom Morris is, treating Harris as if he's lost his wits, not his leg.'

'But Harris and his mechanic are surely closer than that?' said Constance. 'Why doesn't Harris go and knock on his door? As you say, he is perfectly able.'

'Jock already saved his life pulling him from his burning plane,' said Poppy. 'Harris refuses to take any further action; says he's not going to play on the man's pity.'

'There is a thin line between honour and stubbornness,' said Constance, shaking her head. 'Perhaps, someday, man will be smart enough to see the difference.'

'Well, woman is not waiting for someday,' said Poppy. 'We're going now. Harris needs a friend and, more importantly, we need an aircraft mechanic.'

THE SHOPS, BUSINESSES and houses grew smaller and sootier as they drove east into a shabbier London. Here there were fewer trees, fewer grand squares to relieve the rows of terraced houses. On the main roads the sidecar felt very small and frail against the stream of cars and lorries and the overloaded drays still being pulled by an odd assortment of struggling horses. The streets were dirty with rubbish and dried manure, and the wheels churned a cloud of dust that made Constance press her shawl to her face. Poppy used the side roads where possible. Here the people coming and going from the houses were less apt to smile at two ladies in a smartly turned out sidecar rig. If they looked around at all, it was with tired faces and frowns.

In a narrow road in Lambeth, where the front doors of the terraced houses opened directly onto the street, Poppy pulled the motorcycle to a stop and asked a small boy which one was number seven. He pointed to a house where the front window was shut and the curtains drawn. Most of the other houses had their front doors and their windows propped open. Sheets, or curtains of knotted strings weighted with iron washers, hung in some of the doorways to let in the breeze but keep out the flies. Further down the street two women sat on kitchen chairs in front of a door, cradling babies and watching other small children playing in the central gutter.

Constance stepped from the sidecar, grateful to stretch her legs. She tried not to feel the eyes of the seated women evaluating her. Poppy stepped up to the entrance of number seven and rapped sharply on the door with her knuckles. There was no reply. She tried again, a little longer and louder this time. The sound bounced off the brick house fronts and reverberated down the road. A smattering of pigeons took flight from an attic gutter. It seemed they were to have a short, disappointing end to a long journey.

'You from the council?' One of the women had left her seat and approached them, her baby held against her shoulder and turned slightly away, as if to hide him from the gaze of officialdom. Her chin was up as if she meant to defy them, but an anxious look in her eye said they had reason to fear authority around here.

'Not at all,' said Poppy. She took off her leather cap and smiled as her hair sprang about her face. 'We are friends of Sergeant Macintyre. This is his house, isn't it?'

'Only he's had enough trouble, the poor man, and the landlord already at his throat.'

'I assure you we are not from the council or the landlord, or anyone else. My brother and Sergeant Macintyre served together in the war.'

'Who's your brother, then?' asked the woman, her eyes narrowed.

'I'm not used to being interrogated in the street,' said Poppy. 'I fail to see that his name is anyone's business.' The two stared at each other, bristling like cats.

'Mr Macintyre is lucky to have his neighbours be so protective,' said Constance. She touched Poppy's elbow. 'We've come a long way to find him.'

'Very well,' said Poppy, backing down reluctantly. 'My brother is Captain Harris Wirrall. Mr Macintyre was his mechanic.'

'Well, you should have said,' said the woman, breaking into a gap-toothed smile. 'He come home on leave and told my boys all about his pilot, Captain Wirrall, and his raids on the Kaiser. Proper proud of him, he was.' She introduced herself as Macintyre's immediate neighbour, from number nine, a washerwoman by trade with four children and a husband who travelled as a wheelwright. 'Mrs Black, but call me Fanny,' she added.

'Do you know where we can find him, Fanny?' asked Poppy. The woman sighed and with a kiss shifted the baby to the crook of her arm.

'Oh, he's in there,' she said, nodding at the house. 'Doesn't come out for days. Such a tragedy. I try to do for him sometimes. A bit of cleaning and so on. But it's gotten so bad recently, he won't even let me in.' Poppy frowned.

'What tragedy?'

'Oh, I thought you'd 'ave known all about it,' said Fanny. She grimaced as she lowered her voice. 'Well, he come home from Russia about Easter time. With a box of eggs in his pocket and a rabbit in a cage no less. But 'e was too late. His missus, Arabella, and the two girls, bless 'em . . .' She turned and leaned her back against the brick house, not regarding the sooty brick against her dress. 'Sorry, it makes me weak still to think about it. She was a Lambeth girl born and bred, Arabella. I knowed her since she was a mite. I did my best to help 'em but I had my four to think about. I put food in for them through the window. Good beef bone jelly and an egg custard. Even got 'em an orange from the church society. But I couldn't go in and help.'

'They died?' asked Constance.

'One day Arabella didn't come to the window, but I thought she was sleeping and the girls were too weak to cry much. It was only in the evening my husband called the coppers to break down the door.' With the edge of the baby blanket she wiped her eyes. 'I'll never forgive myself for the hours those babies lay with their dead mother all blue and cold in that bed.'

'And the children?' asked Constance, a quiet horror making her neck cold even in the heat of the afternoon.

'They took 'em away to the hospital,' said Fanny. 'I hope they were together when they died. I hope the nurses held their hands. But you don't know with hospitals, do you?' She looked up as if to find the answer in the narrow piece of blue heaven visible between the rooftops.

'And the sergeant?' asked Poppy, her lips pressed together grimly.

'I'll not blame him for taking to the drink,' said Fanny. 'But it's likely to kill 'im the way he's going.' They were silent. Loss – so much loss – seemed to hum between them. The road was dark as a ravine, the sun now a cruel slash across upper-storey windows. The happy shouts of the small children mocked despair. Constance trembled at the echo of her own grief. Her mother gone, her brother's child. And she could weep angry tears at her own hubris: in mourning a silly job in the office of a small man or a shared room in a boarding house; at being too proud to live with her brother and too weak to absorb and forgive the awkward thrust of her sister-in-law's pain.

'Well, we can't let Sergeant Macintyre succumb,' said Poppy finally, slapping her leather cap against her thigh. 'Is there a back door, Fanny? We need to get inside and rouse him.'

'I 'ave a spare key,' said Fanny. 'But maybe you'd like to wait until one of the men gets home? Number eleven's husband is home at six.'

'After your story, I don't think we should wait,' said Poppy. 'My brother is very fond of Mr Macintyre. I'm sure we will be safe.'

'I'll get the key and leave the baby with her down there,' said Fanny, indicating her friend. 'I'm coming in with you.' Poppy looked like she would demur, but Constance jumped in.

'We would love your help. You know him best.'

'Why do we need her?' asked Poppy as Fanny scurried down the street.

'Even the most independent woman should be willing to acknowledge when she is out of her depth,' said Constance. 'We have no idea what we'll find and, unlike me, Fanny has a washerwoman's strong arms and looks fully able to brawl if necessary.'

'HELLO, JOCK, IT'S only me,' called Fanny. There was no reply. The front door gave directly onto a small, dark front room containing a threadbare settee and two wooden chairs set around a narrow fireplace. Dust furred the chair backs and the dried flowers on the mantelpiece. 'I haven't been in here lately,' said Fanny. She pulled back the curtain and more dust flew up in the shaft of light. The smell was acrid and dry but hinted at worse to come further down the passage.

The back kitchen smelled of sour milk, fish and mould, and Constance steeled herself not to gag. In the sink, cups, plates and saucepans were piled alongside empty tins of beans, sardines and pressed meat. On a small coal stove a large saucepan of dried porridge had developed a green fuzz. A crooked wooden kitchen table held empty brown beer bottles and larger green gin bottles, standing in neat rows as if to be more easily counted. Fanny opened the back door and Constance was grateful for the hot breeze from the small courtyard and alley behind.

'Do you suppose he's sleeping?' asked Poppy as Constance fought the urge to cover her mouth and nose and flee. 'Perhaps we should leave?'

'I hope he's not up there dead,' said Fanny. 'That would really make the street smell.'

'We will find out, Fanny,' said Constance. Her voice was firm, mostly to convince herself. 'We have come this far and our nerves will not fail us now.'

'I don't think I can go up there,' said Poppy. Constance had never seen her so white. 'I'm not good with sickness of any kind.' She sat down abruptly on a dirty kitchen chair.

'I'll go up first,' said Fanny. She nodded at Constance. 'Will you see if there are any embers in that stove and boil a kettle?'

Tea being the universal response and panacea for all English crises, it seemed only mildly unusual to poke at the coals of a stranger's kitchen stove. There was no water in the house and Constance took the tin kettle past a reeking outhouse into the alley, where a single pump served half the row.

When she returned, Fanny was in the kitchen wiping out a copper bowl with a corner of her apron and Poppy was tearing an old pillowcase into strips.

'Passed out drunk in his underwear and seems to have cracked his head open,' Fanny said by way of explanation. 'I'll get him into his clothes and then we'll need some hot water to clean him up. This is the cleanest thing I could find for a bandage.'

While Fanny disappeared upstairs, Constance set the kettle to boil and found a brown teapot and a small paper packet of tea in a cupboard. On a high shelf was a set of wedding china, florid with roses. The kind kept for show and never used. But as the only other cups were cracked and filthy in the sink, she took down four delicate china teacups and set them on the table. There was no icebox or pantry. She opened a tin-lined cupboard to find a bottle of milk separated into stinking curds. Quietly she shut the door again. She did not care to search for sugar. Instead she opened the little window over the sink and then went into the dark front room to open its larger window. The breeze immediately began to run through the house.

'I'm sorry, we shouldn't have come,' said Poppy. She was standing by the open window, her face tipped to catch the air. 'I overestimated my own stomach for this sort of thing.'

'Well, we are here now,' said Constance. 'Just like in the war, we can only keep going one step at a time.'

When the kettle steamed, Constance poured some hot water in the copper bowl and was just filling the teapot when they heard Fanny on the stairs.

'I'll go first so if you fall I can catch you,' said Fanny. 'You hold the banister now, Jock. Steady!'

'Paid the piper, dropped the bottle. Always fit to handle a spanner at dawn . . .'

Hurrying to the front room, Poppy and Constance watched as Fanny came backwards down the stairs, one hand out as if to stop the man from toppling forward. He was bent over, blinking at his own feet. On his forehead loomed a mass of sticky congealed blood and trails of it, already dried, coated his neck and hands. Hindered by the steepness of the narrow stair, they made a halting progress. She gripped him by one elbow and with her other hand braced herself against the grimy wallpaper. As they reached the bottom, the young man looked up and saw Constance.

'Have you come for me, angel?' he said. 'Did you bring me a nip of something for the journey?' He managed a grin, but his eyes seemed to lose focus and he sagged against the newel post.

'Pay attention there!' said Constance, grabbing his other arm. 'Let's get you sitting down.' She and Fanny lowered him onto the settee, where he promptly curled up into a ball and closed his eyes.

'Probably should keep him awake,' said Fanny. 'I had an uncle once, fell down drunk and hit his head. Never waked again.' She shook the man roughly. 'Here, wake up, Jock. Ladies to visit you.'

'Flight Sergeant Macintyre. Wake up. Captain Wirrall's orders.' Poppy's loud command had the desired effect. The young man opened one eye and rolled upright. He began to salute but his trembling hand fell back to his lap.

'Best officer I ever served with. Lost his leg you know.' He made no noise but blinked as his eyelashes grew matted with tears.

'I'll bathe the wound and bind it up,' said Constance.

'I'll bring the tea,' said Poppy. 'Pity there isn't any milk or sugar.'

'I'll nip and get you some,' said Fanny. 'I expect he hasn't eaten nothing either. Look at you, Jock, skin and bone.'

She left and Poppy went to see to the teapot while Constance fetched the bowl and bandages. There was no table in the front room on which to put anything. In the end she carried in a kitchen stool and set the bowl on it.

'This shouldn't hurt,' she told the man. 'It may start to bleed a little again. Head wounds can be nasty.'

'I think you'll find a nip of something left in the kitchen,' said Jock. He waved a vague finger. 'Under the sink behind the crate. To help with the pain.' It was his most lucid remark yet.

'Fanny is coming with some milk and sugar,' said Constance. 'Hot, sweet tea will be just the thing.'

'I can find it for you.' He attempted to rise from his seat, but one knee buckled and he sagged back with a groan.

'Stay where you are, Sergeant Macintyre,' said Constance, rubbing a piece of pillowcase with a hard end of soap from the kitchen sink. 'You've had a blow to the head and it needs attention.'

'We'll leave it alone till later then,' he muttered. She hurried to wash and dry the wound and to bind it with the strips of pillowcase. He sank into a few moments of sullen silence but then, as she finished, he roused himself to add, 'But if you church women tip it out again, I'll not be responsible . . .'

'We're not from any church,' said Constance, patting his arm. 'This is Captain Wirrall's sister, come to visit you.' Poppy had brought in the teapot and cups and arranged them on the mantelpiece. Macintyre screwed up his forehead and blinked at Poppy several times before shaking his head.

'Can't be. Rides motorcycles. Militant as a Pankhurst. Bound to look like a horse.'

'Such a happy conjunction of logic and imagination,' said Poppy, raising an eyebrow at Constance. 'Really, one is constantly in admiration of the mind of man.' Jock appeared confused and a little hurt at this and closed his eyes to mutter,

'Tell a girl she's pretty and she bites you.'

Fanny appeared at the front window and handed in a basket with a quarter bottle of milk, sugar in a twist of paper, and a thick slice of bread smeared with dripping. As Constance took it from her she saw Fanny's eye linger on the bread and she knew such generosity would hurt at suppertime.

'Let me know when you leave and I'll come in and see what he needs,' she said. 'He's a good man, miss. Don't judge him too harsh in his extremity.'

Sergeant Macintyre looked askance at the fragile teacup, into which Constance had swirled plenty of milk and two heaping spoons of sugar as if drunkenness and despair might be relieved as simply as shock. She had little hope of the remedy, but after a tentative sip he drank it down in one go and held out the cup in a trembling hand, nodding for more. It was a hopeful sign. She poured him more tea and offered him the bread. He asked for sugar on it, as if he were a sick child, and she obliged, crushing the lumpy sugar with the back of a spoon and sprinkling it on the rank-smelling dripping. He watched in glassy-eyed fascination and ate it fast, as if she might seek to take it back from him.

Poppy declined tea. As Constance drank a cup, she watched Poppy make several turns up and down the room, even walking into the kitchen again, her brow furrowed in thought. At last she came and sat down. Sergeant Macintyre had finished his tea and his bread and fallen into a doze, his hands curled protectively around the china cup.

'We can't leave him like this,' Constance said quietly. 'I can't be sure how long those bottles have been collecting, but not long enough. There are enough fresh ones to have put a man in the hospital.'

'Maybe Mrs Black or her husband would stay with him for a while?' asked Poppy. 'Or we could call a doctor?'

'They won't be able to keep him from the drink,' said Constance. 'He'll need constant watching.' She looked around the grimy room. 'I'm not afraid of the nursing, but what will your mother and Mrs Fog think if we don't come home?'

'Well, I never thought I would lean on a sense of propriety,' said Poppy. 'But in this case I'm glad to say we can't possibly stay here. Besides, what would we do when he's awake and we're standing between him and the gin?'

'Then what are we to do?' asked Constance. 'Perhaps when we get home your brother will have some idea how to help him?'

'My brother!' Poppy jumped up. 'That's the very answer.'

'Good,' said Constance. She also stood up, glad to be going. They would call on Mrs Black to check in on the man occasionally and then they would be away on the road home. She could almost taste the fresher air of Sussex. But Poppy peered closely at Macintyre and then shook him roughly by the arm.

'What, who is it?' he asked, starting as Poppy caught the teacup falling from his slack fingers.

'Flight Sergeant, we have orders to take you to Captain Wirrall,' she said. 'Can you travel, my good man?'

'Captain Wirrall, is he wanting me?' asked Macintyre, straightening his spine. Some flicker of thought struggled against the thick blanket of intoxication. 'Is it the evening flight?'

'We need to pack him a few things,' said Poppy. 'Could you find him a few clothes, Constance? I'm not sure I'm up to rooting around up there.'

'But how are we to take him?' asked Constance. 'There's no room.' The sidecar might have accommodated an extra small child or a medium-sized dog, but a grown man would not physically fit with her, and the thought of a reeking body pressed against her was enough to make her blanch.

'We'll throw him in the sidecar and you'll take the pillion,' said Poppy. 'See if there's a clean pair of trousers up there. That skirt won't work for riding.' It was hard to say which was the more alarming, the thought of straddling the motorcycle at speed with nothing to hold on to but Poppy herself, or the idea of putting on a strange man's trousers to do so. She must have telegraphed her horror because Poppy took her by the elbow. 'Bear up now, Constance. We have to move fast while he's still in an amenable condition. You go upstairs and I'll pop round and explain things to Mrs Black.'

In the stinking bedroom above, Constance pulled open the drawers of a deal chest and tried not to look too closely as she pulled out shirts, socks and grey undergarments. From hooks behind the door she took down two pairs of wrinkled trousers, one wool and one flannel, a single black jacket and a khaki Flying Corps uniform. Only the uniform looked clean, still pressed along the seams. Almost sobbing, she tucked up her skirt and pulled on the uniform trousers beneath. They were too long and too wide. She rolled up the bottoms, then took the ribbon from under her shirt collar and tied it around her waist. Her thin petticoat she tucked into the trousers. Refusing to remove her skirt, she tucked one side of the hem into her waistband. Fortunately, there was no mirror to display the rather bulky effect.

A watch and a wallet stood on the bedside table alongside a small framed photograph of Sergeant Macintyre and his family. A woman with dark hair, a small girl and a baby dressed in a long christening gown, clustered on a chair with serious expressions, while a younger Sergeant Macintyre leaned on the chair back and smiled with paternal pride.

Constance took a deep breath and some of her horror faded into pity for the little family lost. She added the photograph and the other items to the pile of clothes. In a small drawer in the table she found a leather jewellery box and added it without looking inside. From a washstand she took a ragged toothbrush and tin of tooth powder, a razor and a strap. From the mantelpiece a uniform cap, three medals on wrinkled ribbons and a loose photograph of a smiling row of aviators; she could pick out Harris and, kneeling in the front, a smiling Macintyre. There was nothing else. No women's clothing, no hairbrush. But she had no time to wonder what he might have done with his wife's and daughters' dresses. Ignoring the stained sheets, she took a crocheted blanket from the foot of the bed and used it to bundle up Sergeant Macintyre's paltry belongings.

Downstairs again, she found Poppy in the kitchen. She had collected a pair of dusty black boots and a mackintosh and was now taking down an old tea tin from a high shelf.

'There's always a money tin somewhere,' said Poppy, rattling it. 'We'll give it to Harris to hold on to. The sergeant would only use it to buy liquor.'

'Are you sure he'll come quietly?' asked Constance. 'What if he tries to climb out while we are driving?'

'No use worrying about more emergencies than we already have,' said Poppy. 'Mrs Black is going to come in and give the place a good scrub once we're gone. I gave her some money for the landlord and to keep an eye on things until he gets back.'

∗

THE RUSH OF wind against her face, the bouncing of the wheels against the rough roads, the pressing of her clothes against her body were at first terrifying to Constance. But as she became more secure in the notion that she was not to be dragged under the motorcycle's wheels, or imminently pitched into the road to be crushed under some oncoming vehicle, she loosened her death grip on Poppy's waist and began to feel the exhilaration of flying along, not even the fragile walls of a sidecar between her body and the air. The only worry was the passenger in the sidecar, but no sound or movement came from the sealed carriage, and she could only hope he was being somehow lulled to sleep even at the rattling pace Poppy had set.

The long summer day was settling into evening as they reached the South Downs, and as the motorcycle coasted down the road to Penneston, and along the track to Poppy's barn, Constance felt as if weeks had passed since the morning. London had battered and bruised her but left her undefeated. A new resilience coursed through her tired body. A new determination, forged, perhaps, somewhere between her own disappointment and the anguish and pain of others. Her life held possibilities, her body held strength, and in her veins sang the blood of a woman riding the highways of England astride a roaring motorcycle.

'We can't take him to the hotel,' said Poppy when they came to a halt at the barn. 'I'll telephone Harris and get him to come here.' She stretched her back as she climbed from the machine. 'You stay here and watch in case he gets out.'

Constance was almost dizzy from the ride, the vibration echoing faintly in her teeth and fingers. She shook out her hands and strode around on the grass, her eyes on the sidecar. It remained closed and darkly ominous, like a fat, unexploded mine.

Chapter 15

HARRIS HAD MADE HIS APOLOGIES TO HIS MOTHER ABOUT dinner and retired to his room with a headache, and a tray of sandwiches and a bottle of wine ordered from downstairs. He asked not to be disturbed. He always claimed a headache because it caused less anguish on his mother's face than if he complained about the leg, which often radiated its ache like a blunt iron nail hammered bone to bone through his body. And he could not explain the quicksand drag of his melancholy, which sometimes made going into public an impossible task. She would only try to cheer him up, jollying him along with talk of the aeroplane restoration or, now that he had given her and Poppy a plain talk about the state of Penneston's affairs, discussing her elaborate plans for fiscal responsibility. She could not understand that neither these nor any topic, no matter how encouragingly presented, had any bearing on his pain or occasional despair. Instead he would sink all the lower under her coaxing face. He had been doing better lately, but this evening, he was suffering from all three maladies. While the leg only threatened to do its worst, and the melancholy felt more like boredom than an aversion to life itself, the headache part was for once the truth. He planned an early night and would eat his dinner in his dressing gown.

He was dozing in a chair by the open window, the iron band around his head easing as the sounds of the promenade below merged into his daydreams, when a tentative knocking startled him awake. It came again, a quiet knocking, not from his mother's suite but from the door that connected his room to the hallway.

'I am not to be disturbed,' he called out.

'Sir, I have a private message,' came the low, fervent reply from one of the hotel pages. 'They said it was urgent, sir?'

'Damn,' he said under his breath. He disliked being caught out. He reached for his leg, which he had unstrapped for comfort and let fall to the thick carpet. It was a fine piece of engineering, aluminium for lightness and polished oak for strength, but its several straps required some moments of work. 'I'm not dressed,' he said. 'Could you put it under the door?'

'Yes, sir. Shall I wait for a reply, sir?' The solicitous boy no doubt wanted his tuppenny gratuity.

'Come back in ten minutes,' said Harris. 'I may have something for you.'

The note from his sister, as transcribed by the hotel telephone operator, was discreetly cryptic.

Please come to the barn now.
An old friend sends his regards.
No need to worry Mother. Do not telephone.

He did not wish to get dressed and go all the way out to Penneston. His headache had just lost its grip and he was comfortable where he was. And what on earth was so urgent but could not be explained with the hotel telephone operator listening in? Yet it was not like Poppy to be dramatic. Stubborn, unconventional, inappropriate at times, but she was not prone to hysterics. So he dressed again, in his most comfortable flannels and a slightly disreputable old blazer, and when the boy returned, he gave him sixpence and asked him to have the doorman hail a taxi to the side door so he would not have to parade through the lobby without dinner clothes.

When he got to the barn, the doors were shut. He pushed open the side door, which flew back and bounced against the wooden wall with a loud crack. Constance Haverhill's face appeared over the back of one of Poppy's sagging sofas.

'You startled me,' she said. 'I was dozing.' She did not seem as discomfited as he would have expected to be found sleeping in Poppy's barn, slightly dishevelled from a day's travel, with her jacket off and smut on her cheek.

'Are you all right?' he asked. She had settled back down in a corner of the sofa and was rubbing her eyes like a child. The innocence of the gesture jolted something in him. He wondered what it would be like to watch her sleep. With a cough, he remembered he was annoyed at being summoned. 'Is Poppy all right?'

'She just went over to Penneston to find some old clothing of your father's.' She yawned. 'He didn't seem to have any pyjamas, you see. I was afraid he would wake up and I'd be here all alone, but she said you were on your way directly.' She smiled now as if all were resolved.

'Who doesn't have any pyjamas?' he asked. 'What on earth are you talking about?'

Her eyes widened and she blinked at him.

'I thought Poppy told you,' she said. 'Didn't she telephone you while I was getting him into bed?'

'She told me nothing,' he said. 'Who are you putting to bed?'

'I hope we've done the right thing,' she said, doubt flickering now across her face. 'I won't claim it was Poppy's idea because I could have objected more strongly. In our defence, we thought you were the best person to help.'

'Miss Haverhill?' He tried not to glare.

'It's your mechanic friend, Mr Macintyre,' she said. 'He's come to stay— Or rather, we may have kidnapped him.'

With a set jaw, and a prayer against falling, Harris followed Constance up the rickety stairs to the loft room and found Jock Macintyre asleep on one of the four narrow iron beds, snoring and trembling. He was thinner than Harris remembered, his cheeks hollow. He was bandaged about the head and dressed in dirty, wrinkled clothes. His feet stuck out from under the sheet, and his socks had holes in them. A clean, still-wet basin stood on the floor beside him, an acrid smell suggesting it had been used and emptied. Harris sank onto the neighbouring bedstead.

'But he never really drank. He was always neat. It was a matter of pride for him that the job might be dirty but he was always ready for inspection.' Harris was saying the wrong thing, easier to grasp at small irrelevancies. He felt a hand press briefly on his shoulder.

'After such a tragedy, who can blame him for breaking,' Constance said quietly. Downstairs, she had told him briefly, reluctantly, about Arabella and the two daughters.

Harris had met them once. A smiling woman and a curly-haired toddler, who stared at him round-eyed, the baby in a basket. They had taken the train and a bus to visit Macintyre for a half day at the airfield barracks. Such a difficult journey for just a few hours, and it began to drizzle. Harris had offered them his room to meet in and left them tea and a Dundee cake that his mother had sent him from Fortnum's. After they left he found a small clothes-peg dolly, dressed in a scrap of calico, tucked up neatly in his cot and forgotten. He returned it to Jock, who slipped it into his breast pocket saying, 'Those women, they'll do anything to keep an eye on you!' But he had patted his pocket with pride, a catch in his voice.

In the semi-darkness of the room, Harris cleared his throat.

'Has Poppy called the doctor? We should know how badly off he is.'

'She thought you might telephone if needed,' said Constance. 'It would look better than us calling.'

'You might have thought of that before abducting him,' said Harris. 'He can't stay here. I don't know what she was thinking.'

'I thought there was alcohol at the hotel,' said Poppy, clomping up the stairs and entering the loft with an armful of clothing. 'I thought it might be better if you took care of him out here, locked up where there are no temptations.'

'Me take care of him?' he asked. 'Either he needs a hospital or he'll be fine. The doctor should advise us.'

'He's survived the trip down from London, so I don't think he's dying,' said Constance. 'But he needs help. The drink has a hold on him.'

'I doubt he'll stay, and in my condition I'm not going to be able to force him to.' Harris stopped, not wanting to sound like he was whining. But he looked around the clean but primitive room in dismay. He had done his duty in the war and never complained about the freezing barracks, eating from cauldrons of boiled mush, pushing his chilblained feet into damp boots twice a day for endless sorties over France, but enough was enough. His leg had surely earned him his quiet billet at the hotel.

'Maybe a job is all he needs to stop trying to drink himself to death?' added Poppy. 'You'll remember we need a mechanic?'

'Women have such touching faith in the redeeming power of regular employment.'

'I believe he saved your life, Captain Wirrall?' said Constance. Her voice was low, as if she were utterly disappointed in him. 'Poppy was sure you would want us to bring him.'

'Of course, you just took me by surprise,' he said, improvising hastily. To disappoint her now would be unchivalrous, he told himself. Her brown eyes were blinking sleepily, and her hair was blown and stuck about her face from the riding. Also his sister was glaring at him like an Amazon ready to charge. So he would stay the night, he decided, and see how Jock was in the morning. They'd have a laugh over the women fussing too much. He could put Jock on a train by midday, not forgetting a simple expression of his condolences to be spoken through the train window. No point dragging out the emotion. 'I'll do what I can, Miss Haverhill,' he added.

'I could come back in the morning,' she said. 'I have some experience in nursing.'

'I'm sure he'll be fine,' he said. 'I'll call the doctor to come by first thing if he's not.'

'Don't be silly,' said Poppy. 'I'll just pack a bag, then I'll take Constance back to the hotel and stay in your room tonight, Brother. It's lucky Iris hasn't forgiven me and come back yet, so the barn is all yours. Tomorrow we'll both be back with more supplies. There are eggs and bread in the pantry and half a bottle of milk if either of you is hungry. Be careful with the gas ring, it can be temperamental. Have an extra match ready.' She opened a pine wardrobe and began to stuff clothes into a large satchel, then added a brush and pot of cold cream from a narrow shelf under a window.

'But you can't leave me here alone like this,' said Harris. 'I didn't bring so much as a toothbrush.'

'It's lucky the peace treaty talks were successful, Constance,' said Poppy, 'because our military men are turning soft as blancmange. Don't worry, Harris, I'll bring you a toothbrush and some smelling salts in the morning.' She ushered Constance down the stairs, and Harris heard their voices fading into the soft evening. The loft was made dark by the glow of sunset coming in at the small open windows. Jock Macintyre, sweating and trembling, with hands curled like claws, snored heavily. Harris hoped he was out for the night, but he had seen men in this condition too many times. He moved to a bed further away from the ripe stench, hung his blazer on the bed knob and lay down in his clothes. It was liable to be a long night, struggling up and down the stairs with a bucket and water jug.

IT WAS DARK as the motorcycle pulled up the hotel driveway. After a word with the doorman, Poppy parked it in the service driveway.

'Do you want to come along to Mother's suite and have some supper with me?' she asked. 'I'm going to have a quick tidy-up and order a few things.'

'If you don't mind, I'm thinking of a hot bath and a bowl of soup,' said Constance. 'It's been quite a day.'

'I'm sorry about the job,' said Poppy. 'I know you were counting on it.'

'I still have a few weeks to go, living in a hotel at the seaside,' said

Constance. 'When I think about poor Jock Macintyre's little girls—
Well, I will count my blessings and think no further than a long hot
soak.'

'That's the spirit! I knew you were a trouper.' Poppy took Constance
by the arm. 'I do think Harris will do wonders for the poor man,' she
added, 'but is it selfish to hope that we may have a mechanic to go with
our aeroplane?'

'Yes it is, and you are a terrible person,' said Constance, and they
strode together into the hotel foyer, grubby, exhausted and laughing.

'Constance Haverhill, where on earth have you been,' said a piercing
voice. From the wine-coloured velvet depths of the circular settee at the
heart of the lobby, a woman rose in a swirl of grey silk and gardenia perfume. Flanked by the hotel manager, Mr Smickle, and the undermanager, Dudley, the woman glared and pointed her fan across the room like
a bayonet. 'What have you done with my poor mother?' It was, Constance realised with horror, Lady Mercer.

'Never fear, I shall stand with you against the Gorgon,' whispered
Poppy, squeezing her arm.

'I appreciate the thought, but please don't,' said Constance. 'I'll have
enough to explain to Lady Mercer without her being distracted by your
trousers.'

She gave Poppy as confident a smile as she could, but to walk across
the marble floor alone felt like doom. She knew she was as dishevelled as
a banshee, coming in after dark, unchaperoned, and having abandoned
Mrs Fog. With every step the enormity of her conduct seemed to grow,
and she knew there would be no avoiding the consequences. She con-
centrated on breathing and keeping her chin high as her new-found confidence seemed to drain out through her boot soles.

Mr Smickle, careful to avoid a scene, ushered them into the small Blue
Salon used for meetings.

'This is much more private and comfortable,' he said. 'We are so glad
to see you, Miss Haverhill. As I told Lady Mercer, I was sure some inno-

cent explanation would spare us from reporting your disappearance to the constable.'

'Thank you. I was merely out for the day. I was not aware I needed to report my intentions to the front desk?'

'Of course not—' He squirmed.

'Where is my mother and why are you not by her side?' said Lady Mercer. 'I was not aware you were sent here to abandon a helpless woman while you go off day-tripping.'

'She is perfectly fine.' Constance hesitated, but it was clear that Mrs Fog's desire to keep her affairs private from her daughter would shortly involve hysterics and the police if Constance did not tell some sort of truth. She began with as bland a version as she could manage. 'Mrs Fog was kind enough to allow me the day, as she was going to stay overnight with old friends in Cabbage Beach.'

'What are you talking about? She has no friends in the area.'

'An old school friend and her brother,' said Constance. 'I've met them and they are very lovely and very respectable. She'll be home tomorrow and can tell you all about it.'

'What old friend?' asked Lady Mercer. 'Why would she not return to her perfectly good hotel at night?'

'They have a lovely home,' began Constance.

'Their names, girl!' There was nothing for it, and Constance sank onto a chair in defeat.

'Their name is de Champney,' she said. 'Mr Simon de Champney and his sister, Miss Mathilde de Champney. A school friend from Mrs Fog's childhood.'

Lady Mercer sat down abruptly in a chair, her face drained. Mr Smickle fussed.

'Some water, dear lady? Dudley, fetch some water.'

'Please leave us,' said Lady Mercer. The fan was employed again, waving the manager away. 'We will not require the constable, I now see. The negligence in allowing my mother to be removed from this hotel is Miss

Haverhill's. I will no longer hold you at fault, sir.' If this was as inadequate an apology as he had ever heard, Mr Smickle did not object but showed his seasoned shrewdness by merely bowing and signalling Dudley to join him in withdrawing.

'We had no notice of your arrival,' said Constance. 'What brings you to Sussex?'

'Those who would change their behaviour on notice of inspection must be doing something wrong,' said Lady Mercer. 'Rachel is coming home unexpectedly early. Her fiancé has a mission to the American delegation in Paris and they arrive next Tuesday by ship at Southampton, from where he goes immediately to Dover. It seemed convenient to meet him here, and to spend a few quiet days beforehand with my mother.'

'Mrs Fog will be so excited to see them,' said Constance. 'I'm not sure what time she had planned to be back tomorrow, but I can send a message first thing in the morning.'

'I cannot express enough my disappointment that you have abandoned my mother, in her frail condition, to the home of these strangers.'

'Friends, I assure you—' began Constance.

'An unsuitable connection severed many years ago.' Lady Mercer's face creased as she held a hand to her eyes. 'My mother promised me, when I was a young woman getting engaged.' She looked up sharply and stared at Constance. 'You've seen them, of course. What has she told you about him?'

'Nothing!' Constance was puzzled now. 'Only that Mathilde is her old school friend and Mr de Champney is the brother,' she added. 'But she seemed so happy to go. I assure you she is safe with them.'

'Convenient for you, no doubt.' Lady Mercer stared up and down, and Constance knew she was begrimed and sweaty. 'Where have you been?'

Constance bit back a retort as to it being none of the lady's business and opted for a simulated meekness. 'I have been to London to look for employment,' she said. 'I was chaperoned all the way by Miss Wirrall, whom you may have seen with me in the lobby. She is the daughter of the late Sir John Wirrall of Penneston.'

'Wirrall? I've never heard of him. A mere baronet, no doubt. Wasn't there some divorce scandal involving a Wirrall . . . ?'

'I'd like to take a bath and get out of these dusty clothes,' said Constance. 'Is Lord Mercer with you or would you like me to accompany you to dinner?' Lady Mercer gave a grim smile and Constance realised that the Lady Mercers of this world would not be denied a place in the dining room because of their sex.

'I certainly do not need you,' said Lady Mercer. 'Please give the front desk instructions to send for my mother first thing in the morning and tell her of my arrival.'

'I will,' said Constance.

'Tomorrow we will make some changes. After this debacle I think it best if we make other arrangements for my mother. We shall see about tickets and put you on a train home.'

'But Rachel is coming . . .' There was a pause.

'And you will be allowed to see her, of course,' Lady Mercer said, frowning. 'I believe my generosity and my fondness for your mother has always led me to treat you like family.' Her gaze shifted away. 'But after Tuesday, as my mother seems to have no need of you, we will not keep you from your brother and his family.'

'I will go home if Mrs Fog has no more use for me,' said Constance. 'I have many things of my mother's to sort through at the cottage.'

'As it happens, we have employed a new estate manager with a rather large brood,' said Lady Mercer. 'I meant to write to you. They required immediate housing, so we have had to make the cottage ready for them. But do not worry, I have already had your things very carefully packed and moved to your brother's farm.'

'I do not believe I have done anything to deserve such callousness,' said Constance, anger breaking through her exhaustion. All her mother's things, that she had kept so carefully in place; putting off the day she would go through them, with reverence and love, and pack them away. Now they had been seized by uncaring hands and tossed into the straw of packing crates to be stacked in some cold, damp shed. Her home gone, emptied in haste and invaded by strangers.

'Callous? This from the young woman, entrusted with my mother's care, who abandoned her side for a jaunt to London?' Lady Mercer also raised her voice. 'Even as you disappoint me, I have thought only of your mother and provided for your proper happiness.'

'My mother would not appreciate such treatment of her daughter,' said Constance, her voice calm now but firm. She was surprised at her own boldness. 'But I will leave if Mrs Fog wishes me to.'

'With Rachel's return I'm sure my mother will be amply attended,' said Lady Mercer. She rose with clamped lips and shook out her skirt. 'We will sort this out tomorrow after I see my mother safely returned.'

'Of course,' said Constance.

'You are dismissed,' said Lady Mercer. Constance walked to the door, her heart pounding with anger and hurt to be so disgraced. As she left the room, Lady Mercer launched one final insult disguised as a gift.

'And, of course, your train fare will be paid.'

Chapter 16

SLEEPING FITFULLY, HARRIS AWOKE AT EVERY GROAN
from Jock, who snored and rolled and tested the squeaking bedsprings
to their utmost with his flailing. He seemed to struggle at times, his
breath snagging and his face purple and wet with sweat. Harris's left leg
ached but he had not dared to remove his prosthetic. Once or twice he
got up to poke Jock, just to make sure he was alive. Not since the war had
he slept in his clothes, itchy, bunching, the chafe of rough seams. It had
once been easy to sleep in the barracks, knowing the dawn raid was inevitable, consumed by the rhythm of the sorties, nowhere else to be,
nothing else a worry. When death was the largest concern, he supposed
everything else was simple. Now, in the peace, every small thing in life
was a difficulty, every step forward met with a blow to set one back. He
sighed and stretched his limbs, his own bedstead launching a volley of
squeaking. He would rouse himself to action in the morning, he thought.
He would make Jock the only focus and to damnation with all the rest. In
the small window, the moon was fading as the dawn came up. A single
bird began to warble in an unseen hedgerow.

When he woke again, the sun was pitching hot on the barn roof. He
remembered where he was, but Jock Macintyre was not in the other bed.
He wondered for a moment if it had been some sort of drunken dream,
but an acrid odour, warmed over and not improved by the morning sun,
was as sharp as smelling salts. In addition, there was a great clattering

downstairs and, though his sister was clumsy as women go, he was fairly sure a man was ransacking the cupboards. He swung both legs off the bed and eased his way to his feet as he had to do every morning, gingerly testing his muscles, his good ankle, as if he was an old man. Pausing on two feet, finding his cane, using a bed rail and a chair back, then holding on to the stout door, he found his balance and a stronger stride and made his way downstairs.

Jock had left drawers and doors open around Poppy's minimal kitchen; pots and pans half out, a colander rolling into a corner. He was already deep into a mechanic's cupboard, pulling out and pushing aside toolboxes and crates of spare parts.

'Good morning, Jock,' said Harris, deliberately nonchalant. 'Did you find the teakettle?'

'Do you not have a single bottle of stout or a drop of your fancy sherry in the place, Captain?' He scowled and blinked in the strong morning light. 'With the hammers going in my head, it's either the hair of the dog or the grave for me, and believe me, you don't know the price of coffins these days like I do.' He continued his rummaging.

'What you need is tea and bacon,' said Harris. 'Did you find any during your search?'

'I need a drink,' said Jock. 'I got the shakes, see? I swear I'll go mad if I don't have something.' He held out his arms. His hands trembled violently.

'Make the tea, Sergeant, there's a good chap,' said Harris. 'Then maybe I can find a spot of something to go in it?'

'Yes, sir,' said Jock, military compliance still ingrained in his very muscles. He filled the battered black teakettle at the tin sink and set it on a gas ring. He emptied a large brown teapot by hurling the tea leaves out of the door into the grass.

'Leave the door open,' ordered Harris. The smell of Jock Macintyre was beginning to fill this new space too.

Jock took up a brown packet of tea, which was lying sideways on the kitchen table, almost spilled from his earlier efforts, and spooned a large quantity into the teapot. He took down two tin mugs from hooks on the bare board wall and found the half bottle of milk in the dark pantry. While the kettle began to steam he sat himself down in a chair with heavy carelessness, as if he were a sack of potatoes.

'I haven't seen bacon since I came home,' he said. 'When we were first married, her uncle used to send us a whole slab of smoked pork-back every Christmas.' He hung his head and, to Harris's horror, began to weep.

'I'm so sorry,' said Harris. 'I wrote to you.'

'Writing paper was not exactly high on my list,' said Jock. 'I weren't up to much. I just like to sit very quiet like and see if I can hear 'em around me.' He looked up and did not try to wipe away the tears that left streaks down his face. 'Can't hear nothing here, not with the bloody sheep and the wind. Where the hell am I, anyway? I don't remember much.'

'My sister and a friend brought you here. They were worried about you,' said Harris. 'You're at my home in Sussex.'

'Thought you were better off than this,' said Jock.

'This is my sister's barn. She thought it would be discreet.'

'I thought they were angels.' He shook his head slowly. 'You can't always trust the liquor in Cheapside.' The kettle whistled and Jock got up with some effort and poured it, with trembling hands, into the pot. There was a biscuit tin on the table, and Harris was relieved to find a paper bag of plain biscuits inside.

'My sister will be back this morning with real food and such,' said Harris.

'I'm really sick,' said Jock. 'You got a nip of brandy?'

'I'm afraid not,' said Harris. It was nominally true. His silver flask was in his jacket upstairs. 'Look, I'm glad they brought you here, Jock. I'd like to ask you to stay a bit. Get free from the booze, get yourself well and so on. You've had a bad time of it and I'd like to help.'

'If you had a bit of brandy, you'd be helping me,' said Jock, wiping his face with the back of a hand.

'What would Arabella want you to do?' he asked gently. 'Would she like to see you this way?' Jock's face seemed to grow blank, and he stared as if at an unpleasant stranger.

'What would you know about it?' he asked. 'You have no idea what it is to lose everything.'

'You're right, I expect I don't.' Harris felt a small creeping shame, conscious that he spent much of his time thinking he did. It was funny, he thought, how each person saw their own circumstances loom large, as if through a telescope, and the tribulations of others as if backwards through the small end. Viewed through some universal lens, he doubted that his own suffering was anywhere near as pitiful as he had thought, indulging it night after black night.

'I'm sorry, losing the leg is hard all right,' said Jock. 'But I tell you, I'd give all my limbs to see my girls one more time.'

'Well, to get my leg back I might be willing to give up my sister,' said Harris. 'Strictly on a temporary basis of course.'

'Don't joke about it,' said Jock, but his lips twitched and Harris was relieved to see some brightness return to his eyes. 'She's quite a force, your sister. At least I seem to remember being forcefully shoved into some sort of box as I was being kidnapped.'

'Sidecar,' said Harris. 'My sister's friend, Constance Haverhill, had to ride pillion all the way from London. Quite a sacrifice for the young lady. I suppose you might hang about a few days and pretend they helped?' He had not expected to be so happy to see Jock and, in the light of day, the idea of keeping him around seemed less ridiculous.

'I got things to do,' said Jock. He did not volunteer any details, by which Harris understood he had no job to go to. 'You can't keep me here, you know.'

'I just thought if you're looking for work, I could use a mechanic,' said Harris. He stood up. 'Come and see my sister's latest project.' He moved to the big doors at the front of the barn and opened them out, squeezing his eyes shut against the glare of the sunny morning. He moved quickly to pull the tarpaulin from the aeroplane.

'Well, I'll be . . .' Jock walked over to pat the fuselage. 'Do you want help breaking it up for the parts, Captain?'

'No, my sister wants me to fix it. She seems to think I can fly again, which is endearing, as everyone else assures me I'm finished.'

'Remember when we used to send the cadets out in old fuselages with no wings to trundle about on the runway?' said Jock. 'But I expect you will want to actually get up in the air.'

'I hope so.' Harris was surprised to find that he spoke the truth. A new glimmer of optimism sat uncomfortably inside him, worrying the edges of his comfortable melancholy and threatening to lighten his usual bleakness. He frowned, as if to squash the thought.

'You'd think after all we've seen that never would be too soon to see another aeroplane, but it doesn't work that way, does it?' said Jock. 'This one's a real wounded comrade, isn't she?'

'Can she be fixed up?' asked Harris. 'My sister wants me to set up a flying school for ladies.'

'Blimey! Just because it's got dual controls doesn't mean it's not a Sopwith Camel,' said Jock. 'Would you put a child on a wild stallion, or your grandmother behind the wheel of a racing car?'

'Let's worry about fixing her first, Jock,' Harris said with a laugh. 'And I dare you to make any such comparisons in front of my sister.'

Jock hiked himself up into the cockpit and then leaned out over the hump to peer deep into the crevices of the rotary engine.

'I'd have to strip the engine down and see what's what,' he said, climbing down again. 'But then there's the spars and cabling. She'll need new linen in places. It's not a one-man job if you want it done this side of Christmas.'

'My sister has someone who's a whiz with engines who can help you,' said Harris. 'And she's got a person who worked in linen sewing and doping. I'm sure we can round up a few others.' He thought it best not to mention that they might all be women. There was no need to spook Jock before he committed to staying.

Jock walked away to a tree stump and pulled a tobacco tin from his pocket. He had some trouble rolling a cigarette with his shaking hands and Harris bit back an urge to offer his help. After lighting a match and taking a draw, Jock turned aside and retched into a clump of nettles.

'I'll be sick as a dog for days,' he said. 'And who says I'm ready to join your temperance army?'

'Good God, man, anyone can see you're trying to kill yourself,' said Harris. 'You saved my life, Jock. At least give me a chance to return the favour. Try it a week or two. If you don't like it, I'll drive you back to London with a crate of gin and no hard feelings.'

'D'you have a wee something to seal the deal, then?' asked Jock.

'Yes, an hour's hike over the Downs and a cold bath should do it,' said Harris.

'All right, we'll see who's the bigger invalid then,' said Jock.

'Oh, I'm not coming,' said Harris. 'I can't go far yet without getting tired.'

'If I go, you go,' said Jock. 'And if you fall down, don't expect me to carry you.'

SITTING ON A chair he had dragged into the sun, Harris closed his eyes and tried to ignore the throbbing in his left leg. It had not been hard to keep up with Jock. The man suffered a combination of hangover and withdrawal that caused him to stumble often, to occasionally stop and blink hard to recover his vision, and once or twice to bend over gasping for air and clutching at his chest. Harris had taken the lead, stepping carefully but swinging his stick at a good pace. Leading the way, he had offered one or two words of manly motivation. Jock returned the favour by pushing him along with a robust profusion of profanities. All in all, he had enjoyed the walk out, following the gentle slope of the fields down towards the Morris estate and the distant Hazelbourne airfield. It was the walk back that did the damage. The hill might have looked slight but soon the two of them were finding reason to pause. The rolling land seemed to tip ever upward on a new axis, as gruelling as an alpine pass, and by the time they regained the barn, Harris found himself as sweaty and out of breath as Jock. Unwilling to admit he could go no further, he had sent Jock in to take a bath.

His sister arrived in a cloud of dust and Harris could see Constance Haverhill in the sidecar, along with a large hamper and his Gladstone bag. Mortified by his dishevelled appearance, he levered his way upright, one set of joints at a time, and hastily tucked in his shirt. He was conscious of being rumpled and possibly odorous. Jock strolled out of the barn, nonchalant in a somewhat cleaner change of clothes, with wet-combed hair and smelling of soap.

'You might want to see to your collar stud, Captain,' said Jock. 'The ladies are quick to draw the worst conclusions about a man.'

'You bear complete responsibility for my dishevelled looks,' said Harris, fishing about to reattach his collar and wondering who decided it was necessary to make men's studs fit only the narrow-fingered dexterity of a child. 'The smell of carbolic won't let you off the hook, I can assure you.'

'I'm not here to be charming,' said Jock. 'I didnae ask to be here.'

'But they come bearing breakfast, so perhaps a veneer of politeness just until we've got a plate of bacon in hand?'

Poppy seemed nervous. She was usually quite bossy, but this morning there was a layer of anxious feminine fussing that seemed to Constance to be quite foreign. She hovered over the carrying in of the hamper and worried over the contents of the bag she had packed for Harris. And she proposed to make breakfast herself as if the domestic sphere were quite normal to her. Her brother laughed out loud.

'Dear me, I fear you are to be punished now, Jock,' he said. 'My sister is to torture us by murdering our breakfast.'

'Do go and change, Harris,' said Poppy. 'Constance and I have to be gone in less than an hour and we have much to discuss.'

Wirrall's Ladies Conveyance was expected in Cabbage Beach at ten to pick up the truant Mrs Fog, and Constance had allowed herself to be persuaded to come along. When she had answered an early knock at her door this morning, she found Poppy dressed and reporting a large hamper of food already stowed on the motorcycle. Given that the world seemed so much changed by Lady Mercer's arrival, it had been irritating, Poppy's blithe assumption that Constance would be free to jaunt off to the barn to deliver breakfast and support to Harris and Jock.

'I had better stay close and wait for Lady Mercer to summon me,' Constance had said, though she trembled with unhappiness. She was too ashamed to admit that she was to be sent away, like a servant.

'No, no, you must come and help me face them,' Poppy had urged. 'Besides, I got a message to pick up Mrs Fog at ten o'clock. Come with me now and then we can go there straight from the barn.'

'I should like to speak to Mrs Fog before she sees Lady Mercer,' said Constance, wondering if she dared hide for a few more hours.

'That's settled, then,' said Poppy, seeming relieved. 'Meet me by the side door in a quarter of an hour.'

Now Poppy cracked eggs in a bowl and sizzled bacon in an old black frying pan, her sleeves dangerously close to a high gas flame.

'I can't toast the bread, and I could fry it but there isn't another pan; do you think they'll mind if it's just buttered?' she said. She seemed bent on breakfast as the key to diplomacy, as if a good spread might make Jock decide to stay.

'It will all be fine,' said Constance. 'Unless you burn the place down with that flame.'

'Just pour the tea, will you?' asked Poppy. 'Take some out to our guest, and for goodness' sake keep him happy.'

Outside, Constance offered a cup of tea to Jock and stood awkwardly with her own cup.

'The prisoner is to be fed and watered, I see,' he said. He gestured for her to sit on the bench and moved slightly away to a convenient tree stump. 'I suppose you think it's more than I deserve, miss, given my conduct.'

'You were not taken prisoner, Sergeant Macintyre,' said Constance. 'We thought you were in trouble and in need of rescue.'

'I'll apologise for you having to see me in such a state, but I'll not apologise for being in any state I like in my own house, minding my own business.'

'Would you say that to a fireman if your house was ablaze?' said Constance. 'Some things are an emergency.'

'I've told the Captain I'll not be staying more'n a few days,' said Jock. 'I don't need you nor him to save me.' He took a swallow of the strong tea and shook his head. 'It wouldn't work anyway, miss. Some of us are just beyond saving.' He appeared a little too satisfied with this pronouncement and, as he looked away over the fields in noble resignation, Constance felt her anger flash.

'Your losses are unimaginable, Sergeant, and were we to stack them side by side, no one would begrudge you the larger share of pain,' she said, wondering what they had become that there was an urge to sort and rank the sorrow. 'But has it occurred to you yet that perhaps Poppy brought you here not to save you but so that you can save your friend?'

'The Captain?' he said, and turned towards her, frowning. 'He seems fine. I mean he lost the leg, but he nearly walked me into the ground this morning. What would he need with me apart from getting that pile of junk – which it will take a miracle to save – into the air?'

'It's not for me to say,' said Constance. 'But you are not the only one who feels they have lost too much.' Though she would be ashamed to compare her own troubles to his, the man could not know how hard it was to face disgrace and to contemplate leaving these people and the humble barn he was so keen to despise. Frustrated, she rose to her feet and threw the dregs of her tea into the weeds. Inside the barn, a spoon rang against a pot and Poppy's voice called them to breakfast. 'Shall we go in?' said Constance. 'I hope you like your bacon cooked to cinders.'

In Cabbage Beach, Simon de Champney waved Constance into the house. 'Eleanor is in the garden,' he said. 'Her bag is packed, but I'm not quite sure she can be persuaded to leave. She has been rather upset since getting the message.'

At the end of the lawn, Mrs Fog was standing looking out at the sea, her hat and gloves tossed aside on a deckchair. Her hair ruffled in the breeze, but her back was rigid. Constance cleared her throat, sensing her unhappiness.

'Poppy and I have come to fetch you. Are you ready to go?'

'I don't like to be ordered home like a schoolgirl,' said Mrs Fog, her voice cracking. 'Why does my daughter insist on descending without notice?'

'Rachel telegraphed her arrival in Southampton next Tuesday,' said Constance. 'I'm not sure Lady Mercer had much notice herself.'

'I hoped I would have more time,' said Mrs Fog. 'More days to just be happy. No explanations, no family difficulties. Just a few more days outside of time and the world.'

'So did I,' said Constance. 'But surely you will be overjoyed to see Rachel again?'

'Yes, perhaps with Rachel arriving my daughter will be too busy to make a fuss over me,' said Mrs Fog. 'And I suppose if you are leaving for London, matters would have come to a head anyway.'

'I'm not going to London,' said Constance. 'It turned out not to be a suitable situation.'

'I'm sorry,' said Mrs Fog. 'So we may go on together some while yet.'

'Lady Mercer has told me my services are no longer required,' said Constance. 'I am to return to Surrey immediately.'

'Return home?' asked Mrs Fog. 'What nonsense.'

'She was rather angry with me for leaving your side, and I don't altogether blame her,' said Constance, unable to keep a tremor from her voice. 'She thinks I allowed you to be spirited away by the de Champneys and I get the impression she does not approve of them?'

'Yes, she does not approve,' said Mrs Fog. She smiled enigmatically.

'I'm sorry if I have been somewhat difficult to manage.' She took Constance's hand in both of hers and gave it an encouraging pat. 'I will explain to my daughter that you are not to blame. I will not allow you to be sent home.'

'I'm sorry for telling her,' said Constance, feeling a worse traitor for Mrs Fog's kindness. 'She was about to send out a search party.'

'No one has anything for which to be sorry,' said Mrs Fog. 'Not you, not I, and certainly not Simon and Mathilde. Shall we go and face the music together?'

Simon de Champney was in the living room. He appeared to be reading, but Constance noticed that, seeing them in the doorway, he snapped the book shut without marking the page. He got to his feet and reached out to take Mrs Fog by the hand.

'Do you wish me to accompany you?' he asked, his face grave.

'No, this is for me to set right,' said Mrs Fog. 'It always has been, and I have been remiss too many times, my friend.' He kissed her hand and then, to Constance's surprise, he leaned in and gave her a lingering kiss on the cheek. Hand in hand they walked ahead of Constance through the house and out to the waiting Poppy.

'You will return to us soon, I hope,' he said, handing Mrs Fog into the sidecar.

'I only wish I had gone visiting with Mathilde this morning. Then I would not have been home to be called away.' Constance stowed the small travelling bag at Mrs Fog's feet and climbed behind Poppy. 'Goodness,' added Mrs Fog. 'You had better not let my daughter see you with your skirt all hitched up, my dear. I fear we will be completely undone.'

Chapter 17

ᴏɴ ᴛʜᴇ Pᴀʟᴍ Tᴇʀʀᴀᴄᴇ, ᴛʜᴇ ᴜꜱᴜᴀʟ ʙʀɪɢʜᴛ ʙᴜʀʙʟᴇ ᴏꜰ conversation seemed muffled, an alteration so subtle as to be invisible to the casual observer, but which Constance recognised as a humming resentment.

At the centre of the room's dislocation sat Lady Mercer, installed in a prime window-front location by Dudley, who was even now presenting a padded footstool while the waiter, Klaus, followed with a large tray of hot chocolate and éclairs. The regular denizens, who had been nudged aside as ripples on a pond might displace surprised ducks, fidgeted, ruffled in unfamiliar chairs, looking askance at their complimentary bouillon as if it were the thin gruel of the workhouse.

Mrs Fog's whist group had their heads together a few windows away, and Constance could see the gossip shimmering about them. Mrs Fog, her lips pressed, sat quietly with her daughter and accepted a cup of hot chocolate that was sure to roil her digestion. Constance fought an urge to smooth her hair again. She had changed into her second-best white summer dress and added a bright pink ribbon and silver brooch to the lace collar. She had intended such finery as armour, but now it felt more like capitulation.

'Ah, Dudley, could you bring a chair for dear Miss Haverhill?' said Mrs Fog. 'Constance, we are just talking about Rachel's impending arrival.'

'Any chair will do. We really shouldn't make so much work for you,' said Lady Mercer to Dudley, and Constance wondered if she was about to be offered the footstool instead. Dudley brought a light wicker chair from one of the small tables and Constance thanked him. 'I'm sure Constance will prefer bouillon,' Lady Mercer added. 'These girls are so protective of their figures.'

'Yes, madam, the waiter will bring it right away,' said Dudley, clicking his fingers at Klaus. 'And meanwhile, ladies, do remember to look out the window when you hear the klaxon.' He went away along the room to speak to other groups.

'Ah yes, we are to be assaulted with the noise of that dreadful submarine on the beach being blown to pieces,' said Lady Mercer as Klaus approached with a bouillon cup on a saucer. 'But the young man assured us we need only cover our ears briefly.'

'Yes, madam,' said the waiter. 'I believe they expect to slice it in two with a single cannon blast. 'You will enjoy a front-row view from here.'

'Extraordinary!' said Lady Mercer, in a voice that carried to all the neighbouring tables. 'I can't imagine such a thing passing as entertainment in Brighton or in St-Tropez.' Constance suppressed a grin, having never personally seen Lady Mercer leave her gardens in Surrey to visit the seaside either at home or abroad.

'I suppose it's entirely safe,' said Mrs Fog. 'Perhaps we should move away from the windows?'

'Nonsense, Mother, the view is in obvious demand.' Indeed, there were more hotel guests and others crowding at the door and Klaus moved away to assist the undermanager in finding seats for the new arrivals.

'Rachel coming home is such an unexpected pleasure,' said Constance, looking to distract Mrs Fog from her nervousness. 'I thought she couldn't get passage home for months?'

'Her fiancé, Percival Allerton, obtained permission to bring her with him,' said Lady Mercer. 'He is on his way to join the last of the American peace delegation still at Versailles.'

'I thought the newspapers said that was all finished and signed,' said Mrs Fog. 'Peace signed and a new League of Nations.'

'Something vital remains about the Balkans I'm told,' said Lady Mercer. 'All very hush-hush, Rachel says.' Constance wondered how secret it could be if Percival had told his bride, who had told her mother, who was now broadcasting it in public.

'So gallant of him to bring her too,' said Mrs Fog.

'They are an old family from Virginia.' Lady Mercer sighed. 'One must be modern about these things. I had hopes of a dukedom for her, but the war has taken the flower of our aristocracy. At least Rachel tells me the Allerton family is wealthy beyond fault, and she assures me they have not a whiff of industry about them. They have substantial lands near Richmond, so they are versed in the ways of the country.'

'I understand they are influential in politics?' said Constance. 'I expect that will be very new and exciting for Rachel.' It was not kind to mock, she knew. Rachel had never shown an interest in politics and indeed had hated the war mostly because of the shocking inconvenience it imposed on her social calendar. But Lady Mercer nodded with enthusiasm.

'Personally, I've always found politics almost as undesirable as the factory floor,' she said. 'But apparently in America it is quite acceptable, even in the finest families, and Rachel tells me Percival is to be groomed for his father's seat in the Senate.'

'Such a pity he does not have the time to visit Surrey,' said Mrs Fog.

'The fate of nations rests on the talks at Versailles and Rachel assures us that nothing less would have prevented him presenting himself at Clivehill,' said Lady Mercer. 'Some might have felt the slight, but I saw it as an opportunity.' She bit into an éclair and chewed, patting her lip with her napkin. 'One of the advantages of an American engagement I think is that we have no need to rush an announcement to *The Times*. We shall take his measure here, in perfect anonymity. These days one must take what advantage comes, but we will weigh the value of the match before any final blessing is given.'

'I hope Rachel will stay for a while,' said Constance. 'She must have missed home as much as she has been missed.'

'I shall insist upon it,' said Lady Mercer. 'Let Percival come for her in Surrey when the treaty is finished and ask her father properly for her hand. Then and only then will we talk about posting the banns.'

'Speaking of which, I have some news to share,' said Mrs Fog. She took a deep breath and Constance braced herself. 'As I believe you know, dear Hildegarde, I have been visiting an old friend here in Sussex.'

'I have been so apprised, Mama,' said Lady Mercer. She shook her head with a fond smile, as if her mother were a child caught in a small but comical infraction. 'But upon a night of reflection I should reassure you that I have no intention of scolding you for it.' She reached out to pat her mother's hand. 'You were left alone too much. I do not blame you for seeking an old acquaintance.'

'You must not blame Constance either,' said Mrs Fog. 'She has been completely attentive and manages me better than most, but as you know, I am quite stubborn.'

'Of course, with Rachel coming, we shall be a merry party and very busy,' said Lady Mercer, blithely ignoring this request. 'I'm sure your friend will understand that you will have to cease your visits.'

'I shall do no such thing, Hildegarde!' said Mrs Fog. 'Life is too precious. I have done my duty and now that I am an old woman, I shall do as I like.' This refusal made Lady Mercer freeze; only her mouth moved, open and shut like that of a carp on the surface of a fish pond.

'Please keep your voice down, Mother,' she said at last, looking around to make sure they were not overheard. 'We must think of Rachel now. At least until she is safely married, there cannot be even the hint of impropriety.'

'Impropriety indeed,' said Mrs Fog. 'There never was any impropriety. Only snobbery of the worst kind.' She sighed and took her daughter's hands in hers, lowering her voice. 'But I have been welcomed, my dear, and forgiven. It is such a weight off my shoulders.'

'But surely you can wait until Rachel is safely married?' Lady Mercer whispered. 'You know these Americans have the most extraordinary attitudes.'

'You aren't even sure you approve the match!' said Mrs Fog. 'At my time of life I don't have the luxury of waiting. And I will not take such generosity and throw it away a third time. You must understand.'

'You see what you have done,' whispered Lady Mercer fiercely to Constance. 'Your inattention to my mother has allowed that man to resume his attentions at the risk of all our reputations.'

'Don't keep blaming poor Constance,' said Mrs Fog. Her sharp tone carried, and Klaus the waiter looked up from where he was setting two chairs just on the other side of a large palm. He raised an eyebrow as if to ask her if she needed help, and Constance gave him a smile of reassurance.

'What on earth are you doing, my good man?' asked Lady Mercer, noticing him. 'Are we to have strangers in our laps?' Klaus stiffened, then bowed and withdrew the chairs to a more private distance. The two ladies at the table now nearer to him did not look pleased but glowered into their cups.

'It is not my affair,' said Constance. 'But Mr and Miss de Champney seem quite lovely people and their home a place of culture and tranquillity.'

'I don't think we need to elaborate for your edification,' said Lady Mercer. 'Let's just say that as my mother is well aware, an unsuitable connection may undo everything.'

'I know your mother has grown stronger and seems happier for her visits.' Constance knew she should remain quiet, but she could not stand to see Mrs Fog's hands tremble and her lip quiver. 'Perhaps friendship is the best medicine.'

'Indeed it is,' said Lady Mercer. 'And in a case such as your mother, and her insistence on marrying your father, I was more than happy to defend her and continue our friendship with no thought to my own reputation. But this is Rachel's happiness at stake. And the de Champneys are so much less suitable than your father, who was of good yeoman stock after all. An Englishman through and through.'

'I don't understand,' said Constance. 'Were your mother's family not also Barbados planters?' Lady Mercer swallowed a piece of éclair awkwardly and began to choke quietly, behind her napkin. As Constance jumped up to pat her on the back, the watchful waiter, Klaus, materialised at her side.

'Constance, you're being much too delicate,' said Mrs Fog. 'Give her one good blow to the back, would you, Klaus?'

'I'm fine, I'm perfectly fine,' whispered Lady Mercer, warding off Klaus with a waving napkin and lying back in her chair to recover her breath.

'Our families were indeed all planters,' said Mrs Fog. 'Since delicacy, and evasion, have contributed to the blighting of a friendship, and worse, I shall tell you the whole story, dear Constance.'

'Oh, that's entirely unnecessary,' squeaked Lady Mercer.

'Constance is like family,' said Mrs Fog. 'She is to be trusted, Hildegarde.'

'I despair of you, Mother,' said Lady Mercer as Mrs Fog leaned close to explain.

'Simon and Mathilde are the children and acknowledged heirs of their father, Roger de Champney, a Barbados planter of great prominence when I was a girl,' she said. 'However, their mother, who died of typhus when they were young, was not formally married to Sir Roger.' She sighed. 'And she was of African blood.' She paused, and Constance was unable to conceal her surprise.

'I thought they were Spanish?' She could see Mathilde's cheek tanned under her floppy hat and hear again Simon de Champney's sharp laugh about the Lady of Spain in his front hall.

'Both children were sent away to England at a very young age, so I didn't meet Mathilde until I was also sent to boarding school at twelve,' Mrs Fog continued. 'I suppose so far from home it was natural Mathilde and I should gravitate to being friends.'

'Spanish, indeed!' said Lady Mercer.

'I assure you, Constance, that any mark against them was largely over-come by wealth, distance from the islands and a proper English educa-tion,' said Mrs Fog. 'It was only when their father suffered certain financial reverses that their social position was viciously cut from them.'

'I'm so sorry,' said Constance. 'It must have been hard for them.'

'Really, Mother, do we have to exhume such old history,' said Lady Mercer. 'They are perfectly respectable people in their own way, but we agreed . . .'

'After our having been forced apart in our youth, I found them again, many years later, after my husband died, and hoped to rekindle my friendship with them, but my daughter was about to marry, and Lord Mercer's family declared my renewed connection an impediment.'

'I am grateful for all you did for me,' said Lady Mercer. 'We mothers do what we must for our daughters. There is Rachel to consider now . . .'

'I don't understand the opposition to such a friendship,' said Con-stance. 'I am sure you did not mean to force it upon the Mercer family in any way.'

'Ah, but you see, I meant to marry Simon,' said Mrs Fog. 'But first as a girl, and then as a widow, I deserted him.'

'Mother, I beg you to say no more,' said Lady Mercer. 'If Father were here . . .'

'But deserting him twice was not my worst betrayal. In our youth, though I was unaware at the time, I contributed to their financial ruin.' Lady Mercer looked aghast as Mrs Fog pressed on with her story as if compelled. 'Simon and I were in love, and my father persuaded Sir Roger to resolve his financial difficulties by selling him their lands upon the promise that the lands would become my dowry.' She turned to her daughter. 'I have always held your own dear father blameless in the af-fair, Hildegarde. He assured me later he did not know when he agreed to marry me.'

'I should hope so, Mother,' said Lady Mercer. 'It has always seemed to me that my father saved you from your own foolishness.' There was a silence as each woman pursed her lips and set her face against the other.

'Simon and Mathilde knew nothing either,' Mrs Fog continued. 'We were all so young and ignorant.'

'And your father lied?' asked Constance.

'He would claim he did not, but certainly Sir Roger was gravely misled. Father promised to settle the estate on me and indeed he did. But when Simon asked my father for my hand, he was refused. My father had already given his blessing to Rachel's grandfather.'

'But what did you do?' asked Constance. 'Didn't you object?'

'I don't think you understand how it was in my day,' said Mrs Fog. 'It was unthinkable that I should defy my father. Of course, I cried and stormed to my mother, but even as she comforted me she too was immovable.'

'I can't imagine how painful that must have been,' said Constance. Lady Mercer gave an impatient snort.

'It is a parent's highest responsibility to ensure their children marry well,' Lady Mercer said. 'Look how fortunately it all turned out. Your daughter a viscountess and your granddaughter to be a senator's wife. I think we have reason to be content, Mother.'

'I am content because my friends forgive me,' said Mrs Fog. 'Or rather, they insist there is no grievance to forgive. In this they show themselves to be of such superior character that we should be doubly ashamed.' She shook her head before she continued. 'Were they possessed of heirs I would have no hesitation in returning their property to them.'

'You are not in your proper faculties, Mother,' said Lady Mercer, turning the colour of cold rice pudding.

'Never fear, Hildegarde. The offer has been broached and they have already most patiently declined to touch any part of the property or its income,' said Mrs Fog. 'I am too old for a dowry, Simon jokes, so the property will remain with me and the income will be settled on Rachel as it was settled on you at your marriage.'

'A dowry, Mother?'

'As I've been trying to tell you, Hildegarde, Simon and I are to be married,' said Mrs Fog. 'Congratulate me!'

In the moment of shocked silence that met this news, the sounds of the Palm Terrace seemed to fade and Constance could hear only a teaspoon somewhere, tinkling against the bone-china rim of a teacup. All hung still except for a small vein pulsing in Lady Mercer's temple.

'Oh, Mrs Fog, I hope you'll be so very happy,' said Constance, jumping up to break the spell. She ran to hug Mrs Fog, but the celebratory moment was lost as Lady Mercer appeared to faint outright and the waiter, Klaus, startled by her slumping among the cushions as he passed, dropped a whole tray of teacups on the stone floor. This crash was scarcely remarked by the turning of the crowd when a booming explosion of sound jarred the teeth in their heads, blew all the curtains into a whirl and caused three of the tall windows to shiver and crack. Constance had barely registered the pall of smoke over the pier and the U-boat's turret before the window in front of them trembled. She threw herself as best she could to cover the two older ladies as the window shattered and slid to the floor in a shower of glass.

No one was badly hurt. As the screaming subsided, Constance assured herself that Mrs Fog and Lady Mercer, on whom she had landed, were unharmed. She held a clean napkin to the back of her own hand, which had been stung by a piece of flying glass.

'Oh dear me, oh, dear.' Mr Smickle, tottering through the room in a daze and waving his hands, came directly to Lady Mercer's side. 'They promised us it would be safe. Are you hurt, my dear madam?'

'We are hit, we are hit,' said Lady Mercer, waving a feeble hand at Constance, who only now became aware that the napkin on her hand was stained with blood. 'Oh, my heart won't take the strain.'

'It's only a scratch,' said Constance. 'I'll go and wash it.'

'You see, Hildegarde. Constance is fine and we must bear up,' said Mrs Fog. 'Perhaps we should wave our hankies out the window, Mr Smickle? Just to let them know we surrender.'

'I believe only one cannon blast was planned, but I've sent a pageboy to the command post to be sure,' said Mr Smickle. 'And to ask them to use the klaxon as promised if they feel the need for further action.'

He moved away to speak to Klaus. 'Clean up this mess and then bring tea to everyone immediately with my compliments.' He lowered his voice, but Constance heard him add, 'And offer the cognac, but mind you charge for it.'

Mrs Wirrall came hurrying in to see the damage, and Constance was surprised to see that Harris was with her.

'My dear Mrs Fog, is everyone all right?' asked Mrs Wirrall. 'There are broken windows all along the promenade.'

'Idiots,' said Harris. 'Someone should be court-martialled for firing on a town full of people.'

'We are only a little shaken,' said Mrs Fog. 'Mrs Wirrall, this is my daughter, Hildegarde, Lady Mercer.'

'How do you do?' said Mrs Wirrall.

'They assured us it was perfectly safe,' said Lady Mercer, not seeming to see Mrs Wirrall's outstretched hand. 'One expects the military to know what it is doing.'

'And that has always been the problem,' said Harris.

'We are all fine,' said Constance. 'No major injuries.'

'You're bleeding,' said Harris.

'Just a scratch.' She held her hand close against her chest, but the bloom of crimson on the white linen made her feel slightly sick.

'We have bandages and iodine in our suite,' said Mrs Wirrall. 'Harris, take Miss Haverhill up and have Suzette see to her.'

'It's nothing,' said Constance, but Mrs Wirrall was adamant.

'As a member of the committee that sanctioned this morning's action as a spectator event, I feel responsible,' she said. 'And the merest scratch can become septic. Do go up and then I can reassure Lady Mercer and Mrs Fog that you are being attended to.'

⁂

IN MRS WIRRALL'S suite Harris rang for the maid.

'I'm pretty sure they won't fire again,' he said. 'What do you think?' On the beach, the U-boat seemed unchanged by the attack. A blush of smoke from the seaward side of the hull indicated a small fire, and a line of men were passing buckets of water from the sea. The navy frigate was already a small smudge on the horizon, steaming away from any responsibility. The promenade seemed to be resuming its normal pattern, with people walking, children running and bowling hoops, a man in a colourful jacket and straw boater selling ice cream from a bicycle cart.

'Do we pretend it never happened?' asked Constance. 'Or do we just forget so quickly?' She felt suddenly weak.

'Here, sit down,' said Harris, his face concerned. 'You are shaking.'

'The explosion was louder than I imagined,' said Constance, sinking into a chair by the large open French windows of the balcony. 'I expect you're used to it.' Harris sat down in the chair opposite and considered the view for a moment. Then he held out a hand that trembled slightly.

'I confess that I am not immune to the sound of so much destruction either.' He clenched his fist shut again. 'I just came to pick up a few more things that Poppy thought necessary, so I can stay up at the barn for a while. I had no idea I would be walking into a war zone.'

'So you've persuaded Sergeant Macintyre to stay on?' asked Constance. 'I'm so glad.'

He raised an eyebrow. 'Somehow, between your arrival and the end of breakfast, he unaccountably became much more amenable, for which I am grateful, though now forced to live in squalor.' She laughed, and Harris's face flashed an answering smile before he jumped up, frowning. 'Where is that maid? Propriety demands I go and find her, but you might bleed to death while waiting.'

'It's really not necessary,' said Constance. 'If you just have a bandage, I can see to it myself.'

Harris disappeared into another room, and she heard the opening of doors and sounds of rummaging. When he came back, he was carrying a bowl half filled with hot water in his free hand and, in the hand using the cane, a clean handkerchief of supplies dangled. A large towel was imperfectly secured under one arm.

'Because of me we always have plenty of medical supplies.' The joviality chafed the edges of embarrassment.

'Let me help you,' said Constance, jumping up. She twisted the napkin more securely around her damaged hand, freeing the other to take the towel from under his arm. Harris moved carefully to set the bowl on a gleaming lacquered table. The handkerchief contained a bottle of iodine, some scraps of linen for bathing the wound and a clean bandage.

'The maid appears to be gone,' he said as they sat down. 'But we have three good hands and three good legs between us. If you would not object to my help?'

'That would be very kind,' said Constance, unwrapping her hand, which had begun to throb. The short, deep puncture had stopped bleeding, but it gaped open and made her woozy to look at it.

'It doesn't seem to have severed any tendons,' said Harris, holding her hand in his two hands and examining it closely. He bathed it in the hot water and then Constance suppressed a gasp at the sting of iodine. 'I'm no expert, but from my experience I think it needs a couple of stitches.' He looked up at her and smiled. 'I've stitched up two comrades and a dog these last few years, but for a lady I recommend the more delicate touch of the hotel doctor.'

'Oh no, I'm sure it will be fine,' said Constance. She did not want to add the expense of a doctor to Lady Mercer's list of grievances. 'I don't want a doctor. I'll just bandage it up.'

'But it's deep enough that it risks infection, and it may leave a scar.'

'Well then, will you please sew it up for me?' she said. 'I'd like to just get it over with.'

'My stitching may also leave a scar,' he said.

'I'll take that risk.'

He sterilised a sewing needle over a candle and dunked some of his mother's best white sewing thread in the iodine bottle. He brought an electric lamp close, to add to the daylight, and pulled reading glasses from his pocket.

'I can stop anytime you wish,' he said and, moving his chair close, he set the towel and her hand casually on his knee and bent his head to the task. Constance thought it prudent to turn her face away from both the procedure and the curly head so close to her. She could smell his soap and the salt air. She could feel the warmth of his leg under her hand. She would have blushed but the sharp pinch of the needle was all she could feel and she bit her tongue to keep from crying out.

Three stitches and then he rinsed the wound once more with iodine and bound it with the clean bandage, turning her hand in his to make sure it was secure.

'I think we are finished,' he said. 'You look a little pale. Do you need some brandy?'

'I don't think drinking will endear me to Lady Mercer,' she said. He still held her hand and the heat she felt had little to do with her injury. She withdrew her hand gently. 'I really should go and find them. I think Mrs Fog may need my support.'

'Do not leave until you are ready,' he said. 'I am happy to sit here until you are quite sure you are well.'

'Shouldn't you get back to your patient at the barn?'

'I left him busy going over the aeroplane engine with that amiable girl Tilly,' he said. 'I don't think he'll drink the methylated spirits in the presence of the young lady, but I hid the bottles just in case.'

'Do you think he can be saved?' asked Constance. 'They say dipsomania is a terrible curse.'

'I don't think he's gripped by the devil as the temperance ladies would have us believe,' said Harris. 'God knows he has more reason to drown his sorrows than me, I'm ashamed to say. But Jock has the stamina of a brick chimney, and if we can just turn his admirable work ethic to a purpose other than his own oblivion, I think he'll be fine.'

'Like Poppy, I truly believe in the hope and inspiration of real work for both men and women,' said Constance. 'I just wish I could find mine.'

'We are in much the same position, I think,' said Harris. 'People are unable to see beyond what they deem our limitations.'

'You have the advantage of your sex and position . . .' said Constance.

'Ah yes, it gets quite tiring hearing people tell me I should be happy to live as the country squire. But what they mean is that I am a cripple and an invalid. They look at me as if my brain has gone missing along with the leg. Or rather they refuse to look at me at all.' His face, turning to the window, looked hollow and tired again. He had probably been tired for a long time, she thought.

'Have I done so?' asked Constance. 'If I have been so unwitting, please instruct me.' He turned back, and she held his eyes with hers and steeled herself not to blush. In her head, Lady Mercer's voice shrieked its disapproval of so direct a gaze.

'You have not, Miss Haverhill,' he said, smiling. 'You are sometimes direct but always kind. I, on the other hand, am my usual brutally rude self. Can you forgive me?'

'Perhaps you could agree to moderate your rudeness to mere astringency for a few days?' she asked. 'I am on thin ice with Lady Mercer and I would welcome a truce.' He laughed and his face relaxed for a moment.

'I shall do more,' he said. 'I shall sing your praises to the heavens in all corners.'

'Please don't,' she said. 'People will think you have gone mad.'

'I shall start by saying your hair sparkles,' he added. He peered more closely, taking her chin in his hand and turning her head.

'Mr Wirrall!' She drew back, her cheeks aflame now.

'No, really, you have glass all over your hair,' he said. 'We should get it out before you hurt yourself or others with your radiance.'

WHEN CONSTANCE RETURNED to the Palm Terrace, Mrs Wirrall rose from where she had been sitting with Lady Mercer and Mrs Fog.

'Here she is – and all bandaged like the heroine she is.'

'It was nothing,' said Constance. 'Just a scratch.'

'I stitched her up myself,' said Harris. 'The maid was not anywhere to be found, Mother.'

'Ah yes, I believe I gave her permission to go and watch the torpedoing from the promenade,' said Mrs Wirrall, all breezy unconcern. She turned to Lady Mercer. 'No doubt she will tarry as long as possible. You know how maids can be.'

'Your hair is peculiar,' said Lady Mercer to Constance.

'I had to get the glass out,' said Constance.

'So very brave,' said Mrs Wirrall. 'Mrs Fog has regaled me with the story of how you threw your body across these dear ladies to protect them.'

'It happened so fast,' said Constance. 'I just thought to cover our faces.'

'No, indeed, we owe her our very lives,' said Mrs Fog. 'We might have been cut to pieces, might we not, Hildegarde. We are so lucky to have her with us.'

'I suppose we are grateful,' said Lady Mercer.

'Well, all's well,' said Mrs Wirrall. 'Though I fear we will be stuck with that submarine at the heart of our Peace Day celebrations. I don't know how we will incorporate its hulking presence.'

'My mother is hosting a ball, afterward,' said Harris. He looked at Constance and smiled. 'You must all come. We insist.'

'Yes, you must come, Lady Mercer,' said his mother, looking quizzical. She turned to Mrs Fog. 'And dear Mrs Fog, Poppy asked me to send an invitation to your friends in Cabbage Beach. I hope you will urge them to join us.'

'How lovely of you,' said Mrs Fog.

'Too kind,' murmured Lady Mercer faintly.

After Mrs Wirrall had made her goodbyes, pressing them to come to tea in her suite one afternoon, Constance asked the ladies if they felt well enough to go up to their rooms to get ready for luncheon.

'I think enough has been said for one day,' said Lady Mercer. 'Not that I have ever done laundry, but we shall, as they say, cease doing ours in public.'

'I just want to know we understand each other,' said Mrs Fog. 'I am to give Simon my answer soon.'

'Can we at least cease all talk of marriage until Rachel is married and gone to America?'

'When will that be?'

'Obviously we have no date set, yet. We will know more when she arrives.'

'You wish us to go on as we were for a few weeks more?'

'Well, obviously, Mother, you cannot go on visiting Simon de Champney unaccompanied. It isn't done.'

'Oh, don't be silly. Mathilde is usually there and I take Constance with me sometimes.' She reached to pat Constance's hand. 'But she is not to be overworked on her holiday. She does too much already.'

'But we must not take advantage,' said Lady Mercer, struggling against complete vanquishment. 'Perhaps she is needed at home?'

'Constance is not going anywhere,' added Mrs Fog. 'And I shall go to Cabbage Beach so long as I am invited.'

'It's a pity Rachel's fiancé can't be asked to negotiate this particular peace,' said Constance. 'But, dear Mrs Fog, I don't want to come between you.'

'You shall stay and we shall invite the de Champneys to lunch so that Hildegarde can see for herself what wonderful people they are.'

'I begin to think the influenza has eroded your mind, Mother,' said Lady Mercer. 'One cannot merely do as one wishes.' Her mother's placid responses seemed to boil Lady Mercer like a teakettle. Had she not been sitting down, Constance was sure she would have stamped her foot. Mrs Fog only smiled beatifically.

'You must feel it too, Constance, how every day we are given is precious? The war and this dreadful epidemic have only made that clearer. You are not as old as Hildegarde or I, but like us, you must already feel how time is always slipping away, the weeks are as days and the year turns as fast as a season. Wasn't it yesterday, Hildegarde, that she and Rachel were swinging on that low bough in the apple orchard, their pinafores covered in juice and their little legs smeared with lichen?'

'I'm sure I have no time for such nervous introspection,' said Lady Mercer, affronted by mention of her age.

'Do you not see the yachts out there on the sea?' said Mrs Fog. From their vantage at the tall empty window, they could see the sailing yachts and pleasure boats, which had gathered to watch the earlier action, and which were still cruising back and forth, sails and pennants flying. She trembled. 'Our individual lives are the merest puff of breeze against a sail.'

'Neither hot chocolate nor unexpected explosions are good for your blood pressure,' said Constance, anxious now as she took Mrs Fog's pulse. The fight with her daughter seemed to have drained her more than the explosion. 'I think perhaps you should miss luncheon and rest in your room?'

As they left the Palm Terrace, the waiter, Klaus, began to sweep up the shattered pile of glass.

Chapter 18

AFTER A QUIET SUNDAY, WHICH TRANSLATED INTO LADY
Mercer securing a front pew at morning church services, and a prominent table in the hotel dining room, from which she studiously cut
any smiling overtures from the other guests, the luncheon with the
de Champneys was scheduled for Monday. No doubt Lady Mercer hoped
the dining room might be more deserted. That morning, she sent a note
asking Constance to stop at her suite beforehand.

'You have met the man and his sister,' she said, without preamble. Her
maid, Constance noted, was leaving the room as slowly as possible. Lady
Mercer had an astonishing capacity to ignore those who did not matter
to her, allowing a sharp servant to be privy to all the gossip. 'What sort of
people are they, in truth?'

'They are of independent means but live very quietly,' said Constance,
putting the de Champneys' characteristics in the order she thought most
important to Lady Mercer. 'They are very respectable and very kind.' She
thought it prudent not to mention their artistic endeavours.

'To you they must appear romantic. To me they have always been a
small cloud, just on the edge of the horizon. I was a girl when I first overheard my parents argue about whether to sell the Barbados lands outright. I didn't think much of it, but then, after my father died, my mother
found them again – barely a year of mourning. I told her I would rather
jilt my fiancé than have to be so humiliated.'

'Things have changed,' said Constance. 'After so much war and death, surely things must change.'

'You are naïve, my dear. I fear my Rachel will pay the price for my mother's foolishness.'

'I trust your mind will be put at rest in meeting them,' said Constance.

'As my mother is intransigent, it is best I do meet them,' replied Lady Mercer. 'I shall put the matter to the man himself, most plainly. If he is not amenable to reason, I shall find a way to allude to my mother being not in her faculties. Perhaps mention a guardianship of her affairs. That should scare him off.'

'Might it not push your mother away also?'

'You might be right. I had thought to offer her the merest hint of having to leave Clivehill, but I have the appalling apprehension that she plans to do just that.' She gave a sighing sob. 'You must help me, Constance. For Rachel's sake. This could jeopardise her marriage as it threatened mine. Such a connection must always drag a family downward and compromise a young girl's reputation.'

'Surely given their respectability and Mrs Fog's age, there can be little to worry about?' said Constance. She could not resist adding a small provocation. 'And after all is not the Empire one big family?'

'Don't be stupid, girl,' said Lady Mercer. 'Please fetch my mother and make sure you stay with her to greet these people. I must go ahead and see the headwaiter about our table as I have no confidence in the man, left to his own devices.'

Luncheon in the restaurant was almost as elaborate an affair as dinner. Despite shortages, the hotel managed to offer four pages of menu, and while there was one less round of cutlery at lunch, the fish and meat courses being collapsed into one, it was a lengthy meal. Fortunately for families wishing to discuss important matters, it was a good deal quieter than at dinner. Lady Mercer had gone in ahead and was to be found seated at a discreet table in the rear. Constance noted that a couple of potted palms seemed to have been moved to give the table even more privacy. Being introduced at the table to Mr and Miss de Champney, Lady Mercer did not rise but gave each a silent bow and pulled off her gloves. Then she nodded at the headwaiter, who directed Miss de Champney and her brother smoothly to seats behind the palms, where Klaus was waiting to pull out their chairs.

'We thought you might appreciate a view of the sea,' said Lady Mercer. On the other side of the table the headwaiter handed Mrs Fog to her seat. Constance, as usual, was beneath his notice. Klaus arrived to put a hand to her chair as she slipped into her seat. He smiled and took care with the unfolding and placing of her napkin in her lap.

'Thank you,' she said.

'We are so honoured to finally meet you,' said Mathilde to Lady Mercer. 'Eleanor has told us so much about her Hildegarde and her Rachel. I believe you are to have the happiness of your daughter's arrival tomorrow?'

'Do you go to church, Miss de Champney?' Lady Mercer blinked her eyes slowly and peered down her long nose as if at a scientific specimen. 'We went to St Michael's twice yesterday and will possibly go on Wednesdays for Bible study while we are here.'

'We usually attend St George's Church in Bexhill, but we have been to St Michael's sometimes,' replied Mathilde. 'They have a very good organist.'

'And occasionally we spend our Sundays at home contemplating in our own garden,' said Simon. 'For God is to be found, I think, in the blue infinity of a summer sky.'

'You are very poetic, sir,' Lady Mercer replied. 'But one should not trifle with the Almighty.'

'Don't listen to him,' said Mathilde. 'He only likes to play the incorrigible.'

'I have explained to our friends that Rachel arrives tomorrow from Southampton and we are to have our first look at this fiancé whom she has thrust upon us,' said Mrs Fog. 'I for one expect him to be a portly young man in a very loud suit.'

'Let us not make fun of Americans as if they were all donkeys,' said Lady Mercer. 'It isn't Christian.'

'No, indeed it is not fair to judge people merely by their heritage,' said Mrs Fog. Constance looked down into her lap to hide a smile.

The waiter came to take their orders, and Lady Mercer led the way, signalling lunch would be brief with her choice of a single course of baked cod and salad. After the waiter left, a silence grew to uncomfortable proportions.

'Mr and Miss de Champney have a lovely garden,' said Constance, feeling the topic of gardens to be slightly more interesting than the weather and more or less safe. 'It is quite an accomplishment so very close to the seashore.'

'Thank you,' said Mathilde. 'Our old gardener was very knowledgeable about our local conditions and taught Simon everything he knew.'

'I'm writing a small book on the subject,' added Simon. 'Putting the local ways through testing by scientific methods.'

'This has recently necessitated several odorous experiments in fish compost and now I can hardly stand to enter the tool shed,' Mathilde said with a laugh.

'How extraordinary,' said Lady Mercer. 'I don't believe I would even know where our gardeners keep the tools of their trade.'

'Two doors down from the tack room,' murmured Constance under her breath. Lady Mercer blinked at her.

'Speak up, Constance, if you have something to add?'

'I was just recalling how nice the potting shed at Clivehill is, Lady Mercer. The estate office is right across the stable yard,' she added for the benefit of the de Champneys. 'I did a regular inventory of tools as Lord Mercer worried about theft, especially with most of the gardeners conscripted.'

'Can you imagine such a slip of a girl running our whole estate?' said Mrs Fog. 'I hear the staff are a trifle less happy with the new man.'

'You have been corresponding with our gossip of a cook again, Mother,' said Lady Mercer. 'And she is wrong. As my husband says, no matter our debt of gratitude to women for stepping into the breach, there is relief in the country that we can all get back to having things done properly, by professionals.'

'I imagine women will go on running the world quietly behind the scenes as they have always done,' said Simon. 'I pity the man who would sit at this table and imagine otherwise.'

The waiter, Klaus, and two assistant waiters arrived in a flourish of plates, and the table was consumed for a while with the offering of various sauces and the passing of the cruet set, with the tasting of the dishes and pronouncements as to their perfect adequacy. When the waiters were again out of earshot, Lady Mercer set down her fork to continue her cross-examination of her guests.

'I think you are quite the diplomat, sir,' she said. 'However, a silver tongue has ne'er prevailed against this daughter's loyal heart.'

'You are as fierce as your mother, Lady Mercer. And I admire that in her as in you. Shall we speak plainly before the waiter comes again?'

'Very well,' said Lady Mercer. 'I disapprove of your attachment to my mother. It can procure no advantage to her and may wreck her only granddaughter's chance at marriage.' She extended a hand towards Mathilde. 'Would you please pass the pickled cucumbers?'

'Did you mean to add that it will bring shame on your family to marry into mixed blood?' asked Mathilde, handing her the little silver dish. 'As long as we are speaking plainly.'

'Thank you,' said Lady Mercer, reddening about the neck. 'I cast no aspersions on your family but merely point out that the connection your brother seeks with my mother is not to her advantage nor to Rachel's. You will agree it could be seen as unseemly to pursue one where all the advantage lies with you.'

'Well, there you are wrong, Hildegarde,' said Mrs Fog. 'I had thought that life itself was lost this winter. But I had good nursing' – here she smiled at Constance – 'and now I find life flowering again. The advantage of happiness is all mine.' She reached her hand, and Simon took it and kissed her palm. Lady Mercer was ineffective at suppressing a small gasp and took refuge in a glass of water.

'We seek no advantage,' said Mathilde, her face stony as she attacked a breast of chicken with unnecessary force. 'My brother is too much of a gentleman to refute you as sternly as you deserve, but I know no man of better character and I will not hear him defamed.'

'Be calm, dear sister,' he said. 'I refuse to take any offence from dearest Eleanor's own daughter. Lady Mercer, you are magnificent in your defence of your family and I salute you for it. I further concur that all the advantage is mine should Eleanor agree to become my wife. Thus I stand ready to make any compromise that will smooth our way.' He waved his hand as he spoke, as if all troubles were mere trifles – which Constance saw made Lady Mercer grit her teeth even further.

'It simply cannot be,' she said. She set down her knife and fork together, firmly.

'You would not want me to live with him without benefit of marriage?' asked Mrs Fog, calmly pressing peas to the back of her fork and taking a large bite of her fresh trout.

'Don't try to be shocking, Mother. It doesn't suit you.'

Mrs Fog chewed, then dabbed her lips with her napkin. 'Also I may have given our cook a whisper or two about my visits to Cabbage Beach, and you know how she embroiders the truth in search of any good story,' she said.

'You are bluffing, Mother.' Lady Mercer's lips were so tightly pressed as to almost disappear.

'No indeed, I have told her my friends may visit and advised her that I will wish to make them a sugar cake from Mathilde's old nanny's recipe. I thought she might need some extra time to track down the required coconut shavings and pineapple in a town as small as Dorking.'

'Mother, I swear I will have you declared hysterical,' said Lady Mercer.

'There is no need to agitate yourself, dear lady,' said Simon. 'Mathilde and I enjoy a life of quiet seclusion without resort to drama and strife. We have no wish to see you unhappy or disturbed.'

'Thank you,' said Lady Mercer, her face frowning with doubt.

'I know Eleanor wishes to leap on time's galloping back so as not to lose the crumbs of hours remaining to us, but I understand your daughter's visit and her marriage are the matter of weeks or months at most?'

'No, Simon, we've spoken of this, and I won't have you and Mathilde hide away,' said Mrs Fog.

'Dearest Eleanor.' And he did not lean, but his whole being seemed to bend towards her.

'I won't let you,' added Mrs Fog.

'My sister and I are not naïve, Lady Mercer. If only you are agreeable to your mother's choice, we would be more than content to be discreet until your daughter is safely gone to America as a married woman. Then I think, a small ceremony and your mother retires to the seaside permanently to make her home with us. We live a quiet life, but we have enough pleasant social connections in the town to ensure your mother will not be a hermit.'

'And what dowry are you expecting her to bring, Mr de Champney?' Lady Mercer's tone was acid.

'Hildegarde! Such coarseness does not become you,' said Mrs Fog.

'She is your daughter,' said Mathilde. 'I, too, would risk any common rudeness to defend my family.' She lifted her chin at Lady Mercer and met her gaze steadily.

'Any monies Eleanor has will remain hers,' said Simon. 'My portion is modestly generous, and I assure you it can maintain three as well as two.'

'You will give up Clivehill, Mother?' asked Lady Mercer. 'And desert me just as I lose Rachel too?' For a moment Constance saw the flicker of real pain across her face and was reminded that the most difficult of people may suffer underneath their armour. Mrs Fog could not answer as the waiter, Klaus, returned to clear their plates. Lady Mercer waved away his proffered dessert menu. As soon as he left, Simon spoke.

'Madam, I would never seek to separate mother from daughter, and I have pressed Eleanor to visit you without me whenever she wishes.'

'As I have made plain to Simon, I will not visit where my husband is not received, but you will always be welcome to come visit us at any time,' said Mrs Fog. 'Whether you choose to do so, I must leave that to you.'

The silence and the unhappiness hung over the table. As far as Constance could tell, Simon's graciousness had failed to pierce Lady Mercer's resolve, but Lady Mercer had won no ground against her mother. Constance felt tears prick her own eyes.

'I lost my own mother, as you know,' she said to Lady Mercer. 'If she were here, I know and you know that she would beg you not to lose yours by estrangement.'

'If you don't mind, I think I would like to retire to my rooms,' said Lady Mercer, rising from the table. 'Mother, would you accompany me?' They all rose, Mrs Fog hesitating as if unsure how to cover such abruptness.

'Thank you for luncheon, Lady Mercer,' said Simon. Lady Mercer only inclined her head and said, 'Miss de Champney, Mr de Champney.'

'I will accompany you to the lobby Miss de Champney, and wait with you while a taxi is found,' said Constance. Mrs Fog threw her a grateful glance.

They were separating at the dining room door when loud halloos and shouts of surprise came from the foot of the lobby stairs.

'Rachel!' Lady Mercer, betrayed into a joyful shriek, was soon engaged in a twirling, dancing embrace in which all that could be seen of the new arrival was a flounce of travel cape and the top of a straw hat.

'Rachel!' Mrs Fog offered Constance a look of some anxiety. It was too much to hope that Rachel would not see the de Champneys.

'I think we must leave you here,' said Mathilde softly. 'Goodbye, Eleanor.' She did not offer to shake hands. She and Simon merely nodded and moved discreetly across the lobby to the hotel's open doors. Constance followed them as she had promised, but Simon turned and raised his hat in farewell.

'You should go to them before they notice,' he said. 'Discretion for Eleanor's sake.'

As he and Mathilde left, they were forced to stop and stand aside for a young man who came in with two large and awkward briefcases. He was accompanied by the undermanager and closely followed by a porter wheeling a trolley of expensive suitcases. Only the porter nodded his thanks. That this was Rachel's fiancé was obvious even before he spoke. Not just in the cut of his jacket, but something about the wide set of his shoulders, and the pink fullness to cheek and jaw of a body that has not known deprivation. As Constance shrank behind the large central sofa, she heard the steel twang of his voice, calmly interrogating Dudley.

'Those individuals who just left, are they guests at the hotel?'

'No, sir, I do not believe so,' said Dudley.

'Only I've heard about certain lax European ideas when it comes to who is allowed in good hotels.' The young man dangled a banknote that made the undermanager's eyes widen. 'I can't have my fiancée staying somewhere without standards.'

'I will make some enquiries, sir,' said Dudley, pocketing the bill. 'But I assure you we are the most respectable hotel in the town.' Signalling to the porter to take the suitcases upstairs, he hurried out to the portico, where the doorman was handing Miss de Champney into a taxi. The young man, still carrying his briefcases, went to meet his future mother-in-law.

Constance, staying out of view, sat down on the sofa for a moment to gather herself. She was sick with shame at the American's open hostility. But her own conscience also wriggled: What if she had not come to like the de Champneys so much? What if she were not secretly happy to see Lady Mercer a little thwarted? What if she had been less blind to the difference in their complexion? Rachel's fiancé might inspire disgust with his open hostility, but what if she and others were merely more circumspect in their various prejudices? She made a silent promise now to examine her own heart for any such equivocation.

＊

PERCIVAL ALLERTON'S MANNERS were as charming as an expensive education and elocution lessons allowed.

'Everyone who meets him wonders if he is English educated,' said a radiant Rachel, holding fast to his arm as they all retired to sit on the Palm Terrace. 'I tell him he could claim to be an Oxford man and no American would be able to tell.'

'But I am far too proud an American to claim any such thing,' said Percival, shaking his head as he pulled out a chair for Lady Mercer to sit. 'My father is from an old Virginia family, but my mother is from Boston and I may have inherited some of her inflection.' Everyone nodded as if this had made things clear.

If she had not heard the discussion with the undermanager, thought Constance, she would have been as charmed as anyone by his firm handshake and the way he looked her in the eye as he professed to already love her from Rachel's affectionate descriptions.

'You are as pretty as Rachel described,' he said.

'She is the beauty,' said Constance. And indeed she meant it. Rachel also seemed to burst with a milk-fed health. From her clear hazel eyes to the blush in her cheek and the sleek shine of her dark hair, she exuded a radiance that made Constance feel thin, dowdy and bone-tired.

'It is so wonderful to have you both here,' said Lady Mercer. 'I was unclear from your telegram as to how long you are staying. I think, Mr Allerton, you plan to return shortly?'

'We will both be returning,' said Percival. 'Unfortunately, I am not the master of my own time at the present. Though the Peace Treaty is signed, there are many pressing matters of state that require my presence in Versailles and then I am expected home to make my report to the President. It is our good fortune that you can be here along the railway line between Southampton and Dover.' With his thumbs tucked in his waistcoat, Percival seemed to bloom with his own importance and Constance wondered if his condescending smile hid any anguish that he had missed the big ceremony by days, and that he and President Wilson had been literal ships passing in the night.

'I told Percival I must be married on English soil with my parents and my dear, dear grandmother about me,' said Rachel.

'Indeed, we must have the banns read at home,' said Lady Mercer.

'There isn't time, Mother,' said Rachel. 'I wrote to you and Father from the ship but perhaps you left home before my letter arrived?'

'If there were any other practical way . . .' said Percival.

'I don't understand.'

'Percival will have one day when he returns from France to pick me up and then we must rush to catch the ship home. We will marry two weeks from next Saturday, here in Hazelbourne, by special licence.'

'But your father!'

'Father will surely understand when he receives our letter,' said Rachel. 'And I have written to three of my dear school friends, but if they cannot come, Constance can be my maid of honour.'

'In the last resort I shall stand with you,' said Constance, her voice teasing and one hand on her heart. Rachel's careless comment stung a little, but her oblivious ways were of such long standing that Constance had learned to find such unexamined insults as amusing as a tale from Mr Pickwick.

'Constance is always so funny,' said Rachel to Percival. 'We are like sisters.'

'Don't worry, Mr Allerton,' said Constance, as gravely as she could manage. 'It is the very definition of sisterhood to be taken for granted.'

'It isn't right,' said Lady Mercer. Her face was grey. Only a grim pressing together of her lips prevented her chin from trembling. 'One can't plan a wedding in only three weeks. What about the announcement in *The Times*?'

'I had hoped to see Lord Mercer today,' said Percival. 'It's very important to my family that I ask his blessing and do everything as proper as may be.'

'I think one or two missteps might have already been made, dear,' said Mrs Fog, patting his hand. 'But we will forgive you, I'm sure.'

'I have a letter of introduction from my father for him, which gives us his blessing on the whole thing, and I have a box of very special cigars for him,' said Percival. 'Direct from our ambassador to Cuba.' He frowned. 'I suppose I can leave them with you to give him.'

'I am not the Post Office, Mr Allerton,' said Lady Mercer.

'Oh, Mummy, please don't make things difficult,' said Rachel, and though she remained breezy, Constance knew her well enough to feel a tension in her voice. 'You wouldn't want us to just elope.'

'I will telephone Lord Mercer before dinner and explain everything,' said Percy. 'He will understand, I'm sure.'

'Percival's father is a senator,' said Rachel. 'One day Percival will serve in Washington. And everyone says he is so brilliant he may ascend one day to the highest echelons.' Percival had the grace to blush slightly as he demurred.

'I look only to serve as I am called,' he said. 'And the electorate is a fickle beast.'

'Percival's mother assures me I'll be an asset in the drawing rooms of Washington,' Rachel added.

'You are British,' said Lady Mercer. 'Your rank must command precedence in any educated drawing room in America.'

'Oh, they think I'm marrying a princess,' said Percival. He crushed Rachel's hand between his own to kiss her fingertips. Lady Mercer looked pained at this display. Mrs Fog clapped her hands though a tear stood in her eye.

'We will be so unhappy to lose you, my dear, and so soon. But we must all be happy in the face of your obvious joy.' Rachel left her chair and dropped to her knees to hug her grandmother.

'It's only a five-day crossing to New York, Grandmother,' she said. 'I hope and pray you will all come and visit us one day?'

'We shall see, my child,' said Mrs Fog, and a tear fell then because, as Constance understood, the truth of Rachel's leaving forever was hard to bear.

'This is all too much,' said Lady Mercer, who seemed to have lost her usual bluster under the twin matrimonial assaults. 'I cannot comprehend such a rush, Rachel. I shall telegraph your father immediately for his guidance.'

'Well, I am so sorry not to meet Lord Mercer in person,' said Percival. 'I am leaving this evening to catch the last boat to France. As you can imagine, though Rachel is my whole world, the needs of the wider world make demands on my time.'

'It must be a tremendous honour to go to Versailles,' said Constance. 'You are making history.'

'It is a great responsibility,' said Percival, shaking his head as if he felt the full weight of the peace process on his shoulders. 'So many countries to please and so many of them having, I dare say, their own interests uppermost. However, President Wilson believes we can bring all nations together.' He did not sound convinced and smiled as if his President were some elderly relative who wanted to go out in the rain without his coat.

'When we are married, I am to be invited to the White House,' said Rachel. 'I hope to wear the family diamonds if you allow me, Mama.'

'The Mercer diamonds in America?' Lady Mercer sounded faint again.

'I told her, "Rachel, I can buy you diamonds," but she is so sentimental about these things,' said Percival.

'I must speak to your father,' said Lady Mercer. 'Papers need to be drawn up.'

'I'm happy with whatever Lord Mercer wants to settle on Rachel. You'll get no arguments from my family.' Even Mrs Fog blanched at such a public discussion of money, though she stepped in to smooth the proceedings.

'Well, that's all for a later time, isn't it,' she said. 'Should we order some tea?'

'I've taken the liberty of ordering champagne,' said Percival, as Klaus and a pageboy in brass-buttoned uniform and cap, came in carrying an ice bucket apiece.

'Champagne at two o'clock in the afternoon?' said Mrs Fog. 'What a wonderful place America must be.'

Chapter 19

IT HAD BEEN THREE DAYS AND CONSTANCE BEGAN TO CHAFE under the close control of Lady Mercer, who now wished to personally supervise her mother and Constance at every moment. To Constance's surprise, Rachel's wedding had been approved by Lord Mercer, and if Lady Mercer appeared more grim than usual, she made no further argument against it. To make sure preparations ran smoothly, activities were planned to the minute and required them to do everything together. Constance was now expected to remain on the Palm Terrace in the mornings, chatting with Rachel while Lady Mercer inserted herself into Mrs Fog's whist group at the expense of whichever lady could be persuaded to give up her hand to 'my poor mother's desire to spend some precious moments with her devoted daughter'.

Rachel ran out of conversation after the first breakfast and so she merely began her stories again from the beginning.

'Did I tell you I was so homesick in the beginning I couldn't even eat? The cousins feared for my life and fed me beef broth and milk custards in tiny teacups.'

'I think you did mention that,' Constance said.

'The first time Percival saw me he said he thought I must be an angel because my skin was so fair as to be translucent.'

'A dangerous response to someone who is obviously ill,' said Constance.

'Everyone said it was the most delicate compliment,' said Rachel. 'But he soon encouraged me to try corn pudding and he was so charming I just stopped thinking of home and determined to make myself strong enough to go out driving with him.'

'You were missed at home, of course,' said Constance. 'No matter how hard things got, every week the farmers would remember to ask me how the young miss was doing out in America.'

'It was terribly hard, wasn't it?' said Rachel. 'The shortages – why, there were times we would run out entirely of something strange – no hams, or a shortage of molasses – and Cook would be hard-pressed to keep the dining room properly supplied. I think brandy was also in short supply for a time. There was grumbling after dinner once or twice.'

After luncheon Lady Mercer dictated that they retire to deckchairs in a sheltered part of the garden, where Constance was usually begged to read aloud while the others dozed in the shade. There had been no room for Constance to slip away, and though she and Poppy had exchanged pleasantries while passing in the lobby, Poppy had been discreet, and there had been no opportunity to hear news from the barn.

This afternoon, they had arranged their deckchairs in sight of a croquet match on the hotel's lawn, and Constance, offered a break from reading, tipped her face to the sun and breathed in the fresh-mowed grass, enjoying the click of mallets on balls and the muted laughter of the players. Her reverie was disturbed when the undermanager, Dudley, trotted down the garden path holding a silver salver on which was a small white envelope for Lady Mercer and Mrs Fog. In it was an invitation from Mrs Wirrall for all four ladies to join her and her daughter the following day for tea in her suite.

'One must wonder at the short notice,' said Lady Mercer.

'Oh, we are very good friends,' said Mrs Fog. 'We must go. Mrs Wirrall has the most marvellous view from her suite.'

'Do let us go,' added Rachel. 'Mrs Wirrall is such an extravagant presence in the hotel. I am so curious to see her up close.'

'She is not a zoo exhibit,' said Constance. 'She is much respected in the town.'

'As she has already invited us to her ball, it really should be us asking her to tea,' said Mrs Fog. 'As she overlooks our faux pas and extends herself so generously, I don't see how we can refuse.'

'Very well,' said Lady Mercer. She withdrew a key from her bag and handed it to Rachel. 'Would you be a dear, run up to our rooms and write a suitable note on our behalf?'

'Can't Constance do it?' asked Rachel. 'She's so much better at composing notes than I am.'

'Rachel, Constance is not your servant,' said Mrs Fog.

'No, but she is also invited to tea and she knows where Mrs Wirrall's suite is, so perhaps she would not mind making herself useful?' Lady Mercer's eyebrows disappeared under her hat as she waited for an answer.

'I would be happy to do it,' said Constance. Any chance to escape from under Lady Mercer's hand was welcome.

'Mind you keep it short and formal. No need for any flourishes.'

SHE COULD HAVE had Dudley or a hotel pageboy deliver the note, but Constance tapped on Mrs Wirrall's door herself. The maid answered.

'Who is it, Suzette?' called a voice, and when the maid gave her name Constance was ordered into the room.

'I'm so glad to see you,' said Mrs Wirrall. She was seated at her dining table with a small pile of bills at one hand and a large Japanese cachepot, which seemed to be overflowing with more papers. 'Any excuse to turn away from this chaos.' She sighed. 'I promised to put my bills in order for Harris, but I am apparently very bad at managing money and men. My renovations at Penneston are making me old before my time.'

'I'm so sorry,' said Constance. 'Are you sure you want the bother of hosting us all to tea tomorrow?'

'Of course I do, my dear. I haven't seen you and dear Mrs Fog for days.

The walls of reserve must be breached and Lady Mercer and her daughter folded into our little social circle.'

'Thank you,' said Constance.

'I hope you are all recovered from the unfortunate U-boat incident,' said Mrs Wirrall.

'We are unscathed,' said Constance. 'As is the U-boat, I believe?'

'Barely a dent,' said Mrs Wirrall. 'Our town's leaders are mortified that it should remain to spoil our Peace Day celebrations. Now our illustrious committee insists it be incorporated and have added to our small air show with a full-scale bombing attack from the air.'

'Might attacking an empty wreck not look a little unsporting?' asked Constance.

'To that end Mr Smickle has dragooned our poor waiter, Klaus, to dress up as the boat's captain. He is giving special tours twice a week to various dignitaries. Then on the day of our celebrations, he will man the decks, mount a modest defence and ultimately run up the flag of surrender.' Mrs Wirrall gave a guilty smile. 'I am assured he is happy to do it and will be amply compensated; and that it will be almost a holiday for him.' Constance felt keenly that the poor waiter would have had little choice but to agree, with perhaps more humiliation than happiness.

'It's supposed to be a celebration of peace, not another war,' she said quietly.

'I fear where women celebrate peace, men will always veer towards victory.' Mrs Wirrall brightened. 'My entreaties have fallen on deaf ears, but at least I obtained an invitation for Harris to join the air show. That is if his machine is airworthy by then.'

'Poppy had great hopes of Captain Wirrall's mechanic,' said Constance. 'I haven't heard anything since we came back from London.'

'Ah yes, Poppy told me about your disappointment in London and she begged me to help her find you some opportunity locally.' She smiled. 'My daughter is not always discriminate in choosing her friends, but I believe you are a very good influence on her and I am happy to assist you.'

'I couldn't ask you to,' said Constance, as a flare of hope mingled with the small humiliation that must, she thought, afflict all recipients of charity.

'Well, I have possibly found an opportunity right here,' said Mrs Wirrall. 'Mr Smickle's bookkeeper is emigrating at the end of the season. I have prevailed upon him to interview you for the position.'

'That's wonderful,' said Constance.

'Good. If you're happy, I'll ring down and see if he's free.'

'You mean now?'

'Strike while the iron is hot,' said Mrs Wirrall. 'Let's pin him down before he finds a way to wriggle out of it.'

SITTING BEHIND HIS carved and gilded mahogany desk, Mr Smickle was not as imposing as he thought. Instead he looked small and distant across the polished leather surface. He pressed his fingers into a steeple and cleared his throat.

'Mrs Wirrall is an important patron of this hotel, and she was most insistent that I speak with you.' He paused and raised an eyebrow as if he had said enough and was merely waiting for Constance to agree with him.

'Mrs Wirrall said your bookkeeper would be leaving and that you had been unable to find a competent replacement,' she said, remaining calm and opening the paper file on her knees. 'She thought I might suit you, as I have the experience and qualifications.' She slid her certificates carefully across the desk. 'I have the required London Certificates in accounting and mathematics, as well as in economics and shorthand.'

'Shorthand is a useful qualification for a young woman,' said Mr Smickle.

'I have been doing the daily bookkeeping for the Clivehill estate for some years. Lady Mercer will be able to provide a reference.' Whether Lady Mercer would do any such thing was of some concern. Constance had a brief vision of her staring at Mr Smickle as if he had asked the measurements of her undergarments. Or of her denying Constance's existence. More likely she might frown and reduce three years of professional work to some version of 'the girl made herself moderately helpful about the place'.

'Yes, the war's left us all a bit upside down,' said Mr Smickle. 'Young ladies crowding out the young men, getting qualifications they won't use as soon as they get married.'

'It was all by correspondence course,' said Constance. 'I don't think I supplanted anyone.'

'The boys of course were away fighting,' said Mr Smickle. 'Now they are back, many with families, and they want me to hire them with no training.' He sighed. 'My choice is reduced to some battle-scarred veteran who thinks he can just learn triple-entry ledger overnight, or a girl with a certificate who might be gone to the altar next week.'

'I assure you, sir, I have no immediate plans to marry,' said Constance. 'And I fear that, for many of my generation, a husband will be harder to find than a job.' She stood. 'I'm sorry if I have wasted your time.'

'No, no, please don't take offence,' he said. 'Mrs Wirrall vouches for you and I have tremendous respect for the lady. Here you are . . .' He rummaged in his desk and pulled out a sheaf of papers. 'Here's a little test I devised long ago. Read this ledger and tell me your thoughts. I'll give you a few minutes to look it over.' He handed her the papers and a pencil and walked over to the window, where he clasped his hands behind his back and looked out at the busy seafront. The slight rocking on his heels served as both metronome and timer and she felt the pressure as the figures danced before her.

'I'm done,' she said. It had taken only a few minutes to focus and to run her pencil down the rows. She had spotted an invoice placed in the wrong column, a subtotal incorrectly transposed and a column of figures added to an incorrect total.

'How did you add up those figures so fast?' asked Mr Smickle, looking over the circled errors.

'I didn't, I thought it would take too long,' she said. 'But the pennies were wrong so the entire figure must be too.'

'Well spotted,' he said. 'What is this figure you've written at the bottom?'

'I think that's roughly the amount stolen from this ledger,' she said. 'Someone has been making small errors to hide the fact, but again, I didn't have time to add everything up.'

'You are right,' he said in undisguised surprise. 'In my first job as a general manager, our bookkeeper and a sommelier conspired to steal from the wine cellar and hide the discrepancies in inventory. I missed it for months and almost lost my position.' He put the papers back in his drawer. 'I copy these pages over from time to time to remind myself not to skim my ledgers.'

'It would have been smarter of them to never put the wine in inventory to begin with,' said Constance. 'At Clivehill I made sure to often check supplies against invoices myself and to write or telephone all our merchants once a quarter to thank them and to casually make sure our figures agreed.' Mr Smickle peered at her, astonished and not quite sure whether to be pleased, as men seemed to do, she had noticed, when a woman said something of import. It was as if when offering a dog a biscuit, the dog had thanked them and begun to quote from the *Encyclopaedia Britannica*.

'I would be willing to give you a trial next month at two pounds a week,' he said. 'And perhaps we'll even give you the opportunity to use some of that shorthand when the bookkeeping is slow.'

'Thank you,' she said slowly. 'I appreciate the opportunity. I must do my own accounting and see if I can live on two pounds a week.'

'Where will you live?' he said. 'It must be somewhere completely respectable. Mrs Wirrall may know of one or two ladies who might take you in.'

'I had not thought that far,' said Constance. 'I imagine when Mrs Fog leaves she might underwrite my room for a week or two until I can find alternative accommodation.'

'Oh, no, no, I'm afraid you can't stay here in the guest rooms,' said Mr Smickle. 'We have a hard-and-fast rule here: no staff in the hotel. Not even Dudley, and he is my nephew. It doesn't do to encourage fraternisation with the guests, you know.'

'Not even when I am not on duty?' asked Constance. 'I had thought, since it is a professional, not a service position . . . ?'

'The guests don't need to see us taking tea on the terrace or drinking at the bar. Even I – who am expected to be sociable with the guests from time to time and raise the occasional glass – even I would not presume to take my meals in the dining room, and you'll never see me lounging in the garden, smoking. No, no, my dear, once you join us I'm afraid you must use the service entrance to come and go, and you will not be able to visit other guests on the premises. Mrs Wirrall will understand that, won't she?'

'I am sure she will,' said Constance. Humiliation began to rise in her veins like floodwater.

'And we would have to be firm with that daughter of hers,' he added. 'Miss Poppy could not apply her somewhat indiscriminate view of social boundaries in this case.' It was a significant blow to Constance, and it was with difficulty that she kept her composure as she rose from her seat.

'May I have some time to consider your kind offer? I must consult Mrs Fog as to her plans before I commit myself.'

'Of course! And for a reference besides that of Mrs Wirrall, a written line or two from Lady Mercer will suffice.' He led her to the door and bowed. 'I do hope you'll join us on this side of the green baize door. It's a demanding life but I believe there is true nobility in the service of others.'

'Of course,' she said, ashamed to find that perhaps she agreed with him only in the abstract.

SHE COULD NOT bear to go back yet and explain her absence to Lady Mercer. She needed some air and the chance to cool her hot cheeks. The sudden sting of tears propelled her off the crowded promenade and onto the beach, where she walked slowly, her shoes sliding and sinking into the pebbled bank. It was clear now that neither the war nor the more casual, ephemeral mores of a seaside town offered anything but a temporary and conditional loosening of society's strictures. She had immersed herself in the beauty and fun of the summer's grassy green days, but underneath, the past and the future rolled out like a hard road and there was to be no relief. She would work and be poor; and that would divide her from Poppy, who worked and owned her own business because she wanted to make a point. Poppy would always use the hotel's front door.

She went down towards the water, under the shadow of the U-boat, where the black hull, hotly radiating the stink of paint and rust, and the lazy grey flop of low tide were the perfect backdrop for self-indulgent distress. She sat down, sank her head into her hands and breathed in seaweed and oxygen as she breathed out her anger and self-pity. She was ashamed to find how bitter she felt now that a perfectly good job threatened to formally divide her from the idling classes. She had rolled her eyes and chafed at her mother's grateful attitude to the friendship and largesse of the Mercers. She had perhaps absorbed too well her mother's philosophy that intelligence and education made one the equal of all; now she saw it was probably just the hollow illusion of people without money.

The sea continued to flop on the shore as it had for millions of years and the pebbles continued to roll and clatter in the foam, and she sighed to feel herself so frail and inconsequential in the mighty scheme of earth and heaven. But then was not immutable England itself also frail? Edged in cliffs of soft chalk and pebbled banks constantly scraped away by the endless tides. Hollowed out, scarred and almost lost to a war too vast to have been properly understood. She shivered to think of it.

'Excuse me, miss. Are you all right?' A familiar voice with the faint German accent made her start and raise her head. It took a moment to recognise Klaus, the waiter, in some sort of naval officer's uniform. A large tin cross on the dark blue coat said he was a German, and the copious gold braid on the arms, and white cap under his arm, suggested a captain, but the darker outlines on the coat, where several previous patches had been unpicked, and the unmatched grey trousers, suggested the whole thing had been cobbled together from the town theatre's costume department. Slightly more *HMS Pinafore* than U-boat, Constance thought. He was accompanied by a plump middle-aged woman dressed in Sunday best though it was the middle of the week. A young boy peeked from behind her skirt.

'I am perfectly fine, thank you,' she said, scrambling to her feet. She was aware that her face was probably blotchy. 'I did not recognise you, Mr...?' She was nonplussed as to how to address him outside of the hotel.

'Forgive me for accosting you, but I was not sure if you were well,' said Klaus. 'My name is Zieger, miss.' The woman with him chuckled.

'The way people have been raising their hats to him all along the promenade, I think he should call himself "Captain" Zieger,' she said.

'An officer's uniform, even vaguely German, does seem to command a respect of its own,' said Klaus. He smoothed down his brass-buttoned jacket with nervous hands. 'I was opposed to taking on the role, but people have been more pleasant than I expected, and one understands that life, and perhaps war, is different for officers.' There was a hint of reluctant pride in his face, and Constance was glad for him.

'Very pleased to meet you, Herr Zieger,' she said, shaking his hand.

'Miss Haverhill, may I present Mrs Wilson of Wilson and Sons Bakers. I was just about to give her a tour of the submarine,' he said.

'My husband was to come with us, but he was called away to Brighton,' said the woman, and a blush crept into her sturdy face. 'Herr Zieger is such an old friend of the family but I'm not sure we should go aboard without Mr Wilson.' Klaus looked distraught that she might change her mind.

'Oh, it will be a rare treat for your son,' Constance urged, smiling. 'I'm sure Captain Zieger will take the utmost care of you.'

Mrs Wilson was persuaded, and as the little group made its way up the stairs of the submarine, Constance was aware how incongruous it felt, not that Klaus the waiter should have transformed into a U-boat captain, but that a hotel waiter should have been revealed to have a life and friends outside the hotel walls. She was ashamed at how little she had bothered to imagine it until now. And she would be suitably punished for her obliviousness, for when she took the job at the hotel, no doubt she too would become invisible.

THE FOLLOWING AFTERNOON, Constance, Lady Mercer, Rachel and Mrs Fog sat drinking tea with Mrs Wirrall and Poppy in the Wirrall suite. The French windows were open to the sounds of the sea and the bustling promenade, while the light was filtered by a striped canopy lowered over the balcony. After a good night's sleep, and having decided to at least consider the position at the Meredith, the brief letter of recommendation was now essential for Constance, and Mrs Wirrall was doing her best to persuade Lady Mercer to cooperate. The discussion, Constance thought, was not going well.

'It's wonderful to see a young lady so independent and so determined to make her way in the world,' said Mrs Wirrall. 'My daughter is just the same. She is determined to run this ladies' motorcycle club and now to offer flying lessons to ladies. It is a far cry from our day, when all we were expected to do was embroider our trousseaus and play the piano moderately well.' She sighed. 'But these days, Lady Mercer, as you know, they can hardly count on getting married.'

'Constance knows I fully expect her to provide for herself and contribute according to her talents and her upbringing,' said Lady Mercer. 'But I cannot give my blanket recommendation to just any outlandish scheme. For some of us, a lady's reputation is still vital. It reflects on the whole family.'

Mrs Wirrall did not blanch but only blinked her eyes a little hard. 'I can assure you, Lady Mercer, that Mr Smickle is a highly respected man.

I know him and his wife personally. I believe Constance would be very well treated here.'

There was a pause as Mrs Wirrall's maid came in with another plate of small cakes and a new pot of hot water to refresh the teapot. Constance bit her tongue and kept her eyes demurely lowered.

'I had hoped, or rather I had fully expected, to see Constance settled with a suitable family. Her mother was an admirable governess, you know. I had even made some enquiries and forwarded some expressions of interest.'

'For which I am truly grateful, Lady Mercer,' said Constance. 'But my certificates and my experience now allow me to pursue a more independent and sustaining career.'

'A woman lodging alone in a town so far from home, and in paid employment,' said Lady Mercer. She shivered. 'It may be common in your town, Mrs Wirrall, but where we come from it is scarcely respectable. I have a duty to your mother's memory, Constance, to see you properly situated.'

'Times have changed, Lady Mercer,' said Mrs Wirrall. 'Young women have proven their worth these last few years and are making their way into many new professions.'

'It's not for the better,' said Lady Mercer. 'I can scarcely get a housemaid any more. It's as if domestic service is now considered serfdom. If we do not take a firm line, they may revolt like in Russia.'

'I am not planning on fomenting revolution,' said Constance. 'I just prefer not to be a governess.'

'I had hoped you would support Rachel when she has her children,' said Lady Mercer, sighing. 'Your mother was so wonderful to me, but I suppose such loyalty is passé now, is it not, Mrs Wirrall?' Constance felt her cheeks burn. She clenched her hands together in her lap.

'Oh, how wonderful that would be,' said Rachel. 'You should come to America. I know Percival's family would be thrilled to have an English governess.' She stopped, blushing. 'I mean in a few years, of course.'

'With the greatest respect, Lady Mercer, I believe my mother was bound to you in friendship, not fealty,' said Constance.

'Well! I have never heard such ingratitude.' Lady Mercer's agitation jiggled her cup and tea slopped into the saucer. 'After we agreed you would stay on here through Rachel's wedding. Now I suppose you mean to abandon us wholly, including my mother?'

'Don't worry about me,' said Mrs Fog. 'I shan't be lonely.' Lady Mercer paled at this. Mrs Fog peered innocently at the plate of pastries and selected a yellow-and-green petit four.

'My employment would not begin until after the wedding,' said Constance. 'The fact remains that I must earn my living. With all the soldiers coming home, it is only with Mrs Wirrall's kind intervention that Mr Smickle even agreed to talk to me.'

'Mrs Wirrall knows better than most, from her career on the stage, the perils that attend a woman's reputation,' said Lady Mercer. 'I must in good conscience see you installed in some nice family. Not a lodger in some boarding house.'

'If it would make your heart easier, Lady Mercer, I would be happy to invite Constance to stay with us at Penneston for a while. I know my daughter would like the company when she moves into the house and, after hotel living, even I will find the house a bit too quiet.'

'That is so generous, Mrs Wirrall,' said Lady Mercer. 'But Constance would not wish to be a burden on another family.'

'I haven't agreed to move in yet, Mother,' said Poppy, munching on two cucumber sandwiches stacked together. 'But if Constance moves in it would certainly be more fun.'

'It would be conditional on your also moving in,' said Mrs Wirrall. 'So you see, Constance, you would be doing me a huge favour in helping extract my daughter from that awful barn of hers.'

'You live in a barn, Miss Wirrall? How extraordinary,' said Lady Mercer. Constance felt her chances of receiving a suitable reference sink, and perhaps her face gave her away, because Poppy moved swiftly to recover.

'No. My brother has taken up residence at the barn while he works on our aeroplane,' said Poppy. 'In the war, we women of the Messenger Corps used the barn as our headquarters and barracks, and spent many a night around the coal stove waiting to be despatched. Now I'm staying at the hotel with my mother, but I run my business, Wirrall's Conveyance, as well as the Hazelbourne Ladies Motorcycle Club, from the barn.'

'What fun,' said Rachel. 'Being secretary of the local War Bonds Committee was a lot of work and I'm happy to say we raised the most money of any county in Virginia, but it was not as exciting as whizzing around the countryside on a motorcycle at all hours.'

'You should come out and see it,' said Poppy. 'We also hope to begin flying lessons for ladies very soon. My brother, Harris, will be our pilot.'

'What would a young lady want with such horrible, noisy, smelly machines?' asked Lady Mercer. 'It is altogether too loud and noxious in a closed automobile as it is.'

'Ah, next to fresh-baked bread, there's nothing better than the smell of petrol in the morning,' said Poppy.

'Extraordinary!' Lady Mercer peered at Poppy as a lady naturalist might peer at a new sort of insect, doing something disgusting. 'Such manly arts are incomprehensible to us, are they not, Mrs Wirrall? What would your poor late husband say of your daughter, I wonder.' Mrs Wirrall stood up abruptly, her eyes blazing. But as Constance braced to hear Lady Mercer receive the sharpest of dressings-down, Mrs Wirrall only turned aside to look out over the seafront.

'My husband had his share of incomprehensible appreciations' was all she said, and a silence fell over the tea table.

'He bought me my first motorcycle,' said Poppy, her face hot.

'To keep her from running off to nurse in France,' said Mrs Wirrall, carefully bland. 'My children were both eager to serve.'

'My husband was insistent that we get our daughter to safety in America,' said Lady Mercer. 'She has always been of a delicate constitution.' If they observed that Rachel was happily munching on her fourth éclair from the dish, no one commented on it.

'I wanted to come home, of course,' said Rachel, swallowing hastily. 'But after the *Lusitania* . . .'

'Perhaps if Constance were at Penneston, we would all sleep a little more soundly at Clivehill,' said Lady Mercer, changing the subject abruptly. 'If you are sure she would not be a burden, Mrs Wirrall?'

'I prefer to earn my keep and be independent,' said Constance. 'As Lady Mercer says, I should not be a burden.'

'Then I have a brilliant idea,' said Poppy. 'Perhaps you could help Mother and myself with our accounts too.' She laughed. 'Shall we say that neither of us has much patience with matters financial and we are really in rather urgent need.'

'Perhaps Constance might begin to help at once,' said Lady Mercer. 'Lying around in luxury at a hotel all day is not the best training for a life of work.'

'I have never found Constance just lying around,' said Mrs Fog. 'She is usually to be observed with a book in her hand.'

'You are very kind, Mrs Fog,' said Constance.

'I think it's a splendid idea,' said Mrs Wirrall. 'You could, of course, work strictly part-time and on your own schedule, Constance. You must come and go as you and Mrs Fog please.'

'It's not as if she is indispensable,' said Lady Mercer, her voice curt. 'Besides, Constance's work will give Rachel some uninterrupted time with her grandmother.' She turned to Mrs Wirrall. 'As she did for me, my dear mother is to endow Rachel with a very generous dowry. All she asks in return is a little time with her granddaughter before the occasion of her marriage.'

'Some time after would have been nice,' said Mrs Fog. 'But love must go where it will and, in this case, it seems it will go across the sea.' Her eyes were full as she spoke.

'Oh, Grandmother, you must come and see me,' said Rachel. 'Washington in spring with the cherry trees all in bloom is a wonderful sight. You shall see me set up in my own home and meet your great-grandchildren.'

'Thank you, dearest,' said Mrs Fog. 'A lovely picture to be sure.' She did her best to sound perfectly cheerful, and only squeezed Constance's hand rather hard.

'Well, that's settled then,' said Mrs Wirrall. 'I was thinking Constance would enjoy working up at the house or barn. That way I can remove all those irritating papers from my hotel suite.'

'All that's left is for Mother and me to fight over who gets Constance first,' said Poppy. 'I assure you my receipts are in urgent need of attention.' Her raised eyebrow was as good as a wink and Constance felt a thrill at the thought of escaping Lady Mercer's eye. But she resisted a grin and, the reference being promised, she remained demure and silent as Rachel launched into a lengthy description of the homes and social niceties of the American capital city.

Chapter 20

HARRIS STRUGGLED, SUSPENDED FROM A BROOM HANDLE hung precariously between two tree branches in front of the barn, wondering if his arms would pull from their sockets entirely. The green land lay asleep under the white haze of a sunny Sunday afternoon, and a blackbird trilled encouragement from the canopy of leaves overhead. Both were nothing but annoying set against his suffering.

'Been a long time since I could beat you, and me in my fragile condition,' said Jock. He spat into the dirt and rubbed his sweating head and bare chest with a rough towel. Jock himself had polished off two dozen pull-ups, attacking the bar with a ferocious stream of epithets. Harris struggled silently to pull his chin above the bar one more time.

'And twelve.' He collapsed downward, hanging like a sack of potatoes.

'Eleven and a half maybe,' said Jock. 'I wouldn't say you've gone a bit soft, but you look like an albino bat hanging there.'

'Help me down, you unfeeling bastard,' said Harris. 'I'm an invalid, haven't you heard?'

'Did you lose an arm then?' asked Jock, steadying him as he dropped onto his good leg. 'You make me work with a belly full of acid and a head fit to explode, so I'll take none of your womanish excuses, sir.'

It had been Harris's idea to exercise. In the first few days, fixing the aeroplane had commanded Jock's attention, and his natural manners had responded to the young women Poppy had rounded up to help them. But his nights had continued to consume him, and he tossed with strange fevers and angry scratching of his own skin. He woke from nightmares shouting and crying, and threw himself against the walls and windows. Every morning, Harris had to rouse himself from his own torpor to beg Jock not to leave. Walking seemed to calm him, but Harris was loath to let him go alone in case he bolted for the train, and so he had suggested instead a plan of rigorous gymnastic exercise and used his own weakness as an excuse.

'I need your help,' he had begged. 'There is no one else I trust to see me struggle. We can do it together.'

Now, lying on his back on a bench, pressing two petrol cans above his head while Jock counted off one-arm push-ups on the rug, it occurred to Harris that he was doing more work than Jock, who often took the role of drill sergeant and pushed Harris, with harsh words and a sly grin. It was worth it to see the damned man smile, and to be wakened less often with his unholy despair, but Harris's body ached from the punishing toll of trying to keep up. Even his stump hurt from where Jock made him balance on one leg at a time, despite his protestations of it being impossible.

'Everything's bloody impossible, but we have to go on trying, don't we?' Jock had said. 'Work on your balance and we'll have you waltzing round the dance floor before you know it.' While dancing remained impossible, for even if he could do it, he would not risk the public scrutiny, Harris could not but feel the slight increase in his own willingness to get up in the morning and face living.

When they were done, Harris rinsed off his head and torso under the outdoor tap, where the water came cold and clear from deep under the Sussex clay. With the water dashing over his head and ears, he did not hear the motorcycle approach. It was only as he stood up and began to towel off, enjoying the warm play of the afternoon sun across his back, that he heard the ringing voice of his sister pierce the summer air.

'For goodness' sake put some clothes on, Harris, there are ladies present,' she said, and he saw, to his horror, that Constance Haverhill was climbing from the sidecar, grinning. He found it hard to resist the urge to clutch the towel to his chest. Instead he aimed for nonchalance as he hung it over his shoulders.

'Ladies would have made themselves scarce on spying a gentleman at his ablutions,' he said. 'I will not be shamed at my own residence.'

'First of all, it's my residence,' said Poppy. 'Secondly, I was only thinking of your self-respect, dear brother. You look like raw chicken.'

'You are a wasp,' he said. 'If you'll excuse me, Constance, we weren't expecting Poppy to bring visitors on a Sunday.'

'We didn't see you at church?' Constance blinked in a display of innocence, but her lips twitched.

'Mother thought I should check for signs of life,' said Poppy. 'Constance is here to help me sort out my expenses.'

'For the record, Poppy owes me almost as much as the German reparations,' said Harris. He reached for his cane and followed them into the barn. Poppy had been firm in refusing his offer to go halves on the aeroplane and accepted only a small loan. Made a little speech about being taken seriously as a business owner and ensuring women were accommodated in flying lessons and air taxis. He was hurt she would think he might not support her if he owned part of the machine, but he suspected it was mostly just satisfying to her to provoke Tom Morris. He couldn't quite work out what Poppy was playing at with Tom. They had been rivals since childhood, matching wits and crossing swords, but always seemed closer friends than Poppy and the twins. Though Tom liked to make a joke of it, he and Poppy were well matched, and Tom had been pretty direct in his intentions, both at the start of the war, when Harris had expected an engagement, and now more recently. Harris sighed. Tom could be a bit of a buffoon and even a bore, but as his mother would say, most men were, and who better to keep him in his place than Poppy? He was both a challenge and a familiar quantity and Poppy could do worse. But Harris knew better than to offer any such advice to his sister. It made him wince just to think of the slicing blade of her response.

Jock emerged from upstairs, dressed in carefully cleaned and pressed work clothes, a cotton jacket over his shirt and his boots polished, as if he were still under orders. He had begun to shave again these last few days, though his unsteady hand was visible in patches of stubble on his neck, and he had combed his shaggy hair back with water. The presence of women at the barn seemed to have done much for his appearance but had not relieved his twitchy anxiety.

'I saw you arrive, Miss Haverhill. It's good to see you again.' Jock's tone was cautious, and Harris hid a grin. Constance and Poppy had managed to terrify his mechanic more than the Kaiser had ever done.

'I hope you are feeling better, Sergeant Macintyre,' said Constance. 'You look much better.'

'Let's hope you are as well as you are sartorially splendid,' said Poppy.

'Miss Tilly's maid offered to do some washing. I'm very grateful.' He reddened and straightened his jacket. 'They used to do it for us in the service – best sixpence a week I ever spent – but since I've been home . . .' His voice faltered and he blinked as if just remembering anew the circumstances of his homecoming. 'Well, there's nothing like a woman's touch, is there?' Harris understood what he felt; the sudden assault of memory was like a jolt of electricity, coming at the most unexpected and quotidian of moments. 'I'll put on the kettle, shall I?' added Jock, escaping to the kitchen.

'I find it highly unlikely that Tilly's mother's twice-a-week char offered to go anywhere near the spit iron,' Harris heard Poppy whisper to the Haverhill girl. 'I recognise Tilly's hand in the cut of those trouser creases.'

Harris also dressed, and perhaps he too, weighing the limited options in clothing from his hastily packed and unpacked bags, chose the newer, crisper shirt, gave an extra stiff brush to his dusty trousers and pulled a rag across the toes of his boots a few times until they shone. It did not escape his attention that he would have been unlikely to do so because of his sister's presence and that therefore the Haverhill girl must be once again pricking at his attention. She did not demand his eye, or work for his regard. She did not show any particular attention towards him at all. It was, he decided, a very great relief.

As he came downstairs he could see her at the Victrola, from which a Viennese waltz burbled up to the rafters. Constance and Poppy were waltzing in a tight circle on the small rug as Jock nodded his head in time to the strings.

'Good pace, nothing too fancy,' he said as they spun around laughing. 'We don't need to be galloping.'

'Is this what you call working?' Harris asked, surprised at how annoyed he felt. It was bad enough to sit at dinner at the hotel and have to watch people dancing. He supposed the barn had been a refuge from the constant reminders of his limitations.

'This is a test,' said Jock. 'You've done so well with your balance, it's time to put it into practice.'

'No, thank you,' said Harris.

'Oh, come on, Harris,' said Poppy. 'I'll hold you up. Jock says you're perfectly able.'

'Is this how you repay me?' he asked Jock. 'Do I gossip about your health to the ladies?' Jock looked more aggrieved than ashamed.

'I didn't speak out of turn,' he said. 'I only said to Miss Poppy how strong you've become.'

'Entirely my fault,' said Poppy. 'I mentioned Mother's party.'

'You've no cause to be afraid of it,' said Jock.

'I am not afraid,' said Harris.

'Good,' said Jock. 'We must test your balance and see that your head is on straight. Make sure you're not going to get vertigo in the cockpit.'

'Can't I just hang upside down from a tree or something?' asked Harris.

'Well, thank you for that compliment,' said Poppy. 'Makes a girl feel so good.'

'I'm not dancing with Poppy. She always leads anyway,' said Harris, knowing his tone was veering towards petulant child.

'Well, I'm too short for the purpose,' said Jock to Poppy. 'He really needs to start out upright so he doesn't fall over before he begins.'

'So much for my being ready,' said Harris.

'Constance will have to do it,' said Poppy. 'If she's ready to risk a few broken toes.'

'Oh, I don't think . . .' The girl trailed off uncomfortably.

'If I'm to be tortured in this way, please would you help me, Constance?' Harris asked and was surprised at his own eagerness. 'Poppy will only find ways to trip me up.'

'Well, if it will help your flying,' said Constance. 'What should I do?'

They began slowly, Jock and Poppy fussing with directions and advice, Constance with a tiny frown of concentration, her gaze firmly over his shoulder as they turned. At his first stumble she only looked at him briefly and nodded her reassurance.

'A bit faster now,' said Jock. 'We're not a pair of eighty-year-old dowagers.'

'One of us may be,' said Harris and was rewarded with a laugh as Constance followed him in a more vigorous swinging around. Faster they spun and Harris felt his body flood with the fizzing joy of momentum. A moment later, a heel caught in a fold of the rug and he was sprawling backwards, Constance falling onto his chest. With both hands he grabbed her close to stop her pitching further onto the hard floor. Her hair swung about his face as her chin came dangerously near the ground.

'Don't move, don't move.' Poppy's concern was sharply felt. 'Is anything broken?'

'Waltzing in three dimensions, are we?' said Jock. 'Anything to impress the young lady, eh?'

'Could you just help us up?' said Harris. 'My apologies, Miss Haverhill. I'm not able to help you to your feet.'

'It's perfectly all right,' said Constance, her face lifted just above his now, her eyes alight with laughter. 'I must be squashing the breath out of

you, but I'm not sure of the most ladylike way to extricate myself.' Poppy
and Jock leaned in to help, laughing.

'Are you sure you're not hurt?' Harris asked Constance as Jock hauled
him up too. 'I should never have asked you to risk yourself.'

'Nonsense,' she said, pinning a handful of hair back into place above a
small ear. 'I think we had better continue right away. Getting "back on
the horse" as they say.'

'All right, but let's try not to break anything,' he said. His left knee felt
bruised in its leather brace and he rubbed at a bump on the back of his
head that was hot and egg-shaped. 'Flying will be less dangerous, I think.'

IN THE DAYS that followed, Constance spent her mornings with the
Mercers and most of her afternoons in the barn. She was strangely happy,
and wondered how much of her satisfaction came from the continu-
ation of their brief dancing lessons. Harris's confidence seemed to have
grown, and today he began to really turn her about the room, imparting
a glow to her cheek. Now, a few hours later, she had a niggling desire to
hum the waltz tune aloud. The barn's usual smell of dust and oil was
overlaid with the scent of fresh wood shavings and the acrid odours of
glue and the strong-smelling lacquer they called dope. A new energy
seemed to have taken hold of Tilly, who was black with dirt from working with Harris and Jock to put the finishing touches on the aeroplane
engine. Jenny and another girl, formerly employed at Hazelbourne Aviation, were busy doping some final patches of the wings. While Constance worked diligently, entering receipts into the large leather-bound
ledger, which Poppy seemed to have barely cracked open for months,
Poppy managed the ringing telephone and a chalkboard showing a full
day's worth of booked rides. The women who rode for Wirrall's came
and went, and Constance began to recognise them: the friend of Iris's,
who raced every other day to the end of Kent to bring Whitstable oysters
to the better hotels; the two girls from a nearby farm who ran taxi services in the middle of the day but had to get home in time for evening

milking; the shy girl whose father dropped her at the barn by horse and trap twice a week and shook his head at all the women working.

The more leisured members of the Hazelbourne Ladies Motorcycle Club also dropped by: to have their motorcycles tuned, to sit with their feet up and talk over tea, or for the occasional committee meeting. All seemed drawn moth-like to the aeroplane, where Jock and Harris were pestered with eager questions. Tilly, spanner in hand, wandered over to the large table at which Constance was working and shook her head.

'So much for sisterhood,' she said. 'If those girls want to ask Jock to check on their spark plugs, I suppose I'll just go home for the afternoon and put my feet up.'

'It's just the novelty,' said Constance. 'It will wear thin soon.' She was distracted, trying to check again the long columns of numbers, but a brief look showed her that Tilly was genuinely glum. 'Cheer up. It looks to me as if Jock really needs you.'

'Not really,' said Tilly. 'But he's been awfully good about showing me everything, and he says I'd be sure to get my air mechanic licence first try.' She examined her fingernails, which were black with grime. 'He did say he'd get along faster if it was just me and him. Captain Harris is well meaning, but Jock says pilots just love getting in the way.'

'I'm not sure if it's the aeroplane or the men who have made the biggest difference,' said Constance. 'But the place is humming. I might need to take this work up to the house to get some peace.'

'It's not the same with men here, is it?' a voice behind them interrupted.

'Iris, where did you come from?' asked Tilly. She did her best to hug Iris without touching her with oily hands.

'I just came by to bury the hatchet with Poppy,' said Iris. Poppy was on the telephone but waving at Iris, her face alight. Iris turned away and Poppy's face fell. 'No need to make things too easy on her,' she added. 'But it doesn't do to let things fester among friends. Before you know it, they've replaced you with a couple of men.'

'It's just Harris, and Jock is a bit crusty, but he's been through so much,' said Tilly. 'My mother was upset at first, as you can imagine, wanting me to stop coming, but I told her that man lost his whole family. We have to be understanding.'

'Still, they are men,' said Iris. 'It was really special to have just a bit of a place that was for us women alone. Even in the war, with all the difficulties and being afraid half the time, this was a sanctuary for me.' She hitched up her narrow trousers and sat on the edge of the table as Constance leaped to move a large pile of papers out of the way. Iris took out her slim silver cigarette case. 'I don't mean to whine.'

'We can't smoke in here now,' said Tilly. 'The dope is highly flammable.'

'Well, I shall whine now,' said Iris. 'It's one thing for Poppy to put a man in my bed without permission. It's quite another to forbid me smoking.'

Poppy finished her telephone call and came over. Her hesitant smile made it clear to Constance that the rift with Iris was a source of real hurt.

'I hope this means you forgive me?' she said, her bravado unconvincing.

'No, and I'm not going to forget it either,' said Iris. 'But friends don't stay angry and they don't stay away.'

'Thank goodness,' said Poppy, enveloping Iris in a long embrace. 'It isn't the same without you here.'

'Appreciate the sentiment,' said Iris. 'Of course we are not here, are we? You've given the place over to the men, I see.'

'It's just temporary, but don't tell my mother that,' said Poppy. 'She is thrilled I've moved into the hotel. You can share my room if you like. It's quite nice to have a real bathtub just for a bit.'

'I can pay for my own room,' said Iris. 'That's my news – a newspaper has offered me a large sponsorship.'

'Well done,' said Tilly. 'That will show the racing circuit women mean business.'

'I can't wait to watch Gwinny and Evangeline having to congratulate you,' said Poppy.

'It's not just for motor racing,' said Iris. 'Since Alcock and Brown conquered the Atlantic, flying is all the newspapers care about. To sell papers, they want a "Lady Aviatrix", the "fastest woman in flight" – that sort of thing.' She raised her eyebrows and waved her hand in her usual jovial style, but Constance could sense her tension as she waited for Poppy's response.

'So just to be clear, am I still an idiot for buying an aeroplane with your money so you now have an aeroplane in which to fly?'

'Yes, you are,' said Iris.

'I completely agree,' said Poppy. 'But, Iris, oh, how amazing this is going to be. You'll be our first student.' She dragged Iris up and spun her around.

'We'll have to hurry, though, they want to photograph me in the air in three days,' said Iris, dragging Tilly into their laughing, dancing circle.

'Three days?' Poppy stopped short in astonishment.

'Not that they can expect me to fly the damn thing right now,' said Iris. 'But they want me to be ready to take part in the air show for the Peace Day celebration on the nineteenth. Help bomb the Hun or some such thing.'

'But we don't even know if it will fly yet,' said Tilly. 'We have to test it first.'

As if in answer, a great spluttering roar went up from outside the barn. The rebuilt engine had fired up for the first time in a cloud of white smoke and the sudden stench of castor oil. There was a cacophony of shouting and clapping, and Constance clapped too, surprised to find herself emotional at the sound of the engine. It was as if the machine were a great beast come alive. Though she shook her head, wondering how she was to tally invoices in such a madhouse, she was happy to be dragged from behind the table to join the applause and celebration.

Chapter 21

A CLEAR EVENING WITH NO WIND PROMISED TO BE AUSPI-
cious for the first test flight of the Sopwith Camel. It was supposed to be
a highly guarded secret, so Constance had not invited Mrs Fog, nor Rachel and her mother, but some other members of the Hazelbourne Ladies Motorcycle Club, who had been in and out of the barn at all hours,
had perhaps been more lax about the secrecy. When Constance and
Poppy arrived, accompanied by Mrs Wirrall, who brought them in her
car, a crowd had gathered. Constance waved at Iris, who was dressed to
fly, in clean new coveralls of a distinctive bright blue colour, much
nipped in through the torso, and with a pink silk scarf tucked in the
front. She was talking to the Morris twins and, judging by their pinched
expressions, Constance thought she might have let slip that the newspaper was coming any minute to photograph her with the aeroplane. Tom
Morris and Sam Newcombe were chatting amid the colourful hats and
dresses of the ladies. In the barn there was much brewing of tea and dis-
tribution of cake. Jenny was in charge of the kettle as Tilly, guiding one
wing, helped Harris and Jock with the towing of the aircraft by two cart
horses to the edge of the long field in front of the barn.

Constance had joined the field inspection party two evenings ago;
walking the length of the grass, the golden light and the long shadows
before her, marking each obstruction and hole with a small flag on a
dowel. She was conscious both of the responsibility of the task and of

Harris walking beside her. Now emptied of sheep and obstructions, the field was mown to one uninterrupted velvet expanse. At the boundary fence several farmers and local children were accumulating. The crowd from the barn moved closer around the machine. It seemed to Constance that Harris and Jock, making last-minute inspections in their coveralls, were none too pleased with all the attention.

'Oh, don't mind them,' said Iris. 'For all their gruff insistence on the mechanics of the thing, they're as superstitious as a couple of old palm readers. Women especially are a jinx.'

'But they kindly told me they don't consider me as a woman,' said Tilly, coming over to accept a tin mug from Constance.

'Lovely,' said Poppy. 'What a gentleman my brother is.'

'I take it as a compliment,' said Tilly. 'Whatever lets me work.'

'Well, personally I think it should be unlucky to shun women in this case,' said Constance. 'So many women have made this machine possible.' Though she did not mean herself, even she had helped. Having cleaner hands than Tilly and more patience than Poppy, she had been assigned to spend an afternoon painting Harris's wartime insignia – a phoenix rising over a white cliff – on the tail.

'Agree, but don't tell the Scottish mechanic,' said a voice, and Sam Newcombe appeared at her elbow to raise his hat. 'Make us all run around a tree three times clockwise and spit.'

'You men are all incorrigible,' said Poppy. 'Children in big boots.'

The machine being ready, Harris beckoned Tilly and Poppy to stand with him and Jock, as he invited his mother to break a bottle of champagne carefully over the fuselage.

'Not too hard, Mother. We don't want to bash a new hole where we've just fixed the old one.'

'And may God bless all who fly in her,' said Mrs Wirrall to the cheers of the gathered crowd.

'Terrible waste of perfectly good alcohol,' said Jock. 'But the gods must be appeased.'

There were hands to be shaken and photographs to be taken, and even Constance was dragged into one of all the women who had worked on the machine. The newspaper photographer took several pictures of Iris standing by and on the wing and shaking hands with Harris. The Morris twins pouted until they were also invited to be photographed, and then they demurred and fussed and had to be suitably begged until they posed, clinging one on each side of Harris. The sun sank further towards the west, the shadows lengthened on the grass and Jock looked at his watch with impatience.

'Let's hope it's not hubris to take photographs first,' said Harris. 'If you'll all excuse us, I suppose we'd better get her off the ground.' As the crowd stepped back, Constance noticed Tom pulling Harris aside. She couldn't hear what was said, but Harris did not seem pleased as he shook his head and turned away. Tom shrugged, raising his hands in defeat, and stepped back as Tilly produced a step stool, from which Harris climbed up onto the wing. He swung first one leg and then the other into the cockpit. Constance was sure no one noticed him use his arms to support his weight, or the hitch and swivel to his movement. Next to her, Poppy let out a little sigh of relief and pressed her hand.

Jock hopped on the wing to lean over for a last-minute discussion before making his way to the front to turn the smooth ash-wood propeller. After a few rotations to ready the engine, he called out to Harris.

'Contact?'

'Contact!' One hard pull down and the propeller sprang to life. The now familiar deafening roar filled Constance's ears. Harris ran the engine wide open for a few moments, white smoke from the vaporised castor oil spitting, as the rotary engine spun around. Jock and Tilly held the wings steady. Then at his signal, they dodged smoothly underneath to remove the wooden chocks from the wheels. The aeroplane began to roll forward on the grass, Harris blipping the engine on and off to control her speed. The small boys at the fence began to run alongside, cheering and waving. Constance felt a wild urge to do the same.

⊰⧏⊱

A HUNDRED YARDS at most to focus and get the bird in flight and Harris's head was filled not with Jock's shouted reminder to keep some left rudder on the right turns but with Tom Morris's last-minute offer to come along.

'Just in case you get in trouble with your leg. In case she gets ahead of you?' Ahead indeed! As if he and Jock had not fully prepared to compensate for the lack of feeling in his left leg. He had been lifting weights and pounding around the fields to build his strength. Still aggravated, he adjusted his boot in the small brace Jock had welded on to stabilise his left foot against the rudder. The tail elevator waggled wildly. He rebalanced both feet equally and flexed one set of fingers at a time against the stick, the better to relax his hands.

'No need to be a martyr to your pride,' Tom had said, and he had been forced to turn away so as not to show the flush of anger that might be taken for shame or weakness. Now he let the engine run wide open again and, with a roar, the machine picked up speed. He exhaled sharply, blowing out his lips; anything to expel Tom's voice, which burrowed wormlike and insidious into his mind. What if he was weak? What if experience and hard work did not make up for his physical loss? The grass blurred away under him and the small boys fell behind. He fought to hold the stick steady as the mass of hedge and trees loomed ahead. But the sky seemed more infinite and blue, and he sensed a lightness beneath him. On the cusp of flight, a familiar stillness came to him and Tom Morris fell away at last. A brief thought of Constance Haverhill, watching, caused a smile to cross his face. He dropped his shoulders, braced his legs evenly and pulled back smoothly on the stick. The machine gave one jarring hop on the uneven ground then soared, as steep and as fast as he remembered, into the air.

By the second flip around the field, he had ceased sweating and adjusted his compromised left leg to the remembered nuances of the rudder. The Camel remained nimble and responsive to his touch. He had forgotten how intense and thrilling it was to defeat gravity, and he welcomed the hard pressure of air drumming against his cheeks and nostrils. His confidence blossomed and, keeping the nose of the biplane up, Harris tested the yaw to left and right.

'Here we waltz,' he shouted over the sound of the engine. 'You can do it, girl.' With a left-right waggle, he threw the stick to starboard, touched the rudder, and the aeroplane obligingly turned and began to spiral down. A whoop of joy escaped him, not so much for the arcing swoop as for the way his hands and legs automatically moved to stop the machine from spinning and to pull it up high into the air again. He could feel his knee ache against the cup of his false leg, but the metal brace had worked. His strength had held. 'Let's go again,' he added and fell away to port this time before soaring up and over the barn; over the sea of tiny faces, waving hats and handkerchiefs. He turned one wing up and waved to them sideways and then pulled the machine into a climb to launch the final test: a diving spin down and away towards the sea.

In the release of the climbing, the air beating against his face, his eyes blurred even beneath the goggles, his happiness became indistinguishable from sorrow, and he felt the presence of all those who had not come home, who had left him behind. As if they were a silent squadron beating up into the sky behind him. At the apex of his climb, as the nose rolled over and all weight left his body for a moment, he felt the loss strangle his throat and tear at his chest. The aeroplane began to spin and all the sky was gone from his vision. Only the green earth wheeling beneath him, the ground blurring into a green river and the blood pounding in his ears as he counted the circumlocutions one-and-a-two-and-a-three-and-a . . . Time seemed to expand and he thought how easy it would be to crush his linen wings against the velvet grass and join his brothers.

As the engine roared and the wires sang with the wind, his mind flashed on the face of the girl, breathless in the field below. His body took over, his hands centring the stick and his legs resisting a natural urge to push against the rudder. Calm now, he pulled back on the stick and the spin became a dive, the grass so close he could see a rabbit racing for the shelter of a gorse bush aflame with yellow flowers. Then slowly the nose rotated upward, the dive became a sweep and he roared back up and over the barn and the upturned faces below, raising a gloved hand to wave. They would see only his nonchalance, and his white scarf streaming, he thought, and no one would know how desperate the choice had been or the exhilaration of choosing, finally, to live. The grass was edged with pure white chalk now and he was up, up, up again over the cliff and soaring for the joy of it, out into the blue freedom of the English sky.

CONSTANCE WATCHED THE small plane dive and soar in the sky and her heart lifted at the magnificence of human flight. She had seen the little red seaplanes, with their cargo of seaside visitors, buzzing along on their smooth elliptical journeys back and forth along the seafront, but she had not been prepared for the magnificence of the Camel making its defiant acrobatic arcs and turns so close above their heads. The crowd gasped and ducked, the ladies holding their ears against the barrage of noise, the children wrinkling their noses as the smell of petrol, hot castor oil and smoke came and went amid the scents of fresh grass and wildflowers. Tom Morris stood with folded arms and spoke quietly to Sam Newcombe. Sam waved his hat once or twice as Harris flew by. They could see the salute of Harris's glove and the long white scarf rippling behind him in the rush of air.

'Isn't it magnificent?' Poppy said, her voice filled with a child's delight. In her fist she clutched handbills offering ladies flying lessons. 'We can rename ourselves now,' she added. 'We shall be The Hazelbourne Ladies Motorcycle and Flying Club from this day on.'

It was hard to remember, Constance thought, how recently such God-given ingenuity had been wasted in grim slaughter. And hard to picture the taciturn Harris at the controls of such a wild machine. Another hand tugged at her. It was Tilly, whispering loudly to follow her to the barn. She was reluctant to tear her gaze from the sky, but Tilly was already hurrying off. Inside the barn, she hurried to the back, and as Constance caught up she heard the unmistakable sound of retching.

'It's Iris,' said Tilly. 'Almost fainted as soon as the plane took off and now she can't stop being sick.'

'Is it something she ate?'

'No, it's nerves,' said Tilly. 'She's petrified.'

'I don't understand,' said Constance. 'You can't mean she's afraid to fly?'

'Who'd have thought it,' said Tilly. 'I'll get her some water.'

Groaning, Iris appeared gingerly from the passageway, holding the wall, her face drained and colourless.

'I'm going to ruin everything,' she said, slumping into a chair.

'Just put your head between your knees,' instructed Constance, trying to keep her voice firm. 'You'll be fine in a minute. I expect it's all the excitement.'

'I can't do it,' she whispered. 'I just can't do it.'

'Nonsense!' said Constance, handing her the glass of water Tilly had brought. 'I've seen you race that motorcycle at seventy miles an hour over a cart track. Flying with Harris will be like pottering along the promenade on the Morris girls' machine.'

'I'll die,' said Iris. 'I just know I'll die.'

'Well, I'm sure the newspaper will make even more money in that case, but if you don't go, they will not be happy,' said Tilly. 'Come on, Iris, it's not as if you have to actually fly the thing. You're only in the passenger seat and you'll be in good hands with Harris in control.'

This caused Iris to groan again and she shook her head as if her mind were made up. Tilly looked at Constance in despair.

'I'm sure it's only a passing weakness,' said Constance. 'Perhaps she isn't feeling well. We'll just let them know it's to be postponed.'

'There's no time,' said Iris. 'They want pictures now to advertise the upcoming Peace Day celebrations. I'm going to lose everything.'

'I'd go for you in an instant,' said Tilly. 'I'm dying to fly, but I think they'd notice we are a different shape.'

'I could do it,' said Constance. The words were out before she could think them, and she felt herself blush at her own audacity.

'Constance, you're brilliant,' said Iris.

'Brilliant and reasonably tall,' said Tilly, squinting. 'You're just about the right size, give or take three inches.'

'But we're not twins,' said Constance. 'I can't be in the pictures for you.'

'No, but you can fly for me,' said Iris. 'We'll figure out the rest later.'

'Or perhaps we should fetch Poppy?' Constance was beginning to regret her offer. The idea of flying thrilled her, but the crowd outside would surely see through her immediately and she was in enough trouble with Lady Mercer.

'Poppy's too much in the limelight,' said Iris. 'They'll notice if she's gone. No one will be looking for you.'

'Thank you,' said Constance, trying not to be insulted by the truth.

'It could definitely work,' said Tilly. 'Shouldn't be a problem on the way out. She can just wear the hat and goggles and run to the aeroplane. But on the way back?'

'Easy,' said Iris. 'Just meet the Camel with your motorcycle and whisk "Iris" up to the barn to wipe the oil from her face. They'll believe that.'

'Let's do it,' said Tilly.

'I'm feeling nauseous as well now,' said Constance. 'Perhaps it's not a good idea.' But even as she said this, she realised the roiling in her stomach might be excitement more than fear. Her thoughts were already racing with how to make her way through the crowd undetected.

'You aren't actually getting sick though, are you?' said Tilly. 'So that's a start. Let's see if the flight suit fits. I'll have to sponge off that lapel.'

'Yes, sorry about that,' said Iris, immediately more cheerful as she began to unbutton her coveralls.

'This is probably a terrible idea,' said Constance. But she was already unhooking her skirt and kicking off her shoes.

'The best ideas are,' said Iris. 'And don't worry, I'm pretty sure you won't die.'

WITH THE WIND on her nose, the machine came down in the smoothest of three-point landings, and Harris took pleasure in his own skill as he rolled up the field. He had calculated the distance and slope well and, with a few blips of the engine to lower his speed, the Camel rolled almost to a stop as Jock ran forward to grab the outer wing strut and help him spin the machine around.

'How did she feel?' asked Jock, stepping up to lean in the cockpit as Harris switched off.

'Smooth as a baby,' said Harris.

'Took you long enough to get out of the spin,' said Jock, frowning.

'I was enjoying the waltzing,' said Harris.

'Well, don't be doing it again. I can get another pilot but it's expensive to get another aeroplane.'

'Heart in the right place, as ever,' said Harris. 'Are we ready to take up Miss Iris?'

'Sort of,' said Jock. 'Here they come now.' In what Harris assumed was a last-minute flourish of showmanship, Tilly came roaring through the crowd on her motorcycle with Iris, in her bright blue coveralls and pink scarf, seated in the sidecar. She was already in her cap and goggles and waving at the enthusiastic crowd. As they pulled up, he could see a newspaper photographer lumbering behind, looking to get another photograph, but Tilly was already helping Iris from the sidecar and Jock was showing her where to step up on the wing. As she climbed into the front seat, she gave him a brave smile.

'What on earth?' It took a second look, but he realised it was not Iris stepping into his machine. It was the Haverhill girl, doing her best to hide the fear in her big brown eyes.

'Small deception, Iris is ill,' said Tilly, rapping her knuckles on the flange of the cockpit. 'When you come back try to stop down by that tree and I'll come pick her up.'

'Is she going to be all right?' He gestured at the shivering girl in the front cockpit.

'She's a trouper,' said Jock, who had finished strapping her in. 'Petrol on? Ignition off?' Harris confirmed and Jock ran to the front while Tilly stepped away and waved off the rapidly closing photographer. Three or four rotations on the propeller again and Jock called for ignition.

'Contact!' confirmed Harris. Once more the machine burst to life and began to roll along the grass. This time there was only calm as he roared down the field gathering speed. Calm and also a determination to make this second flight as smooth and controlled as possible so as not to petrify the girl in the front seat.

THE NOISE WAS overwhelming, battering her ears even under the padded earflaps, vibrating in her chest. Then the release from the weight of the ground and the leap into the air, weightless, as if tossed like a child from her father's arms. The wind pummelled her cheeks and pressed against her nose as if to suffocate her. For a moment all was panic and then, remembering the fear and the joy of cresting the Downs in a motorcycle sidecar, she took a deep, slow breath and opened her eyes to look about in wonder. The Sussex countryside spread below like a model. Tiny houses huddled in villages, tiny church steeples, miniature sheep running in fields stitched together like a quilt. The thick grey seams of roads, the rivers glittering like silver. As the aeroplane banked right, her heart thumped against her ribs. The sea came into view and the sharp white edges of the cliffs, and with another deep breath, she raised her arms and gave a long whoop of sheer joy.

They flew on, and slightly below them a small flock of blackbirds flew in parallel and she marvelled to watch their small shoulders working their wings up and down. The machine turned back towards the barn, and as they swept low she remembered her duty and waved energetically to the crowd with both hands. One more circuit, slipping sideways at a somewhat alarming angle to lose height, and, to Constance's sorrow, Harris brought the aeroplane smoothly in to land. She blinked as the wheels hit, as if waking reluctantly from a dream. The machine came to a stop well short of the barn and Tilly and Jock were already waiting for them. Constance stepped out onto the wing and hopped to the ground. Behind her, Harris stood up and reached down his hand to shake hers.

'Well done,' he said. 'I hope you enjoyed it?'

'I didn't want to come down,' she said. 'I had no idea it would be so wonderful.'

'Let's go,' called Tilly, her engine revving. 'They're waiting for Iris to make her report.'

'I have to go,' she said. 'I'm not allowed to tell anyone about this, but I may just burst with excitement.'

'I'll find you later,' he said. 'We'll talk all about it, I promise.'

IN THE DIM shelter of the barn door, Constance watched as Iris, surrounded by excited well-wishers, was given a large bouquet and smiled for more pictures on Harris's arm. She was trying not to feel a touch of resentment when Evangeline Morris appeared at her side, flustered and frowning.

'Since Iris is always beating the drum of the independent woman, I have no idea why she's clinging so tightly to Harris. It's almost unseemly.'

'I think it's just for the newspapers,' said Constance. 'She doesn't mean anything by it.'

'I've known Harris forever, of course,' Evangeline added. 'It was so devastating when he was crippled.'

'He seems to be doing much better these days,' said Constance. Perhaps he was not smiling as broadly as might be expected given the press of young women around him, but he was standing straight and did not look as tired as usual. 'I'm sure Poppy will be relieved to see him managing all the attention so well.'

'My father told me Harris would never fly again,' said Evangeline. 'That he would always be an invalid.' She seemed puzzled and not a little put out that Harris had failed to accept his fate.

'You've seen the men at the convalescent home,' said Constance. 'A simple amputation might seem not so devastating.'

'Yes, only as Father said, no sort of sensitive girl could be expected to stomach it.' She sighed. 'I suppose if it had only been an arm, he would still have been able to dance. I for one can't live without dancing, can you?'

'In this war, most women found a strong stomach,' said Constance. She paused, finding herself at the same time driven to defend Harris and reluctant to share further. 'Actually, Harris has been dancing. It's good for his balance and he's become quite proficient.'

'And how do you know this?' asked Evangeline.

'I've been here all week in the afternoons,' said Constance. 'I'm helping Poppy put her finances in order.'

'Ah yes, I think Poppy said she had taken you on in her latest batch of unemployed girls,' said Evangeline. 'Such a charitable heart, I've told my father they should make her a trustee of the almshouse.'

'I'm just making myself useful until after my cousin, Rachel, gets married,' said Constance, conscious that, in her desire to avoid humiliation, she had found sanctuary in the same faded myth, of uncompensated equality and family connection, that had sustained her mother for decades. 'Then I intend to take up a real career.'

'I can't imagine having to join the ranks of the employed,' said Evangeline. 'It's delightful to make money – my sister and I are quite determined to build an absolute fortune of our own – but I imagine it's a complete bore to be forced to grub about doing someone else's bidding day after day.'

'Millions of us worked during the war,' said Constance, feeling her face redden with a barely suppressed anger. 'We would not have survived without the work of women.'

'Of course, one wanted to do one's part,' said Evangeline. 'But if we have learned anything from these horrible few years, it's that there is no time to waste one's life. We must dance, and travel and fall in love – seize the day and damn tomorrow.'

'If I were amply provided for, I might well feel the same,' said Constance. 'But I am not ashamed to say I must plan for my tomorrow.'

Once again, she pinched out shame, which tended to sprout like a weed under the niggling judgement of others.

'Given the swiftness of her marriage plans, I think your cousin – though I believe she is not a real cousin? – would agree with me?' Evangeline's face bore an unpleasant smirk and she tossed her hair as Constance glared.

'Rachel's fiancé works at the highest echelons of government,' she said. 'He is needed back by the President himself.'

'So say the rumours around the hotel,' said Evangeline. 'Gwinny and I have not been introduced, of course, but we are both sure there's nothing untoward in the hasty timing.' She adopted a look of concern. 'Not that we would judge,' she added. 'For all a girl tries to be careful, you never know, do you?'

Constance was rendered blinking and speechless, both by the notion that the Morris girls themselves might have need of being careful and by the outrageous slander against Rachel. It was an impossibly cruel piece of gossip to repeat, and it had done its work as the poison seed began to sprout in Constance's mind. Now she wondered why Lord Mercer had capitulated so swiftly to Rachel's marriage. And why Lady Mercer had dropped all argument and begun to order flowers, and Rachel – happy Rachel – was there perhaps a tinge of desperation in her endless adoration of Percy?

Evangeline did not seem to notice Constance's confusion and went blithely on. 'How good is Harris's dancing, by the way? Will he be able to dance at his mother's ball, do you think?'

'It's not my place to guess,' said Constance, not caring if she sounded rude. 'I don't gossip.'

'Oh, I'll never tell,' said Evangeline slyly. 'You can count on me.'

'I really shouldn't have mentioned it,' Constance added. 'Dancing in public is quite another thing.'

'But if the man can dance, perhaps a girl might reconsider her natural delicacy. Who knew there would be such a limited supply of suitable gentlemen. What are we all supposed to do? One wouldn't want to end up marrying a tradesman or something worse, like an American. Not to disparage your cousin. Her fiancé being from, we are assured, as high a family as one can find in the former colonies.'

'Perhaps we should support ourselves and stop worrying about finding a husband,' said Constance. 'Independence has its attractions.'

'An unheated bed-sitting room and baggy lisle stockings,' said Evangeline. 'My old governess lives in Clerkenwell.' She shivered. 'Just her and a mangy cat cooking porridge on a hot plate.'

'Does the cat also boil eggs?' asked Constance. Evangeline looked puzzled, then laughed.

'I shouldn't be too gloomy. I'm sure you'll find a lovely room somewhere, and I know they have lots of clubs and activities for working girls these days. I just wouldn't recommend getting a cat. Somehow the cat hairs on her skirt hem were the saddest thing of all.'

'Evangeline, the man from the newspaper was asking the spelling of your name.' It was Poppy, and the arch look on her face indicated she had overheard quite enough. 'I think you had better make sure he has all your information.'

'Thank you, Poppy darling,' said Evangeline. 'I suppose one must keep up with the press, even though it is all quite exhausting.' With that she sallied forth from the barn as Poppy rolled her eyes.

'Don't pay any attention to her,' said Poppy. 'She thinks she's a princess in a castle and we are all her serfs. I swear Evangeline is enough to make one understand the revolutionaries in Russia.'

'Yet she's not altogether wrong,' said Constance. 'Not everyone will be as gracious as you once I am a working woman.'

'Well, damn them, I say,' said Poppy. 'You are worth twice a Morris girl, which is why they probably had to have two of them.'

'You are truly terrible,' said Constance.

'I am. So let's go and ask Iris more questions about how wonderful it was to fly,' said Poppy. 'Just to make her squirm a little.'

After the crowds were gone and Jock and Tilly were putting the Camel away under its tarpaulins, Constance saw Poppy and Harris standing on the track talking to a man in an ill-fitting brown suit, who carried himself as stiff as the high celluloid collar around his red neck. He was stroking his moustache as if to calm his anxiety. Even from a distance, Constance could see Poppy was upset, and she went immediately to offer her support. As she approached she could hear Poppy dress him down in the firm manner of a woman confident in her class and education.

'So you see, my good man, my enterprise is entirely new and separate. It did not exist before the war.'

'With due respect, madam, begging your pardon and all . . .' He hesitated and turned to Harris. 'You'll have read, sir, that taxi service, moving and drayage, motor repair, flying, are all to be covered occupations.'

'My sister's efforts are to provide a living for young women,' said Harris. 'Surely there are exceptions?'

'We employ several war widows,' added Poppy.

'Well now, you see, your war widows, they get the pension.' He brightened as if they might find common ground.

'We are, for all intents and purposes, a charity,' said Poppy. She noticed Constance and beckoned her over. 'Here is our bookkeeper now. She'll tell you we've made barely a profit in the last six months.'

'How do you do, miss,' the man said, raising his fedora. 'I was explaining to Captain Wirrall and Miss Wirrall that the Labour Board is talking to businesses in advance of the new law that's about to come in. Covered occupations to be offered to returning servicemen.'

'Wirrall's is hardly a giant factory or shipbuilding yard,' said Constance. 'Shouldn't you be focused on the larger, unionised employers?'

'Law's the law,' said the man. 'When we get a complaint we have to investigate. You'll have to provide evidence of compliance or be summoned to appear before the local board.' He tried to hand Harris an official-looking letter.

'The letter goes to the owner,' said Harris. 'I'm just the errand boy, so to speak.'

'Substantial fines may be assessed,' said the man, grim-faced now as he was forced to offer his letter to a woman.

'You can't be serious,' said Poppy. 'This is an outrage.'

'If I were you I'd make plans now to call us at the Labour Exchange. We'll be glad to send you the men you need to keep things running, and once they are hired you can send your girls home without any interruption to your business.'

'My business is my girls,' said Poppy.

'We all have to do our part for our boys coming home. Even those of us as don't have pensions, we have to put that aside, don't we?'

'But there are women and girls who need to eat and pay rent, sir,' said Constance, weak with a sudden fear that bookkeeping might also be covered by the upcoming law.

'Well, there's always domestic service,' said the man. 'Meanwhile it seems you have a couple of men there to run the aeroplane. I'll make a note of that. It's a good start.'

'And if I won't comply?' asked Poppy.

'Prison is also an option,' said the man, cheerfully. 'Now, if you ladies and the gentleman will excuse me, I've a long ride to Eastbourne. Report of a brickyard entirely staffed by girls. Can't imagine what their mothers are thinking letting their daughters be turned into great Amazons carrying hods of bricks all day.' With that he mounted a large black bicycle, touched his hat and wobbled away down the track.

'What will you do?' asked Constance. 'How will you fight it?'

'If I do, I risk another scandal for the family,' said Poppy. 'I don't think I'll win, and I can't afford to be bankrupted by fines.'

'So that's it, then,' said Constance, taking the letter to scan. 'You're just going to turn all the girls out into the street? What about Jenny and the other girls you just hired from the airfield?' By her count there had to be at least ten women who relied on some sort of paid work at the barn. Perhaps because of her own uncertain future, she felt keenly the loss of every small, weekly pay packet. 'It's an absolute outrage. After all they have given.'

'What can she do?' asked Harris, taking the paper from her gently, as if he feared she might tear it in half, and frowning as he looked it over.

'It says here you may have a month or two before the law really takes effect,' he said. Poppy seemed to slump, and Harris put an arm around her shoulders.

'Some of the girls – who just need to earn petrol for their rigs – we can help within the social club, I think,' said Poppy. 'But riders like Jenny I'll have no choice but to let go when the summer is over.'

'And Tilly?' Constance saw now that while she had lived like Poppy these past few weeks, she had seen her future most in Tilly. And though she had not known any of the women long, she felt the blow to Tilly's future the most.

'Poor Tilly, I wish I could do more. I thought once the flying lessons were successful she might take over from Jock as mechanic and I could at last employ her full-time. But I can't risk the fines or being shut down entirely.' Poppy sighed. 'We still have the club, and we have the aeroplane, so Harris can fly. We can still offer lessons to ladies.'

'Wealthy ladies,' said Constance.

'You sound just like Iris,' said Poppy. 'But I have no choice. Perhaps Jock will agree to stay on and run the barn, and I'll keep Tilly on as long as we can, but when they come to inspect again, she'll just have to go back to the library.'

There was a muffled sound, somewhere between a sob and a groan, and Constance turned to see Tilly walking swiftly away from them.

'Oh my goodness, Tilly,' shouted Poppy. 'Come back.'

'I'll not stay where I'm not wanted,' Tilly shouted over her shoulder and kept walking.

'Aren't you going to go after her?' asked Constance. 'Explain that you'll find a way?'

Poppy hesitated. 'I would, but no good can come of it.'

'She's your friend,' said Constance, trying to keep the anger from her voice. 'She would ride through fire for you.'

'Yes, and I love her like a sister too,' said Poppy. She ran her hands roughly through her hair and gave a small roar of frustration. 'Why,

why, why does everyone look to me to fix everything and then blame me when I can't?'

'I just meant she needs words of comfort,' said Constance.

'I won't mouth platitudes about how it's going to be all right when really it is not,' said Poppy. 'I wish Tilly hadn't found out like this, but I don't have anything comforting to say to her.' She took a deep breath. 'I think it's best if I just wait for her to calm down and hopefully she won't tell anyone else. I don't need Iris screaming at me again.'

'My sister doesn't mean to sound flippant,' said Harris to Constance. 'I can assure you these girls mean everything to her.'

'Well, Brother, just promise me you'll keep flying,' said Poppy. She shook his hand and clapped him on the back. 'That would be one bright spot in the demise of all our hopes.' She sighed. 'Shall we go and put the kettle on?'

Constance saw the sadness in his face was all for the others, not for himself. He gave her an encouraging smile. 'Not the end we wanted to such a successful day but while we lick our wounds, we should at least take a moment to sit over a pot of tea and talk about how magnificent Miss Haverhill was as an aviatrix.'

Chapter 22

ON MONDAY MORNING, CONSTANCE WAS ALONE ON THE
Palm Terrace, reading a letter from her brother, when Mr Pendra appeared, frowning as he looked around for an empty table. Constance
caught his eye and smiled, whereupon he came over and shook her hand.

'Infernally busy in here today.' His brow was knitted and his eyes dark.
'I'll probably have the chap send a pot of tea to my room.'

'Would you care to join me, sir?' she asked. 'I've rather spread out, but
I can move my things.' She was already transferring the newspapers and
writing paper to a spare chair as she spoke. She folded her letter and put
it in her pocket. Pendra hesitated.

'Are you sure?' he asked. 'I wouldn't want to impose on a lady.' She
nodded, and some of the thunder cleared from his face.

'Not at all,' she said. 'It saves me from the indignity of having the
empty chairs removed to busier tables, thus highlighting my lonely sta-
tus.'

'The rest of your party?'

'Gone to view the South Downs in a carriage,' she said. 'I stayed behind.' She was proud enough not to mention that Lady Mercer had
sought to exclude her on the grounds that while the carriage could hold
four people, it was so much more comfortable with three people and a
picnic basket. Mrs Fog, of course, had begun to quibble, but Constance

had pleaded much accounting work still to be done and hidden her hurt behind a wide smile.

'You'll join me in some tea?' he asked as the waiter hovered. 'Klaus knows I like my tea good and hot.' She assented and he ordered Darjeeling for two.

'And where is your companion, Mr Basu?' she asked.

'Basu is taking a day off,' said Pendra. 'We are both out of sorts so I told him to go take the air or whatever he wanted. Some days there is nothing to be done.'

'Something troubles the Hazelbourne business world?' she asked.

'No, no, though there is plenty of trouble there to be had if one chooses.' He sighed. 'I received word that the Indian delegation to the Peace Parade in London will not arrive in time.'

'Oh no,' she said. 'What bad luck.'

'Isn't it?' A grimace twisted his fine features. 'A question of shipping delays and a sudden outbreak of influenza, they say. Nothing to be done.'

'I'm so sorry.'

'We were to march some eighteen hundred strong.' He shook his head. 'A small contingent given that British India and the independent princely states together contributed over a million men to this war.'

'I had no idea,' said Constance.

'The normally sanguine Mr Basu has quite boiled over in rage at the carelessness of the British government in mislaying us.'

'It's surely no one's fault,' she said. 'No one can control the influenza, and shipping has been quite disrupted.'

'As civil servants we understand that hitches and delays in a bureaucracy are inevitable,' he said, and Constance noted that while he usually mentioned his profession with an underlying humour, today he seemed merely derisive. 'And yet, as Basu notices, the dominions – the Anzacs, the South Africans and even the Chinese Labour Corps – have been delivered in good time. Of course they are well behaved and do not agitate for home rule.'

'This is what Basu thinks?' Constance spoke cautiously to this new anger. The newspapers, which she read every day, had written of protests in India being put down hard. In her heart, she deplored the lack of mercy and feared worse to come in each day's crowded print columns, but she was careful never to share her opinion, especially with a man.

'I warned him that it may be merely fate and that, in our disappointment, we are unfair. That the West Indies are forbidden from the festivities, and their mutinous soldiers shipped home, does not directly prove our own deliberate exile.'

'But you agree with him?'

'I am not in a position to embrace such radical ideas.' He shook his head in mock sorrow. 'Basu is not always as politic as required. Then I have to send him off to scream into the wilderness.'

'Could you and Mr Basu not represent India since you are here?' she asked.

'We have been politely declined in London,' Pendra said, his face a mask of neutrality. 'Fortunately, Mrs Wirrall has invited us to join her in the grandstand.'

'Well, I think it's wonderful that India will be represented right here in Hazelbourne,' said Constance, angry that these most polite of men, who had served as nobly as any British officers, could have their invitation to march in the national parade withdrawn. The thought surfaced that no Englishman would have been treated so casually, and she blushed as if she herself had dismissed them.

'I fear two men could not possibly represent all of British India and the independent states,' he said. 'But as India is such an exotic terra incognita to the English mind, Basu and I will do our best.'

'I looked up Kochi Benar in the atlas,' said Constance. 'I think you are in the hill country?'

'You prove yourself the exception, Miss Haverhill,' he said. 'I hope I was not rude.'

'I must say, you are a very strange sort of civil servant, Mr Pendra,' said Constance.

'You are, I think, both perceptive and trustworthy, Miss Haverhill.' He gave her a long quizzical stare. 'So I will share with you, in confidence, that mine is a small state and a government that must be very careful about its place in the Empire. Let us say I prefer to go about as a civil servant of a lower rank than I might claim because I have seen how senior officials too often receive only flattery, inflated prices and empty promises. Basu and I hope instead to get an honest response in the social realm and an honest price in the business one.'

'And do you succeed or suffer, Mr Pendra?' She remembered he was not allowed to fly at the airfield and wondered what other insults he and Basu might have endured.

'We have had some successes,' he said. 'But sometimes, they do not want the colonies to have access, at any price, to the things that might make us too strong.' He sighed. 'And then I must restrain Basu from dressing them down and remind him of our mission. If we must humble ourselves and even pursue success through a competent intermediary, so be it.'

'And will you reveal yourself someday to those who were less than kind?'

'Ah, once again you see my real plan.' He laughed. 'I believe my business will be successfully concluded before the Peace Parade. May I count on your discretion until then, Miss Haverhill?'

'You may, Mr Pendra,' she said.

'And – if I may be bold – who are you behind your disguise, Miss Haverhill?' he added, smiling. 'Do you live with Lady Mercer at Clivehill?'

'My family owns a large farm nearby.' She paused. 'My brother and his wife have it now. It will always be home, but one does not wish to impose.' The letter in her pocket from her brother was the first he had written since her departure, though she wrote to him every few days. In his lumpy farmer's script, he had expressed some regret that she was not home to advise him on the pricing of the summer's corn and barley crops. This she took as an expression of real warmth. In an awkward postscript, in which his hand became more spiky and anxious, he announced that his wife was pregnant again and suffering from the usual nausea. No specific invitation home was extended, but his words eased her exile. As she felt the colour rise in her cheeks, Mr Pendra's warm brown eyes seemed to sympathise. He placed a hand on his chest as he answered.

'I fear that young ladies often have a similarly uncertain and tenuous relationship to home as second sons and nephews. I have been both of those, so I do understand your pain.'

'Thank you,' she said. 'You are a sharp observer of human nature, Mr Pendra.'

'In this I believe we are also similar, Miss Haverhill,' he said. 'Two peas observing the rest of the scattered pod?' She laughed and felt that here was someone who shared her sense of amusement at the world.

'Mr Pendra, you have been very honest with me in a manner you yourself would describe as impolitic,' she said. 'I believe I can count on your trust in return?' He nodded, so with an unaccustomed sense of glee, she told him about flying in Iris's place and how wonderful it had been.

'Well, good for you, Miss Haverhill. You are exactly the dark horse I thought you were,' he said. 'And am I to understand that the committee expects Miss Iris to fly the aeroplane herself at the Peace Day parade air show? Will she be recovered from her sickness and able to take to the skies in a week's time?'

'Would I be a terrible person to hope she will not?' she asked. Pendra laughed aloud.

'Then I think Captain Wirrall should prepare you immediately to take her place,' he said. 'It will be no small thing to take the controls of the Sopwith Camel, even for the shortest time. They are tricky work for the most accomplished fliers.'

'I must hope I have the strength to hold her steady for just a few minutes,' she said. 'It isn't real flying, of course, Captain Harris will always be at the dual controls, but Poppy hopes it will be enough to make people believe that women can fly too.'

'You'll get no argument from me,' he said. 'Despite my experience as a pilot, when I first applied to the Flying Corps, it was suggested I become an air mechanic instead. Some imputed weakness of my race, or perhaps a disinclination to train and empower a colonial. Either way I would never presume to tell someone they are not allowed to fly.'

'With what argument did you prevail?' she asked. 'We could perhaps make use of it.'

'I went to the French and obtained an immediate commission,' he said. 'Horrible embarrassment to the government to have a British subject forced to fight for an ally, so they quickly reconsidered.'

Constance laughed. 'I doubt the entire Hazelbourne Ladies Motorcycle and Flying Club can up and move to Paris,' she said. 'Though it sounds wonderful to me.'

LADY MERCER HAD agreed with the utmost reluctance to attend the hotel's Tuesday afternoon tea dance, and Constance was asked to forgo her afternoon bookkeeping to support Rachel.

'Nothing looks worse than a girl alone,' said Rachel. 'One must have companion girls around one.'

'Hotel dances! Shopgirls and divorcees I shouldn't wonder,' sighed Lady Mercer as they were shown to a prominent table. 'This is what the war has done to us.'

'It must be harmless, surely, if Mrs Wirrall and her daughter attend?' said Rachel, looking around with undisguised happiness at the filling room. 'Of course, it's not the same as a private ball. I'm told Mrs Wirrall's will be the event of the season here.'

'My point is made,' said Lady Mercer as Rachel turned away to order a lemonade from the waiter. 'As you know, before the war, Clivehill was recognised throughout the county for its private balls. I suppose with Rachel moving away it will hardly seem worthwhile to open the ballroom again.' Her face slackened, and Constance knew her anguish was real. She was surprised, not that Lady Mercer should be affected by her daughter's departure, but that she herself had not allowed for it. She was so busy thinking of her as an adversary to be managed, that she had not allowed any compassion for the mother about to lose her daughter for good. She reached over to discreetly squeeze Lady Mercer's hand.

'There will be steamship crossings again,' she said quietly. 'You and Lord Mercer will surely visit her in Washington.'

'My grandchildren will be strangers and my daughter a foreigner,' said Lady Mercer. 'But I need neither your platitudes nor your pity, my dear. A sense of duty will sustain me.'

'Constance, you and Poppy must introduce me to everyone,' said Rachel. 'My last chance to dance before becoming a bride.'

As Constance introduced her to the Morris girls, and to Harris and Sam, Rachel sparkled. The glow of being so nearly a bride gave her a confidence that Constance envied. It seemed she even had some school friends in common with Evangeline and Guinevere, which quite won over the twins and made them all squeal with happiness. Unlike her mother, Rachel showed no hint of sorrow in telling of her upcoming nuptials and her move to America. She was even smooth and polite to Mr Pendra, who made the rounds of the room, providing conversation and ordering refreshments but declining to dance, despite any number of friendly protestations.

'He's actually a very intelligent man,' Rachel confided to Constance, as Mr Pendra busied himself fetching them glasses of punch from the passing tray of Klaus the waiter. 'Percival says being a diplomat's or politician's wife often requires presenting an affable front despite any natural distaste. Americans of course do not have the tolerance we do, given our Empire. They do not understand them as we do. But in this case it isn't hard to like the man; even if he is Indian.'

'I doubt Mr Pendra would find our tolerance any more palatable than the most crude expression of distaste, Rachel,' Constance whispered, her tone sharp. 'If you're going to practise diplomacy, you might start by treating the man as an equal.'

'What an extraordinary thing to say,' said Rachel. 'If you're going to spout such alarming ideas, perhaps it is better you do not become a governess.'

TIRED FROM DANCING, and perhaps from smiling at all the compliments about Rachel, Constance decided to sit out the next dance and waved off Sam with an excuse about her bruised feet. Sam, whom she suspected had asked her out of a lack of courage, was then forced to ask Poppy, who was sitting next to her. He was visibly delighted when she agreed. Tom Morris, who was bearing down on Poppy, contained his chagrin and promptly asked the bride-to-be for the dance instead.

'If poor Constance doesn't mind being left all alone?' asked Rachel, already rising from her seat.

'I'll be just fine,' Constance assured her.

'Your cousin seems truly happy,' said Harris, appearing at Constance's elbow as Rachel was carried off into the group assembling for the mazurka. 'It's unusual, if pleasant, to see.'

'It's as if the war has not touched her,' said Constance, inviting him to sit. 'The rest of us have been aged and scarred. She is what the world could have looked like.'

'She will not miss her home?'

'She is too young to weigh the cost of leaving,' said Constance. 'And then she is the one leaving. I think it is much harder to be the one left behind.' He blanched and she saw she had touched a raw nerve.

'You have a way of speaking truth,' he said. 'It's a rare quality.'

'In a woman?' she asked, laughing.

'No, in anyone,' he replied, looking surprised. 'I think you would know me better than to accuse me of such a lazy insult.'

'Yes, your insults are usually well honed and direct,' she said.

'Being direct, can you get away from the financial books tomorrow and come for a flying lesson?' he said. 'If we are to have "Iris" fly the Camel on Saturday, I need "her" to know the basics. We can pretend you are just another paying student.' The flying part of the club had begun the same day as the test flight, with at least three ladies, including Gwinny Morris, signing up for lessons and others going up for brief pleasure flights. Constance envied the young women crowded with Iris around the blackboard, learning the finer details of flight, and leaving with their new goggles and their instruction books under their arms. It seemed a cruel irony that Iris, who had yet to brave the cockpit, had all the sponsorship, but none of the stomach, for flying. To Constance, flying was another passion for which she would never have the funds. Still, she had pilfered an extra copy of the instruction book.

'I would be thrilled,' she said. 'But your mother wishes me to be finished with her ledgers tomorrow as I believe your family banker visits on Thursday? I may be working until very late.'

'I can imagine,' he said. 'But perhaps you can spare an hour or two in the afternoon to walk down to the barn? The lesson is important, Constance, and we are out of time and options if we are to help Iris.'

'I've read the instruction book,' she said, blushing. For the last three nights, she had read late into the night by the light of a single lamp. She had lingered over the chapters on navigation, dreaming of flying across to France, or along the coast to picnic on the Isle of Wight.

'Most of our boys had only that book and two weeks of training before flying combat missions,' said Harris. 'Two hours or so should prepare you to take the stick for a few minutes. Any more and you'll be begging me to let you fly alone.'

'I don't beg,' she said.

'No, you don't,' he said and leaned in closer. 'But those deep brown eyes do command.' Before she could summon a response, he got to his feet and moved away. 'I'll ask my mother to invite you to dinner. That way we'll have plenty of time to talk about flying.'

DURING A REFRESHMENT break for the orchestra, the gentlemen escaped to the snug and the ladies joined Mrs Wirrall and Lady Mercer over tea and several tiered stands of mushroom puffs, cucumber sandwiches and selections of small sponge-cake dainties. Mrs Wirrall unbent enough to Lady Mercer to acknowledge some fatigue.

'I hardly know how I will fulfil my duties on the reviewing stand and also prepare for my party,' said Mrs Wirrall. 'I may have overestimated my powers.'

'Constance could help you,' said Lady Mercer. 'I understand she's already been invaluable.' The smile she directed at Constance did not crinkle her eyes.

'She has indeed,' said Mrs Wirrall. 'But all the girls of the motorcycle club, including Constance, are in the parade, you know. I would hate to deny her that pleasure.'

'How the times have changed,' said Lady Mercer. 'Our mothers would never have countenanced such public display, would they, Mrs Wirrall?'

'It is for the larger patriotic cause, Lady Mercer,' said Mrs Wirrall, and she too smiled with just her lips, and if she worried that her career upon the stage might be remembered, she showed no such concern.

'I seem to recall you performing half-naked in theatrical tableaux when you were younger, Hildegarde,' said Mrs Fog. 'They were supposed to be classical themes and old master paintings but were an excuse for all the girls to dampen their muslins to a shocking degree, I remember.'

'Those were private parties, Mother,' said Lady Mercer. 'Not a display before the unwashed classes.'

'Well, the parade would be dull indeed without the young ladies with their flowers and the children,' said Mrs Fog. Children were to parade with flags and decorated hoops and be given a tea afterward. 'I think we can be assured that Hazelbourne-on-Sea will make sure all is perfectly proper.'

'I would be happy to go to Penneston instead,' said Constance, trying not to appear too eager. 'If Poppy can spare me?' If she was to fly in Iris's place she needed an excuse to miss the parade.

Poppy was quickly into the breach. 'Of course,' she said. 'Though your absence will leave a gaping hole.' Evangeline Morris paused in selecting a single cucumber sandwich.

'Would Miss Rachel consider taking your place? We would be delighted to have such an elegant replacement, and I'm sure the crowd would be delighted to see the bride-to-be.'

'Wonderful idea,' said Gwinny. 'Though we will miss Constance.'

'Oh, do let me, Mother,' said Rachel. 'We mustn't let the people down.'

'That would be very unorthodox,' said Lady Mercer. 'We had planned to be as retired as possible before the wedding. Mr Smickle said he could find us a very private corner in the hotel grandstand.'

'No, no, you must come and sit with me,' said Mrs Wirrall. 'I have extra tickets for the Grand Reviewing Stand. You would honour us if you would agree to sit with the Mayor and the other dignitaries.'

'How wonderful,' said Evangeline. 'And Rachel will be the highlight of the ladies' troop. There is nothing like a bride to express our faith in the future.'

'She can ride with us,' said Gwinny. 'We will be her handmaidens accompanying her to the altar.'

'Very well,' said Lady Mercer. 'Rachel will cover Constance's absence and I will be happy if my presence in the stands supports the town.'

'I shan't risk my actual wedding dress in a dusty parade,' said Rachel. 'Perhaps I can wear your parade dress, Constance?' She frowned and continued, 'Of course it will be too big for me. You have a bigger bone structure, you know. I shall probably have to have one or two tucks made if there is time.' Constance was ready to snap at her, but Poppy wriggled her eyebrows, which took some of the sting away, and made her lips twitch.

'That would be fine,' she said, her voice a study in calmness. 'It was your dress to begin with. I haven't altered it at all.' Evangeline giggled and Gwinny had the grace to look uncomfortable.

'Evie and I share clothes all the time,' she said to Constance. 'Sometimes they are a little tight on her.'

'You are a witch,' said Evangeline.

'I was also a slip of a girl at Rachel's age,' said Lady Mercer. 'Even without a corset, my husband could almost fit his two hands around my waist.' Lady Mercer's frame had been substantially padded in flesh for as long as Constance could remember, so it was disconcerting to see her blush the mildest pink at some secret memory of hands.

'You must go to Poppy's friend,' said Mrs Wirrall. 'A lovely young seamstress with a delicate touch and very fast.'

'Jenny is not the most sophisticated girl, but she does superb stitching and is very artistic,' said Evangeline.

'I was going to ask her to add a ribbon or two to my evening dress just to make it a little fresh,' said Constance. 'But I know she's very busy with all the celebrations and the ball.'

'I hope you won't mind if my dress comes first,' said Rachel. 'As I'm to be in the public eye.'

'Well, I was trying to practise the Charleston in my new dress and I already tore a seam up to the thigh,' said Poppy. 'Let's all go to Jenny's tomorrow morning. If I drop her a note, and bring her a pint of petrol, I'm sure she'll fit us all in.'

'And tomorrow afternoon I hope Constance might join us up at Penneston to finish up my accounts?' said Mrs Wirrall. She leaned in confidentially to Lady Mercer. 'I am going to stay up at the house beginning tomorrow, just to see that all is in place and the staff are up to snuff before Saturday.'

'Perhaps Constance can stay the night,' said Poppy. 'We can give her the lay of the land, so to speak, well before Saturday's chaos.'

'If Mrs Fog can spare me?' asked Constance. Lady Mercer frowned and seemed about to refuse.

'She should be introduced to the new servants,' said Mrs Wirrall, speaking as if Constance were herself a servant. 'They will need a firm hand and I believe you have trained her well.' Lady Mercer nodded at the compliment. Evangeline Morris smirked. They failed to see Mrs Wirrall's broad wink at Constance.

JENNY LIVED IN a small cottage in the old town across from a large bakery. Constance, glancing briefly, was jolted to recognise the woman behind the bakery window. It was Mrs Wilson, whom she had met on the beach with Klaus. A red-faced man stood close to her, scowling as she carefully placed a stack of small pies in the window. Constance would have liked to wave, or support the woman by popping in to buy something. But she had the suspicion that to do any such thing would make life difficult for Mrs Wilson; and possibly for the waiter too.

The bow window of the seamstress's cottage was heavily draped in lace curtains, and the narrow sill held a miniature model of a tailor's dummy. Both dummy and sill were draped in a roll of cheerful muslin, sprigged with yellow and pink daisies. A small needlepoint sign, colourful wools on a white canvas, indicated *Ladies' Tailoring and Alterations.* Poppy pulled the doorbell.

'Thank you for seeing us on short notice,' she said to Jenny as they were shown into the tiny front parlour, which held three upholstered chairs around the fireplace, a large mirror and a sewing machine along the stairway wall, which was hung with a white curtain. Against the curtain were hung all sorts of dresses and skirts in various stages of construction. A large cabinet of sewing supplies filled another corner almost to the ceiling. It was cramped and did double duty as living and work room, but it was sparkling clean and the round rug, though threadbare, was well beaten and newly fringed.

'Welcome,' said Jenny. 'This is my mother.' A diminutive elderly woman bobbed an arthritic curtsy from the door to the back kitchen.

'I'll make some tea,' said the old lady as she hobbled away. The kitchen, glimpsed through a bead curtain, seemed equally well scrubbed, with polished copper pans above a range and a pine table that bore more fabric, pinned to a paper pattern, and a large pair of pinking shears. A wicker bassinet held a sleeping baby.

'It's like a doll's house,' said Rachel. 'I do so envy people who are able to live so simply, so charmingly. It is so much less difficult than managing a large house.'

'We are happy here,' said Jenny. 'Would you like to show me what you need?' Her pleasant smile and brisk tone suggested she was used to absorbing the vagaries of lady customers as a normal if unpleasant part of commerce.

She pulled the curtain all the way to the front door, creating a small alcove where Rachel could slip on Constance's best white dress. Then a footstool was produced from beneath one of the chairs and Rachel stood on it, in the middle of the rug, while Jenny pulled and straightened fabric and pursed her lip as Rachel described all the nips and tucks she required.

'I think we should leave some room in the shoulders,' Jenny said at last. 'You will be waving at the crowd from the parade.' She had Rachel practise waving in the mirror.

'I see what you mean,' said Rachel, doubtful. 'But perhaps I can just wave from the elbow?' She added a low, slow flexing of the hand, her elbow tucked to her waist.

'Very ladylike,' said Jenny, adding pins to the shoulders. 'I don't think you need any darts in the back, it's already quite tight.' She pinched at the back of the dress.

'That's so strange. My mother must have had it taken in for me before she gave it to Constance,' said Rachel, smoothing the front with her hands and, it seemed to Constance, sucking in her stomach. 'I can't imagine how you ever got into it, Constance.'

'I suppose the lack of food for the last four years has whittled us all down a little,' said Constance. Rachel had always made it her mission to keep as small a waist as possible. Now, as Constance peered at her plump middle more closely, Rachel blushed and hurried behind the curtain.

'Well, I have a serviceable brown walking skirt that I planned to give the hotel maid,' she called, her voice peevish. 'But if you are finally that slim, I'll leave it for you instead.'

'Ooh, if you have that, then maybe you'll pass me on that blue walking skirt of yours,' said Poppy. 'It's so comfortable, I just love it.' Constance looked with gratitude at Poppy, who was lounging in a chair, picking at a loose gold thread on her own party dress.

'Don't ruin that,' said Jenny, slapping at her fingers. 'Go put it on now.'

Poppy's dress was a shimmer of green tulle banded with heavily embroidered gold silk at the dropped waist and hem. It brought out the lights in her hair and the colour of her eyes, and though she did her best to slump and scowl on the box, she looked shockingly good.

'You're a vision,' said Constance.

'What an extraordinary dress,' said Rachel. 'Is it French?'

'Poppy refuses to spend money on what she calls frippery, so I made it for her from two of Mrs Wirrall's old dresses,' said Jenny.

'They're actually costumes,' said Poppy. 'Don't tell anyone but while the green is from *A Midsummer Night's Dream*, I believe the gold was from when she played Salomé.'

'It's beautiful,' said Constance. 'You'll be the belle of the ball, Poppy.'

'Which is far too much pressure for me,' said Poppy. 'I asked Jenny to make something serviceable.'

'And I said she'll wear it, take all the compliments and repeat my name everywhere,' said Jenny. 'You know I need the work, Poppy.'

'All right, all right,' said Poppy. 'But I don't promise to like it.'

'What are you wearing, Jenny?' asked Constance. Jenny dropped her eyes to her pins.

'Oh, I'm not attending the ball,' she said. 'Tilly isn't working at the barn any more – too much work at the library – so I'm managing Wirrall's taxis that evening.'

'It will be very busy,' said Poppy. She looked awkward, and Constance understood she had not told the women of the club about the coming demise of her business. 'A great chance for those of our girls who need to make some money. Many of them have agreed to work.' There was a pause, as the reality of divisions between the women thrust through the illusion of camaraderie.

'Personally, with my fair skin I have never favoured green,' said Rachel. 'But it really suits you, Miss Wirrall. Were I competing for the attention of young men, I should be quite jealous. But I will be Mrs Percival Allerton, and I will have to hope that my wedding dress, which is modest to a fault, will suffice for the ball.'

'What style is your wedding dress, Miss Mercer?' asked Jenny smoothly, and as the old lady brought in tea they passed several minutes discussing Rachel's wedding dress, which had been ordered from Paris and which her fiancé was to collect in some spare moment from what she described as duties personally overseeing the final days at Versailles.

'Not at all showy,' said Rachel. 'The expense is in the silk and the quality of the workmanship. Such tiny hands they must have, the French, to make such exquisite seams and beading.'

'I have heard that said.' Jenny pinched and pinned a seam in Poppy's dress.

'Ouch!'

'Oh, I am sorry, did I catch you?' said Jenny as Poppy flinched. 'Sorry, these pins are so fine for my rough old hands.'

'Constance has alterations for you too,' said Poppy, hiding a grin.

'I was looking to perhaps add a ribbon,' said Constance. 'My dress is from some years before the war, and I just want it to look fresh.'

'It's good to blend in with the guests,' said Rachel. 'Though you are helping Mrs Wirrall, are you not? So really that old blue gown of mine is not even absolutely necessary. A black ensemble would be perfectly adequate.'

'She and I are both helping my mother,' said Poppy, her tone dry. 'But we will not be donning cap and apron.'

'Of course not. I meant only to reassure Constance. The blue is quality Belgian lace. I would have scolded my mother for giving it away, but when she told me it was handed down to dear Constance, I was very happy. It will serve you many years, I hope.'

'Pop it on then and let me have a look,' said Jenny.

The blue gown felt heavy and restricting and, against Poppy's modern dress, it looked to Constance like a relic from another age.

'I doubt they'll make dresses like this again,' said Jenny. 'There's enough yardage here for two dresses and a couple of pillowcases.'

'I hoped maybe to shorten the hem?' asked Constance. 'And perhaps a silver or pink ribbon at the neck or waist might make a difference?' Jenny tucked a few pins in the hem and pinched about the waist. Jenny's mother, coming in to clear the teacups, stepped up to feel the stiff boning in the bodice and peer closely at the tucked and stitched ruffles of the neckline.

'Don't see real whalebone any more,' said the old lady. 'Built like a battleship. Shame to touch it.'

'Don't mind Mother; she appreciates good tailoring and actively dislikes fashion,' said Jenny. 'You'll have to leave it with me, and I will see what I can do to freshen it up.'

'Thank you,' said Constance. 'You have complete carte blanche.'

'Don't tell her that,' said Poppy. 'Look where that got me.'

Chapter 23

It was late in the afternoon, the breeze dying, and the sun a deep gold dazzle over the green countryside. They were stationary in the field, parked under a tree as Harris showed Constance the Sopwith Camel's dual controls. In the tiny space, with Harris crammed in behind her, she felt a tide of rising panic. How could she possibly fly in public in three days' time? It was so different to read about flying in the instruction book, or even to fly as a passenger, than to sit in the small wooden cockpit as a student. Now she had to focus as Harris explained the dials and switches; she had to place her feet on the rudder and feel it give beneath her shoes. Harris's hand closed over hers on the stick in front of her and she could feel his warmth, and his breath on her cheek, as he took her through the positions.

'Forward down, aft up, and left and right to bank the craft,' he said. 'She requires the lightest of touches. If you grip too hard she'll lurch about in an instant.' He squeezed her knuckles and she relaxed her tense fingers in their short leather gloves.

'How does one remember it all?' she asked, trying to control the tremble in her voice. 'I thought a motorcycle was dangerous enough, but one wrong move in the air could spell disaster.'

'I have full control and I'll make sure you can't do any real damage,' said Harris. 'I'll get us up to a good height and then you just feel your way to keeping her good and level.'

'I'll do my best,' she said.

'Remember, I'll point for directions, but if I pat you on the shoulder like this, just give up all your controls and let me take over,' he said, patting her firmly three times. 'Nothing worse than having to fight for control of the stick with a student who's welded to it in panic.'

'I promise not to panic,' said Constance, and a sudden joy made her laugh. 'But I warn you now that if I throw my hands in the air and scream, that will also be a cue to take charge.'

They practised her required moves in the cockpit first by taxiing across the grass. She tested the feel of the stick and watched the elevator flap and the ailerons twist. She braced against the rudder and turned the machine in a ragged circle around the field as Harris blipped the engine on and off to keep their speed low. And all the time she could feel him behind her, his legs almost under her elbows. Finally she felt the three heavy pats on her shoulder from the palm of his hand and she snatched her hands and feet from the controls as Harris turned into the wind and let the engine run wide open. In a brief and glorious instant they were flung into the air and began a sharp climb and a slow turn about the field. When he tapped her once on the left shoulder, she put her feet on the rudder and took the stick in front of her into her hands as gently as if it were a baby bird. The stick seemed to beat and vibrate against her hand – more eagle chick than sparrow – and she fought to keep her shoulders loose and her hands firm, but calm, as she held the fierce machine on a gently curving right-hand circle around the field. Anything more than the slightest move and the Camel started to roll and yaw wildly. Constance more than once feared for her control and then the machine would right itself and she knew Harris was keeping a check on the controls. She relaxed, and as he tapped her and pointed left, she took a few slow breaths and turned the finely tuned machine smartly to port.

They made three short flights, stopping in between for Harris to critique her performance and to talk over their manoeuvres. She appreciated his bluntness in pointing out her mistakes and his lack of effusiveness about her few successes. But she wondered, with a suppressed smile, if other ladies might expect more encouragement.

'I think you'll manage adequately on Peace Day,' he said as he handed her down from the cockpit for the last time. She was ready to take this as a compliment but Jock the mechanic, bringing towels to wipe the hot spray of castor oil from the undercarriage, gave a mild snort.

'Aye, for a woman,' he said. 'But do we have to risk our only aeroplane on it?'

'If you disagree, Mr Macintyre, we can set you up with a pink scarf and a long wig,' joked Constance. She knew she had barely held the Camel straight, but she had worked too hard to take Jock's dismissal quietly. 'You are free to take my place,' she added.

'With Jock's ham hands she'd be upside down in a minute,' said Harris. 'You on the other hand have the right touch, Constance. You did well.' She glowed with pleasure at the unexpected praise as Harris turned to Jock to add, 'If all the women are as dexterous with the controls as Constance, Poppy's little school might be a success after all.'

'I think I'd make a lovely woman' was all Jock said, glowering. But he winked at Constance and she, in her happy exhaustion, was content to take this as an apology.

SOMETIME PAST MIDNIGHT in the Penneston library, Constance sat alone in a pool of yellow light, putting the final touches to her book-keeping. Between the flying lessons, the intense hours of accounting work, and being invited to join the Wirralls for their first family dinner back at Penneston, it had been an exciting and exhausting day. But Constance found she could not sleep. Her thoughts ran on with her future and with the fear of Saturday's air show – not the flying so much as the trying to disguise herself as Iris. She decided to quiet her mind by going over her ledgers one last time.

It had taken her many afternoons, and several long evenings, to put

Mrs Wirrall's pot of receipts and bills into some sort of order. In among the Penneston refurbishment receipts, there were personal bills for hats, dresses and expensive hair treatments, which might explain Mrs Wirrall's lavish black locks. There were months of the hotel account, for which Mr Smickle never seemed to press for payment, while there were urgent letters from other purveyors, including a threatening note from a psychic reader. It was not her business to judge the rich, but now that her future loomed, Constance sighed over a summer hat expensive enough to furnish a good wool winter coat, stout leather boots and several pairs of gloves.

For the Penneston refurbishment, any expense spared had been due to the difficulties of post-war supply, not cost. The new Moorish garden room was floored not in Italian marble but Portland bluestone, hand-cut to a lotus pattern – for which the stonemason made copious apologies, while billing a small fortune. And new sheer curtains of muslin came from Lancashire, not India, and were trimmed in hand-spun wool pom-poms instead of silk tassels. Yet they too were sewn by hand and hand-embroidered with the Wirrall coat of arms. There was a note from the mill too, thanking Mrs Wirrall for making it possible to re-employ four weavers. From the copper roof and bronze windows to the large orders for potted trees and flowers – and the elaborate lead pots and troughs to contain them – the bills kept emerging, flowering from the cachepot as if from a bottomless magic jar.

Now, Constance was reviewing the careful ledgers she had made one more time, checking her figures and writing out copies of the summary as carefully as if making art. As the clock chimed once she laid down her pen and blotted the last underlined total. In less than a year, Mrs Wirrall had spent more than would be needed, if cautiously invested and spent, to generate a lifetime's independent income for a single woman of modest habits. Constance drew the tapestry collar of her late mother's purple velvet dressing gown tighter around her neck and tucked her legs up under its old, generous skirts. She felt no resentment towards Mrs Wirrall as she indulged for a moment in the quiet contemplation of what such a sum might buy. Two attic rooms in a tall house in London or a tiny cottage like those here in the old town, perhaps? Not a library like this, where the books slumbered on their mahogany shelves in the darkness, but maybe one wall of books and a small fireplace, a clean galley kitchen, and a strip of garden or a balcony. A public library within walking distance and a job not too far away by bus or train. For, of course, she would still want to work, and with the salary perhaps take a small holiday each year; somewhere different each time, by train. And one year as far as Paris? She sighed, allowing no further indulgence in dreams of such bounty. She could not join the many, including Mrs Wirrall and Poppy, who seemed to delight in a blissful ignorance of their own limitations. It was the curse of the numerate, she thought, to know exactly one's circumstances.

The quiet creak of a door startled her as she rose to close the ledgers and tidy away her pens. She shrank from the light and stifled a cry.

'I'm sorry, I didn't mean to startle you.' Harris's voice identified him before she could register his face. 'I was walking around and I saw the light. I came to check all was well.'

'I couldn't sleep so I came down to work,' she said, feeling caught, like a schoolgirl out of the dormitory. 'There is nothing like accounting to soothe the mind.'

'Being useful again,' he said. 'Most people would have settled for a cup of hot milk.'

'I didn't want to wake anyone bumbling about in the dark.'

'Can I make you some now?' he asked. 'As you can probably guess, I am something of an incurable insomniac. There is a certain bitter note to the loneliness of the dark.' His face was etched into haunted planes by the light of the single lamp. She felt an urgent need to drag him into some light and warmth and hold him there.

'Thank you. I'd like that' was all she could say.

In the kitchen he turned on the electric light, lit the two stumps of candles left on the large pine table in the centre of the room and invited her to sit down. She watched him stoke the coal stove, take down a small copper pot from the overhead rack and retrieve a bottle of milk from the cool north-facing larder.

'I think there's cocoa, if you'd prefer?' He was proficient, deft even, stirring in the cocoa, putting some oatcakes on a small plate. 'We may have some cake left from dinner?'

'You're very domestic,' she said. 'Did you learn all that in the war?'

'We had all the usual offices,' he said. 'But there's camaraderie in doing for yourselves. Something about creating order in chaos. Or re-creating a memory of home. Anyway, I can iron a shirt collar in a pinch and scramble eggs over a kerosene heater.'

'How truly great our Great Britain will be if all the men are boiling cocoa for their wives and helping with the ironing,' said Constance, unconvinced. He laughed and his face creased into roundness.

'I imagine most married men are trying strenuously to hide any such talent,' he said.

'And the unmarried?'

'I believe boiling cocoa is sometimes used as a romantic gesture, but the plan would be to discontinue the habit right after the wedding night.'

'Another blow against marriage,' she said. 'If only all men would speak such truth.'

'If men and women spoke the truth to each other, I fear populations would crumble and Empires would fall.' He poured the steaming cocoa into two large cups and put the empty saucepan on a cool spot on the stove. She noted that his kitchen technique did not extend to rinsing the pan. Cook would have to deal with the hardened residue in the morning.

'It would be nice to think that something good might come out of all these years of misery,' she said. 'World peace is all very well, but for the average person – let us say, the average woman – it would be nice to think there might be some enduring changes. Some additional respect, some freedom, some scope for a larger life.'

'You do not feel that motorcycle clubs, ragtime and bobbed hair are enough?' His smile was gentle and took the sting from the jibe. 'I think you are a serious person, Miss Haverhill. You have my respect, for what that might be worth.'

He joined her at the table and, as they sat in silence for a moment, she weighed the comfort and pleasure she felt against the sense that he was still a man in darkness. That he viewed her, viewed everyone, from a very great distance. The fear she felt for him was larger now, in proportion to her greater care. And yet to try to reach him across the divide might turn him away from her. She could imagine the curled lip, the cutting remark, if she said the wrong thing.

'What would you like to see come from these shadowed years of misery?' she asked as gently as she could. 'You who have given the greatest sacrifice should design our future.'

He laughed sharply, but his eyes, when he looked up from his cocoa, did not blaze with contempt. He took a moment to consider her question, turning it in his mind as if it was a thing of many facets.

'Those who have given the greatest sacrifice are not here to speak,' he said, his voice hoarse. 'Those of us who are— Well, I must rack my brain every day to discover if I am a coward. If I made some decision to save myself. Because why else am I here and better men are gone?' He buried his head in his hands and made a low animal moan of pain. Without thinking, Constance flew to his side and put her arms around him.

'No, no,' she almost crooned, as if he were a small child. 'Please, no.' Something had cracked open in him. She could only press her warm arms into his cold back, her cheek against his ear, her breath encouraging his to slow and deepen. It seemed like a long time crouching at his side, or perhaps it was just a moment. Eventually he lifted his head. Gently he placed his hands on her shoulders and she loosened her hold. Her hair dishevelled, she searched his face for hope. And like a Good Samaritan plunging into the river to save a drowning man, she took a deep breath and kissed him.

IT WAS LIKE FLYING, he thought, as he buried his face in her neck and kissed her all the way along her jaw, and held her cheek with his hand and kissed her mouth again. Just the moment and the complete freedom from any other thought. He gathered her, warm and yielding, onto his lap, and her hair fell around his face as she matched him kiss for kiss, long and slow. Then, too soon, she pulled away, as if shocked awake from a dream, and blinked at him. Her mouth was open and round and bruised red from his lips, and she rubbed the back of a hand across it as she scrambled away from him.

'I'm sorry,' he said, because he was a gentleman, but she had kissed him first, he was sure of it.

'Don't apologise to me,' she said. 'I'm the one who kissed you uninvited.'

'I invite you now,' he said, laughing. 'Come kiss me again, please.'

'In my nightgown, in your mother's house?' she said. 'What sort of girl must you think me?' In the sort of simple, bubbling happiness he had forgotten since the war, he wanted to offer to dispense with both house and whatever nightgown hid beneath the long velvet robe that made her look like a medieval abbess. But he sensed her distress was real and growing.

'I think you a girl so generous she wished to save a man from himself,' he said. 'You have given me your friendship and your trust – and now comes hope.'

'I don't expect anything of you,' she said, and her voice was firm, but her eyes were large and wary as she backed behind a chair. 'You must believe me.'

'I don't claim anything of you either,' he said gently. 'Please don't run from me. I assure you I don't make a habit of chasing girls around tables, not with my leg.'

'I hold you in the utmost regard, Captain Wirrall.' That she did not flinch from his disability was rare and her face rebuked him for using it to coax her.

'And I hold you in the utmost respect, Miss Haverhill,' he said, placing his hand on his heart. 'I give you my word that your compassion will never be held against you by me.'

'Then I will wish you goodnight, Captain Wirrall.' He would be gentleman enough to let her go but he ached to ask her to stay, and when she paused by the door and turned back, a cautious gratitude in her brief smile, his heart leaped. 'And we will never speak of this again,' she said.

THE NEXT MORNING, after breakfast, the family was to gather in the library for the discussion with their banker. From the library window, Constance could see Harris walking up from the barn, his steps confident, his cane advancing smartly. Her breath quickened and she could taste his kiss on her lips. She felt desire pull at her, like the insistent tug of a rushing stream. But she could not quell the fear that he might choose to wink at her all day, or tell someone, and that he now held her reputation in his hands. She had come too far this summer to feel so powerless. By the time he reached the house, she was ready to be angry with him.

Mrs Wirrall had taken an inspection tour of the gardens early and now bustled indoors, under a flowering of gauze shawls and parasol, all of which seemed to heighten rather than mask her air of anxiety. Constance squared up the ledgers on the desk and fanned out the three hand-written summaries she had made of Penneston expenses, and Poppy's outlays for Wirrall's Conveyance, and the motorcycle and flying club. She had no idea as to the income side of the ledgers but, given Poppy's air of distraction over the toast and marmalade and Harris's deep frown as he disappeared into the front hall, she feared they would be in for a long and possibly uncomfortable family discussion.

Such a discussion would not be helped by today's arrivals of furniture, fittings and plants for the final staging of the house. The ball was in two days, and she doubted it could be called off at this stage even if the Wirralls were willing to eviscerate their reputations to do so.

Everything was committed, and as she leaned out of the library window, she could swear she saw, in the misty distance of the valley below, a lorry full of palm trees making its waving and nodding way towards the house.

'Ah, Constance, I am quite delighted with how you have managed to tame my little maelstrom of financial papers,' said Mrs Wirrall, coming into the library ahead of her children. 'Harris tells me you burned the midnight oil to review it all over again?' Constance's cheeks burned as Harris raised an eyebrow at her and smiled. Poppy marched over to the desk and picked up a set of pages.

'I told you last night she's a whiz at this stuff.'

'Miss Haverhill is a very intelligent woman,' said Harris. 'Though how you two are to appreciate it when you can't tell a column of figures from the weather forecast, I don't know.' He picked up a set of pages and went to study them by the window.

'Yes, indeed, he's quite right,' said Mrs Wirrall. 'Everything you explained to me last night has gone right out of my head again. Constance, I feel you should join us this morning so you can explain everything.'

'Oh, I don't think I should . . .'

'Please do,' said Poppy. 'We know you are discreet and absolutely know how to keep a confidence. Mother and I will be completely at the mercy of Harris and Mr Llewellyn if you leave us alone.'

'I hardly think Miss Haverhill wants to watch us turn out our pockets,' said Harris, avoiding her gaze. Constance understood his natural reluctance and would have demurred again, but Mrs Wirrall interrupted.

'Yes, do stay or else Harris will simply berate us for being fools and we will have no answer except to remind him that he has absented himself from all responsibilities since his return.'

'The small matter of the leg, dear Mother?' he said.

'You don't need a leg to hold a pencil,' snapped Poppy.

'Very well, if you wish a complete stranger, like Miss Haverhill, to know all our dark secrets, I have no objection.' He looked at her, but his smile was gone and his face seemed to have closed into its usual stern frown.

'I would be honoured to help,' said Constance, her pride bruised by such a retreat. Privately she thought it highly likely that much foolishness had occurred but now she was provoked into ensuring that Poppy and her mother were not treated as children.

'A most useful woman,' muttered Harris, and she shot him a glare that had no memory of warmth in it.

MR LLEWELLYN ENTERED with all the bonhomie of a favoured uncle, and it took some time to settle him in a stout chair at the table, to instruct the new maid as to his preferences for tea and to make mutual enquiries into health and plans. Constance noticed that Mrs Wirrall did not mention the upcoming ball; perhaps some sense of her financial position was becoming apparent.

After an initial perusal of the ledgers, Mr Llewellyn was most complimentary about the presentation of the accounts and the summaries made, both of Penneston's expenses and those of Poppy's endeavours. Mrs Wirrall was generous enough to credit Constance with the work, and Mr Llewellyn tried not to look too surprised. Harris had totted up his own accounts, which he presented on a much rumpled and ink-blotted page torn from a notebook. No copies had been made, and Mr Llewellyn did not pass the numbers around.

'Well,' he said at last. 'I thought it best to come in person and have a chat. As Harris and I have already discussed, the estate, which is now his, cannot go on bearing such a level of expenditure. He has authorised me to share the income numbers with you.' He raised an eyebrow at Harris and pointed a discreet finger at Constance.

'Yes, let them all see,' said Harris.

'I thought you said we looked very tidy?' said Mrs Wirrall, accepting a thickly laid paper with bank letterhead. Constance and Poppy shared a copy. Constance was not astonished by the income of Penneston – after all, she had managed the books at Clivehill – but it did cause a pang to see the separate trust funds of Poppy and Harris. She doubted even Rachel was treated so generously.

'The numbers are presented with perfect clarity,' said Mr Llewellyn. 'Which is why, dear lady, I know you will see the issue. The renovations to Penneston, and the perfectly understandable costs of maintaining a second household at the hotel, have taken a bite out of the estate's capital. And I'm afraid capital does not generate quite the income it did before the war. We have extended two loans for the work, and payment on those loans begins in September. From these very clear numbers, I believe Harris will need to halve expenses going forward.'

'For how long?' said Mrs Wirrall.

'For the foreseeable future, Mrs Wirrall.'

'I can help,' said Poppy. 'Mummy has never asked us for any sort of contribution from my trust.'

'Your own income is also badly overdrawn,' said Mr Llewellyn. 'Your funding of this charity effort, Wirrall's Conveyance?'

'It's not a charity, it's a business,' said Poppy. 'We are to be closed down, I'm afraid, under the new laws. But I hope the flying lessons will compensate.'

'Just as well, I fear. According to your own accounting, the busier you become, the more into debt you seem to go,' said Mr Llewellyn. He turned to Constance. 'Miss Haverhill, perhaps you might explain to Miss Wirrall?'

'I'm not an idiot,' said Poppy. 'Any business has expenses to begin.'

'I think Mr Llewellyn is concerned about ongoing monthly costs,' said Constance. She looked again at her own figures and made a hurried calculation in her head. The result was dismaying, and she looked at Mr Llewellyn with alarm.

'Ah, the young lady sees the bigger picture,' he said, and she would have been gratified by the grudging approval in his eyes had she not felt as if she had failed to warn Poppy.

'I'm so sorry,' she said. 'I was focused on finishing the bookkeeping, and did not have time to study the results.'

'But we are growing rapidly,' said Poppy. 'We are adding more deliveries every week.'

'If one averages the expense per delivery, they cost more than they bring in. So adding more deliveries just increases your deficit.' Constance squeezed Poppy's hand.

'I can't charge as much as others because then we get no business,' said Poppy. 'I've already accepted that being a woman is worth fifteen per cent less in this world.'

'Were you paying your drivers fifteen per cent less?' asked Mr Llewellyn. 'In this economy, we must all wring the last drop from our resources, including labour.' Poppy reddened.

'I'm ashamed to say I have been,' she said. 'And now I must throw them all out of work.' She sighed. 'These women have families who count on their support. Everyone acts as if women work to make pin money – to buy a new dress or provide fancy cakes for tea. But the most well-off of my girls is looking to keep herself in a good winter coat and to afford her motorcycle, and some are supporting a widowed mother or are widows themselves.'

'I believe the war widows receive generous pensions,' said Mr Llewellyn.

'If you believe any of the war pensions are generous, you have not tried to pay the rent with one,' said Poppy.

'With Wirrall's Conveyance no longer a drain on funds, there is still the matter of the aeroplane,' said Mr Llewellyn. 'The cost, the mechanic's salary . . .'

'I can pay for Jock,' said Harris. 'I'd be happy to.'

'Again, that would be an act of charity, not part of a sustainable business,' said Mr Llewellyn. 'The price of fuel alone is a burden.'

'I don't understand the fuss,' said Mrs Wirrall. 'Penneston needed so much work after being knocked about during these past few years. I've just been making it habitable for Harris. It was an absolute horror.'

'Your taste and your purpose are unassailable, dear madam,' said Mr Llewellyn. 'But perfection has come at a steep price.'

'Well, we shall simply stop spending,' she said. 'Right after – right after we move in.'

'Even after we get rid of the expense of hotel living, I fear it won't be enough,' said Mr Llewellyn. 'I had suggested your going abroad?' He looked at Harris, who shook his head.

'Get rid of the hotel?' Mrs Wirrall looked white about the gills. 'I have been refurbishing Penneston for Harris and, I hoped, his bride.' She stopped and seemed lost in her thoughts. Constance saw Harris redden and knew he and his mother were thinking of Evangeline.

'Mama, I thought you wanted us all to live at Penneston,' said Poppy.

'As long as you wish it,' agreed Harris. 'I wouldn't have it any other way.'

'But I like hotel living,' said his mother. 'I hate the thought of being trapped in all these cold rooms, shut away from people.'

'Then perhaps we should lease or sell Penneston,' said Harris. 'A bachelor has no need of an old pile.'

'You can't sell Penneston,' said Poppy. 'It's our home. If I have to shut down the motorcycle and flying club entirely to help, I will.'

'I can't let you do that,' said Harris. 'It wouldn't be fair when it's not – it's not your obligation.'

'You mean it's not really my home,' said Poppy, and her voice was bitter with hurt.

'Hard choices will have to be made,' said the banker. 'As the legal owner, your brother is the one who will have to make them.' He looked at Harris. 'A sale might allow you to purchase a small cottage outright for your sister. We might carve the dower house from the estate for your mother or your own use.'

'I prefer the hotel,' said Mrs Wirrall. 'And we're not turning out those poor crippled servicemen onto the street.'

'I don't see any rent here for the dower house?' asked Constance. She was scouring the income statements for some hidden source or opportunity that might offset the family's spending, but nothing seemed too helpful in that regard.

'Well, they were so obliging about moving out of the main house that I didn't have the heart to charge them,' said Mrs Wirrall. 'Those poor men.'

'We may be foolish, but no one ever said we were not generous,' said Poppy.

'Very admirable, of course,' said Mr Llewellyn.

'There are stocks and bonds here that don't seem to pay much dividend,' said Constance. 'There is a large concentration of shares in the one bank?'

'I wouldn't advise touching the core of your principal,' said the banker, blanching. 'Your father's legacy, so to speak. It would be preferable, I think, to sell some of the less desirable land perhaps.'

'The land is also a principal part of that legacy,' said Harris.

'You are not getting large returns on the rented land,' said Constance. 'And I understand agricultural land prices are particularly high right now.'

'How do you know that?' asked Harris. Stress made him snappy.

'I am capable of reading a newspaper,' retorted Constance. The banker beamed in a way that made her feel awkwardly complicit.

'The young lady is right, and I have been approached with an offer that might solve some problems short-term,' he said. 'The airfield land, which you leased to the government at a generous discount—'

'It was our duty to help,' said Mrs Wirrall. 'My husband also felt strongly.'

'We have not received any income on a regular basis despite my repeated requests to the Ministry,' said Mr Llewellyn. 'They insist that Hazelbourne Aviation is responsible for the lease.'

'My husband was happy to rent them the fields for their runways,' said Mrs Wirrall. 'But he was too much the gentleman to hound Mayor Morris for payment.'

'Indeed,' said Mr Llewellyn. 'What I have received is a written offer to purchase the land outright, along with a cash settlement in lieu of any rent arrears.'

'From whom?' said Harris. 'It can't be Morris. He recently complained of poverty in telling me he could not take me on as a pilot.'

'I believe Mr Morris has new investors interested in a partnership,' said Mr Llewellyn, pushing across some papers. 'Discretion precludes me from saying more at this point. But this offer, from their intermediary, might be worth considering. A little low, but it would be a cash infusion, and as the future of aviation is more uncertain now the war is over . . .'

'If Morris has the money to buy us out, he has the money to pay us what he owes,' said Harris. 'Is it some trick of business that one should not pay one's debts?'

'The intermediary who came to see me did drop a hint that they believe the Ministry may have plans to guarantee the field stays active by forcing a sale under eminent domain if a private sale cannot be facilitated. He did not think it was in any way imminent, or preferred, but he thought we ought to know. The price might be better through a private sale.'

'Ridiculous,' said Poppy.

'That's the thanks we get for charging them only a peppercorn rent,' said Harris.

'It does make one question what has happened to the sense of honour in this country,' said Mrs Wirrall. 'Did we actually win the war?'

'This is unacceptable,' said Harris. 'I shall go and talk to Mr Morris again tomorrow.' He stood up, his jaw set, and Constance was moved to see him for the first time take on the mantle of the master of Penneston.

'I am happy to facilitate, my dear boy. No need for you to exert yourself.'

'I am not an invalid any longer,' said Harris. 'And I need to know, Mr Llewellyn, where the bank stands in this? I know Morris banks with you. He was a client of my father's as well as a neighbour.'

'I assure you I am only seeking the best for all sides,' said Mr Llewellyn, reddening about his stiff collar. 'And to look out for you as your father would have wished.'

'My father wished me to become a partner in the bank,' said Harris with mild sarcasm.

'And yet flying is, I believe, your passion,' said Mr Llewellyn, stammering now. 'To sell the land will resolve your immediate liquid needs. And the land will, after all, remain an airfield.'

'I believe the airfield is already my own.' Harris turned away to the window. He clasped his hands behind his back, signalling an end to the meeting. 'I will see that you are paid on time, Mr Llewellyn.'

'I am always flexible,' said Llewellyn, defeated. 'Your dear father and I had a perfect understanding.'

AFTER THE BANKER departed, Harris returned to the library, where Constance was preparing to leave.

'Oh, but can't you stay and take me through my expenses one more time?' Poppy was asking her. 'I'm sure we will find some redeeming item we have overlooked.'

'The numbers don't change between readings, Poppy,' Harris said, a complicated irritation sharpening his tone. On the one hand he wished Constance Haverhill to Timbuktu. It was a blow to the ego for any man to see his distressed affairs laid out in public, especially in front of a woman one might want to impress. On the other, his feelings were strongly opposed to her leaving so soon and he wished his estate to damnation, wanting only to make her smile and to go into the garden with her and make sure last night's kiss was not imagined.

'I suppose we have no choice but to bother Mr Morris for the rent he owes us,' said Mrs Wirrall. 'One hates to call a gentleman on his obligations. And on the very eve of Peace Day.'

'Do we even have a lease to hold him to?' asked Harris. 'Or am I to settle the matter tomorrow by challenging Morris to a duel?'

'I filed it among your mother's papers,' said Constance. 'And I wrote out an invoice for Mayor Morris, detailing every month's charge, and left it in the drawer of the library desk.'

'Thank you,' he said and hoped she felt his admiration. 'You have saved me from pistols at dawn.'

'What a treasure you are,' said Mrs Wirrall. 'You will stay to luncheon?'

'Now that the bookkeeping is finished, I really must go to the hotel,' said Constance, and her fierce blush was so unusual that he knew he must be the cause. 'Rachel's fiancé is due back tomorrow night, for the wedding on Saturday, and I fear I have been remiss in my role as companion and maid of honour.'

'You can't get blood from a stone, as they say,' said Poppy, a temporary gloom descending on her face. 'I'll take you down to the town.'

'If we listen to Llewellyn, we are to be homeless, landless and depreciated,' said Mrs Wirrall. 'I can't credit it true. He exaggerates, surely?'

'To be fair, it is you who exaggerates, Mother,' said Harris. 'I'm sure Llewellyn would be happy with two out of three of those conditions.'

'Things will turn around, won't they?' said Poppy.

'I hope so,' said Harris, and he smiled at Constance Haverhill with as much pleading as he could manage without raising suspicion. 'With all my heart.'

Chapter 24

THE WORKSHOPS OF HAZELBOURNE AVIATION SMELLED of fresh sawdust, metal filings and doping lacquer. A set of wings for the Avros they built sat almost finished on trestles. A carpenter Harris recognised was planing the curved edge of one, and curls of wood like a child's ringlets fell softly to the floor.

'Beautiful work,' said Harris.

The man touched his cap in salute. 'Smooth as a baby,' he said, and gestured to Harris to test this claim. Harris ran his hand over the silky surface of the spruce spar and breathed in the fresh wood.

'Only the one in production, then?' asked Harris.

'Aye. And a few in the hangar that Tom is testing. We used to turn out ten at a time, a hundred a year or so,' said the man. 'Of course, we're grateful the war is over, but they're not saying what comes next.'

'I'm sorry to hear it.'

'But I shouldn't speak out of turn,' he added. 'I hope you'll forget it.'

'Of course,' said Harris. 'None of my business anyway. I'm looking for Mr Morris Senior?'

'He's in the back hangar checking on a repair,' said the man as he chuckled. 'You might not get the warmest welcome though, Captain Wirrall. Every time you fly that Camel overhead, management gets a bit huffy.'

'I had no idea,' said Harris.

'Good machine you got there. I've a mind to come up there and look her over one of these days.'

'Please do,' said Harris. 'My mechanic and I would value your eye on one or two wing struts that have seen a bit too much action.'

IN THE REAR hangar, Mr Morris was expressing his unhappiness with the doping on one of the seaplanes.

'It's supposed to be a fire-engine red. This looks more like half-dried blood sausage.'

'It's not our usual make,' said the foreman unhappily. 'I did warn the office the cheaper dope doesn't have the same colour saturation.'

'They didn't have more of the old stuff when we ordered,' said Morris. 'This is a disaster. We can't have the fleet in dull unmatched colours for the peace celebrations tomorrow.'

Harris cleared his throat and Morris stopped abruptly.

'Good morning,' said Harris. 'I was hoping for a word?'

'Fix it!' Morris said to the foreman, then turned to Harris. 'Come to sell me that Camel, have you?'

'I might throw it in,' said Harris. 'I want to talk about these investors you've put together. I want to discuss being a part of it.'

'Well now, as I already explained, when you came to see me about flying for us . . .'

'With the greatest of respect, Mr Morris, I am a pilot again and I have an aeroplane of my own to contribute,' said Harris, his jaw set. 'Despite my youth, I am also the owner of Penneston, and as such, I own the airfield land, on which I'm owed considerable back rent.' He did not raise his voice but perhaps projected it with more authority than even he expected. The foreman lifted his head to listen. 'After meeting with my banker yesterday, I think it's time we had a proper sit-down and hashed out a workable arrangement.'

'My investors may have no interest in taking on additional partners,' said Morris, lowering his voice. 'They have their own vision.'

'Well, we can ask Sam Newcombe, can't we?' said Harris. He was rewarded with a frown that indicated he was right. 'Of course, I wanted to talk to you first, Mr Morris. Out of the great respect my father had for you and his early support of Hazelbourne Aviation.'

'Let's go up to the office, shall we?' said Morris. 'This is no place to discuss such important matters.'

TOM MORRIS WAS lazing in an office armchair, smoking a cheroot, his boots on the low table in front of him. His father did not seem amused at his studied nonchalance.

'I know you're on leave, Tom, but could you not flaunt your indolence quite so openly around the works? We don't need a revolution among the workers.'

'I would hope they understand that every man is entitled to his hard-earned holiday,' said Tom. 'I don't begrudge the bus driver in his seaside deckchair with knotted hanky on his head. I fail to see why the proletariat should deny me my brief interlude from the fray.'

'You set a bad example,' said his father. 'From those who are given much, much is expected. Harris here is begging to be put to work. Please get out. We have business to discuss.'

'Oh, do let me stay, Father.' Tom continued to feign boredom, but Harris detected a real curiosity. 'You want me to leave the RAF and join you, so let me sit at the right hand of power and learn.'

'Very well,' said Mr Morris. 'It will concern you in the end, so let's get down to business.'

In the frank discussion that followed, Harris found he was able to stand his ground thanks, in some large part to Constance, whose own accounting skills had shamed Harris into actually studying the pages of figures Llewellyn had provided. Constance had also pointed him to the original airfield lease agreement. He was able to cite the current value of the airfield land and hand Morris a full accounting of unpaid rent. Mr Morris seemed very ill at ease with Harris's new financial acumen, and

Harris found it rather thrilling to be in possession of one's facts and ready to drive a hard bargain. Mr Morris seemed grudgingly convinced that some arrangement might be made to their mutual satisfaction.

'Of course, any agreement we may strike will not be signed until my bookkeeper has had a chance to look over the company books,' said Harris. 'I assume there will be no objection?'

'Well, if you think it's necessary,' said Mr Morris. 'You can send your man in anytime.'

'A woman, actually,' said Harris. 'Tom, I think you know Miss Haverhill?'

'A dark horse, that girl,' said Tom, raising an eyebrow. 'But really, Harris, wouldn't you rather settle this as gentlemen than squabble over the pot like Cheapside moneylenders?'

'Your father never played the banker with me,' added Mr Morris. 'A handshake and a gentleman's word was good enough.'

Harris felt himself stumbling. He walked away to the large window overlooking the airfield and watched a dog trot across the cropped grassy runway towards Penneston. 'We are like family,' he said. 'But I have a duty to provide for my mother and my sister.'

'If that sister of yours weren't so infernally stubborn, we might be actual family,' said Tom. 'I'm happy to take her off your hands and provide for her as soon as she hops down from her high horse.' He laughed. 'Isn't she providing amply for you all with her little ventures?'

'I see those conveyances of hers everywhere,' said Mr Morris. 'My girls don't like it, you know. They worry that paying women to be taxi drivers will cheapen the ladies' club and bring down the reputations of its members. A social club and a business can't really coexist in comfort.'

'She's just helping a few worthy women keep their motorcycles on the road and food on the table,' said Harris.

'Except that in a couple of months, employing all those women will be in direct contravention of the War Practices Act,' said Tom, grinning. 'I believe the Labour Board has already visited?'

'Did you send them, Tom?' With a jolt Harris realised he had known for years, but never acknowledged, that Tom Morris was a bit of a cad.

'Of course not,' said Tom smoothly. 'Family and all that.'

'I apologise,' said Harris, but perhaps it was obvious that he thought Tom a liar because Tom sat up, his jaw tightening.

'What say you we settle this like family with a small wager?' he said, and a note of belligerence crept into his voice.

'Now this is business, Tom,' began his father, looking aghast. 'None of your boys' jests.'

'What sort of wager?' Harris knew it was foolish to ask, but he felt the sting of Mr Morris's nonchalant jab about gentlemen and his pride asked for him.

'Since we are talking about the future of an aviation company, why don't we see who's the better pilot and make tomorrow's little Peace Parade air display a real competition?' said Tom. 'They're already expecting us to bomb the damned U-boat, but how about we give them a real show, the usual ribbon-cutting competition, hitting targets from the air and so on.'

'Peace Day is not really about us, Tom,' said Harris.

'The town will love it,' said Tom. 'Two flying aces duelling it out? It just adds to the general excitement.'

'If I win, you'll accept my proposal to join the partnership owning Hazelbourne Aviation?' asked Harris.

'Yes, the rent will be your partner capital and you get the pilot job you want,' said Tom. 'But if I win, we buy the land, including that infernal barn of Poppy's, at the settlement we have already offered, and you sell me the Camel at twice what you paid for it. Seems as if no one really loses and we don't grub about with bookkeepers and lawyers. What do you say, gentleman to gentleman?'

'I'll have a lady flier onboard,' said Harris.

'Well, she won't be much of a flier if she can't sit through a few acrobatics,' said Tom. 'And to be clear, I'll be flying our newest Avro 504, not the seaplane.'

'The committee is expecting the seaplanes,' said Mr Morris. 'I'm having them all repainted.'

'One can't compete at Ascot if one is riding a mule, Father,' said Tom. 'If we're agreed, we'll have to hurry and let the committee know.'

'We should each choose someone with expertise to set the parameters and judge the competition,' said Harris. 'Would Captain Pendra be acceptable to you?'

'Acceptable,' said Tom. 'And I'll ask Sam Newcombe.' Harris felt a slight nausea, and wondered why it felt like he and his childhood friend were arranging a duel after all.

'But Harris and I already discussed that I can't make room for him in the business,' said Mr Morris, huffing.

'Well, firstly, Father, I would have some hope that you expect me to win,' said Tom.

'It's going to be your company, Son,' said Mr Morris.

'Look here,' said Tom, sitting up straighter in his chair and blowing a deliberate smoke ring as he paused for the right words. 'If I choose to go back, I may be in the lines in a couple of weeks. If anything should happen to me, you'd do a lot worse than to lean on Harris here. He's always been a good man, and a hell of a pilot.'

'Good of you to say so,' said Harris. He wondered how one was supposed to treat a friend who was a complete cad only half the time, and he found himself wishing he could find a way to take back the stupid wager.

'No one is saying otherwise.' Morris Senior looked as if he'd taken a blow to the sternum. His eyes watered as he turned away to snort into a large handkerchief. 'I don't see why you keep volunteering. I thought you'd agreed to demobilise for good and come into the business.'

'I haven't decided yet, so let's not become morbid,' said Tom. 'Besides, Harris and I have outlasted better men – and every statistic – so someone upstairs must be looking out for us.' He grinned, but there was a hint of steel in his eye. 'Maybe when I've killed as many of their friends as they've killed of mine, I'll give it up and be content with offering flying lessons to ladies.' And there it was again; another dig, another elliptical insult, as if the man could not help himself.

'I'll take your wager,' said Harris. 'But don't blame me when I beat you with a woman flying my machine.'

CONSTANCE SPENT A pleasant Friday helping Mrs Fog to keep Rachel, and Lady Mercer, calm before the chaos of Saturday's wedding and peace celebrations. There were reminiscences to share, hair to wash, and, for Constance, much sorting and ironing of Rachel's trousseau, which was all, Rachel insisted, far too delicate to trust to the maids. Percival Allerton arrived just after dinner and Constance had to admit she was glad to have avoided what might have been an interminable meal filled with his self-important stories from Paris. They were now on the Palm Terrace, enduring a tense half hour, over coffee and petit fours, in which all their happy news had been met with frowning objection. Percival, it seemed, found it unseemly that his fiancée should appear in a public parade. He had also lectured his future mother-in-law on the unsuitability of half the persons invited to share the Grand Reviewing Stand. He seemed particularly upset that Captain Pendra would be attending.

'Whoever heard of a colonial allowed to be an officer in the air services?' he said. 'Arming colonials has always been considered dangerous by both our countries. Give them guns today, or aeroplanes, and they will turn them against you tomorrow. Use them in the labour corps if you must, but if you ask me, training them as officers is just a recipe for revolution.'

'No one asked you, Mr Allerton,' snapped Constance.

'Constance!' Lady Mercer looked shocked and Rachel pained. Even Mrs Fog gave a slight shake of her head, and Constance tried to quell her anger.

'I merely mean that Captain Pendra has been invited by Mrs Wirrall and the Mayor,' she said. 'I'm sure that is adequate in diplomatic protocol to assure his welcome.'

'No, no, you are right,' said Percy. 'I should apologise for bringing up such weighty matters at the tea table. Such questions are not for the delicate ears of the ladies.'

'Oh, Percy, so you'll escort Mother to the parade?' asked Rachel.

'I will, but I shall be sure to insist that we be seated at a good remove and for goodness' sake, Rachel, please tell me he is not invited to the wedding.'

'Of course not,' said Lady Mercer. 'But I can't vouch for Mrs Wirrall's ball. The woman may be the leading light of this town, but she has some extraordinary opinions.'

'Oh, I must go to the ball,' said Rachel. 'Our wedding is so small, I want to give everyone a chance to see my dress.'

'I think I saw Harris Wirrall heading to the snug,' said Mrs Fog. 'You could ask him, I'm sure.' This proved a fortuitous remark, for it sent Percy off in haste. The tension seemed to lift immediately, and the women were enjoying talking about wedding plans when Constance excused herself to fetch Mrs Fog a shawl.

As she approached the staircase in the lobby she saw, outside the telephone booth, Percival Allerton talking in a low murmur to the undermanager. As she watched, Dudley passed him a sealed envelope. Percival gave him some folded bills in return, which Dudley stuffed in his jacket pocket with an awkward nod and then hurried towards the front door. Constance turned her head away as he passed and went swiftly and silently up the stairs. She could not guess what a man such as Percival Allerton might exchange with an undermanager, but she could not abide underhandedness. Rachel's fiancé, already a subject of her dislike, fell to a new low in her estimation, and she went away shaking her head at Rachel's choice.

Chapter 25

THE INVISIBLE CHORUS OF BIRDS SEEMED TO SING A LITTLE louder and the morning sun to filter more brightly through the curtains. Perhaps this is how it feels, thought Constance, seated at the open window and feeling the freshness of the morning, to be just a young girl with no other thought but the looking forward to a party.

She dressed in a simple white blouse, her blue walking skirt and a stout pair of shoes. Into a small bag she crammed her oldest shirt, a cotton scarf and a pair of much-mended kid gloves to wear with Iris's flight coveralls. It still worried her to continue a charade that could not help Iris in the long run. But truth be told, she had to acknowledge that much of the glow of the morning was the anticipation of Harris's strong arm helping her into the aeroplane and then that weightless moment of being flung into the sky.

She would skip breakfast so as not to offer Rachel and Lady Mercer any opportunity to catch her lying about the day's activities. But first she went to see if Mrs Fog required her help. As Constance knocked on her door, Percival Allerton came from the opposite direction.

Constance could not forgive him his remarks about Captain Pendra, but she reminded herself sharply to be civil and nodded good morning. She was surprised when he did not pass by but also stopped at Mrs Fog's door.

'If you don't mind, Mrs Fog and I have an appointment just now,' he said and raised an eyebrow as if she should scurry away.

'I don't mind at all,' she said. 'I'll just go in and see if it's convenient.' With that she opened and slipped through the door, shutting it carefully in his smug face.

PERCIVAL STOOD AT the French windows looking out at the sea. He rocked on his heels, hands held behind his back. Mrs Fog was silent on the settee, twisting her handkerchief around her knuckles as if tying some elaborate knot. It was rude, Constance thought, to request an audience and then keep them waiting. She was sure Poppy was already at the side entrance waiting to whisk her discreetly away to Penneston. She stood up from her chair and cleared her throat.

'Mrs Fog does need to rest before today's festivities, Mr Allerton.'

'Yes, it's a very exciting day, of course, but it does threaten one's stamina,' agreed Mrs Fog.

'As I said, a rather delicate, private matter concerning the wedding,' he fumbled. 'Best not to risk gossip in the back halls, as it were.'

'I do not gossip in any halls,' said Constance. 'Perhaps you mistake me for a servant?'

'No disrespect intended,' said the young man, but as he could not look at her, she rather doubted his word.

'You will understand I am too frail to conduct such an interview alone. But, I assure you, you can rely on Constance's complete discretion, young man,' said Mrs Fog. 'I vouch for hers and I hope she'll vouch for mine.'

'And of course, Rachel vouches for you,' added Constance, smiling boldly and daring him to call her impertinent. She hoped she was being a shrew and that Iris would be proud of her.

'I would hope my own family name—' He frowned.

'Don't worry, we don't hold it against you that you are from America,' said Mrs Fog. 'I have it on good authority that there are many trustworthy Americans.' Constance ducked her chin to hide any twitch of amusement. Mrs Fog's face was a picture of benign attention.

'I come to you, Mrs Fog, out of a desire to protect Lord and Lady Mercer and, of course, my dear Rachel.'

'How may we help?' she said, including Constance more firmly by calling her over with a simple pat of the seat beside her.

'Obviously a man in my position, contemplating a life in politics and with my family legacy to protect, must be cautious,' he said.

'Do go on. We are agog.' Mrs Fog's voice grew more clipped. For a moment she was as imperious as her daughter. She indicated a spindly wooden chair and Percival sat gingerly on the edge of its cross-stitched seat.

'It has come to my attention – that is, I have received information – about Rachel's family connections.'

'You mean you've been investigating,' said Constance. 'Is that why I saw you bribing the undermanager? Have you been spying on us?' Percival ignored her, but his ears turned puce.

'It has come to my attention that you have been acquainted for many years with a brother and sister by the name of de Champney?' He could not hide a sneer. 'And that they are of mixed bloodline?'

'Is that what all the fuss is about?' said Mrs Fog, shaking her head.

'You have not seen them in many years but have recently renewed your friendship here in Hazelbourne?'

'True. I confess it,' said Mrs Fog. 'But out of respect for your American "sensibilities" we have agreed not to see each other.'

'But after Rachel and I leave, you mean to continue a relationship with them?'

'Are you here to give me an ultimatum, young man?' Mrs Fog looked pale, but her lips were firmly set. 'If so, please get on with it. I thought Americans were supposed to be direct?'

'No, no, it is not in anyone's interest to issue ultimatums at the eleventh hour,' he said. 'But you understand that any connection with the de Champneys, publicly flaunted, would be an impossible issue for my family. Relationships across the races being, we believe, against the laws of the state and nature.'

'So once again I am to be asked to renounce them. The first time was at my father's command, the second was for my daughter's marriage and now I must cede my happiness to my granddaughter?' Mrs Fog rose and went to the window, where she seemed to look far out to sea. 'It was the third denial that broke Saint Peter, I seem to remember.'

'You are frankly old enough and obscure enough that we might consider an arrangement that involves no damage to my family. You would plan, I trust, to be discreet in any correspondence with Rachel, and I would rely on your age being a complete impediment to any visits to us?'

Mrs Fog could not hide her look of surprise.

'You do understand I mean to marry Simon de Champney?'

'While I would strongly counsel against such a marriage, if I understand correctly, madam, your plan is to marry privately – nothing sent to the papers – and to live quietly in retirement away from Clivehill,' he said.

'It is,' she said slowly.

'And your marriage would not interfere with the financial settlements for dear Rachel?'

'It would not,' agreed Mrs Fog. 'She will immediately begin to receive a share from the Barbados holdings as her mother does. When I die the estate, with the agreement of her mother, will pass directly to Rachel.' Percival looked nakedly relieved.

'Then only one small issue stands between me and my bride,' he said.

'To what further insult could you subject dear Mrs Fog?' asked Constance, incredulous. 'In your country you must have a very different definition of what it means to be a gentleman.'

'On the contrary,' stammered Percival, 'I think we share an interest in the pedigree and lineage of our leading families. We must perhaps work even harder than your ancient established families to ensure the purity of our bloodlines.'

'Ask what you must, young man,' said Mrs Fog, returning to the davenport and sitting down slowly.

'I must ask you, madam, on your honour as an English gentlewoman, to reassure me that Lady Mercer is not the progeny of de Champney.' He had the grace to redden as he said it, but the words seemed to twist his lips into a strange leer. 'Without such a vow, I cannot marry your granddaughter.'

Constance gasped. She could not help it. Mrs Fog sat rigid, her face as set as a wax mask. The moment seemed to buzz in Constance's ears. From outside she heard the faint tick of a halyard against a flagpole, the whinny of a horse, an automobile door slammed shut.

'How dare you,' Constance said at last, her voice somewhere between a whisper and spitting in his face. 'To insult an Englishwoman of Mrs Fog's stature and reputation with such a base suggestion.'

'Don't be too hard on him,' said Mrs Fog, her voice weary. 'He just wants to be sure he gets what he pays for. Americans are like that, you know. Like to strike a hard bargain. A nation of fur trappers and Nonconformists. They distrust the word of others because they do not feel bound by such bonds of character themselves.' Percival whitened as if struck, and Mrs Fog pressed her advantage. 'I find it strange you would take me at my word?'

'I seek only your personal confirmation, Mrs Fog.' He was sweating and apologetic now. 'I have already sent Rachel's photograph, and that of her mother, to a renowned phrenologist in London and he reports only Anglo-Saxon bone structure and a goodly hint of Norman around the chin. But you will understand that with such an extraordinary impediment, I need to be sure. I deeply regret causing any offence.'

'Your question is so low and vile, Rachel will throw your ring back in your face,' said Constance.

'I doubt she will do that. As Mrs Fog knows, it is very much in Rachel's interest that we marry expediently.' He smirked, confirming Constance's worst fears about Rachel's condition. She felt the power of his position like a blow to the face. Even with her parents' wealth, and a child quietly passed off as a relative's, or passed to a local family to be raised as their own, such a secret shame would likely blight Rachel's heart and her life.

'I could provide you records of my daughter's birth a full year after my marriage, Mr Allerton.' Mrs Fog raised her chin and anger sparkled in her eyes. 'But if you doubt my virginity on my wedding night, I can offer only my word as an Englishwoman.' Percy got to his feet and made a small bow.

'Thank you, Mrs Fog, I accept and consider the point settled,' he said. His genuine relief seemed as vile as the question itself, and Constance felt a rage burn through her veins as his smug voice continued. 'If we agree that Rachel and I will never hear the de Champney name in our married home, I am fully satisfied, and I trust there will be no need to distress my fiancée?'

'You are satisfied?' Constance clenched her hands, wishing she were a man so she might smash her fist into his self-satisfied nose. 'You hope to bully us women, but I can assure you Lord Mercer will not take such an insult to his family lightly.'

'No, indeed, Constance, I think the matter is settled to everyone's benefit,' said Mrs Fog, tugging on the back of Constance's skirt, her voice sharp. 'I see no need to distress Rachel's father or upset the family over a matter already resolved.' She also stood up, indicating an end to the interview. 'We will say nothing more about it.'

'Thank you,' said Percival. He hesitated as if to seek their hands, but Mrs Fog's were clasped firmly together at her waist and Constance felt her own still balled into fists. He compromised by sidling out of the room, bobbing his head like some sort of inferior waiter. Klaus Zieger, thought Constance, would never have stooped to such obsequiousness.

Constance held her tongue until well after the door had closed. She did not rule out his listening in the corridor.

'Surely you will tell Rachel of his underhanded investigations?' she asked. 'She has a right to know who she is marrying.'

'What benefit would it be to her?' asked Mrs Fog. 'Do we hope to shatter her happiness or merely inject it with a small vein of poison that may fester over the years?'

'She is not a child to be protected.'

'No, but she is a young woman already committed to her path in ways that cannot be undone. To upend things now would benefit no one, especially Rachel.' Her voice trembled as she turned away to the window. 'I appreciate your urge to fight for us both, but you are a sharp young woman, Constance, so I know you understand.'

Constance had no further words to comfort Mrs Fog or to help Rachel. She would join them all in remaining silent.

'You will live a lie too,' whispered Constance. 'For the rest of your life.'

'A small prevarication, barely an omission.'

'You can never visit her.'

'I was not likely to visit anyway,' said Mrs Fog. 'The young man is not wrong about my age, my dear. And can you imagine having to meet Percival's family? A whole brace of them?' She shuddered. 'No, she will come home to visit her parents and perhaps I will visit her there. If necessary, I know where Cook keeps the spare key to the servants' hall.'

'It still denies the truth of your love,' said Constance.

'At my age, it will have to be enough.' For a moment her cheerful manner failed, and she looked so wistful Constance was moved to throw her arms around the frail figure and shed a few tears into her starched collar. Whether for Rachel and Mrs Fog, for herself or for the compromises it seemed all women must make, she could not say. Mrs Fog hugged her back and patted her hair.

'There, there, my dear. You are very kind to a difficult old woman.'

'You deserve such kindness,' said Constance, releasing her and drying her eyes. 'You have been very good to me this summer, and I so very much appreciate that.'

'Then perhaps we should continue our friendship,' said Mrs Fog, leading her back to the davenport to sit. 'I should tell you that Simon and I, and Mathilde, of course, plan to remove ourselves from English society and return to Barbados.'

'Oh, Mrs Fog, you mean to restore Simon and Mathilde to their estates?'

'Given the legal constraints of my trust, I cannot return the lands to Simon, but there is no impediment to us enjoying them together; or to my granting them both life tenancies. I would like to invite you to come with us, Constance. We are three elderly folks and would benefit from your companionship and assistance. I would pay you a small salary, of course. I could manage that, I think. And there are many delights to the island.'

'I never thought of reaching foreign shores,' said Constance. 'Only in dreams and in books.'

'There was always quite a social life among the planter families; an endless round of teas, tennis and dancing that I'm sure has been impervious to the ravages of war.' Mrs Fog shook her head. 'I cannot expect that Simon, Mathilde and I will be welcome at the country club or my father's beach club. However, my family name still carries weight, and I am sure I can find suitable ladies to sponsor your introduction. Perhaps we may find you a husband yet, hiding behind a palm tree.'

'It's a generous offer, Mrs Fog,' said Constance. But the dream of foreign shores was already suffocated by the image of small-minded people playing tennis under tropical skies. 'May I think it over?'

'Of course, my child,' said Mrs Fog. 'Now I must go down to breakfast, and you had better escape before my daughter and granddaughter come looking for you. Don't worry, I will tell them I have no idea where you are. Certainly not up in an aeroplane.'

'How could you know that?' Constance gasped as Mrs Fog's eyes twinkled with laughter.

'Gossiping in back halls, I suppose,' said Mrs Fog. 'And sometimes one appears to be asleep and people talk as if one can't hear them.'

'Sharp as a tack,' said Constance.

'And quiet as the grave,' said Mrs Fog. 'Run along now and know that at least someone in the crowd will be cheering for you, my dear girl.'

THE HOTEL'S LOBBY was crowded with parade dignitaries and hotel guests celebrating the day. The white dresses and frothy hats of the ladies could hardly compete for attention today against the gentlemen. In the centre stood Mayor Morris, in his scarlet-and-black fur-trimmed robes; complete with white lace jabot, bicorn hat with gold cockade and a gold chain of office as thick as a saddle girth. Around him, Mr Smickle and the other aldermen, in red robes trimmed with black velvet, and white feathers in their bicorns, mingled with military officers, in gold braid and medals, who apologised for tripping ladies with their long swords. The town crier wore doublet and hose, and it amused Constance to see that every businessman and fraternal leader had dug up some sort of ceremonial costume, topped with tasseled honour cords and brooches of office. Even the dour baker, hovering with his wife, the waiter's friend, had managed to drum up a soft velvet cap and a cape embroidered with the arms of his bakers' union. The lobby resembled an epic medieval tapestry and smelled strongly of mothballs.

Constance was about to slip away when she spotted Percy Allerton, in a plain frock coat, a top hat under his arm, standing with Rachel and Lady Mercer. He looked chalk white, while Rachel frowned and whispered urgently to her mother. There seemed to be some excitement causing their distress, and she edged from behind a pillar to get a better view.

Into the middle of the lobby strode Mr Pendra, the former captain and lowly civil servant, smiling, in a blue dress uniform blossoming, from collar to cuffs, with gold braid. Coils of gold-cord aiguillettes hung from one shoulder, and a large bar of medals was almost eclipsed by several jewelled orders on his breast. A sash and sword belt completed a look so splendid that Constance was sure he must have been made an honorary marshal of the Royal Air Force. Behind him marched Mr Basu, in a long coat of black and silver thread, crossed by a swathing sash of red silk, and adorned with medals and an embroidered girdle with silver dagger and jewelled sabre. On his head he wore a tall red turban, decorated with a small silver medallion, and on his face was a stern look that kept the crowd from pressing in too close.

As Constance watched, Mr Smickle and his nephew, Dudley, made obsequious low bows, while Mayor Morris took off his bicorn hat and mopped his brow as he attempted to bend in the middle. The ladies began to drop into curtsies as the crowd murmured and shifted for a better look.

'So it seems that Pendra's father was the late Maharajah of Kochi Benar, my mother's great friend,' said Poppy, materialising at Constance's shoulder. 'His uncle assumed the throne and Pendra went into the war incognito, fearing they would never allow a prince a flying commission.'

'Harris never knew?' asked Constance.

'No. And the uncle died a few months ago, so Mr Pendra has been the new Maharajah of Kochi Benar all this time.' Poppy grinned. 'He came to the suite this morning to confess to Mother, and there were quite a few tears and protestations of friendship. Hardly what we expected from the quiet captain.'

'He is not the lowly civil servant now,' said Constance, smiling as the new Maharajah caught her eye across the room and winked. 'More than a few people may have cause to regret their cold behaviour.'

Chapter 26

At Penneston, Constance found the house in an up-
roar. The new housekeeper had taken an instant dislike to the temporary
butler and staff hired for the weekend and was in the front hall arguing
with him in front of a bemused Harris over the placement of floral arrangements.

'I won't have them big urns dragged across the parquet,' she said.
'Take them round the back.'

'They are too heavy to carry up the terrace stairs,' said the butler, wiping his forehead with a large handkerchief. 'We have to wheel 'em
through the house.'

'Over my dead body,' said the housekeeper.

'Good morning,' said Constance.

'I don't suppose my mother is right behind you, is she?' said Harris.
'I'm being held against my will and tortured with arrangements.'

'If I might suggest something we used at Clivehill – it is to lay drugget
and then boards on top of that,' said Constance to the two glowering
staff members. 'We never had any damage to the floors that way.'

'That's a capital idea, ma'am,' said the butler. 'May I proceed, sir?'

'Yes, please,' said Harris and turned to the housekeeper. 'I hope that
will leave you free, dear madam, to add a couple of patriotic blancmanges
per my mother's directions?'

'Where I'm supposed to get the extra sugar, I don't know,' grumbled the housekeeper.

'A partial victory,' said Harris as the two servants left the room, like prizefighters retiring to their corners. 'I expect our worthy housekeeper is muttering under her breath about being put in her place by a slip of a thing.'

'I find it works best to ignore any moods,' said Constance. 'Cheerful and direct tends to produce cooperation.'

'That doesn't seem to work on my sister or you,' he said.

'I think you should probably practise the "cheerful" part,' said Constance.

'I would really like to talk to you,' said Harris. 'But I have a list of things to sort out for my mother and I don't know how to get it done in time.' He produced from his pocket an actual list, much crossed and blotted, across three sheets of paper. 'I must get to the barn if we are to be in the air promptly at eleven thirty.'

'I suppose there's no chance that Iris will suddenly decide to go up?' she asked.

'I would much rather fly with you anyway,' he said and took her hand and pressed it. 'I need a woman whose nerve can be trusted.'

'Would you like my help with your list?' she asked. 'I have some experience with these things.' She thought of all the affairs at Clivehill where she and her mother had been prevailed upon to give the 'merest of assistance', only to find themselves exhausted, sweating and completely unacknowledged.

'That would be a complete imposition,' he said.

'A complete imposition,' she agreed, but she laughed and the relief on his face lifted her heart. 'Where do we start?'

Constance spent a consuming half hour with Harris, first going over the extensive evening menus with the housekeeper and then a long list of arrangements with the butler, who kept one eye on the flower urns and so may only have comprehended half. Constance released Harris to the barn about halfway down the list. Only one or two substantial issues remained.

Poppy had demanded a ragtime dance band, from Brighton, whose local musicians seemed to think an American authenticity required them to be already drinking heavily in the garden. Constance suggested the butler order them a large, hopefully spongy, lunch, and she reminded them personally that they would not be paid if they were found derelict. They put away their flasks and made promises. But the rude sounds from the slide trombone and laughter as she left made her nervous. And then there were the maids and footmen in rented liveries, many from the hotel, who were so unfamiliar with the house that the butler and housekeeper agreed they were quite unsure how they would assist any guest who needed it. Having a sudden recollection of the library, Constance had a large framed architectural blueprint of the house moved from a nook beside the fireplace to a side table in the back hall where all the servants might refer to it in passing. Then she used it herself to find her way to a side door and slip out through the kitchen garden and onto the dirt track to the barn.

To one side of the track, Iris was smoking under a tree, sitting sideways on her motorcycle with her legs carelessly crossed. She wore her usual motorcycle leathers and sat with her head down, disconsolate.

'It's no use,' she said as Constance walked up to her. 'I can't go on hiding like this. I'm just going to have to admit defeat.'

'I'm so sorry,' said Constance. 'You are the bravest woman I know.'

'It doesn't feel that way, skulking around taking people's money under false pretences.'

'If you want to come clean today, I can't fault you,' said Constance. 'It will be a blow to Harris, but I'm sure he'd be the first to agree.'

'On the other hand, it would be a shame to spoil the celebrations,' said Iris. 'And I believe there is a gentleman's wager that Harris can beat Tom with a woman co-pilot. So I'm game to carry on if you are. And I'll split my fee with you of course.'

'I'm just thrilled to get the chance to fly,' said Constance. 'I couldn't take any money.'

'Upsettingly noble, but I won't hold it against you,' said Iris. 'Let's go to the barn and get you kitted out, shall we?'

—⁊||⟨—

AGAINST THE SUNNY, pastoral background of barn, fields and trees, it took a moment for the outlines of a disaster to become clear. Constance saw first that the Sopwith Camel's engine cowling was off, lying on the ground. There was a small canvas sheet with engine bits on it. This seemed at odds with a desire to be in the air at eleven thirty sharp. Then the splash of water caught her attention and she saw Harris, in his shirt-sleeves, holding Jock's head under the outdoor tap as if they were boys hazing each other. Jock was sprawled and shouting, Harris looked grim and both were soaking wet and muddy. Iris pulled the motorcycle to an abrupt stop and Constance hopped off the back to approach them.

'What on earth is going on?' she asked. Harris saw her and let go of Jock, who rolled away and struggled to sit up, shaking his head slowly.

'He's ruined everything,' said Harris, his voice bitter. 'After all I've done – after all we've all done for him – this is how he repays us.'

'I'll fix it right up,' said Jock and waved an arm vaguely at the aeroplane. 'It's nay so bad.'

'He's drunk,' said Constance with shock. 'What did he do to the engine?'

'I didnae do nothing,' said Jock. 'I was just taking out that last wee plug to give her a clean and I fell asleep.'

'Someone gave him an entire bottle of Scotch whisky and then either he or they took apart the magneto.'

'It wasn't me,' said Jock.

'Sabotage,' said Iris. 'The bastards.'

'I can put it right in a jiffy,' said Jock. 'I just need a sleep first.' With that he rolled into a sunny patch of dry grass and passed out.

'Even if he could put it together, I'm not going to trust my life or yours to an engine checked by a drunkard,' said Harris. 'I'm afraid the flight is off, ladies.'

'Surely Tom Morris wouldn't stoop so low just to beat you in an air show?' said Constance. 'It's not very gentlemanly.'

'It's the wager,' said Harris. 'Stupid of me to be goaded into it. I deserve my own downfall, but I'm rather afraid I'll be taking Poppy down with me.'

'What did you idiot boys do?' asked Iris. 'I thought it was just a gentleman's wager.'

'If I lose I've agreed to sell them the airfield land for cash.'

'Sounds like you got the best in that deal,' said Iris.

'The land includes the barn, and I have to throw in the Camel.'

'Oh, you are really in trouble,' said Iris. 'Poppy will kill you.'

'We are running out of time,' said Constance. She had never felt so helpless. And in that moment she felt she would give all her future if she could only help Harris save Penneston. A sudden idea occurring, she asked, 'Could Tilly fix the engine?'

'Tilly?' said Harris. 'She hasn't been here in days. Not since the Labour Board man told Poppy to close down. Even if she could get here in time, I'm not sure she would help us the way things were left.'

'I heard about Poppy having to close down,' said Iris. 'Tilly Mulford may be upset, but she is not one to hold a grudge. She has more of a sense of fair play in her little finger than you men apparently do in two heads. Constance and I will go fetch her at once. Twenty minutes at the most.'

'It'll be very tight,' said Harris. 'That'll leave only half an hour to fix things.'

'So stop talking,' said Iris, running for the motorcycle. Constance ran with her.

'Why do you need me?' she gasped as Iris signalled her to climb aboard.

'Because Tilly is the most stubborn woman I know after Poppy,' said Iris. 'You'll push the whole fair-play thing, where I'll just be seen as wanting to help Poppy.'

'Twenty minutes, maximum?' said Constance. 'Doesn't leave me much time to persuade her.'

'We'll just have to ride faster then,' said Iris, grinning as she opened the throttle.

AT PENNESTON LODGE, Tilly was arguing with the Morris sisters while Poppy and the nurses directed patients into sidecars and onto the backs of machines.

'But your sidecar is the most ideal for Arthur with his crutches,' said Tilly. 'You can't want to watch him walk while you ride, surely?'

'The whole thing is a wretched idea,' said Evangeline. 'We were all going to look so pretty.'

'Hello,' said Poppy, coming over. 'Did you hear? They forgot, I assume deliberately, to send transport for the men.' She rolled her eyes. 'So we decided they should ride with us. Our lady passengers are all going to walk alongside, carrying flowers.'

'Rachel already left us for the grandstand,' said Guinevere. 'She said her silk wedding shoes would be ruined by the walking.'

'I think she'd rather be seated next to a Maharajah than parade with us,' said Poppy.

'My shoes are silk too,' said Evangeline. 'I don't understand why we have to all give up our seats.'

'I'm sure you can walk a few miles before they collapse, Evangeline,' said Iris. 'Or run home and get a pair of boots.'

'Yes, do buck up, girls,' said Poppy. 'You will look silly if you don't participate.'

'It's a wonderful idea,' said Constance. 'Just think, everyone will see how charitable you are.'

'Yes, I'm sure it's worth extra publicity,' said Iris.

'They may be right,' said Guinevere. 'Come on, Evie, we'll just have to make the best of it. Angels of charity and all that.'

'The aesthetic of the rig will be ruined,' said Evangeline. 'Sam won't be happy.'

As the two sisters left grudgingly to assist their allotted passenger, Tilly came over to hug Iris. 'So much fuss over an overgrown wicker baby carriage,' she said. 'No sense of duty.'

'Now we need you to do your duty too, Tilly,' said Iris. 'Tell them, Constance.'

'Someone sabotaged the Camel,' said Constance. She told them briefly what they had found at the barn.

'Someone gave whisky to Jock despite his history?' said Tilly. Her lips pressed together in anger.

'By "someone" we assume Tom Morris?' said Poppy. 'I'll run the man over.'

'We don't know that for sure,' said Constance.

'Poor Jock,' said Tilly. 'Surely Harris doesn't blame him?'

'Tilly, can you come and look at it?' asked Constance. 'If Harris fails to fly, it will be a disaster for him.'

'It won't affect my future,' said Tilly. 'My future is in the library, remember?'

'Come on, Tilly. We know how much you care,' said Constance. 'We have less than twenty minutes to get airborne.'

'But who'll take my passengers?' asked Tilly. 'I have one in the sidecar and one on the pillion. I'm not letting Gwinny Morris handle my machine under a load.'

'I'll do it,' said Iris. 'You take Constance back on my motorcycle.'

'You never let anyone ride your beast,' said Poppy. 'And aren't you supposed to be flying?'

'It's too late for all that, Poppy,' said Iris.

'Tilly, you're the only one who can get us airborne,' said Constance. 'Harris and I are willing to put our lives in your hands if you'll help us.'

'Please help Harris,' added Poppy. 'I've no right to ask but you know how important it is to him and to Jock that today is a success.' Constance looked at the ground and hoped her face would not betray how much worse the situation was than Poppy could imagine.

'I suppose I have no choice,' said Tilly. She undid a buckle at her waist and without flourish dropped her white skirt to the ground. Underneath she wore linen knickerbockers, white gaiters and her thick motorcycling boots. 'Here you go, Iris. It's a bit short for you, but you'll need it for the parade. Better ask Poppy if she has a comb for that hair.'

'I'll even find you a spare hat, Iris,' Poppy said with a laugh.

'Some sacrifices are a ribbon too far,' sighed Iris. 'You'll all owe me for this later.'

HARRIS TOWELLED HIMSELF off as best he could while Jock leaned against the barn worktable and hid his head under his towel for perhaps longer than necessary.

'I'm sorry, Captain,' he said at last, blinking in the day's strong sunlight. 'I meant to keep the bottle for you, then the more I looked the more I thought a wee dram wouldn't hurt and, well, I knew what I was doing, I'll not pretend I didn't.'

'I know what it is to be gripped by something. To want to give up and let it have you,' said Harris. 'People tell you "just don't drink" or "just be cheerful and get out more". It's not that easy.'

'It's like Jekyll and Hyde,' said Jock. 'The extra voice in your head telling you to do it. To go ahead and burn it all down.'

'I didn't take you for a reading man, Jock,' said Harris.

'It's good to know a little literature, my dad used to say,' said Jock. 'When you're in the dock it always softens up the magistrate.' He staggered off into the back of the barn, making further retching noises.

Harris shook his pocket watch. The thing seemed to be ticking too fast, the hands moving inexorably towards his being late. In the distance he could hear the sounds of an Avro being run up at the airfield. He tried to breathe and unclench his jaw, to control the strong desire to pace back and forth. Fatalism, he decided, was not his strong suit. He was beginning to lose hope when he heard the distinctive growling sound of Iris's motorcycle. It was Tilly driving; in clothes too pressed and starched for riding or for mechanical work. But as she and Constance hopped off, she simply beat the dust from her knees and walked over to the Camel with a frown.

'Few bits removed,' she said. 'Hope you have them all.'

'Everything should be here,' said Harris. 'I searched around on my hands and knees anyway. Found this washer.' He handed her a ring of black rubber he had found in the grass.

'No, that's from a fuel cap, not the engine. It may be from a motorcycle,' she said. 'I'll start putting this back together and just hope Jock is lucid enough to check my work.' She nodded to the barn, where a very white-faced Jock could be seen stumbling towards them.

'He's not his usual self,' Harris said, as ashamed as if it were he, not Jock, drunk at eleven in the morning. 'He's a good man, really.'

'Don't you worry,' said Tilly. 'Leave Jock to me. Between us we'll get you in the air.'

Harris left her smartly assembling the small parts on the tarp, and Jock, kneeling beside her, nodding his head at her questions.

'I'm not sure we'll get up,' he said to Constance. 'And if we do, I'm not sure it's safe to take you with me.'

'I have every faith in Tilly, and in Jock,' she replied. 'And having the lady flier aboard is part of your wager, I believe?'

'I can't risk your life for a wager,' he said. He took her hand in his. 'Not just because you are a woman, but because you are a friend.' He put his arm around her, and she softened against him, the press of her body releasing a wave of warmth that coursed through him. After a moment, at once too long and too short, he drew away and cleared his throat. 'I couldn't possibly let anything happen to you. Poppy would kill me.'

'Let's see what they say,' she said, glancing towards Tilly and Jock. 'I don't want to be a burden, but I want you to know it is a great privilege to fly with you. Iris is riding with the club so the charade will be over today. This might be my last chance to take to the sky.'

'You are a constant surprise, Miss Haverhill,' he said.

AFTER AN AGONISING half hour and with not a minute to spare, it was Tilly who declared the machine ready. Jock seemed unable to speak, whether because of physical effects or shame was hard to tell. He gave Harris a look as mute and unhappy as a kicked dog and, as Tilly helped her into the front seat, Constance noticed that Harris took the time to shake the man's hand and clap him on the shoulder.

'Strap in tight,' said Harris to Constance, climbing up onto the machine. He leaned over and pulled hard on the buckles of the strap across her lap. To be touched by Harris so matter-of-factly felt more intimate to Constance than if he had kissed her again. 'We'll be pulling some pretty acrobatic manoeuvres today, but remember, I won't fly upside down. You're perfectly safe.'

She tried to answer his worried frown with a smile. 'I trust you, Harris.' He paused as if he would like to say something more, but then seemed to shake it off.

'When I tap you on the shoulder, you'll balance your feet evenly and hold the stick steady,' he said, brisk as a sergeant. 'Stay relaxed, count to twenty just as we practised, and try not to compensate if we wobble a bit as I release the bags.'

She nodded. This was the bonus pass designed to show off Iris the Aviatrix. The proof that a woman was actually flying the machine would be Harris waving 'look no hands' and then dumping flour bombs as she held the machine steady. In their practice she had fought to keep the Camel level, the nose always pulling down to the right, and the machine responding too fast and far under her clumsy hands. It had felt at times like walking a large, unruly mastiff.

'You'll be great,' he said. 'You are one of those useful women, remember?' There was no insult now in his grinning face. Perhaps the raised eyebrow offered a hint of apology for the time before they were friends. She shook her head.

'Is this how you compliment a woman before covering her in the hot spray of castor oil?' she asked.

'Not a woman now,' he said, a hand on her shoulder. 'A fellow pilot.'

He clambered into the rear seat with his usual hitch-and-pull motion and strapped in.

'Contact!' called Tilly from in front. As she pulled down on the blade, the engine coughed twice and then burst into a loud and steady roar. The propeller disappeared into a smooth blur. A thumbs-up from Jock said the machine sounded good. He and Tilly ran to pull away the chocks from the wheels and waved them clear for take-off. The Camel began to roll forward.

HARRIS TOOK A cautious flip around the field, just to test the engine, then steered away for the seafront, taking a slight detour over the airfield, all the while ready to set the machine down at the first sign of engine trouble.

In front of him the girl, Constance, looked about her eagerly, Iris's pink scarf close around her neck. There was no time now, he thought, to examine the feeling she created in him. He had often felt the fluttering of attraction in the presence of a pretty girl. Even in the depths of his melancholy, it had seemed an almost instinctive reaction. But Constance inspired something deeper. She had pierced his armour as much with her barbed wit as with her beauty, and in the slicing, she had let sunlight into the darkness.

Chapter 27

K̲L̲A̲U̲S̲ ̲C̲O̲U̲L̲D̲ ̲N̲O̲T̲ ̲U̲N̲D̲E̲R̲S̲T̲A̲N̲D̲ ̲T̲H̲E̲ ̲D̲E̲S̲I̲R̲E̲ ̲T̲O̲ ̲C̲E̲L̲E̲-brate peace with the trappings of war. Or rather, he was disappointed that they called it a peace celebration but kept adding the elements of a victory parade, like the flying contest that included a simulated attack on the U-boat. And he, Klaus Zieger, symbol of German defeat, was to raise the white flag of surrender. Mr Smickle, volunteering him for today's performance, had promised him an extra day off and half a sovereign for his trouble and made it clear he could not refuse. He could not articulate whether it was the white flag itself or the reduction of war to seaside pantomime that caused a hot tide of humiliation to now roil his stomach. He could only wonder what Odile would think of him from her grandstand seat.

He had made such a quiet request that Mr Smickle had quite thought it his own idea to invite the baker and his family. When Klaus stopped at the bakery, to buy a loaf of bread he did not need, he found Odile flushed and happy, whispering that the invitation to sit with the rest of the town's prominent business families had created great contentment in her husband. Klaus did not tell her it was his doing; the secret had fed the small flame of his happiness.

From his position on the conning tower, Klaus had a fine view of the seafront promenade, which was loaded with bunting draped from every lamppost, and pennants fluttering from every kiosk and pavilion. Temporary grandstands flanked the Meredith Hotel, Mr Smickle having taken care to ensure the repaired windows of the Palm Terrace would not be obstructed. Every gatepost, lamppost and garden was bursting with flowers, and every square inch of promenade and beach had been picked clean of litter and weeds and trimmed to perfection.

The parade was moving, in a slow tide, along the seafront. The crowds cheered and bobbed, children shouted and screamed. Klaus raised his binoculars to look for Odile in the grandstands, but she was indistinguishable in the general profusion of hats and best dresses. At the centre, Klaus could just make out the Mayor, in his gold chains of office, Mrs Wirrall in a hat the size of a cartwheel, and, on the other side, the young Maharajah, whose ornate uniform blazed in the sunlight. A shock to all the staff to see the almost invisible Mr Pendra revealed as foreign royalty. They had joked in the service hall about the chambermaids being blind to have missed the swords and turbans kept in his rooms, along with more jewellery than the richest women in town. And there was some low grumbling about the sneakiness of it from a couple of porters who, Klaus was fairly sure, had been curt to the young Indian and now feared to have lost some generous gratuity.

A troop of Canadian soldiers and airmen accompanied by a regimental band, playing 'O Canada', were followed by the local Boy Scouts playing 'Land of Hope and Glory' on tin whistles. Klaus winced at the discordant assault on his ears. After troops of returned local soldiers, it was the turn of the schools, girls carrying floral garlands, boys holding wooden rifles and a band of drums and fifes playing a ragged 'Rule, Britannia'. Behind them the applause and cheering seemed to pause and then resume with a slight change in tone.

The cause of this ruffle in the crowd was soon revealed to be the Hazelbourne Ladies Motorcycle and Flying Club, marching behind its banner decorated with ribbons, flowers and a new insignia, featuring an aeroplane flying over a young woman waving from her motorcycle. Many of the young ladies were walking because the ladies who did ride had their pillions and sidecars full of wounded soldiers, distinctive in their blue hospital suits. From his high perch, Klaus was not as close as the crowds, but he could see the missing limbs, the bandaged heads, the scarred faces. There were some audible gasps at the ravaged bodies. As the ladies drew even with the grandstands, there was a commotion, and Klaus could see the young Maharajah making his way from his seat of honour down to the road. The Mayor and one or two officials scrambled to follow him. The young man, accompanied by his turbaned aide, came down to walk among the machines, shaking hands with each and every wounded man. The Mayor was forced to do likewise, and the crowd, so instructed by their betters, began finally to cheer in a loud and sustained manner.

As the parade ended, a persistent buzzing heralded the arrival of the aeroplanes. Though it was just a show, Klaus could not help but stiffen. The voice of the town crier, calling to the crowd through a large megaphone, caused all eyes to turn towards the beach. A brass band in front of the grandstand burst into a frenzied marching tune. The street filled in now, those uniformed and costumed from the parade mingling with the crowd, all pressing to view the show. Klaus stood taller, chin high in the air, scanning the horizon for the oncoming attack. Tucked away below the promenade, next to the deckchair rental hut, a small colour guard were busy unfurling their flags and testing their bugles, ready to board the U-boat.

There were two aeroplanes. Klaus could not tell them apart but he had only to remember the choreography in order to play his part. After criss-crossing above him, performing loops and turns, they would compete to sever rolls of falling crêpe paper and then count spins from a great height. Then in a mock attack they would pass over the submarine and drop bombs of coloured flour on him, competing on the number of hits and effect of the imitation explosions. Klaus had to light four fuses to set off loud fireworks fore and aft on the vessel, creating sound and pillars of smoke. He also had a flare pistol, which he was to fire over the sea; the flares, it had been agreed, would show up more brightly against the noon sun than any firework. It was presented as a raucous but jovial show, but to Klaus the droning engines heralded the final humiliation, when he would have to step to the mast and, alone and despised by the roaring crowd, raise the white flag of surrender.

He felt the thrill and the menace of the machines as keenly as the vibration of their engines. Like large birds of prey, or small dragons, the aeroplanes buzzed and dove and seemed to dance with each other. The heads of the pilots tiny, seemingly tied on with white scarves; in one aeroplane a woman too, her scarf fluttering a bright pink against the blue sky. The crowd cheering and clapping, great waves of applause now as the woman's machine flew back and forth, its propeller cutting cleanly through the long streamer of crêpe paper. Two and three times it sliced, each time lower, the paper slipping down the breeze, now perilously close to the sea. One more time the pilot banked steeply, turned over into a steep dive and sliced the streamer so low that Klaus was sure some of the crowd could not see it happen behind the bulk of the pier and the U-boat. A great cheer went up as the megaphone barked again: 'Captain Wirrall in the Sopwith Camel wins the streamer challenge with four clean cuts to Captain Morris's three.'

Now the action required Klaus's participation. He was not anxious but instead a new energy coursed in his veins. As both aeroplanes climbed higher and higher into the sky, his hand was steady on his fuse box, and then, as each machine rolled over to begin a death spiral towards the sea, something primal seemed to sharpen his focus.

'Closer, a little closer,' he said aloud. As the Avro, painted a distinctive red, and then the Camel, broke their spins to roar up and away over his head, he threw his first two switches.

A ten-foot flare of flame burst fore and aft, followed instantly by the loud, percussive bang and columns of thick black smoke. It was so unexpected to the crowd that it caused an audible hitch of silence in the general roar. The slightly larger red aeroplane wobbled slightly as it climbed again; the pilot's face, briefly seen, was white and hard. In that moment, Klaus took his hand from the switches and thought he should not contribute further to this charade. It seemed to him that the Victory Committee had made a dreadful mistake in bringing the war here. How many soldiers, flowers in their buttonholes, were now fidgeting on the seafront? How many widows sickened by the smell of cordite?

But just as in the war itself, there was no choice for the individual soldier, he thought, as now the Sopwith Camel came sweeping overhead and the commentator barked again:

'Ladies and gentlemen, we are all even after the death spiral. Now please note the Camel will be flown by Miss Iris Brenner, champion motorcycle racer and aviatrix.' And to the roar of the crowd, the Sopwith Camel made a level pass, with a somewhat alarming wobble each time the bags of flour were released. Three fell along the deck, and one on the beach, each landing with a great *whumpf* and exploding clouds of red, white and blue. Klaus braced himself not to flinch, but the male pilot had been as kind as he was accurate, spacing the bags to fall well clear of the conning tower.

Then the aeroplane banked upward and banked sideways into a steep dive. It was to be the last and lowest pass. As the Camel came screaming low overhead, it dropped a larger bag, which missed the submarine by inches, exploding on the shingled beach in a great cloud of confetti. Klaus flipped two more switches, sending up two answering columns of paper confetti as cannons by the bandstand sent their own barrages of paper towards Klaus. He was strangely comforted by the clouds of confetti, drifting like cherry blossom towards the crowds. It was, after all, a mere circus entertainment for children, he thought. He took the flare gun from his holster and, as scripted, fired two flares low and well to either side of the departing aeroplane. There was a faint smell of sulphur, two long streaks of white into the sky and the loud crack of red fireballs falling slowly over the sea. But the crowd was wild and happy now, the men waving hats and shouting, the women clapping and gasping. Children reached from their fathers' shoulders to grasp for paper fragments as if for prizes.

'Take that, Mr Hun,' said the town crier. 'Three hits for Captain Harris with Miss Iris Brenner in command.'

'That is Captain Hun to you,' said Klaus quietly. On the beach below, the colour guard was getting into formation. Klaus had not expected to feel so unhappy at the prospect of their boarding. Of his own surrender. He squared his shoulders. He would maintain his dignity and get through it.

The red Avro made its pass now, the exploding bags grouped far too close to Klaus. He choked in the billowing flour, struggling for a handkerchief to hold over his nose and mouth. Disoriented, he pulled and fired the flare gun again. The flares arced high into the air, and though they were still well clear of the aeroplane, the pilot dove sharply towards the ocean as they exploded above him, then pulled up into the sky, twisting away from the red fire.

'Captain Tom Morris with four hits and some impressive flying there to escape a singeing,' said the commentator. 'Poor sportsmanship from the German Navy.' There was booing from the crowd. As the aeroplane banked around for another pass, the announcer shouted again, 'Watch out, Mr Bismarck! I have just had it on good authority that Captain Morris has a surprise for you. It's all even, folks, so if this bomb strikes the target, it's a win for Captain Morris!' It was to be the last diving pass of the show. Klaus wiped his face and brushed the thick dusting of flour from his shoulders. As the crowd roared and screamed, he lifted a stern chin to the oncoming machine. Lower and faster it came. Hard to remember it was just a pageant as the ear-splitting roar vibrated into every fibre of his body. He leaned forward, bracing against the sound as if into the teeth of a gale. Then the aeroplane was overhead, and from a canister slung underneath came a rotting, stinking deluge: a foul-smelling wave of water, blood and fish guts strafed the centre decks and took Klaus full in the face.

'Howzat!' shouted the commentator, aping a cricket umpire. 'A little surprise, I'm told, from the fishing ports of England and a knockout blow for the German Navy. Captain Morris wins. Germany surrenders!' The band broke into a rousing rendition of 'Rule, Britannia', but the colour guard, who had already advanced across the pebbles, now stood awkwardly, unwilling to climb the slippery, befouled stairs to the deck.

'Raise the white flag, mate,' the bugler shouted.

'Come and do it yourself,' said Klaus, wiping blood and flour from his face. The flare gun hung loosely from his hand. He did not point it at them but neither did he point it away. There was a huddle of urgent whispering on the pebbled shore. On the seafront, Klaus thought he saw Odile being pulled away by her husband. The glimpse of her face recalled him to his senses and, in her honour, he laid down the flare gun and climbed down from the conning tower. The band concluded its song, a little raggedly, and did not begin another. Perhaps the National Anthem did not seem appropriate until the Union Jack had been hoisted on deck. The town crier coughed into his megaphone but, without the signal of a white flag, the commentary was stalled.

Then a strange hiccup of quiet in the crowd. Over the sea came a cough, a series of sharp coughs, from the Sopwith Camel. Klaus, already on the stairs to the beach, turned his head to watch the machine flying no more than five hundred feet up, as if for a final pass. There was another pulse of sound, a revving of the throttle and a last burst of white smoke from its engine. Then only a shocking silence.

'WE'VE LOST THE engine,' Harris shouted. He could not be sure Constance had heard, so he leaned forward and tapped her shoulder. She turned her head, and her face was very pale, her eyes big with fear. Automatically, he checked the air-and-fuel mix lever, flipped the fuel shut-off a few times and tapped the gauges. He had switched to the second tank just before the last pass but the gauge showed empty. He switched back to the main tank but no fuel flowed. It would soon be useless anyway, once the engine stopped windmilling. He made one last attempt to switch the engine off and on again. Nothing. It was quiet enough to hear the sea underneath them as they glided forward. He had already set the nose down to maintain their airspeed, and while the Camel felt heavy, she was steady in her shallow glide. 'It just died on us,' he added.

'Can you restart it?' The slight panic in her voice was controlled. Good girl, he thought.

'Can't restart these engines without the propeller,' he shouted. 'But we're not on fire, so that's good.'

'Poppy says you're the absolute best.' She smiled, and he thought her courage was beyond all expectation.

'Don't worry, we can land without an engine,' he said. 'I've done it before.'

A deadstick landing, they called it. He had always thought it a poor choice of words, even before the last fiery crash, in which he had lost his leg and nearly his life. They were lower in the sky than he'd ever begun one before. No room for error, and Constance sat in front, where she would take the brunt of any mistake as he brought the nose-heavy machine down.

Only one chance to glide down, keeping a straight line; any turn a real danger of slipping into a deadly spin. They were heading at a shallow angle towards the shore, the pier looming ahead. Not enough height to make the airfield, he calculated. Ditching in the sea was the last resort; the fixed wheels would catch hard and likely cause the entire machine to flip, drowning them both. He could aim for the shore, but the entire seafront was teeming with people. The time to decide was now. At the end of town, he remembered the cricket pitch, parallel to the shore and set in a scrubby open park. The centre would be regularly mowed and would be smooth and grassy under the wheels. But would it be long enough? And would the ground be full of families, or had the parade pulled everyone away?

Without the engine it should have felt like silence, but the roar of the wind through the wires seemed to grow and rush at him like a squall. For a moment his head spun and the old thought invaded his mind and clutched at his throat; his number was overdue. But the girl in front was counting on him.

'I think I can make the cricket ground,' he shouted. 'Brace yourself.

With the crosswind off the sea it's going to be bumpy.' She turned and he wondered what it cost her to give him her brief smile and a raised thumb. Land or crash, he would not let her trust be undermined by his own fear. With gentle pressure to the rudder, he turned the machine further towards the shore.

They needed to be high enough to clear several lampposts, a wind shelter and an ice-cream kiosk topped with flags; and to make a final turn on approach. But they needed to be low enough to then immediately drop onto the handkerchief of green grass. Even for the Sopwith Camel, nimblest of machines, it would be close. There were only a few families and there were signs they saw him approaching. Children were grabbed, picnic baskets abandoned, a small dog braced its paws, barking. The crowd on the seafront shifted like liquid and was now flowing towards the park. A few men running formed its lacy edge. He could hear the sea, the hollow call of a hungry gull on the wing. He could feel the Camel vibrating around him, the wires humming, the spars creaking. His left knee throbbed now, his right foot ached against the rudder and his arms felt stiff from holding the stick steady. He blinked to clear his vision and took a deep breath.

Just clearing the flags of the kiosk, he crossed the blur of the sea road, swept over a red line of beech hedge and turned sharply to starboard to align with the long velvet swath of the cricket pitch. He brought the nose up to slow down and blessed the nimble Camel as it dropped lightly onto the grass on two wheels, bouncing once in the wind, but staying down, the tail wheel dropping in behind. Rolling fast, too fast across the grass, they crossed the groomed run of the cricket pitch and up an incline towards where the park ended in a small headland. With little rudder control now, he could only pray that they would not yaw and catch a wingtip on the ground, and that the rising slope would stop the brakeless machine in time. Slowly, the Camel began to lose momentum. The slope grew steep and the aeroplane still pushed forward, the propeller now nosing into a substantial gorse bush under a tree. Sounds of breaking branches and a green blur and then the Camel came to a lurching stop as a large branch gave one last snapping scrape across the cockpit.

Then quiet. A slow tick from the cooling engine. The disgruntled squawking of a displaced blackbird in the thicket. Harris unbuckled himself, sniffing the air for any smell of leaking fuel.

'We have to move,' he said, reaching to release Constance's straps. 'Can't be sure she won't spark a fire.' Constance had removed her goggles and had her scarf clamped to her eye. Blood soaked the pink silk and trickled down her cheek.

'I can't see out of my left eye,' she said. 'I think a branch cracked my goggles.' She held them out and he could see the left lens shattered.

'First we get out, then we'll see to it,' he said. She nodded, standing up to feel for the cockpit's edge, and shaking her head as she swung a leg over onto the wing. He held her by the elbow, reaching to steady her as she slid to the ground and then sat down abruptly. 'We must get further away,' he said, climbing after her. He hauled her up by her shoulders, rough in his haste to get her away. Clinging to each other, they stumbled across the grass towards the wave of people surging to meet them. At a safe distance, he lowered her to the ground and knelt, stiff and awkward, to gently pull her hand away from her eye. With her eyelid pressed shut and the socket full of welling blood, there was no way to tell the damage. He pulled off his own scarf and pressed the cleanest section gently to her eye.

'I can't see,' she said softly.

'I know,' he said. 'Don't try. Wait for the doctor.' He found himself praying it was just a cut and not a piercing shard of glass to blight her life. Grim hypocrisy, he knew, for a man with one leg to recoil from a girl with one eye.

The crowd began to swell into the cricket ground, and he looked up to see Jock and Tilly on a motorcycle sweeping across the field, shouting and waving at them to keep back. Then Poppy and Iris, scattering people as they roared up. In the confusing moments that followed, Constance clung to him silently as Poppy produced bandages and they wrapped

Constance's head. Jock dragooned some men into pulling up the ropes and stakes from around the cricket pitch and using them to fence off the machine. Flashbulbs exploded in Harris's face as newspapermen pressed forward shouting questions.

'Tilly will take her to the hotel,' said Iris. 'Harris, you and Jock should secure the Camel, and Poppy and I will hold off the press.' Poppy and Iris drew Constance from his arms and helped her to stand.

'Could you manage a wave at the crowd?' Harris heard Poppy ask her. 'For Harris's sake.'

Constance waved as she was loaded into the sidecar and Tilly drove her away through the clapping, cheering crowd.

'It may be bad.' His throat thickened around the words.

'Wait and see,' said Poppy. 'Not your fault.' She shook his arm.

'Completely my fault. I should never have risked her life.' He straightened his aching shoulders. 'I will stand by her.'

'We will all stand by her,' said Poppy. 'But let's not play this as tragedy. You are both safely landed. If anything, this should show how safe it is for ladies to fly.'

'I've lost my wager,' he said. 'The Camel will belong to Tom Morris.'

'So I heard from Iris,' she said. 'But this too shall be resolved.'

'You have a steel in you I did not imagine,' he said.

'Did you imagine the war only hardened the hearts of men?' She waved at the crowd, who now clapped and cheered for Harris. 'Smile and wave,' she added. 'Our future depends on it.'

A reporter broke forward to ask, 'Is she all right, the young woman? What happened up there?'

'I have to go,' muttered Harris.

'Take my machine,' said Iris. He nodded, and as he left, ignoring the crowd, he heard Poppy take charge of the questions.

'They are both fine,' she said. 'Just a few scratches and bruises. Sudden engine failure is not common, but I assure you that the pilots of the Hazelbourne Ladies Motorcycle and Flying Club, both ladies and gentlemen, are trained early on in the mechanics of the emergency landing.'

Chapter 28

PROPPED UP AGAINST SEVERAL PILLOWS IN THE COOL SHADE of her room, Constance watched the closed curtains flap lazily at the open window, a hem of light indicating the sunny afternoon. Her left eye throbbed beneath its bandages. She was not supposed to sleep but was drifting in a pleasant daze.

The hotel doctor arrived and, with Tilly's help, sponged away the mass of blood while Constance held her breath and squeezed her eyes shut. At last she felt the soft swipe of wet gauze across the eyelid and the doctor's cool fingers gently pressing her cheekbone and eyebrow.

'Just missed the eye,' he said. 'You can open it, my dear.' She did so, her lashes pulling apart slowly, still matted and sticky. The doctor smiled, one finger still pressed firmly under the inside corner of her left eyebrow.

'I can see,' she said, the gratitude sighing out of her.

'Luckily, it must have angled up into the brow bone,' said the doctor. 'These head wounds bleed like the devil. I'll have to put in a couple of stitches, but hopefully it won't leave more than a small scar.'

'She'll wear it as a badge of honour,' said Tilly.

'Or cover it up with a little cosmetic powder,' said the doctor. 'I know how important your looks are to you young ladies. Don't worry, with my help you won't need to be a wallflower.' He patted Constance on the leg, took a needle and thread from his bag and sat down on the bed. She thought briefly of Harris and her hand, lying on his knee, as he made his stitches with care and slow, sensitive movements. What followed was very different; an agonising few minutes in which the pain of the stitching was compounded by the discomfort of having to remain still as the doctor pressed thigh to thigh against her, bracing now his elbow on her chest, now one hand across her face as he stitched and tied. Always the avuncular tone, but his breath hot on her face and his moustache dangling up and down above her lips. She grasped Tilly's hand, determined to be rigid and silent under his hand. When he was done she resisted the urge to scramble away.

'Thank you,' she said as he pressed sticking plaster over a small gauze.

'I probably should examine you for any other injuries or internal damage,' he said. 'Are you able to undress?'

'No, thank you,' she said. 'I'm perfectly fine, really. The landing was quite gentle. I just got caught by a stray branch.' The doctor seemed disappointed.

'Very well,' he said, shaking his head. 'I don't know why you young ladies risk your lives and your future as mothers insisting upon these strenuous male pursuits. If God had meant women to fly . . .' He left the rest unsaid as he packed up his bag and left.

Tilly giggled.

'I've thought of two or three ways to finish that sentence, but all of them would make a strong man blush,' she said. 'Speaking of which, Harris has been pacing the hallway this entire time. He's probably ground a muddy track right into the carpet.'

'Am I even faintly presentable?' asked Constance.

'Not in the least,' said Tilly, smoothing a stray curl gently behind Constance's ear. 'And of course it's entirely inappropriate to visit you in your bedroom. But the man is distraught. I say we let him in for just a minute so he'll actually leave you in some peace.'

HARRIS WAS ACROSS the room and picking up her hand before she could say anything.

'Are you sure your eye is fine?' he asked. 'I can get a second opinion. A specialist?' He sat on the bed and, with his other hand he turned her chin gently to look more closely at the eye. She held still to suspend the moment.

'It's perfectly fine,' she said at last. 'Just a nasty deep cut that needed stitching.'

'If anything had happened to you—' he said. 'I shouldn't have agreed to take you up.' She blushed under the intensity of his gaze.

'You had better get over such gallantry if you're going to teach ladies how to fly,' said Tilly. The way he released her hand so promptly told Constance he had forgotten they were not alone. Tilly's wide smile said she was not fooled.

'But we didn't win, did we?' Constance said. 'Your land and the barn will be lost.'

'It's not important,' he said. 'Not right now anyway.' He stood up. 'You will have quite a spectacular black eye,' he added. 'You'll be the talk of the town tonight.'

'I will be hideous,' she said.

'Wear it with pride,' he said. 'It's a badge of courage.'

A peremptory knock on the door and Lady Mercer and Rachel swept into the room, seeming to shrink it to the size of a bus shelter. The air grew warmer, more stifling under the assault of ruffled linen, perfume and angry voices. Constance was sure Lady Mercer was already appalled, but to find Harris in her room seemed to threaten her with apoplexy.

'My abject apologies, ladies,' said Harris. 'I came to check on Miss Haverhill's injury. Felt it was my duty.'

'A gentleman in her room. As if we have not suffered with the effrontery and the irresponsibility...' Lady Mercer addressed her remarks to Rachel, who looked torn between scowling distaste and a reluctant admiration. Or perhaps, thought Constance, the admiration was just for Harris, still in his flight suit and boots.

'Will you be all right?' he leaned down to ask, and she tried to keep from blushing again.

'You should go,' she said, her voice quiet but urgent. 'This is a crash from which you cannot save me.'

'Then I will see you this evening, I hope?' He left, making hurried excuses, to which Lady Mercer returned only a stiff nod.

'Excuse me, ladies. She's suffered a head wound and is under doctor's orders to rest,' said Tilly, manoeuvring her short body between Constance and the visitors. 'Perhaps give her an hour or two?'

'Who are you to talk to me like that?' said Lady Mercer. 'Do we know you?'

'She's a librarian,' said Rachel.

'Thank you, you may go,' said Lady Mercer.

'I jolly well will not,' said Tilly.

'It's all right, Tilly,' said Constance, though it really wasn't as her head began to spin and a wave of nausea hit her. She retched hard twice, and Tilly flew to stick a basin under her chin just in time.

'Well, this is most unpleasant,' said Lady Mercer, clutching a handkerchief to her mouth. 'How could you behave so scandalously, Constance, and on your cousin's wedding day. We couldn't believe it when we heard your name rumoured.'

'I can't have a bridesmaid who looks like a pirate,' wailed Rachel. 'Whatever will I tell Percival?'

'And after we lost the chance to invite the Maharajah,' said Lady Mercer.

'How could we have been so cruelly misled as to his identity?' said Rachel. 'Such a connection would have been a coup for Percival.'

'I am so very sorry, Rachel,' said Constance, biting her tongue so as not to make a retort as to Percival's own small-mindedness. 'I am afraid I have been very thoughtless.'

'Perhaps I can ask Evangeline and Guinevere to stand in for you,' said Rachel. 'The twins would make quite an impression in the photographs, don't you think, Mother?'

'I will be happy to step down and sit with Mrs Fog instead,' said Constance.

'You are in no state to attend the wedding at all,' said Lady Mercer. She turned to Rachel, her forehead wrinkled with thought. 'Our reputations could hardly withstand her presence after today. But if she stays hidden, it will take time for her identity to be confirmed, and we may hope Percival hears very little of it.' She turned to leave, and as she did so she said, over her shoulder, 'And of course you will not be well enough to attend the ball at Penneston. You will rest tonight, Constance. And may you use the time to think seriously about how your actions may ruin not only yourself but the lives of innocent others. How unforgivable it would be if your outrageous behaviour were to taint your cousin's marriage.' As they swept out into the corridor, she heard Rachel consoling her mother.

'Perhaps we may run into the young Maharajah on the Palm Terrace, Mother, and bring up the subject in passing? At least we might ask him to stop by for tea afterward?'

'Charming,' said Tilly. 'Sometimes I think there's a direct inverse correlation between wealth and manners. Sorry, I know they are like family to you.'

'They may be right this time though. I went too far,' said Constance. 'It was completely thoughtless of me to agree to something so dirty, if not dangerous, the morning of Rachel's wedding. Even without the stitched eye, I fear I have a ring of castor oil along my hairline.'

'We'll just brush that out,' said Tilly. 'Your hair will have more shine than usual.'

'I'll be sorry not to see her married,' she said. 'I've spent so much time thinking of ways to get away from them all, but it is hard to give up on family, however much one dislikes them.' There lingered a residual hurt in Constance's heart to be discarded and to think they might not miss her.

'They can't keep anyone out of the church,' said Tilly. 'If you want to go, I'll come back and take you myself. '

'I suppose I can sit in the back and keep my hat over my face?' A small wave of nausea threatened to surface again. Her face felt clammy and her eye ached. 'But maybe I'll sleep first and see how I feel?' She was already drifting down as she heard the quiet click of the door closing.

THE WEDDING, IN a church stuffed with an undignified amount of hothouse flowers, was, in the end, a quiet affair. Rachel, in her ruched and beaded French gown, the long veil secured over her hair with her grandmother's diamond combs, carried a bouquet of tiny pink roses and blue larkspur. Though the gown was more suited to a cathedral wedding than the simple seaside church, she looked beautiful, thought Constance. She was transformed as all brides are by some mysterious internal glow of happiness, though her father, Lord Mercer, who had arrived in the early afternoon, could not manage more than a stern stare. The twin bridesmaids preceded Rachel down the aisle in their white dresses from the parade, with fresh flowers pinned to the shoulders, to match their nosegays, and fresh white stockings and gloves. They were practised in their smiles and poise and well aware of every eye upon them. Mrs Fog had been inclined to make a fuss about Constance's absence but had been persuaded to sit up front with Lord and Lady Mercer, while Mrs Wirrall and Mayor Morris sat across the aisle and so filled in for the groom's absent family. Behind the sparse front pews of invited guests was a no-man's-land of empty seats, and then the back pews filled with assorted parishioners and townspeople who liked to observe weddings. Constance, who had slipped in the side door with Tilly, sat in the last row, half hidden behind a huge stand of gladioli.

It was a brief service and then, as the bells pealed, there was the usual cheering, throwing of confetti and photographs in front of the old church door. Constance hung back among the gravestones, unnoticed beneath a large yew. It was strange to see the Morris twins leaning into nymph-like poses in her place and to know she would be always absent from this moment. But the women of Poppy's barn had taught her a new resilience, she thought – or perhaps she had flown above the earth and seen her place on it more clearly – for she felt at peace.

'You are the ghost at the wedding?' It was Poppy, her dress stained with oil and her hair sweaty at the ears. 'I've been helping Jock and Iris get the machine back to the barn,' she said, brushing futilely at her skirt.

'I was well and truly uninvited.' Constance laughed. At the church door, Mrs Fog was now posing with the happy couple. 'I've been ordered to stay home from your mother's ball too, but I feel no compunction about ignoring such a command.'

'Well, good, because I'm sent to fetch our famous lady aviatrix and newest full member of the Hazelbourne Ladies Motorcycle and Flying Club,' said Poppy. 'All the girls voted you in after today's flight. It was unanimous.'

'Thank you for having me,' said Constance, hugging Poppy. 'I could use another family.'

'But first, let's prove a point and haunt the wedding party a bit more vigorously, shall we?' said Poppy. With that she waved hard at Mrs Fog, who spotted them and beckoned them over.

'No, no, no . . .' said Constance to deaf ears as Poppy dragged her across the grassy cemetery.

'We must have a photograph with Constance,' said Mrs Fog loudly, and in her new happiness Rachel seemed to forget any quarrels, waving to her over the spluttering of her mother.

'Yes, do come and stand by me on this side, my dearest cousin. That's it. Now if you turn your head towards me, we shall only see your good profile.' As the photographer worked she added in a whisper, 'I saw you in the church and I'm so glad you came. Mother doesn't always mean what she says, you know.' And Constance forgave her obliviousness wholeheartedly, for what was the point of quarrelling with an almost cousin you would never see again, and whose loss you could already feel? Whether from their years together or the lingering effects of the blow to her head, she was overcome with affection for Rachel. As they leaned their heads together and smiled for the camera, she let a tear trickle down her cheek.

Chapter 29

PENNESTON GLOWED IN THE SETTING SUN, EVERY WINDOW glinting gold and the stone frontage warm against the bright green lawns. The shadows were long across the grass, and the earth exhaled a fresh moisture as it cooled. Cars and carriages and motorcycle taxis made a slow procession up the driveway to drop their passengers at the open front door. Constance, who had hurried in at the side door with Poppy, lingered in the shadow of the library windows, watching the shimmer of gowns and jewels emerging from the back seats, ladies being handed up the shallow steps and into the music spilling from the front hall.

'I suppose I had better join the receiving line?' She turned at the unexpected voice to see Harris smoothing the lapels of a well-tailored dinner suit. She wanted to ask him about the lost wager, but Harris did not seem upset. In fact he was grinning broadly as he tugged his collar like an impatient child. 'Not sure I can breathe well enough in this collar to dance, but I hope you'll do me the honour, Miss Haverhill. I know I can trust you to hold me up if I stumble.'

'You know you are agile enough to dance with any lady you care to,' she said. She had to force herself not to turn her bruised and stitched face away.

'But will there be ladies who look as lovely as you do, Miss Haverhill?' he said. 'The dress is very becoming.' Jenny had somehow taken all the boning and stiffness from the blue lace dress and slimmed it down into something as easy to slip on as a nightgown. Silver beading on an almost invisible netting now sparkled on a lengthened bodice, and a thin ribbon of unexpected silver ran down each side of the dress. It was almost decadently short, fluttering around her calves, and she only hoped her ankles did not look as naked as they felt.

'Lady Mercer has warned me I am hideous,' she said. He took her chin in his fingers once again and moved her head gently side to side.

'I think the sticking plaster only adds an air of mystery and danger,' he said. 'You must remember you are an aviatrix now.'

'I grow less employable by the minute.'

'But not less popular.' He smiled. 'I think you will find you are quite famous and your dance card will be too full to shuffle around with this decrepit wreck.'

'I will hold any dance you wish,' she said, looking him straight in his deep blue eyes. She held his gaze, long enough to pick out flecks of topaz and gold and see the black pupils widen, long enough to feel heat rise in her neck.

'I don't suppose we can just hide in the library all evening,' he said, lowering his face to within inches and breathing on her cheek. With difficulty, she recovered and gave a sharp laugh, fumbling for the dance card hanging from her wrist.

'I might suggest we avoid the mazurka.'

So Constance came into the blaze of the hallway with her hand on Harris's arm, and she acknowledged a less than honourable satisfaction in doing so as Lord and Lady Mercer, Mrs Fog and Rachel arrived, Percival ushering them in through the front door with outstretched arms, like a sheepdog. The placid look of bridal smugness on Rachel's face broke just for a moment into shock as Harris drew Constance to his mother's side and the party was welcomed by the receiving line.

'Lord and Lady Mercer, how kind of you to come,' said Mrs Wirrall.

'And my bride, Mrs Percival Allerton,' Percy was saying loudly, to each hand he shook.

'Lovely, my dear,' said Mrs Wirrall to the bride. 'And dear Lord and Lady Mercer, we have you to thank for introducing my family to Mrs Fog and to the redoubtable Constance. Such a wonderful young lady.'

'Like one of the family,' Lord Mercer contributed. 'Under one's wing, you know.'

'Also an extremely useful young lady,' added Harris.

'We are very proud of her,' said Mrs Fog and kissed Constance on the cheek.

'Quite indispensable,' said Mrs Wirrall. 'I should never have been able to manage this affair without her.'

'As she was well enough to come, I hope she will continue to make herself useful this evening,' said Lady Mercer. She frowned, but Constance gave her only a bold smile in return, finding herself at last impervious to such put-downs. She felt no fear and would seek no more favour from the Mercers.

'Well, you'll have to give her up now, Mother,' said Harris. 'Believe it or not I am going to dance, and Miss Haverhill, our famous lady pilot, is going to navigate me around and make sure I don't fall down and disgrace myself.' Mrs Wirrall could not compose her face fast enough to hide a confusion of happiness and concern.

'Do be careful.'

'Come, Constance, before she has them strap bolsters to me fore and aft.' He bowed his head to the ladies, and Constance allowed him to lead her away into the warm gaiety of the ballroom. Lady Mercer could only gape, while Mrs Fog gave her an unapologetic wink.

THE LONG BALLROOM was lit in a blaze of electric chandeliers, and great tall arrangements of summer flowers and grasses flanked every door and window. Raised stages held a string orchestra at one end and the ragtime band at the other, playing in turn and competing for dancers and for applause. Waiters, many from the hotel, dodged and spun among the crowd, while in both the dining room, where a cold buffet was laid out, and the morning room, lavish bars were crushed with men ordering champagne and cocktails.

It was easier than Harris had imagined to ignore the crowd and the noise and dance with his eyes firmly fixed on Constance's face. His hand, pressed to the small of her back, felt the warmth of her skin under the thin lace. Her eyes were wide and twinkling at him. The purple bruise, the sticking plaster, the peeking edge of a strong black stitch, gave her an amused, raffish air. The upturned chin, the collarbones peeking from her scooped neckline, and the smell of her, soap and orange blossom and underneath the hint of a more passionate heat, entranced him. He hesitated to break the spell.

'You might loosen your grip,' he said at last. Her arms were stiff and braced, her fingers crushed painfully against his. 'I promise I won't fall.'

'I will if you promise to slow down,' she said, laughing. 'No need to whirl me quite so forcefully.'

'It's like diving an aeroplane, Constance,' he said. 'You have to lean into the spiral to get out of it.'

'I've had quite enough flying for one day, Captain Wirrall,' she said. 'Perhaps you might steer me over to Mrs Fog and then take some other poor girl out to terrify.'

'You're quite right,' he said. 'I'd prefer to dance with you all night, but I suppose it will raise too many eyebrows. You'll save me all the waltzes?'

'I will if you'd like,' she said, and with this mutual understanding there was no need for further words. Harris was content to dance the rest of the song in a comfortable silence.

CONSTANCE WAS DANCING with Sam, and around her guests of all ages waggled and jiggled about in their own ways to match the exuberance of the ragtime tune. She was inspired to smiles and open laughter as

Mayor Morris and one of the whist ladies, she thought the head mistress, strutted by, levering their elbows up and down as if driving a piston engine.

'You look lovely this evening,' said Sam, whisking her in a tight circle and flipping her into a dizzying twirl. 'Good time?' He was a generous lead, and Constance felt the pleasure of having so many eyes on her.

'My poor bruised face thanks you for your chivalry,' she said, ducking back under his arm. 'And I think it's the loveliest evening I've ever spent.'

'Peace of the nation that inspires such happiness?' he asked with an arched eyebrow.

'It must be,' she said, and she could only hope the inner flame of hope was not shining too obviously in her cheeks.

'You are quite remarkable, Miss Haverhill,' he said. 'Were I otherwise situated, I would not – I mean I would – would not hesitate to enter the lists for your affections.'

'By situated, do you mean because your affections are so transparently engaged elsewhere? Or do you mean my disqualifying lack of means and position?' In her happiness she meant only to tease, but she saw him wince.

'Deserved that,' he said. 'Too frank about Father's expectations, wasn't I?' He swung her around to the final bars of the music. 'Sorry. Tried to be amusing. Only managed to be thoughtless.'

'I should apologise for repaying your frankness with cruelty,' said Constance. 'We are all limited by our circumstances, and you have been nothing but kind and generous, Sam.'

He pressed her hand in both of his as all around them the dancers clapped for the orchestra. 'You deserve all happiness, Constance. Really are a gem. Don't let them tell you otherwise.' She was touched that he should put together such a speech for her. He looked quite dizzy with the effort.

'You are a catch yourself, Sam,' she said. 'Why don't you escort me back to Mrs Fog and you can ask Poppy to dance?'

They walked over to where Mrs Fog and Lady Mercer were sitting with Rachel and her new husband. Rachel was talking to Mrs Wirrall and Poppy at the next table, where Harris also stood. As they approached, Constance was acutely aware of his eyes on her.

'Percival doesn't like me to waltz with anyone but him, and he won't tango at all,' said Rachel, with an air not of complaint but of pride.

'We have to guard against low foreign influences,' said Percival. 'Don't you agree, Mrs Wirrall?'

'The one-step is completely American, I think,' said Mrs Wirrall. 'Do sit with us, Constance. Isn't it a crush in here?' As Harris pulled out a chair for her, Mrs Wirrall continued her thought unabated. 'I saw a wonderful ragtime big band in London before the war. All black musicians. Let me think of the name – the Pontchartrain Peccadilloes or some such charming American name.'

'Do you like the new jazz, Mr Allerton?' added Poppy, a sweet, dangerous smile on her face. 'We think it's wonderful that America's most exciting new music is coming from such talented black musicians.'

Percival turned an alarming shade of purple, strangled somewhere between his scorn and his public politeness, and Constance hoped privately that it choked him.

'My husband and I prefer classical music,' said Rachel, slipping smoothly into her new role as diplomatic wife. 'We've enjoyed a number of charming chamber evenings in his mother's drawing room. Do you like Vivaldi, Miss Wirrall?'

'Will you excuse me?' asked Poppy. Tom Morris, in his full captain's uniform, swaggered towards them as the band struck up a jaunty tune that resolved into the aforementioned tango. 'Tom promised to clutch me in a low foreign dance.'

'Now, Poppy, don't be contentious, dear,' said her mother, but she was smiling as Poppy swept away with Tom. She turned to Percival to add, 'Young man, you should enjoy yourself more. You will find the secret to a long life is to dance more and judge less.' With that she rose from her seat and, accepting for her first dance the hand of old Colonel Smith, she allowed herself to be led into a slow and somewhat tottering tango.

'Well, I never,' said Percival. 'I fail to understand why the English have so many rules of etiquette if all they do is flout them.'

'We do it to keep our friends amused and our enemies confused,' said Harris. Leaning down to Constance he whispered, 'I rather doubt that man has a funny bone in his body.' Constance forgot to be amused, lost in the feel of his breath on her ear.

Guests continued to arrive, and the ballroom bubbled like a cauldron. The hired butler had long since dispensed with announcing people; the noise was too great to hear a proper entrance and the crowd too great to see new arrivals. So it seemed quite sudden that the closest cluster of people broke apart and, in a rush, Mr and Miss de Champney were squeezed through and set down in front of Lady Mercer's table.

'Oh, how wonderful,' said Mrs Fog with joy in her voice.

'We had an agreement, Mother,' said Lady Mercer faintly.

'Good God, how did they get in?' asked Percival.

Mr de Champney bowed to Lady Mercer and to Mrs Fog. His sister eyed them with a hint of frost from above her raised chin. She looked, thought Constance, just like the painting of her mother.

'Mathilde!' Mrs Fog waved. 'Do come and sit beside me. I am so happy to see you.'

'This is not what we agreed, Mother,' Constance heard Lady Mercer whisper.

'I kept my word and Rachel is married,' Mrs Fog replied, urgent and low. 'We can be gracious now, I think?'

'We don't usually come to such things, but Mrs Wirrall was quite insistent,' said Mathilde, sitting down. 'And I said to Simon, "Why not just this once? After all, it's to celebrate peace in the world."'

'Peace in the world,' echoed Simon. He turned to Lady Mercer. 'Madam, may we congratulate you on your daughter's marriage. She is as beautiful a bride as I'm sure her mother was, and as I know her grandmother was before her.'

'Thank you, sir,' said Lady Mercer, frowning even as she pinked with pleasure.

'I'll thank you not to stare at my wife,' said Percival. 'Where I come from such an outrage would be firmly dealt with.'

'Well, we're not in the colonies now, Percival,' said Mrs Fog.

'I think we can all agree that decorum must be observed,' agreed Lady Mercer, sending Percival Allerton her sternest look. Constance grinned to see him quail.

'Yes, don't make a fuss, Percy,' added Rachel.

'You're from America, I believe,' said Harris with a studied casualness. 'I knew several pilots who volunteered even before America joined the war effort. Brave lads one and all. Where did you serve, Mr Allerton?'

'If you will excuse me?' Percival was quick to pivot. 'Come, Rachel, we really must find our coats and be on our way. We have an early start for the ship tomorrow.'

'But they're going to serve a late supper,' protested Rachel, who had taken off her left shoe and was massaging her toes against her right calf. 'And fireworks on the lawn at midnight.'

'Immediately, Wife, if you please!' said Percival and strode away. Rachel slipped on her shoe and hurried after him; her face when she glanced at Constance could not hide a certain shock.

'I say, that's quite high-handed, isn't it?' said Harris. 'I can't imagine you responding to such a command, Constance.'

'If you'll excuse me, I should see the bridal couple into their car,' said Lady Mercer, frowning as she hurried after them.

'Should I come too?' asked Mrs Fog, but Lady Mercer was already gone into the crowd.

'No, no, you must stay and do me the honour of dancing with me, Mrs Fog,' said Simon. 'I think the coast is clear now.'

And Mrs Fog blushed like a maiden and rose to take his hand as the band struck up the first waltz of the night.

'A romance for the ages, I think,' Harris said and took Constance by the elbow. 'I believe you have promised me this dance?'

ON THE DANCE floor, Constance felt a shyness descend. There was a strange certainty of more happiness to come, but it was enough now to waltz in Harris's arms, with her eyes downcast, her hand in his and his arm firm against her back. The ballroom dazzled and spun around them, the music lifted them and the warm waves of conversation and laughter sounded the peace just as well as church bells. They danced two waltzes in succession without talking. Harris seemed so many times to start to say something but pressed his lips together again and spun her onward. At last, as the music stopped again, he spoke.

'I must talk to you,' he said. 'There is so much to say.'

'The library?' she asked, and he laughed.

'Too distracting,' he said. 'I want to be on my best behaviour. How about we put my mother's new conservatory to some use?'

THE DOORS OF the new Moorish garden room stood open to the gardens, and a damp breeze freshened the air and set the potted palms to nodding. Constance moved among the strolling couples, enjoying the perfume of the jasmine and orchids, the muted sounds of the band, the swishing of her own dress against her legs and the night air on her bare arms. Harris would come to her soon, bearing champagne, and perhaps walk her into the dark garden, but she was in no hurry. She paused by the marble fountain.

'It's quite astonishing how much you've helped us all.' The voice at her elbow was Evangeline, a vision in celadon silk. She smiled, but two pink spots burned in her cheeks. 'I quite see why the Mercers think you the absolute best sort of companion.'

'Thank you?' said Constance, trying not to let the doubt be obvious.

'With Harris, I mean,' said Evangeline. 'Of course you didn't see him when he came home. He was so shattered. I'm not ashamed to say I was too weak to face him.'

'He has come a long way this summer,' agreed Constance. 'Working on the Camel with Jock and being able to fly has given him such purpose.

I only wish . . .' She stopped. It was not her place to beg nor Evangeline's place to bestow a waiver of Harris and Tom's wager.

'But the way you leapt into the task with gusto, and then you have that direct manner not allowed to girls of our set, well, you and Tilly are both absolute bricks. Or brick walls as Harris says.'

'Does he?'

'You have given us the most wonderful gift, Constance. You have given us time.' She wiped a tear from her eyes. 'Harris time to heal and me time to find my strength and my duty.' From a gold chain around her neck, she pulled from her bosom a sapphire ring set about with tiny pearls. She sighed, kissed it with her rosebud mouth and let it hang visible against her dress. 'Now we may go forward.'

'Poppy said you threw him over,' said Constance, her voice thin in her throat. 'You gave no sign of being attached.'

'Many months ago dear Harris offered to release me from our engagement, but I was too overcome to answer him then.' She frowned. 'In good conscience one could not walk away and besides, many people would be quick to damn such an action. And yet what life is it for a young woman of delicacy to be bound to nurse a poor broken invalid?' She shook her head. 'Harris saw my dilemma and, gentleman that he is, he suggested we say nothing at all and let the matter lie. I thought it would wither naturally over time and be forgotten. He kept his promise. Never a word or look to claim me or limit me. That is true love, my dear.'

'You cannot mean to hold him to this claim after all he did for you.'

'I only hope I can make up for my immaturity in the years to come and that I will once more be his dream dancer, as he always called me.'

'You still have to hold him up a bit.' It was a rude betrayal of Harris, but Constance felt a little desperate. 'Help him balance.'

'We shall have too much to plan to dance anyway,' said Evangeline. 'Of course, Tom will drop his silly wager. Daddy will make him. And Harris will be a partner and fly for Hazelbourne Aviation. So you see, "All's well that ends well" as the bard once said.'

Constance felt chilled and numb. The warmth and gaiety of the party faded to a dull buzz in her ears.

'You can't just decide for Harris,' she said. 'He's a grown man.' Evangeline's laugh tinkled.

'That's the trouble with you summer girls. You don't really know the real us at all, do you?' said Evangeline. 'Poppy has been a bit of a minx this year. As I said to Gwinny, always another girl to tempt his eye, as if a pretty skirt might get him to drink his beef broth and take his exercise. I believe Poppy quite made it a part of his convalescence, and of course she hoped to nudge my affections.' Harris was in the doorway now, champagne glass in each hand, scouring the room for her. Constance could barely see him through blurry eyes.

'Poppy would never do that,' she said as she tried to quiet an echoing whisper of doubt. Evangeline seemed to ignore her.

'I wonder if he'll want to make an announcement at supper or if he'll just slip the ring back on my finger, and we'll giggle together over how long it takes anyone to notice?' For a moment Constance caught his eye, his face brightening in recognition. Then Evangeline stepped in front of her to wave at him. As his face grew still, Constance turned and fled into the garden.

ONE MINUTE HE was crossing the ballroom with no thought other than the immediate puzzle of manoeuvring through the oblivious, tottering crowd. A glass of champagne in each hand, his cane tucked firmly under his arm, he walked with care, but here a cigarette holder waved in an expansive gesture within inches of his face; there a woman tripped on her own shoes and bumped against his back; now a man swung his partner vigorously towards the dance floor, brushing at his arm. As he focused on keeping bubbles from slopping over rims, the German waiter from the hotel, Klaus, balancing a large tray of champagne glasses above his head, exchanged a knowing glance and a nod. Admiring the man's calm resilience, after the despicable prank with the fish, Harris thought he would confront Tom later about coughing up a suitable gratuity.

The next minute there was a stillness, as if in the eye of a storm, and a vision of present, past and future collided. He saw Constance across the Moorish garden room, the strained whiteness of her face and her sudden disappearance, like a rabbit bolting under a hedge. And there was Evangeline, waving and smiling with a warmth and air of possession as if it were before the war, when he was whole and in love. And he saw the sapphire ring on her bosom. A ring he had been too much the gentleman to ask be returned, even after all hope was gone. In a slow dawning of understanding, he saw a future he had once been denied and had already discarded. Now, a sudden weakness in his hands spilled champagne from the glasses.

'Watch out,' said a woman whose shoe tip he had splashed.

'Sorry, so sorry,' he blathered, but Evangeline was already upon him, taking the glasses from his hands.

'Silly darling, why didn't you have a waiter carry those?' she said, as indulgent as a mother with a favoured child. 'Captain Harris insists on doing far too much,' she added to the woman. Perhaps she glanced at his leg, he could not be sure, for the woman began to make effusive apologies to him.

'Oh, be assured I was always clumsy, even with two good legs,' he snapped. The woman made a swift escape.

'Oh, Harris, can you ever forgive me for being such a silly girl,' said Evangeline. She handed him a glass and hung on his other arm. Her face turned away, she blithely watched the ballroom through the open doors, nodding at people she knew.

'There is nothing to forgive,' he said. 'I never wanted to tie you to me.'

'I'm only glad you gave me the space to reflect,' she said. 'When I saw you go down today, I realised that it should have been me in that aeroplane with you. Not literally, of course, I don't have the masculine stomach for danger. Some girls do, of course, and I don't judge them as being any less a woman. But you are so brave, and I am so sorry to have been so weak and silly.' She turned, and her eyes were damp with unshed tears. 'I can be brave too, I'm sure of it now.'

'You are not obligated,' he said. 'I mean, you never were. It was difficult for both of us at first, but I believe we are comfortable now, letting go.'

'On the contrary, I see my duty clearly now,' she said. 'I am only sorry it took me this long. I want you to know I've demanded that Daddy ignore Tom's stupid wager. He agreed at once when I told him, and he'll make room for you in the business as you wanted.'

'You shouldn't have done that.'

'Well, of course I should. It's not enough these days to sit on one's lands and laurels,' she said. 'If one is not to moulder away in the country, one must have interests and ambition. You are perfectly capable of being in the thick of things, and I shall defend you to anyone who thinks otherwise.'

'I believe I released you from all obligation to me.' A slight sensation of falling bothered him, and he stiffened his back against it.

'You have been so utterly patient, my darling,' she said. 'You told me it was my choice when and if to release you, and you have never made any sort of demand of me. I did not deserve such kindness, and I plan to spend the rest of my life showing my appreciation.'

'You mean marriage?' The word landed as inelegant as a brick between them. But he could not allow her answers to go on flitting away like quicksilver minnows in a stream.

Her tinkling laugh turned several heads to smile in their direction as she stood on tiptoe to kiss his cheek. 'I'm ready to set a date for next spring, but since you've been so patient, I'll understand if you'd rather we elope right now.' He shook his head, struggling for the right words to counter the elegant pincer movement of such a choice. It was like a physical blow to realise that what she said was true. He had never demanded she release him. He could do so now, but he would be the cad who threw her over. She turned and looked him full in the face, and he saw a steel in her pretty jaw that he had never noticed before.

'After all Poppy has tried to do for you, with her little business and buying the Camel to get you flying again, I expect she'll be so relieved that you have saved Penneston and assured your future,' she said. 'And all in our simple acquiescence to a marriage long expected and a cherished love restored!'

He felt a great cold settling in his veins. In his mind a pair of laughing brown eyes called to him, a different future he had barely begun to envisage. A girl who was by no means fearless but therefore even more courageous.

'It's not unwomanly to fly,' he said, his voice cracking. 'It's absolutely brave.' Evangeline widened her eyes with surprise and her laughter pealed again.

'Then you shall teach me yourself,' she said. 'I intend to place all my life and my happiness in your hands.' He looked at the open doors to the garden, and if she had been there, the girl, he might have had the strength to break away. But there was only the pale moon and the deep breath of the dark garden to set against the bonds of his own word and his family's financial position. He felt the reality of his future grip him as hard as his melancholy had ever done. And then, just as in the heat of a dogfight over the Channel, fear dissolved and, in the face of the inevitable, his mind grew quiet. The band struck up a raucous ragtime tune to great shouts and laughter in the ballroom.

'I suppose we should go in,' he said.

'Yes, let's go and tell your mother at once,' said Evangeline. 'She might want to add an announcement to the evening's speeches.'

Chapter 30

THE BROAD, UNEVEN FACE OF THE WANING GIBBOUS MOON
and scattering of stars visible in the darkness offered Constance their
usual reminder that her troubles were small and insignificant. In the war,
and through many losses, she had often counted her blessings under
such a night sky. But tonight, when she had felt so strong and come so
far, she could only tamp down an urge to scream. She sat on a stone
bench hidden in a beech hedge and dug her heel into the gravel walk,
kicking up the small stones as if she could afford to damage unlimited
pairs of dancing shoes.

'Constance, I've been looking for you.' It was Poppy, flushed either
from dancing or from a mild shame. Constance hoped it was the latter.
'Why are you hiding out here?'

'You knew about Evangeline all along,' said Constance, her voice dull.
'They were always engaged and now they will be married.'

'I've just heard the news,' said Poppy. 'I'm so sorry, Constance. Lately I
thought things might turn out otherwise, and I would have been very
glad of it.'

'Evangeline says you only befriended me for Harris, so she would be
jealous.'

Poppy sat down on the bench. 'Only the mind of Evangeline could
believe such a devious plot,' she said, twisting her hands in her lap and
gazing into the garden. 'I mean, when I invited you to dinner, perhaps it

crossed my mind that you were pretty. My mother and I would have done anything to spark some life into Harris. But I had long given up on Evangeline coming around. I think that was all your doing. What with the dancing lessons and the flying, I think you rubbed her little snub nose in it until she couldn't bear it any more.'

'You're happy about it,' said Constance.

Poppy seemed to consider carefully before she spoke. 'I couldn't know, when we first met, how much I would come to like you, Constance,' she said. 'But I owe you nothing less than full honesty, so I will not pretend I am not relieved that Harris's future will be assured.'

'The wager will be moot,' said Constance.

'I believe so,' said Poppy. 'And he will have a full partnership in Hazelbourne Aviation.'

'But now Penneston will be Evangeline's home.'

'Yes, silly really, isn't it. I've been working so hard to save it and it was never really mine, was it? With his injury I suppose I did sometimes think that Harris would never marry and I could run Penneston for him. I didn't think this far ahead.'

'If the wager had been lost, I imagine Tom might have pressured you again to marry him, to save your barn and Harris's future?' Constance asked.

'He knows I would never have married him under duress,' said Poppy. 'Lucky for me the wager is moot now. I'm free to accept him if I want and I think I shall.'

'Evangeline was right,' said Constance. 'I don't understand you people at all.'

'Tom once made the mistake of counting me a sure thing,' said Poppy. She paused a long moment. In the darkness a bat flitted overhead like a snapped handkerchief. 'Tom and I were each other's first great love,' she continued. 'When the war came we thought he was going off to certain death and we gave ourselves to each other fully.'

Constance hid her shock in the darkness. She did not want to seem prim, but for all the girls' talk, she had thought only maids and factory girls succumbed to such a common soldier's ruse. 'I can only imagine your anguish,' she said.

'But then I heard stories from my brother and his friends, the women at every airfield,' Poppy said. 'When I tackled Tom about it, he laughed that I would object to a few wartime wild oats and begged me to marry him right away. He swore he would be true, as if mere protestation would work where his love for me had not.' She laughed. 'I was an incurable romantic when I was younger, but by then even I could see that being married just meant being stuck at home, unable to work, while he went on doing whatever he wanted.'

'What's changed?' asked Constance. 'Because it doesn't seem as if Tom has.'

'Perhaps the war has made us all more cynical?' said Poppy. 'Or made love more practical? I still love the man despite his flaws, and we have understood each other for years. Morris Manor is right next door, so our children will have the run of both estates. And it may be easier and more acceptable for me as a married woman to run the Hazelbourne Ladies Motorcycle and Flying Club. With the business gone, I can at least help some of the girls with cheap petrol or to pay their membership fees. I can do a lot under the guise of charity work. Being Mrs Morris is not the worst outcome for me.'

'Sam would buy you any Penneston you wanted.'

Poppy shook her head. 'I told Sam to his face that he needs an estate with all the furniture included,' she said. 'Only I'm not a Regency chair.'

'You are too harsh, Poppy,' said Constance. 'He cares for you.'

'He'll move home again after the end of the season.'

'So summer ends and everything is neatened away,' said Constance bitterly. Like the deckchairs on the beach, or a parasol, she too had been welcome for a short time but had now served her purpose.

'You must believe me that I did not mean to cause you heartbreak,' said Poppy, tears in her eyes.

Constance would not afford her that privilege. With her new strength, she would not show anger or sadness. She took a deep breath to force down her grief and spoke in a voice she hoped was hearty rather than grim.

'I believe it's time for me to go home.'

'I wish you'd stay on,' said Poppy. 'We would be happy to have you stay with us for as long as you need.'

'Thank you, but though your mother is so much preferable to Lady Mercer, I will no longer presume on the generosity of others,' said Constance. She stood up, tugging at her dress as if she could brush off her feelings with the straightening of a seam. 'My heart is nothing but happy for Evangeline and – everyone.' She found herself unable to say Harris's name and managed a smile before turning away to hide her own welling eyes. 'I shall go in now and find Mrs Fog. She will want to drink to your brother and his bride's happiness before we leave you.'

THE BALLROOM THAT had seemed so sparkling and joyful now seemed to Constance to be only hot and noisy and crushed. She pushed her way through a crowd that was growing loud and tipsy, laughter as piercing as a shriek, faces beaded with sweat about the lips. There were sticky patches on the polished parquet and a droop to the tall floral arrangements. All the promise of the evening seemed as limp and bedraggled as a morning after. She kept moving, focused on finding Mrs Fog.

A heraldic flourish from a trumpet in the orchestra and a tapping of spoon on crystal brought the swirling guests to a halt, and the room settled like a flotsam-filled puddle. Constance saw her quarry just in time and, sliding neatly behind a pair of matrons gossiping on a settee, she reached Mrs Fog's side just as the butler, restored to his voice by the silence, announced the Maharajah of Kochi Benar.

The young Maharajah entered in a long coat of shimmering silver thread, wrapped in yards of pale green silk sash, held in place by a diamond-encrusted sword belt. Layers of pearls glimmered amid the fine white linen of his collar, and his hands flashed with heavy rings. For the social occasion, both men had left off their sabres, but Basu, in heavy black silk coat and turban, kept one hand on a small, jewelled dagger. The Maharajah was also in a turban this evening. It was silver and finished with an ornament of white feathers and diamonds, set with an emerald the size of a hen's egg.

Enthusiastic applause greeted their crossing of the floor to Mrs Wirrall, who stood on the raised bandstand with Harris and Poppy. She came down to curtsy to the young prince, and there was a clasping of hands as if they were old friends. After some private words, spoken low, and the hands of Harris and Poppy shaken with vigour, the young Maharajah addressed the room.

'Ladies and gentlemen,' he began. 'Dear friends and residents of Hazelbourne-on-Sea. I want to thank you all for your welcome these past few weeks. My late father was most appreciative of his welcome here and so am I.' More applause greeted him, and he raised his hands to quell it. 'Most of all,' he continued, 'I am grateful to meet the woman of whose friendship and counsel my father spoke so fondly. Like me, Lady Wirrall understands the benefit of assuming a more ordinary honorific, and many of you know her by her preferred Mrs Wirrall. However, she is of such noble character that she is, and would be, a true lady regardless of title.' Warm laughter encouraged him on.

'I will not take more of your time,' he promised. 'But in recognition of Lady Wirrall's service and friendship to the princely state of Kochi Benar, it is my honour to present her this small gift, cut from the same stone I wear today.' He took from Basu a velvet case and displayed to the crowd an emerald the size of a walnut, set in gold and surrounded by white and yellow diamonds. Gasps and murmurs were drowned by more applause as he handed the box to Mrs – or rather, Constance supposed, Lady – Wirrall. With her permission he took the brooch and pinned it to her left shoulder. The band played a rousing march and the room took up the rhythm with handclapping. After a while, Lady Wirrall signalled for quiet and thanked her royal guest.

'Your father was too great a leader to need my help, but he was magnanimous enough to say my advice had been useful, and that is all the gift I needed.' She paused and added, 'But I will be keeping the brooch.' After more laughter and shaking of royal hands, the Maharajah stepped aside to stand with Poppy, and Mayor Morris hustled his son, Tom, forward for the presentation of the Air Cup.

'Very admirable display. Good fun, of course, and all's well that ends well for Captain Harris and his aviatrix,' said the Mayor. Shouts of 'Where is she?' went up, and Constance was given a standing ovation and urged onto the floor. 'Yes, please welcome Miss Constance Haverhill of Clivehill, Surrey,' he added. Deeply aware of Harris trying to catch her eye, she crossed the floor, keeping her gaze firmly fixed on Poppy, who welcomed her with a brief hug and a smile.

'But on this special occasion, to mark the peace, we ask Lady Wirrall to present the Peace Day 1919 Air Cup to the winning pilot, Captain Tom Morris.' Poppy produced a large silver cup from the stage, and Lady Wirrall presented it to Tom. More applause as Poppy went to Tom, whispered something in his ear and allowed herself to be crushed in his embrace and thoroughly, publicly kissed.

'To the King!' said the Mayor.

'To the Peace!' said the Maharajah.

The ragtime band gave a ribald trombone riff and the first bars of a merry two-step, but as the guests began to dance, a shout went up from the entrance hall and the butler and two footmen could be seen struggling with a man who was pushing into the room.

'A damn cheat and a murdering bastard,' shouted the man. The band came to a ragged stop and the words rang around the room.

'It's all right, let him through.' Harris strode across the room to separate the men, and Constance saw it was Jock Macintyre, in his full Flying Corps uniform. He had ripped the butler's collar and given a footman a black eye.

'Let me go, you bastards. I'm here to let you know the truth.' Harris pulled him free and shook him.

'What do you mean by this, Jock?' he asked. 'In my mother's house?'

'Sorry, Mrs Wirrall. Sorry, Your Royal Highness.' Jock waved and started up the room.

'Get him out of here, Harris,' said Tom Morris. He handed the silver cup to Poppy and stepped forward, straightening the cuffs of his uniform. 'He's a drunk and he's spoiling the party.'

'I'm cold sober,' said Jock. 'No thanks to you, you damn cheat. And almost a murderer too. Let's not be forgetting that detail.'

'The man is mad,' said Mayor Morris. 'Someone restrain him.'

'I found sugar in the reserve tank we added,' shouted Jock. 'Must be half a pound caked all over the bottom, clogging the valve. In case you polite fools don't know what that means, I'll tell you . . .'

'It means the fuel lines will clog and the engine stall,' said Maharajah Pendra, stepping forward. 'They call it a prank, but I've seen it before. It's the most despicable sabotage.'

'There must be a mistake.' Harris spoke automatically, but his eyes darkened as Tom stood silent, his face drained of colour.

'No officer would do such a thing, let alone to a friend,' said Poppy. She was still holding Tom's arm. Constance caught Harris's eye and felt her own eyes fill with tears.

'Are you not going to deny it, Tom?' said Harris. 'For heaven's sake, say something, man. I had a woman aboard.' His voice fell. 'Constance could have been killed.'

'Tom would never want to hurt you,' said Evangeline, appearing at Harris's elbow. 'Please, Harris. We should discuss this in private.' She tugged at his arm, insistent.

'She's right, surely?' said Poppy. 'We have all been family for a long time. Tell them, Tom.' She looked at him, her eyes wide with fear. Constance felt any resentment of Poppy fall away. She understood by Tom's face that Poppy's happiness was already gone. Tom took Poppy by the shoulders and looked at her, pleading.

'It was just a harmless prank,' he said. 'There's only one fuel port, and

I had no idea they'd added a second tank. The machine was supposed to conk out on the runway.' Poppy stepped back and pulled from his grasp. Her slap across his face echoed like a shot.

'So just a simple cheat, not a would-be murderer?' said the Maharajah. 'The deaths would have been a regrettable accident?'

'I wouldn't have held him to the wager,' said Tom, as he felt his stinging cheek. 'Not entirely, anyways. I just thought it would make life easier.' He frowned at Pendra. 'I did it for you as well. Don't tell me you're not Sam's secret investor. Sam insisted on us getting title to the airfield.'

'Don't involve the Maharajah, Tom,' said Sam Newcombe, stepping from the crowd. 'Best, as a gentleman, just to own up to one's actions.'

'How would you know?' sneered Tom, then his face seemed to crumple into anguish. 'Sorry, Sam, old man, you know I don't mean anything by it.'

'I think you'd better leave now, Tom,' said Harris. He signalled to the butler. 'Please escort Mr Morris out.'

'I'll take him.' Sam looked grim. 'Come on, Tom, my friend. Best for Poppy and for business if we leave quietly.'

'Now look here, that's my son . . .' began the Mayor.

'You may want to rethink your position if you wish our business,' said the Maharajah. The smiling Pendra was gone, and Constance saw, in his place, the implacable face of royal power. 'We do not willingly align our state with cowards.'

'We'll settle this tomorrow,' said Sam Newcombe mildly. 'Like friends and gentlemen.'

'Are ye not going to call the police,' said Jock. 'Rich people, you are enough to drive a man to the bottle. Saw it in the war. Always play by your own rules.'

'Sergeant Macintyre, if Captain Wirrall can find us a quiet spot to talk, I'd like to speak to you more about your experience of military leadership,' said the Maharajah. 'Shall we go to the library, Harris?'

'Mother, we should strike up the band again,' said Harris. 'And, Poppy, take Evangeline somewhere quiet. Gwinny too. We must protect them from this.'

'Of course we must,' said Poppy, but the sarcasm in her voice was faint, as if all the fight had left her. Harris turned to the assembled guests and spoke with authority.

'Please let's all enjoy this wonderful night, everyone.' There was some hesitation and angry murmuring as the band struck up an elegant waltz.

'Ladies and gentlemen, my son, Captain Wirrall, and Miss Constance Haverhill, winners of the 1919 Peace Day Air Cup,' said Lady Wirrall, handing Harris the silver cup. A relieved roar of congratulation went up around the room, and the band played more vigorously as guests began to once again revolve on the dance floor.

Constance could not move as Harris placed the heavy cup in her hands with only a pained nod. Maharajah Pendra shook her hand, and Mr Basu gave her a low bow as they followed Harris out of the room. All around her people clapped her on the shoulder and congratulated her. All she could see was Harris, disappearing, and Poppy, supporting a swooning Evangeline on the far side of the ballroom.

'Congratulations, my dear,' said Mrs Fog, coming up to her. 'Never forget you earned this.'

'I have to go,' said Constance. She put the cup back on the edge of the stage. 'I'm so sorry, Mrs Fog. I don't feel well.'

'Well, it's all been rather shocking, of course,' said Mrs Fog. 'Take one of Poppy's taxis and charge it to my account. I'm going to stay in Cabbage Beach tonight.' Her cheeks were pink with happiness, and the girl she once was shone in her face again. Constance managed a smile, and Mrs Fog kissed her and patted her hand. 'I'll see you at the railway station tomorrow,' she added. 'We shall give Rachel a wonderful send-off and also get rid of that horrible Percy.'

OUTSIDE, ON THE steps of Penneston, Constance drew her shawl around her and tried not to cower away from the animated gaiety of the small clumps of people waiting for their cars. It was important not to appear upset and to hold down firmly on the quaking sorrow that threatened to brim over at any moment. In desperation she looked for a Wirrall's motorcycle taxi, but there was none among the vehicles in the courtyard. In a dim corner to the right she saw a lorry being loaded with dirty dishes and glasses. Among the workers, Constance saw Klaus the waiter, a crate in his hands and his jacket folded over one arm. He was leaving. Before she could think, she was down the steps and across the gravel, calling his name.

'Mr Klaus. Herr Zieger. Please wait!' He startled and looked around.

'Miss Haverhill?' he said. 'Are you all right?'

'No, I'm not,' she said. 'Are you going to the hotel? Can you take me with you?'

'Miss, it's a delivery truck and rather a dirty one,' he said. 'May I call you a taxi?'

'I don't care. I just need to go *now*,' she said. 'Please take me.' He nodded and opened the door.

'This is Fred, our driver. Move your dinner, Fred. Make room for the lady.' The young man in coveralls and a cap nodded, seemingly unperturbed at carrying away a guest in evening dress along with the empties. He removed from the bench seat a large waxed paper parcel that smelled strongly of liverwurst.

'Evening, miss,' was all he said.

THE HOTEL'S EXTERIOR was packed with milling crowds who appeared to have been celebrating the peace to excess. A horde of English and Canadian soldiers hung, some of them literally, over the railings of the balcony, singing and calling out to pretty women in the driveway and the street. Townspeople who would never enter the hotel now strolled its gardens and collected on the forecourt in knots. Music blared from the hotel windows, and the light and movement of dancing in the lobby, dining room and Palm Terrace spilled into the darkness. The lorry pushed its way slowly up the driveway and around to the service entrance. Twice the young man had to stick his head out the window and yell for people to move.

'We cannot take the lorry to the front door,' said Klaus, as it pulled up by the stairs down to the hotel kitchens. 'I will walk with you, miss, and then I will help Fred unload.'

'I'll be quite all right,' she said, but he helped her down from the lorry and offered her his arm. It was dark in the side alley, and she took his arm without further argument.

'I heard what happened to you,' he said. 'I'm so sorry.'

'I heard what happened to you,' she said. 'I'm sorry about the fish. If I had known, I would not have agreed to take part, and neither would Captain Wirrall.'

'They tell me it was all meant in good fun.' He sighed. 'It was not, of course, but Mr Smickle has given me two days off next week, so I think he also has some remorse.'

'A two-day holiday,' she said. 'Perhaps you will visit your friend, Mrs Wilson?' In the darkness she was not sure if he blushed, but he patted her hand and, as they strolled to the hotel steps, he smiled as he had done on the beach that day.

'Captain Fish Guts at two o'clock,' shouted a man in a Royal Navy uniform from the balcony.

'By God, the Hun has captured a girl.' Two army corporals leered in Constance's direction.

'I know that girl.' The Canadian airman with whom she had danced at the first tea dance peered from behind them. 'What's he doing?'

'That's the man who's been bothering my wife!' replied the baker, in his best suit, waving a beer mug.

'Unhand the woman.'

'Dirty Hun!'

'Get him.' The shouts went up and the men began to push and shove their way back into the hotel to get to the front door.

'I had better leave you here,' said Klaus.

'Yes, do hurry and get somewhere safe,' said Constance with concern. As Klaus headed down the service alley, and the hotel's front door began to extrude drunken men like so many fat pink sausages, she called out to the two doormen, 'Hello, can we get some help?'

A car swung down the driveway and she was thankful to see it was Sam Newcombe pulling up, with Tom Morris. Though furious at Tom, she knew she could count on them both, as gentlemen, to help. She ran to Tom's door.

'Help me,' she said. 'A mob is threatening to hurt that poor waiter, Klaus. They're drunk. You must help me stop them.' The doormen were trying to remonstrate with the group, but she saw them shoved aside.

'Which way did he go?' asked Tom, jumping out and grabbing her arm. When she pointed to the service alley, he laughed and leaned into her face. Her arm hurt where he gripped it. 'You show more concern for a Hun than for me, after I treated you as my sisters' equal,' he whispered. She pushed him away with her free arm.

'You're drunk,' she said. Rage made her voice loud. 'Drunk and a coward. No wonder Poppy rejects you.'

'Steady on,' said Sam. 'First things first. Come on, Tom, let's stop this madness.'

'You all think you're too good for us. You and Poppy will be old maids,' said Tom. Then he let her go abruptly and turned to shout. 'He's over here in the alley. Follow me, boys!'

'No!' shouted Constance.

'No, Tom! You're not thinking straight,' yelled Sam. Constance tried to grab Tom by the jacket, but he swung at her and knocked her into a hedge. He and the bawling mob ran past, up the driveway, as Sam helped Constance to her feet.

'Don't mind me. Stop him.' She was crying now, in rage and fright and frustration. Sam took off, but he was several paces behind the last of the mob. Constance caught a glimpse of Klaus's face, white and shocked, in the darkness as he tried to run. The kitchen stairs were just ahead and the side door to the hotel just beyond. The mob was still behind Tom. He turned to egg them on and Constance hoped that small pause might give Klaus time to hobble to safety. 'Help! Help! Call the police!' she shouted at the doormen. As she began to run too, she saw Tom gain on Klaus. A brief scuffle and Klaus seemed to spin around before disappearing backwards. Tom stumbled and backed away, holding up his hands.

'He tripped,' she heard. 'I didn't touch him.' The mob was brought up short, milling in confusion. Men began to shuffle back towards her as Constance pressed forward. At the railing above the kitchen steps, Sam caught her in his arms and held her back, but not before she saw Klaus, lying crumpled at the bottom, his limbs at strangle angles, like a puppet with its strings cut. 'He tripped,' repeated Tom. 'I mean, I may have tripped him, but I didn't see the stairs.' And now his face was white with shock, all trace of drunkenness gone. 'It was just a bit of high jinks.'

Chapter 31

A LOW CLOUD MISTED THE TOWN WITH RAIN, A SHIMMER on every leaf and gutter, and dusty roads turned to polished ebony. At the railway station a train stood ready, the rain-washed scarlet carriages filling rapidly with passengers and the engine steaming in the drizzle. On the platform, Constance waited with Mrs Fog to see off the newly married couple and Lord and Lady Mercer, who would accompany them to Southampton. Though properly washed, dressed and present on the platform, Constance felt strange and removed, as if she were still living last night. The dark driveway, the shrill bell of a police car and Sam pulling her away into the hot lights of the hotel and calling for brandy. Her legs failing as he helped her to her room. And then there had been only the darkness, and a silence in which she lay awake still hearing her own screams. She must have dozed sometime around dawn, as the birds began to sing, before a knock from the maid shocked her awake and forced her up to dress and wash and attend the happy couple's early departure.

Rachel whimpered softly now; the finality of her new life was hitting her hard as she clung to her grandmother.

'Now do stop making a fuss, darling, people are beginning to stare,' said her mother. 'Remember, I will be with you until the boat.'

'How can I leave you all?' Rachel's voice cracked and her face began to crumple. 'What if I'm not ready to be married; to be a wife, and a mother?' She shivered in the damp and gripped her grandmother's hand.

'Think of Washington, my dear,' said Mrs Fog. 'Remember your lovely house is waiting and all those parties.'

'Percival told me last night that he will buy me two matching white deerhounds to walk in the park,' said Rachel, sniffing as her face brightened. 'I am to pick out the puppies myself.'

'Lovely,' said her mother. 'And we shall all write every week to exchange our news.'

'And you and Grandmother will write to each other too?' asked Rachel. 'I couldn't bear to think of any estrangement between you.'

'I will write to you and so will Constance, I'm sure,' said Mrs Fog, deflecting the question. 'Now hurry and say goodbye to Constance. I see Percival coming.'

'Goodbye, Constance,' said Rachel, and tears threatened to brim again. 'If circumstances persuade you to change your mind about being a governess, please know you will always have a position with our children.' At the mention of children she unconsciously touched her belt and lowered her eyes. Constance pressed her hand, but there were no words suitable to comfort her across the divide of her unacknowledged impending motherhood.

'We should get aboard, my dear,' said Percival.

'Surely we have a few more minutes,' said Rachel. She looked distraught. Percival smiled, as if at a child, and took her arm.

'I already had to have the conductor remove some army corporals from our seats,' he said. 'They were very rude and are likely to launch another sortie unless we occupy our beachhead.'

'I'm not sure I can go,' said Rachel, fluttering her hands. But in another minute her mother and Percival had bustled her aboard, and she was soon waving a handkerchief from the carriage window and calling out pretty farewells to her grandmother.

'Of course I'll visit you,' said Mrs Fog, going to the window to answer yet another frantic invitation. Constance hung back, exhausted, and as she did so she saw a familiar face getting into a carriage further down the platform.

It was Tom Morris, in dress uniform, carrying a kitbag, with a senior officer and a young military policeman at his side. He was accompanied by Sam Newcombe, who reached to clasp Tom's shoulder while Tom, white about his clenched jaw, shook hands. Constance understood that while Tom was not being actively compelled, this was not an ordinary parting of friends. As he turned to step into the carriage, Tom caught sight of her and she shrank from a sudden hope in his face. He said something to the senior officer, but the man shook his head. With a brief word to Sam, Tom went into the carriage with the others. Sam raised a hand in one last goodbye and made his way down the platform to Constance.

'Sorry business,' he said. He stood next to her, and they both contemplated the train. 'Tom wanted to make sure you are all right. They haven't let him see anyone, you know.'

'Looking for some cheap absolution as they whisk him away?' asked Constance, disgust making her voice harsh in her throat. 'No real consequences for the well connected?'

'Some consequence perhaps,' said Sam. 'Troop ship to Cherbourg and then overland to the Russian Front.' He looked away at Tom's carriage and shivered. 'Good chance he won't make it home this time.'

'You may excuse him, but I cannot,' said Constance. 'The man he killed, Herr Zieger, had nothing to do with the war. He had nothing and Tom took even that.'

'N-not honourable to make excuses,' said Sam. His faint stammer suggested she had stung him. 'Just trying to stand by an old friend on his worst day. Be of use to the family.'

'I didn't mean to insult you, Sam.' She turned to look at him and her heart softened at his anguished face. He was a man losing his best friend. 'The twins are lucky to have you beside them,' she added, touching his arm. Despite everything, she pitied the Morris girls' abject misery, for she had a brother too and loved him dearly.

'He took full responsibility, you know. Told the police exactly what happened,' said Sam, growing calmer now. 'But they wouldn't hear of putting him on trial. Kept insisting it was an accident.' He grimaced. 'He asked the Royal Air Force for a court martial, but they wouldn't hear of that either. More valuable in the battle and so on.'

'I'm sorry, Sam, but I for one will not forgive him,' said Constance.

'He can't be forgiven, but I give him credit for facing up to it.' Sam hesitated, and his voice wavered with emotion. 'I would like to be able to tell his father and sisters that people know he is not running away like a coward.'

'You are a good friend and an honourable man, Sam,' said Constance. 'You may tell them at least one person knows.'

'You are the best of women, Constance,' he said. His face brightened now, as if some burden had been lifted. 'I knew I could count on you. Everyone else does.' He put on his hat and hurried away, and Constance went to join Mrs Fog just as the train whistle blew.

'We'll send you a telegram when we arrive,' called Rachel from the train window.

'Or she'll write,' said Percy, thrusting his head out beside her. 'Telegrams are expensive and inspire undue alarm.'

Constance and Mrs Fog stood, arm in arm, waving as the train began its slow, heavy roll out of the station.

'I can't believe she had to marry a man like that,' said Constance.

'What's done is done.' Mrs Fog patted Constance on the hand. 'Come, my dear, you must help me pick out my dress. I promised I would wait to marry and I have. Simon has secured the registrar for noon tomorrow.'

Constance spent the rest of the day keeping close to her room. She feared to run into Poppy and her mother in the public rooms, but they did not return to the hotel. She supposed them busy with the aftermath of the ball and Tom's disgrace. She could have phoned the barn in the hope of talking to Tilly, but she hesitated with an irrational fear that Harris might pick up the call. Harris she would avoid so as not to have to endure his heartfelt excuses. Or worse, perhaps he would have none and feign polite incomprehension. So she packed and repacked her travel bag, tried and failed to read a novel, and at dinnertime, she worked hard to summon a brighter face, and pleasant demeanour, so as not to spoil Mrs Fog's happiness on the eve of her marriage.

As THE BELL struck noon at Hazelbourne's redbrick town hall, in the registry office upstairs, next door to the magistrates' court, Mrs Eleanor Fog and Mr Simon de Champney were married. Constance Haverhill and Miss Mathilde de Champney were the only witnesses. At least the room was thickly carpeted and panelled in well-rubbed mahogany, thought Constance, looking around at the high window, the bare table, the single vase of dried grasses that served as decoration for all couples. The ceremony was brief, the registrar jovial but weary, a thousand hurried war marriages behind him. Yet the vows exchanged, though short and ordinary, contained such joy that Constance felt her lip tremble and her eyes fill. Mathilde wept openly, and Mrs Fog, resolute and filled with obvious happiness, had to be helped to a chair afterward to catch her breath.

'Not another day will we waste, my dear,' said Simon, dropping stiffly to his knee and collecting her hands from her lap. 'Today you have made me a young man again.'

'Let's go home to Cabbage Beach,' said Mathilde. 'We have redone Simon's room for you both.'

'As young as you feel, I don't advise trying to carry me over the threshold,' said the new Mrs de Champney. 'Constance, my dear. Do come and let me embrace you.' Constance did as she was asked, falling to her knees to put her arms about the old lady.

'I am so happy for you,' she said. 'I wish you many, many years of happiness to make up for the years of separation.'

'I want you to know that I appreciate all you have done, including saving my life in the influenza.' She reached to fiddle with her hair, which Constance had so carefully curled, piled and pinned that morning. In a moment she had pulled out her diamond combs. Kissing each, she placed them in Constance's hands. 'I am starting a new marriage now. I can't imagine a better home for these beloved tokens.'

'No, I can't,' began Constance.

'After all you've been through, including the tragedy of that poor man, Klaus, you most certainly will,' said the new Mrs de Champney, her voice firm. 'You are to sell them if you wish. Perhaps buy yourself one of those motorcycles?' She kissed Constance on the cheek. 'Or keep them for the daughters I'm sure you'll have one day.'

'Thank you, Mrs Fog,' Constance said, and felt tears wet her cheeks.

In the town hall lobby they paused for a photographer to take pictures of the happy couple. Constance fixed Mrs de Champney's hair, which threatened to tumble down without its combs. And then she waited patiently, her heavy travel bag at her feet. She would walk directly from the town hall to the railway station where, she had been assured by the ticket seller, her ticket would be allowed on an afternoon or evening train. She told herself it was not wrong to slip away unremarked.

When they emerged blinking in the sunlight, the wedding party was met with an honour guard. Tilly, Iris and Jenny were drawn up in a row next to their gleaming Wirrall's Conveyance motorcycles. At sight of the happy couple, they threw up their finest salutes followed by three loud cheers.

'What's going on?' asked Constance.

'Taxi service for the de Champney party,' said Tilly. 'To Cabbage Beach for the happy couple and Miss de Champney, and up to Penneston for you, Constance.'

'But I'm going to the station,' said Constance.

'Your ticket is good on any train,' said Mrs de Champney, patting her on the arm. 'Go and make peace with your friends, the Wirralls.'

TILLY TOOK THE long driveway to Penneston at great speed and drew up in a flourish of gravel on the forecourt.

'Leave your bag and come down to the barn afterward for a ride back,' she said. 'There is no way you are leaving town without Iris and me giving you a proper goodbye.'

In the house, slight traces of the ball were still evident. On a side table sat a tall vase of blowsy flowers left over from the ballroom. On the floors, scuffs showed in the wax and a small piece of tinsel hid under a chair leg.

'Sorry we're still in a mess,' said Poppy, coming from the library. She looked tired and drawn. Her hair was messier than ever. 'I'm so grateful that you've come, Constance. I was afraid you would leave with things unresolved between us.'

'Mrs Fog and Tilly had other ideas,' said Constance.

'Won't you come into the garden room for tea with Mother? Afterward, I'll walk with you to the barn and we can talk on the way.'

It took all of Constance's willpower not to flinch but to walk calmly into the garden room. It was different in the sunlight, the flower smell less overpowering, the open doors letting in a breeze from the garden. Mrs Wirrall was sitting at a wrought-iron table, supervising a large hot-water samovar and a small teapot.

'Ah, Constance, I understand we are to lose you,' said Mrs Wirrall. 'I'm so disappointed.'

'My brother's wife is pregnant and having some difficulties,' said Constance. 'I'm so sorry to accept your kind invitation to stay and then disappear, but I am needed at home.' Not that Charles had directly asked her help, but she could read the pleading in between the lines of his stilted letters and she understood that her return would be greeted with gruff relief. As for her sister-in-law, Constance would be more understanding and stand impermeable against the burn of any residual anger. She accepted a cup of tea and added, 'Mr Smickle was most understanding, but he was inclined to think my departure was inevitable. I fear I have not advanced the cause of women's employment.'

'Well, we hope you will visit us again,' said Mrs Wirrall. 'You have done us great service with your skills and I know Poppy values your friendship.'

'Thank you,' said Constance. She did not look at Poppy and Poppy did not look at her.

'I hope this is sufficient recompense for your work,' said Mrs Wirrall, passing her an envelope.

'Oh no, I didn't come here to collect money,' said Constance, horrified. 'You offered me a home. I was glad to help you.'

'Nonsense,' said Mrs Wirrall. 'Women must be paid for their work, my dear. Poppy has taught me that. Consider this from both of us.'

'Well, thank you,' said Constance. It was a fat envelope and she was mortified but grateful as she tucked it in her pocket. 'I'm so sorry about the ball and, everything. I hope you are all right?' Mrs Wirrall sighed.

'Tom's sabotage we might have forgiven, but that poor man's death? One feels for the girls, especially,' said Mrs Wirrall.

'It's like a horrible dream,' said Poppy. She looked away, wincing, and Constance understood she had not told anyone else that she was to marry Tom. To avoid scandal, her loss would be endured in secret.

'Mr Morris Senior has gone into temporary seclusion. A sister in Battersea, I believe.' Mrs Wirrall added sugar to her tea.

'Harris will take over at Hazelbourne Aviation and has finalised a partnership arrangement with Sam Newcombe and his investor, Maharajah Pendra,' said Poppy. 'They will develop aeroplanes for use here and in India, and Sam will represent all the Maharajah's business interests in England.'

'Sam is a good man.' Constance spoke fervently and hoped Poppy would hear her this time.

'Sam is going to marry Gwinny,' said Poppy, a wry twist to her lips. 'I was too late to appreciate his worth.'

'I think dear Guinevere saw the wisdom of changing her circumstances,' said Mrs Wirrall. 'They will reside at Morris Manor.' The three women sat in silence for a moment.

'It's not my place to ask, but will there be the funds now to keep Penneston?' asked Constance.

'In a manner of speaking,' said Mrs Wirrall. 'The Maharajah was very struck by the wounded soldiers at the parade, and he and Harris are discussing leasing Penneston for a large rehabilitation hospital and convalescent home.'

'And will you be able to stay on?' asked Constance

'Harris may keep a wing,' said Mrs Wirrall. 'But I prefer living at the hotel anyway. So much more convenient and less draughty.'

'Mother wouldn't take Pendra's offers of direct financial assistance, of course,' said Poppy.

'Well, he already gave me the beautiful brooch,' said Mrs Wirrall wistfully. 'A pity that one could never sell such a gift.'

ON THE WALK to the barn Poppy was silent and Constance knew she had only a few minutes to speak.

'I'm so sorry about Tom,' she said. 'Sam says he did not run away like a coward, but asked to be held accountable.'

'Thank you,' said Poppy, her voice low. 'It's good to know some part of the man I loved remained.' She paused for a few moments, then shook herself as if to clear the shadow of the past two days from her mind. 'I am too often careless with my friends,' she added. 'But I never meant to be hurtful, Constance.'

'You were nothing but kind to a summer visitor,' said Constance. 'I should not have succumbed to the idea that summer can be permanent.'

'I have managed to make things right with Tilly,' said Poppy. 'Harris has promised to employ her as well as Jock at Hazelbourne Aviation.'

'How can he do that?' asked Constance.

'So simple, I should have thought of it myself,' said Poppy. 'Tilly will be officially employed as a secretary even though she'll work in the mechanics' shop. Harris says he'll put a typewriter on her workbench just in case a government inspector comes by.' She gave a short laugh. 'Of course she'll be paid as a secretary too, not a mechanic, but it's more than she makes as a librarian.'

'That's a relief,' said Constance, who had worried about Tilly most of all.

'If I could make things right for you too . . .' Poppy shook her head. 'Harris has no choice now,' she added. 'His duty to Evangeline is only made clearer because of Tom. Others might shirk, but he will not throw her over in the face of such shame.'

'I would expect no less from him,' said Constance. 'Your brother is an honourable man. We must wish them both all happiness.' She tried to keep the bitterness not just from her voice but from her heart as well. Any hopes she might have entertained, for just the sweetest of moments, were only part of the brief illusion of a summer at the seaside. A strong woman could not be bitter simply because life was not a fairy tale.

'Then we part as friends?' asked Poppy. They came around the corner of the barn as she spoke and a great cheer went up. All the ladies of the Hazelbourne Ladies Motorcycle and Flying Club were gathered under a rough home-made banner that said, in letters of decreasing size, GOOD LUCK CONNIE.

'And as fellow club members, it seems,' said Constance, taking Poppy's arm. 'I may have to start a Surrey chapter.'

'Sorry, we ran out of room,' said Jenny. 'But our hearts are in the right place.'

'We'll miss you,' said Tilly. 'I hope you'll come back and visit next summer?'

'If you don't we'll just have to plan a long-distance outing to the home counties,' said Iris. 'And scandalise all your neighbours with our motorcycles.'

'And our trousers,' said Poppy.

The pop of a champagne cork interrupted, and more cheers sounded as cups were passed. Plates of scones appeared, and Tilly brought in the teapot. For one last half hour the barn was loud and filled with laughter and Constance knew that while a summer love might fade, the memory of these women's friendship would sustain her down the years.

Epilogue

THE LAST OF THE HAY WAS BEING GATHERED IN FROM THE lower field. Sloping along the small stream at the bottom of the valley, it was always slowest to ripen, last to be baled and stacked in the barn for winter. The burning of the stubble there marked the end of the harvest on the farm. Constance, pausing with copper pan and cloth still in her hands, leaned out of the kitchen's Dutch door to admire the scene. The horses waited patiently, heads down in the stubble, while her brother and the men forked hay high onto the already overloaded cart. The rolling green landscape was fat and lush from a warm September, but the temperature had dropped this week and the hedges and treetops were tinged a rich gold by the lower angle of the sun. There was a chill in the air as the afternoon lengthened into evening. Autumn was here and the threat of early frost was on everyone's minds as the farmers hurried in their crops and herded their animals closer to the barns.

The kitchen smelled of the apples, cored and sliced, waiting to be steamed in the pot Constance had just scrubbed. She hoped a little broth, followed by apples and custard, might tempt her sister-in-law to eat. A persistent sickness combined with a still raw grief had made the pregnancy difficult. Mary slept much of the day, and though she tried to be cheerful, Constance could see the haunted panic behind her eyes.

Her brother had merely nodded at her return to the farm, as if she were expected, but her sister-in-law had welcomed her with tears and an apologetic clutching of her hands. She had found the house neglected, the dust furred on the picture frames and the floors streaked with muddy boot prints and dog hair. Charles had hired a girl to do the rough cleaning, but she was fourteen and knew about helping with babies more than about scrubbing floors. Her presence was another ghost of their loss. Summoning all she could remember from her mother, Constance had donned an apron and begun to cook and clean. It felt good to scrub and to empty buckets of dirty water outside and refill them with steaming water from the stove and a good cupful of carbolic soap. It felt good to carry wet laundry into the garden and peg sheets on the line to dance and slap in the wind. It felt good to wash windows and rub them dry and clear with old newspaper so that the sun poured into the stone farmhouse and onto newly waxed wood floors. She poured her days into physical labour and went to her narrow bed at night exhausted, with aching feet, a pinched back and no regrets.

Her brother came in as she was emptying the hot, thickened custard into a large stoneware bowl.

'Hay's in,' he said. 'We'll burn tomorrow.'

'Your supper is ready.' While he washed his hands at the sink, she ladled a bowl of soup, thick with chicken and vegetables, and laid a fresh loaf of bread on the old oak kitchen table. Then she sank a ladle carefully into the soup to skim just the broth, which she tipped into an invalid cup, pretty bone china with a small drinking spout.

'I'll just take up the tray,' said Charles. Grateful for his wife's pregnancy, and her retreat from almost madness, he treated Mary as if she were made of glass. He carried her food, found cushions for her head and feet and spoke to her in a hushed voice; touching her as tentatively as if her skin were burned.

'She was awake earlier,' said Constance. 'She took a little bread in hot milk and said she would knit.'

'She's been knitting that same bootie since she found out,' he said as he left. 'I think she unpicks it as she goes.'

'That might be said of many of us,' said Constance.

AFTER SUPPER CHARLES put a kettle of water to boil on the stove. 'You've been a godsend,' he said as she washed the dishes. 'She's glad you're here now.'

'I should not have been so quick to run away,' said Constance. 'I wanted to prove I didn't need a home.'

'I shouldn't have let you go,' he said. 'I think I worried this home wasn't good enough for you. You and Mother were always comfortable up at the big house in a way Dad and I were not. Always reading and wanting more.'

'You're not wrong,' she said and sighed. 'But it's exhausting trying to straddle different worlds.' She spread out her hands and laughed at the reddened knuckles and the new calluses. 'Everyone will know I am a farmer's daughter now.'

Charles went up to sit with Mary after supper. Constance pulled a thin shawl over her shoulders and went out into the golden evening to walk her family's lands. The shadows of trees were flung across the harvested fields. Even the sheep, so white in the lower pastures, each made a long black shadow on the cropped grass. The sun, sinking fast, seemed to etch every inch of the landscape with a sharp blade; timeless, lasting. Larks called over the hills and a dog barked in a distant farmyard. She felt the magnificence of the land and her own small but unyielding claim on it. In time, she would go out from the farm again, but not as far as London. She thought perhaps she would follow Mrs Fog's advice and buy herself a motorcycle and sidecar. She would be able to take her sister-in-law and the baby out for healthy rides around the countryside. And she might ride daily to a bookkeeping job in the nearby market town. She would be an independent woman, but she would go out this time knowing from whence she came.

A low sound, like a tractor, grew louder and she looked around for signs of any such vehicle moving fast along the lanes. But there was no machine in sight, no trace of smoke from an exhaust. And then the roar was too loud and she knew it was an aeroplane. She shielded her eyes, narrowed against the evening glare, and searched the sky until she found it, the silhouette of a small biplane coming in over the ridge to the south. Banking west into the sun, it circled the farm, setting a woolly white tide of sheep to running and startling the birds from their evening perches in tree and hedgerow. As the machine came around east, lit by the sinking sun, she recognised the paintwork and knew who it was. She began to run towards the empty lower field, knowing it to be largely flat and firm and of the longest span. Arriving at the stile, she took off her shawl and waved it above her head, pointing with her arms and body at the field. The machine waggled its wings and the pilot waved a hand. A tighter, lower circle now, slipping down the sky, and the Sopwith Camel came in smoothly, so low above her head that she ducked instinctively. It landed in a spurt of dry soil and rolled smoothly up the field's slight incline before coming to a stop.

She was already hurrying up the field, caught between decorum and a desire to run. She saw him step down, favouring the left leg. Easing his shoulders after a long flight, taking off his goggles and helmet to toss them in the cockpit. Then he was striding towards her, waving, and she was so happy just to see him.

'How are you here?' she asked. 'How did you even find me?'

'I do have some navigational skills, Constance,' he said. 'I flew several missions over the Rhine. I think I can find my way to the home counties.'

'It's just so extraordinary that you're here,' she said. 'My brother will be so happy to meet you. Is everything all right?' She stopped, for there was no need to ask. He would not be smiling so widely if there were an emergency, and she would not, for shame, be seen to ask about Evangeline.

'Everyone is fine,' Harris said. 'Poppy and Iris have left for Loughborough College, where they've decided to allow women to study engineering. My mother has become chairwoman of the new Penneston Convalescent Centre and is running the place like a general. And Evangeline – Evangeline has gone to Paris to spend time with her sister and Sam, on their extended honeymoon in Europe.'

'When is Evangeline coming back?'

'Not sure she is,' he said. 'She released me from our engagement, again. When she understood I was serious about using Penneston as a rehabilitation hospital, she seemed to lose interest.' Constance tried not to show the happiness that sparked like a flame inside. 'I'm so very sorry, Constance,' he added. 'Can you forgive me?'

'Will you come to the farm?' she said. 'You must be hungry.'

'In a moment,' he said. 'I must clean off the old girl and tie her down. It's getting dark.'

'You'll stay with us then,' she said, her happiness blooming. 'There's no hotel nearby.'

'If you'll have me.' His face was serious now, though his eyes were laughing.

'Well, if it saves you having to camp under the wing,' she said, teasing him.

He only reached out and took both her hands. 'Seriously, will you have me, Constance? I've been such a fool, I know. I didn't know how much until you left and all the light went out of my days.'

'I'll make you up a room,' she said. It was hard to stay practical while lost in his blue eyes and the warmth rising in her arms. 'It's only a box room.' He laughed aloud and slid his arms around her and kissed her fully on the lips. And in the setting sun, birds sang invisible in the hedges, the engine ticked as it cooled and the breeze ruffled the field's stiff stubble and hummed in the wires.

Acknowledgements

PENGUIN RANDOM HOUSE AND THE PUBLISHING WORLD mourned the loss of the renowned editor Susan Kamil in 2019. Susan was my editor, and her belief in my writing was everything to me. In writing this novel, I still heard her voice and laugh over my shoulder – especially when I tried to get away with something! Warmest thanks to Whitney Frick, editor in chief of the Dial Press, for sticking with me and taking on the Hazelbourne ladies. Thanks to the whole Dial Press/PRH team: Andy Ward, Avideh Bashirrad, Rose Fox, Evan Camfield, Donna Cheng, Rebecca Berlant, Sandra Sjursen, Virginia Norey, Vanessa DeJesus, Michelle Jasmine, Maria Braeckel, Madison Dettlinger and Debbie Aroff.

I have found it hard to write with my usual love and optimism during our recent bitter political times and global Covid pandemic. I would like to thank my extraordinary agent, Julie Barer, for supporting and encouraging me through the wilderness. Thanks also to Olivia Oriaku and all at the Book Group.

A big thank-you to my British agent, Caspian Dennis, of Abner Stein, and to the team at Bloomsbury: Nigel Newton, Paul Baggaley, editors Charlie Greig and Emma Herdman, Francisco Vilhena, Ben Chisnall, Mike Butcher, Anouska Levy and Grace Nzita-Kiki. Gratitude also to Patrick Gallagher and Annette Barlow of Allen & Unwin, Australia; to my other wonderful editors and publishing houses around the world; and to Jenny Meyer, who arranges all my foreign rights. Fondest regards to retired editors Alexandra Pringle (UK) and Maggie Doyle (France).

Special thanks to Rob Tholl of the fantastic Old Rhinebeck Aerodrome (where you can see early aviation and WWI aeroplanes fly every summer) for talking me through the flying and engine maintenance of Sopwith Camels. All remaining errors are mine.

Thanks also to Dave Richmond, of the Isle of Wight, for producing motorcycletimeline.com – a lifetime's work of uploaded text, artwork and photographs from international motorcycling periodicals, from the nineteenth century to today. A great resource, and often hilarious!

I must mention the Bexhill Museum, in Bexhill-on-Sea, for its inspirational exhibits on motor racing, World War One, the famous visit of a real maharajah and Eddie Izzard's train set.

Writers need to talk to other writers. Through the amazing Roxana Robinson, I've been privileged to meet so many thoughtful, generous women writers, including (but not limited to) Lisa Gornick, Christina Baker Kline, Helen Klein Ross, Rachel Cline and Kate Manning. I depend also on the continuing friendship and advice of the posse in DC: Susan Coll, Mary Kay Zuravleff and Michelle Brafman.

A big thanks as always to all our family friends in Brooklyn and beyond. Love to my husband, John Simonson, who is my best friend; to our two wonderful sons, Ian and Jamie; and to my strong, beautiful mother, Margaret Phillips, on her mountain in rural France.

This has been a time of loss for our family. John's father, David Simonson, died in 2021. A newspaperman and cartoonist, he was ninety-four. He and I always ordered the straight-up gin martini with olives. And in March 2020, my beloved father, Alan Phillips, died in the early days of the Covid pandemic that claimed so many of our loved ones. He was eighty-four, an industrial chemist and proud member of the Royal Society of Chemists. He thought Hemingway wasn't a patch on his writing daughter. He was also a lifelong aviation enthusiast.

All the aeroplanes are for you, Dad.

About the Author

HELEN SIMONSON is the *New York Times* bestselling author of *Major Pettigrew's Last Stand* and *The Summer Before the War*. She was born in England and spent her teenage years in a small village in East Sussex. A graduate of the London School of Economics with an MFA from Stony Brook Southampton, Simonson is married, with two sons, and lives in Brooklyn. She is proud to be a dual citizen of the United States and the UK, and a longtime New Yorker.

helensimonson.com